MW01484224

BLACKSTAR

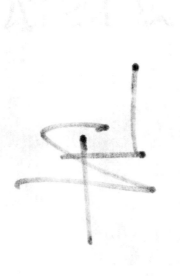

What is the meaning of love and sacrifice in a post-war generation?

The Eastern Isles, an empire of humans, beastkind, and Fae, have recovered from a divisive war caused by an infectious entity. Humans established the Commission as a defense mechanism; however, mistrust of the Fae races has only increased while upholding their duty to protect against dangers.

Beast, Kovuco Blackstar, born of a deviant legend, lives in the shadow of remorse until he meets the enchanting Lady Ameilja Rose Frost, a human seer of the Eastern Isles. Kovuco is unique among his kind, but even more troubling, he harbors an illicit attraction toward Ameilja, whom he's strictly employed to protect.

Ameilja isn't your typical noblewoman; she's an advocate gifted with an unfathomable power, a power that makes her a prominent tool in the Commission's goal. Unknown to Ameilja, her rare ability is also a fatal instrument in an even darker plot that threatens the fabric of all life.

While dealing with internal struggles, Kovuco finds himself increasingly drawn to his lady, until they're both compelled to do something that will irrevocably bind their destinies. The fateful event between Kovuco and Ameilja may be the only hope for eradicating an ancient evil that's risen against the world, all while harboring the most significant obstacle: humans don't give their hearts to beasts.

BLACKSTAR

LUKAS RYAN

ARCHWAY
PUBLISHING

Archway Publishing books may be ordered through booksellers or by contacting:

Archway Publishing
1663 Liberty Drive
Bloomington, IN 47403
www.archwaypublishing.com
844-669-3957

Cover and interior graphics by Brandon Wedge.

ISBN: 978-1-6657-5455-2 (sc)
ISBN: 978-1-6657-5457-6 (hc)
ISBN: 978-1-6657-5456-9 (e)

Library of Congress Control Number: 2023923912

Printed in the United States of America.

Archway Publishing rev. date: 2/29/2024

CAUTIONARY FORWARD

To my readers,

Thank you for picking up Blackstar. I am very excited for you to embark on this adventure filled with peril, action, and love! This is a story that has been built for many years, following me into adulthood, and now here it is in your hands!
    I want to give you a heads-up on what you're about to dive into.

    Firstly, Blackstar is a work of fiction. All elements of Blackstar—including its characters, locations, and objects—are fictional. Certain aspects of this narrative draw inspiration from my personal experiences, travels, folklore, or other sources of influence. This world has been built with heart. Specific parts are incorporated to enhance visual and sensory engagement. Who doesn't appreciate a delectable bowl of ramen accompanied by gyoza or a salmon fillet served along the coast?

    Blackstar includes themes of graphic bloody violence, death, psychological traumas, sexuality including sexual assault, domestic abuse, drug and alcohol use, and strong language. Readers who may be sensitive to this material, have been warned.

Welcome to the world of Blackstar.

Lukas Ryan.

Dedicated to my wife.
The one who showed me the meaning of love.

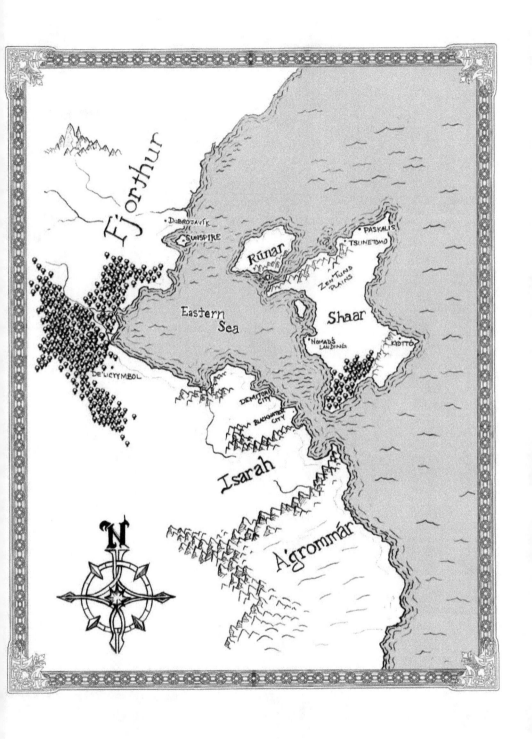

PRONUNCIATION GUIDE

Á, É, Í, Ó, and Ú: Referred to as the acute *A, E, I, O,* and *U*. Adds emphasis to the vowel.
- *Á* sounds like "ah" (*Kristján* is pronounced "Kris-jan").
- *É* sounds like "ey" (*féja* is pronounced "fey-ya").
- *Í* sounds like "ee" as in *sweet* (*Aoustí* is pronounced "Oust-ee").
- *Ó* sounds like "oh" as in the interjection (*Jónsi* is pronounced "Yohn-zee").
- *Ú* sounds like "ew" as in *lure* (*Rúnar* is pronounced "Rew-nar" or "Rue-nar").

Ä, Ö, and Ü: Referred to as the umlaut *A,* umlaut *O,* and umlaut *U*.
- *Ä* (aa) sounds like a long *A* sound, as in *walk* (*Näkk* is pronounced "Nock" or "Naak").
- *Ö* (uu) sounds like a long *U* sound (*Halbjörn* is pronounced "Hal-byuurn").
- *Ü* (oo) sounds like a long *O* as in *wool* (*wülkure* is pronounced "vool-kur").

Æ: Sounds like "eye."(*æsir* is pronounced "eye-zeer").

Ð or ð: Referred to as an *eth*. Sounds like "th" as in *father* (*Pantokraðor* is pronounced "Pan-tock-ra-thor").

J: Sounds like "y" as in *yellow* (*Ameilja* is pronounced "A-meel-ya").

S and Z: Some words and names are pronounced with *S* as a *Z* and vice versa (*Désoto* is pronounced "Dey-zoe-toe"; *Medzio* is pronounced "Met-seo").

W: In some cases, especially when combined with an umlauted letter, a *W* will sound like a *V*, as in *wächter* and *wülkure*. (*wächter* is pronounced "vaak-ter" or "vock-ter"; *wülkure* is pronounced "vool-kur").

PROLOGUE

Fjorthúr
The Sunspire
Lab 2
Harujasa 6

"HE'S OUT! HE'S OUT!" DR. TIEM SCREAMED, frantically alerting his colleagues. "His arm—it's out!"

He tried to gain control of the overpowering male ork's arm, which had slipped from the restraint. Its hulking, calloused gray hand smacked the doctor's chest, instantly winding him. A nearby lab assistant dropped his surgical tools, tripping over his stride toward Dr. Tiem.

"Help me, damn it!" Tiem ordered through gritted teeth as he finally grasped hold of the ork's arm, pressing it forcefully against the metal surgical table.

The ork reacted instinctively to his unfamiliar surroundings by roaring angrily through his muzzle. He thrashed and gyrated violently against the restraints.

The assistant reached for the straps that previously had held down the ork's arm. "How the hell did he wake up?"

"Just get him tied down." Dr. Tiem demanded, using his entire body weight to keep the flinching arm in place.

Just as the assistant was about to secure the ork's wrist, his survival instincts kicked in; he ripped his arm free and swiftly seized the assistant by the hair. The young assistant screamed in anguish as panic surged through his body. In a hurried fury, the ork smashed the assistant's head into the edge of the surgical table, knocking him unconscious.

"No!" Dr. Tiem bellowed as the ork began repeatedly slamming the assistant's head onto the table, smashing his skull to the point that blood and brain matter splattered onto the floor.

Tiem froze, shock holding him captive. The ork laughed hysterically through his muzzle, stretching his thick fingers around the assistant's exposed skull, allowing the brain matter to seep through his clenched fist. The bitter smell of blood and urine swept through Tiem's nostrils. He turned away from the horror just as one of his colleagues, Dr. Baadar, stepped in, grasping a surgical cleaver. With several swift chops, Baadar severed the ork's arm, preventing him from becoming a further threat.

The ork wailed in pain as gore spurted from the bloody stump.

"Do you have the tranquilizer?" Baadar urged, catching his breath.

Dr. Tiem turned to his surgical supplies. There were two syringes: one with a colorless liquid and another with a blended blood-and-orange-colored liquid. He lifted the colorless liquid: the tranquilizer, then looked to the body of his dead assistant. He then cut a glance to the ork, who was still roaring in pain. Tiem tightened his glare, and intentionally drained the colorless liquid onto the floor.

"What the hell are you doing? We need to administer the tranquilizer—"

"And risk him smashing another skull?" Tiem snapped, picking up the other syringe.

He quickly approached the ork and aggressively drove the needle into his gut. He pushed down on the plunger and injected the liquid, then immediately took a few strides back.

Seconds passed, and the ork began convulsing; his body violently twitched. The ork's eyes flooded white, while blood poured from inside his eyelids and out through the muzzle, until he abruptly ceased, dead.

The bright, fluorescent lit room fell eerily silent. They both stood there, stunned.

"What the fuck happened?" Dr. Baadar asked.

"I don't know what happened. The strap must not have been—"

"Don't let it happen again!"

"Yes, yes, of course," Tiem replied nonchalantly, brushing off Baadar's authoritative tone.

"Now, get this mess cleaned up and get back to the evaluation room—quick! We have another ork that's reacting positively to the new emulsion."

"I'll be there shortly," Tiem stated. "I'm not disposing of the assistant's body in the crematorium just yet; we can salvage some of his parts for human testing first."

Baadar eyed Tiem briefly, morally debating if that was the right thing to do. *This assistant had a family.* He immediately suppressed the thought, gaining his composure. "Fine."

"Good," Dr. Tiem said, surveying the scene. His gaze drifted to his shoes. Blood began to pool around his left sole. He took another step back.

"Don't worry," Dr. Baadar said slyly over his shoulder before exiting. "You'll see your little lab assistant in hell one day. We all will if this project doesn't promise anything beyond what we've witnessed—what we've done."

ARC ONE
REFLECTION

CHAPTER ONE

ALL WAS SILENT

Fjorthúr
The Sunspire
The bridge washroom
Lyul'ai 31

Nine years later

KRISTJÁN BAADAR CLOSED HIS HEAVY EYES AS HE sat before his locker. The stench of cautery and blood had finally lifted from him. Although his contract with the Sunspire's nefarious underground operation was still in progress, he would soon be permitted to leave and return to the island's surface.

"What a fucking day," he huffed, pulling his fingers through his dirty-blond hair. Due to stress and his advanced age, strands were beginning to turn gray.

Droplets of sweat lingered along his hairline, while specks of his test subjects' blood seeped into the fibers of his lab coat. Getting the new subjects to cooperate had been difficult. His team was used to their hostility, which forced them to break their will to resist, but some days were much more difficult than others. He didn't blame them for retaliating.

His contract was approaching its tenth year, but Kristján felt as if he had walked through the facility's doors yesterday and sold his soul to the operation. Despite being a highly ranked æsir of the Commission—a leader of the human race's enactment to enforce order and peace—Kristján had been hired under sworn secrecy, pledging himself as one of the lead doctors over the unethical, lethal experiments.

Since then, he'd lived with those contradictory roles, and the deadly risks.

Kristján sluggishly inhaled, expanding his tensed chest cavity. For a brief moment, he held his breath, allowing the daunting memories to permeate his mind, and then he solemnly sighed.

His fingers clenched tighter around his hair as he envisioned the historical events of how he'd ended up in his position in the first place.

Long ago, the world had been united under the gaze of powerful spiritual beings known as Aureates—not gods like their sole creator, Uridei, but ancient, godlike beings endowed with supernatural powers and abilities.

The Aureates had ruled over the lands inhabited by humans, Orkésh, Fae, and other creatures. Their power had been intended only for the blessing and welfare of all, ensuring Uridei's creation transpired fruitfully.

Unity and cohesion had reigned successfully during the beginning times, until the human race's survival had been put to the sword by an infectious force that sought only to destroy them: the Näkk.

The Näkk was a wicked, lethal plague with unknown origins. Sabor, one of the Aureates, had been the first to discover it. Instead of annihilating the Näkk, Sabor learned to wield and control its all-consuming power. He was cast out for his traitorous actions, which had prompted him to vindictively flee to the Eastern Isles and prey on the race most vulnerable to the plague: humans.

The Näkk lived to kill its human hosts, mutilating their insides to bring them back from the dead. It multiplied its insidious power through the biological makeup of humans, infusing their undead bodies with strength and an insatiable appetite for the flesh of anything with a heartbeat.

Through the Näkk's fatal methods, it spread like wildfire, weakening the human race and causing destruction throughout its path. Little had humanity known that the struggle had just begun. The devastating effects of the Näkk had led to a world-altering war that erupted across the lands. It inevitably had drawn in all the ethereal races to try to stop its destruction; however, rather than rallying all the races together, it had birthed division, distrust, and fear among them.

The humans not only struggled against the plague but also struggled to regroup and gain peace with the other races, which had left them to solely defend themselves once again.

"Until Albean …" The name slipped from Kristján's lips like a hushed whisper. "The savior of humanity."

Humanity's salvation was all owed to the devout Aureate Albean, who'd gained notoriety for defending the humans. In desperate times, one must resort to desperate measures. Albean had taken affairs into his own hands. He'd risked opposition by advancing the native wolf species, altering them to be more like the ethereal humanoid race, the Fae, and to be civilized and walk alongside humans. He named this new race the Völfien and gifted them with not only immunity to the Näkk but also the capability to comprehend the frail human race, who desperately needed a stronger defense.

Albean's interference through his Völfien creation and his granting his supernatural power of the Purge flames to worthy humans had led him to finally defeat Sabor. It was a monumental victory, officially ceasing the horrific plague and vanishing Sabor from existence, but it had not ceased the division. The divisive war among the races had raged on for many centuries, eventually earning the name the Great War.

In the decades that followed, the Aureates no longer ruled over the territories, but Albean's influence had left its mark on the hearts of the people. The humans, who were fed up with the division, turned their anger and fear into strength, which paved the path for the rise of the Commission: humanity's last line of defense against any force or race that tried to destroy them.

The Commission, solely run by the humans, was the movement that officially ended the Great War. Its mission stood for order and peace, all while watching out for any dark entities that could try to emerge.

Years of advancements had grown the Commission into what it was currently: Three departments comprised of the Sentry, involving the wülkure and the wächter roles; the Religious Order, involving the paladin role; and the Academy, involving alchemy roles and departmental studies.

Regardless of Albean's intentions for his beloved Völfien race, the humans' intimidation of them eventually had taken precedence, even more so than with the other mystifying races. They labeled the Völfien as beasts, utilizing their mysterious strengths by placing them in a protectorate role under Commission regulation, or by unyieldingly micromanaging their lives.

Kristján scoffed under his breath. "Such irony—order and peace." He spat, keeping his eyes closed while they stirred under his eyelids.

The Commission worked endlessly to keep its finger on the pulse of the lands, making sure they did not fall back to the ways of the war. However, that still didn't stop malice from seeping in.

Nearly nineteen years ago, members of the Commission discovered traces of the Näkk. They had secretly preserved the infectious plague, eager to experiment with its life-altering power. This had resulted in the illegal, underground operation within the walls of the Sunspire and Kristján's current contract as a head doctor.

To the general public, the Sunspire was known for basic facilitation. It was a highly classified facility built into an island off Fjorthúr, safeguarding the Commission's alchemical research. Sunspire's staff had no clue what horrors took place in their underground labs.

The unethical experimentation commenced thanks to the original discovery of the Näkk, which involved a young male ork. He had stumbled across the infection in the desolate caves of the Fjorthúr'an Mountains. Reports had flooded in of the ork boy's unusual behavior.

Prominent Commission members immediately had been sent to investigate under direct orders, but once they'd unveiled the reality, they'd neglected to annihilate or report it further. The discovery of the ork boy birthed the epiphany that the plague could attach itself to the other races, not just the humans. The Näkk had infected the ork boy's body just as it had infected the humans during the early war, a profound yet phenomenal discovery.

The current analysis was that the Näkk still did not infect the Völfien race, just as Albean had intended. Although the team had tried to crack the Völfien's genetic coding, they'd concluded that it was impossible. Instead, they focused on the victory that had proven the plague could infect and reanimate the life of anything else.

Kristján and his team had taken immeasurable steps to wield and manipulate its power, but he knew the Näkk was more insidious than history taught. It worked as an inevitable dark entity, desiring to be found by powerful beings. All would be doomed if the plague were ever to escape into the lands again.

Kristján opened his eyes. He straightened his back, letting his stiff spine crack and relax, as he reached into his pocket to retrieve his badge from his lab coat.

"What have you gotten yourself into, Kristján?" he asked himself, adjusting his spectacles.

He rubbed his thumb over the etched lettering and engraved Commission emblem. The fluorescent light above him reflected off the badge, catching his eye, as if the cold piece of metal were taunting him.

Dr. Kristján Baadar
Commission Æsir: Alchemy Branch

He quickly shoved it back into his pocket. It was only a matter of time before the Commission found out about Sunspire's secret operation and his illegal involvement. He knew he would need to resign if any strain of ethical integrity was left in him to save.

He shrugged off the thought and began undressing. He paused, reached into his other pocket, and clutched his pocket watch in the palm of his hand, ensuring it was still there. He carefully pulled it out and pressed the crown, and the lid swung open to reveal the time as two seconds past the stroke of one o'clock in the morning. He needed to be back in the lab by eight.

"Shit, does sleep even exist?"

He gazed at the picture of his wife tucked into the watch's lid. He had barely seen her since delving into this operation. *I'm sorry, Isabelle …*

Isabelle Baadar—a former æsir legend within the Commission's Sentry—was trained to be a weapon for Isarah's Sentry department. Isabelle had grown up devout to combat, intimidating some of the most skilled men, not only because of her skill but also because of her intelligence. Although she no longer worked under the Commission and was much older now, her fierce skills had never faltered, nor had her beauty. Unlike her surviving broad-built family members, Isabelle was a petite, pale woman who maintained a slender, toned build. She wore her long blonde hair in taut braids along the top of her head and shaved along the sides, a common style of her culture.

Kristján studied the photo of her. It was dated before they had wed thirty years ago. He'd intentionally placed the photo there to admire her beauty in grayscale and keep her youthful smile forever trapped in his timepiece, despite the faults of their marriage.

Just three years after they had married, the Commission had sent her and Kristján on a mission to the South, which had been set to go on for three months; however, in their second week, she'd disappeared. Three years had passed without anyone hearing from her. Then, one day, she abruptly returned with a small child in her arms and resigned from her position with the Commission, with no explanation.

An affair had begun to grow between Kristján and a colleague about six months prior to Isabelle's return, but it had been emotionally going on for much longer. Most wouldn't have been surprised. Isabelle had always treated her career as her first love.

When she came back, the child had changed all of that. Even though Kristján knew the boy was likely her captor's child, he loved the boy. He never pressed for in-depth questions or second-guessed his and Isabelle's love, as he understood both their faults. Isabelle's boy had become like a son to him, and as the boy had grown older, it had become undoubtedly more evident that he was not Kristján's biological son. It didn't matter; the boy had become Kristján's world, even though his relationship with Isabelle was forever damaged by the unspoken affairs he was forced to bury deep inside.

Kristján closed the watch, placed it in his wash kit, and finished undressing to head to the shower hall. He took a single towel from the bench before entering the heated ceramic tile washroom. He leaned in and turned on the water in the nearest stall to test it with his hands, waiting until he could submerge himself under its heat entirely.

Dr. Tiem entered the room. He reached into his wash kit and began cursing aloud. "Ah fuck! Kristján, I forgot to replace my razor. You got an extra?"

Kristján reached into his kit and tossed a sheathed razor. "Use my straight razor. I shaved this morning. It's sharp and clean."

"Much obliged," said Tiem, catching the razor in flight. "Can't ever remember anything down here. I thought I wouldn't notice the depth with my suite overlooking the ocean."

"You're still underground, I'm afraid, and some days we spend sixteen hours in that lab. I barely see the need even to approach my landing. I get nauseous."

Tiem grumbled under his breath and agreed.

Kristján then retreated under the hot water. The thick streams pierced the sounds of the outside world, so for once, he could focus on nothing. He was lulled into a reverie as he closed his eyes, and memories of Isabelle overtook him as the steam clouded his thoughts.

He thought back to the time he had visited his homeland in Fjorthúr to bury his parents, which also had led him to meet up with his wife-to-be, Isabelle. She had been training the next round of Sentry recruits for the Commission. She'd demanded much respect, yet somehow, she'd allowed Kristján into her bed. Even though he was a high-ranked leader within the Commission, she could have had any man she wanted, yet somehow, Kristján, the meek alchemist, had been her choice.

He had married her, and together they'd left to pursue their careers in the well-known city of Demitori.

"Isabelle ..." Her name floated from his throat. Images of her naked figure flashed through his mental realm.

Kristján and Isabelle's first night in bed together had been more intense than he had expected from a virgin woman. She loved nothing more than to have his face forcefully buried between her legs. Isabelle preferred to fuck rather than make love. It made sense with her aggressive nature. He missed the feeling of her fingers grabbing at his hair, begging him to bring her to climax with just his tongue.

He cleared his throat and quickly shifted back to reality to avoid public arousal. He leaned over to turn off the rushing water, when he was abruptly slugged square across the jaw.

"Fuck!" he yelped, losing his footing.

His naked body slammed against the floor tiles of the next stall. He heard a crash as the contents of his wash kit hit the floor, including his spectacles and sentimental pocket watch, which clamored just a yard from his reach. There hadn't been anyone besides himself and Tiem in the showers, and he had unconsciously dismissed the sounds of his invaders rushing in.

The blurs were becoming clear, when a figure swung like a pendulum and bludgeoned him against the face again, loosening some of his teeth. He felt a tooth slip between his lips, and the iron taste of blood drenching his chin followed. A good flow of blood ran down his temple, but he took little notice. He focused more on his pocket watch, now surrounded by hot water and crimson.

Before he could identify his assailants, he was lifted by his hair to his feet. He raised a fist to retaliate, but Kristján was not a man accustomed to fighting. His blow was deflected, and he was kneed in the naked groin. Nausea roiled his stomach as one of the assailants shoved his face against the wall tiles.

Kristján didn't think to say anything, until he felt the point of a knife run down his spine and lower over his buttocks. The clenched fist that gripped his hair slammed him against the tiles again, forcing an anguished groan out of his throat. The knife-wielding assailant pinned Kristján's arm with his shoulder and then pinned his leg with a booted foot. The second assailant had Kristján pressed against the wall with all his weight and twisted his left arm behind his back, locking him in place. An eerie feeling settled in when he heard a third assailant pacing behind him. Thick soles clapped against the tile floor, sloshing against the running water and blood beneath them.

"What do you want?" Kristján rasped. He hoped the fear rising in his throat couldn't be heard.

"Quiet!" exclaimed the pacing man. "Do you have any idea who I am, Baadar?" he asked with a thick accent.

Kristján thought hard. He dissected the accent and the dialect. *His voice is gruff. Perhaps a smoker. A'grommán? The mission with Isabelle— perhaps they were involved with her disappearance. Or is this my punishment from the Commission?*

"I-I don't know," Kristján spilled.

"Dumb motherfucker!" The pacing man slashed Kristján across his lower back with a switchblade.

Kristján shook with terror, trying desperately not to break his composure. "Please don't do this!" he pleaded to the man to his right as he felt the blade press against his inner thigh, piercing the exposed dermis. Blood escaped the puncture and ran down to his ankle.

The man ignored his plea while the pacing assailant loosened his buckle, preparing for his turn in the assault, and said, "Wait, don't kill him yet."

The knife-wielding assailant removed the knife from Kristján's thigh. "What? Why?"

"We all know you want to kill him, but don't hold me back from having a little fun first," he said with hoarse laughter. He gave his zipper a hard yank, pulling it down to free a corpulent erection from its cell. "Don't worry. I'll be rough."

The knife-wielding assailant shook his head. "You sick son of a bitch. Just make it quick, and keep him quiet. After you're done with him, he's—"

A massive force entered the circle, seized the knife-wielding assailant, and smashed his head against the tiles. A grisly crunch masked the running waters of the washroom, and the knife fell to the floor, clamoring loudly.

As the attack happened, Kristján felt the grip around his neck tighten; the assailant's fingernails broke through his skin and then instantly fell limp. The clutch weakened, and the man's body fell to the wet floor. The assailant with the unzipped pants felt a sudden slice, and his steaming innards spilled out of him where he stood. Next was the man to Kristján's right. He released Kristján due to a sudden bludgeon against his head, which forced him into the wall next to Kristján. Kristján locked eyes with the unknown man before a giant clawed fist smashed his face, splattering his head like a melon. It was a horror Kristján would never forget.

Kristján sputtered and fell back from the wall. He found himself lying in pools of running water, blood, and debris of offal and brain matter. He tried to regain his composure as he heard a fourth man's muffled shrieks of terror, followed by a hideous flesh-ripping sound echoing throughout the shower stalls. Then there was silence. A few more thuds echoed, and then ribbons of human meat hit the ground.

Kristján looked up, clearing his vision the best he could without his spectacles, to take in the identity of the new assailant. It wasn't a human, but a creature Kristján knew all too well—a völf!

The Völfien race, whose members were called völves, were tall, limber digitigrade beings birthed with long, clawed carpals and tarsals, which gave them the predatory propulsion to catch their prey by running on all fours, as their ancestors had, except Völfien could maneuver on just two legs. They resembled demonic beasts from folkloric tales; however, these beings were uniquely different, and even more terrifying, they were real.

The mysterious völf before him—a female völf— was covered in fur over a slender and muscular form with a sweeping tail giving her adroit balance. She had a long muzzle known to carry forty-two lacerating teeth, ten more than a human. A Völfien's bite was strong, and they ate fast, gulping down twenty to thirty pounds of meat within minutes.

Kristján inhaled and began to drag himself away from the scene, keeping the völf in his peripheral vision while she occupied herself with feeding on her current prey. He cowered as the massive beast, his perceived savior, towered near him. He continued his crawl through the water and blood while gnashing teeth overpowered the sounds of the running showerheads. He then turned his gaze away from the horror and looked to the exit. The dead naked corpse of Dr. Tiem lay on the floor; his throat had been slashed with Kristján's razor. His beloved pocket watch lay next to the corpse.

Kristján's instinct to escape the large beast suddenly slipped his mind at the idea of being without the closest thing he had of his wife. The völf sensed his escape; her claws began scraping against the tile floors. Her heavy steps crept closer to him. He heard predatory breaths and grumbles as he felt the rising temperature radiating off her form as she moved in.

Inhale. Exhale.

Slurping remnants of saliva hissed in the back of the monster's hot throat.

Inhale. Exhale.

A breath beat against his shoulder blades. He froze, feeling her towering above him. Drips of hot saliva and blood splattered against his back.

It's now or never. I love you, Isabelle!

Kristján lunged for his watch, clutched the chain, and quickly drew it close to his heart. He flipped onto his back after retrieving the watch, clamping his eyes shut. He held his breath, preparing for the consequences of that final maneuver. Droplets of blood sprinkled his face. The sensation led him to open his eyes, and he instantly took in her flared jaw as a deep roar bellowed from the depths of her throat.

Everything went black; all was silent.

☆

Fjorthúr
The Sunspire
The bridge, ground level
Lyul'ai 31

Matthäus stopped and pivoted his gaze down the hall. He walked alongside two other guards, securing the corridors during the after-hours of the Sunspire facility.

The woman accompanying him, Kaja, ex-medic, spoke, "What's got you, Matty?"

Matthäus was a sniper, and, due to his success during the war's final days, he had settled down and become a security lead within Sunspire. "You didn't hear that?" he asked.

The other guard, Rikard, tugged Matthäus's beard as if it were a bell. "Let's go, old man. You're hearing things again."

Matthäus shoved him away. "Step off, Rikard! I bloody well heard something!"

Both Rikard and Kaja had joined the night security crew with sketchy backgrounds. Rikard had been a smuggler at one point, while Kaja had smuggled pharmaceuticals and illegal drugs. Both had aided the Commission and proven themselves trustworthy. With living on-site at the facility, their loyalty could be maintained under Matthäus's leadership and watchful eye.

"Let me radio dispatch Alwin," Kaja said. "I think he's walking the other side of this level. He would've heard it if you did."

"We need to split up," Matthäus directed. "Check fitness and showers, and see if anyone's up. Rikard, you cover her. I'll hit the cafeteria."

The team dispersed.

The Sunspire, which had six levels, was shaped like a pyramidal tower with slightly curved sides. It had been built into the island to make it difficult to access. The only means of leaving or entering was by airship or sea.

The bridge level, also known as the ground floor, had earned its name due to its bridging the gap between the upper and lower levels. The recreation areas, showers, staff housing, and cafeteria were all part of the bridge. The doctors' suites, offices, and main control room were on the upper floors above sea level, while the labs were in the two underground levels. Lab 2, the deepest and most advanced lab, was accessible only to authorized team members. The Sunspire purposely had been designed so that if the labs ever needed to be shut down, any alchemical research would be kept underground, rather than risking release near the surface.

Matthäus charged ahead toward the cafeteria. A group of other security guards were seated at one of the few tables, playing cards. They were off duty and enjoying twin liquor bottles, which, if abused, could result in punitive measures. A record player was playing at a higher-than-appropriate volume. That, mixed with their noisy chatter, made Matthäus go unnoticed as he approached the table.

"Hey!" Matthäus shouted after pushing the needle from the spinning disk. "I doubt you're paying attention to anything with all the noise you're making, but have any of you heard anything outside the area?"

"Like what, sir?" asked one of the men.

Matthäus didn't want to alarm them. "Never mind. Just be on your guard. You should pack it in."

"He's right," one of the men said. "I have first shift tomorrow."

The area beyond the men's table was dark. Matthäus pressed on and headed into the kitchen. The kitchen was immense; it could employ a dozen cooks, two sous chefs, and a head chef. The space was used to feed the entire facility, which could house up to a hundred fifty on-site.

After scanning the kitchen, he came upon the chef's quarters, where three cooks and Chef Ádrez sat outside the kitchen, by ventilation ducts, smoking cigarettes and speaking quietly.

Chef Ádrez noticed him and stepped away, dabbing his cigarette in the ashtray. Matthäus knew him and called him by name: "Ádrez."

"Sir?"

"Anyone beyond the kitchen who isn't a cook?"

"No, just us. We closed the kitchen down pretty late tonight. Since some executives are arriving this week, I wanted to inspect the new shipment."

"Shipment?"

"Yeah. About two hours ago, the shipment—"

"Shipments don't come in for three more days."

"Well, with Dr. Baadar packing in and Dr. Wendtfuss looking to replace him soon, we knew that only the best—"

"Three more days! The log never changed." Matthäus stepped closer to him, correcting him again with a forceful tone.

Matthäus became more suspicious as Ádrez grew more defensive. He took in the chef's eyes. *He's alert. A glimmer of sweat on the brow and upper lip. Always telltale signs of a liar.*

Matthäus's radio abruptly sounded: "Matthäus! We have a breach! Sunspire has been breached!"

The words echoed in Matthäus's head as he caught the overweight chef reaching for the knife at his side. He quickly smashed the butt of his rifle against Ádrez's throat, causing him to drop the knife before he had a chance to use it. The knife clamored sharply onto the floor along with his podgy body.

Matthäus headbutted the nearest standing cook, and he too found the tile floor like a rag doll. He pointed his rifle at the remaining cooks. "Don't move! Has Ádrez been with you this whole time? Answer!"

One cook swiftly drew his knife and pulled the other cook toward him, attempting to take him as his hostage. Matthäus's rifle answered first. The bullet split through one cheek and out the other, and the man emitted a squeal through a gargling weep of pain. The following two bullets pierced through the cook's chest until he hit the ground dead.

The other cook was bewildered about what was happening, but Matthäus expertly observed that he wasn't in on whatever the others had done. "Don't let Ádrez get away. Tie him up, and lock down your quarters. I'll be back!"

"Understood!" The cook nervously obeyed and immediately ran for supplies.

Matthäus took off and ran back through the cafeteria toward the fitness center. The group of men in the café were immediately alerted. Matthäus turned to them. "Apprehend Chef Ádrez. We have a breach!"

"Yes, sir," replied a man who quickly resumed his role while Matthäus continued down the hall.

He got on his headset. "Kaja! What's your location?"

"Lockers. Several dead."

"Hold your position. I'm on my way!"

☆

Fjorthúr
The Sunspire
The bridge washroom
Lyul'ai 31

Rikard maneuvered past a recognized dead colleague who lay on the bench with multiple stab wounds to the stomach. He'd met his fate in the locker room with the obvious assailants, who were also gruesomely massacred in the open shower hall.

Two others were dead in the gym, having been executed at knifepoint. Still, something else seemed to have unfolded in the showers, rendering Rikard and Kaja anxious as they waited for Matthäus, shocked at what they were witnessing.

Kaja's pistol was aimed toward the other end of the shower hall, where the women's half of the lockers were located, while Rikard aimed into the men's half. Suddenly, Matthäus appeared.

"Any bodies over there?" asked Kaja.

"No. What the hell happened?" Matthäus pressed.

Kaja shook her head. "There are five more. Dr. Tiem too." She knelt by a body leaning against the wall. His head was smashed with brain matter sloshed against the wet floors. She pulled up his sleeve to reveal a tattoo on his wrist: a simple triangle. "Opposers of the Commission."

On the Commission's emblem, the Sentry department was the lower half of the symbol; a down-facing triangle. The triangle pointed upward signified opposition to the Commission's purpose. Those who wore it were obsessed with bringing back forces threatening the war's revival.

20

"That crazy fucking cult?" Rikard snapped.

"You got it. The acolytes are at it again," Kaja huffed as she stood up and pointed to the next corpse.

He lay on his back, locked in a gaze of shock as his pupils began to turn white. The evidence of what had killed him was displayed across his abdomen. His intestines blanketed the tiles, while four sizable, thick cuts also lined his chest and extended to his neck, face, and hairline. As the wounds gaped open, they noticed whoever or whatever had killed him had taken parts of his hair.

"Those wounds are not what I think they are, right?" Rikard uncomfortably asked.

"We need to get the hell out of here. Are all the bodies accounted for?" Matthäus urged, meeting Rikard's discomfort.

"We searched the contents throughout the locker. The only unaccounted-for individual is Dr. Kristján Baadar."

"Baadar? What makes you think he's unaccounted for?"

Rikard tossed the pocket watch to his superior. "Check the back."

Matthäus flipped the watch and read the etching in the silver plating: *Dr. Kristján J. Baadar.* "What was he doing down here without an escort?"

"Pool," Rikard answered. "He often finishes his shifts late and likes to go for a swim. He doesn't like anyone—"

"Shifts don't run late. The labs should be closed. Baadar should always have an escort; he's a high profile, Rikard! Where the hell is he now?"

"I thought he was the most loved man in the Spire. I didn't think to make a federal case of his secret late shifts."

"Get fucked!" exclaimed Matthäus, pissed. "Is the pool secured?"

"Yes," replied Kaja with a relieved tone.

"Let's get up to control." Matthäus picked up his radio. "All personnel, lock down Sunspire. We have a breach!" He waited a moment and then turned to his colleagues. "Ádrez is the reason for the cult breach, by the way."

"The fat fuck of a chef?" Rikard sneered.

"Ádrez, the one with the crooked nose? The one you play cards with?" Kaja added, rolling her eyes.

"Lost a week's worth of pay to that cake-eating bastard." Matthäus shook his head.

"Are the ones involved with this cult all dead?" Kaja asked.

"It appears all but Ádrez," Matthäus answered, turning back to his radio. "Control, lock down the Spire. We have a confirmed breach. Do you copy?"

Silence.

Kaja got on her radio, "Control, lock down Sunspire. We have a breach! Do you copy?"

Silence.

"Where the hell is everybody?" Matthäus huffed.

Static suddenly burst through the communication units, followed by a familiar-sounding voice: "Control is gone." Another stream of static broke, and the voice continued. "I implore you to get above the ground level in the next thirty minutes, as I will be releasing the plagued prisoners."

"Prisoners? What prisoners?" Rikard exclaimed, cutting his teammates a baffled look. "Plagued? Is this guy fucking mad—"

"What the fuck is he talking about?" Kaja cut in. "The plague … as in the Näkk?"

"It can't be." Rikard shifted his shoulders uncomfortably, gripping his weapon.

Matthäus returned to his radio. "Who is this?"

Silence.

"Who is this? Damn it, answer!"

"This is Dr. Kristján Baadar. As your superior, I order you to breach level one immediately. You have thirty minutes."

"Dr. Baadar, what the fuck is going on? What did you do? There are people down here! There are—" Matthäus paused and turned to his colleagues, unsure what to say next.

"Matty? Matty, what is it?" Kaja urged. "You must tell him to stop!"

Matthäus swallowed hard and shook his head. He aggressively threw the comm unit to the ground, causing it to shatter into pieces. "Damn it!" he bellowed. "No, there is nothing we can do! We must gather as many people as possible and get the hell off this level. Get to the logs, and check who's on-site—now! This is it; it's happening. Sunspire has fallen!"

CHAPTER TWO

THE VÖLF

Shaar
Tsunetomo
West Wing protectorate tower, second floor
Aoustí 9

"KOVUCO? KOVUCO?" TAM'S VOICE CALLED OUT,
waking me abruptly.

I snapped open my eyes and rose from my pillow, observing the shade still closed around my elongated, oval-shaped cell. My bed had been built into the wall to make more space for my large form; it was the same case for my packmates. We'd joked and called them our coffins.

I pulled back the shade and noticed the light was on in our shared washroom. "Tam?" I said after a massive yawn. "Is that you?"

"Yes. Dancer and Nav'i left to grab breakfast. You'd better be up and dressed before they get back," he said. "Come on! Get moving—it's egg day."

"I didn't sleep in again, did I?" I asked him as I kicked out my foot, pushing the rest of the shade to the end of my cell.

He didn't answer. I swung my legs out and pressed my feet onto the floor; my toes reverberated against the cool bamboo floorboards, crackling with each movement. I scratched my snout with a single claw and let out a quick sniff to clear my sinuses. I then rubbed my eyes with my brawny knuckles before rising from the mattress.

Standing six foot nine, I stretched every toned muscle from my pointed ears, which stretched a few inches above my head, down to the thick pads on the bottom of my clawed feet. My bones cracked and then settled back into their articulated, relaxed state.

I was unmistakably what one called a Völfien.

Our race were linked to the Fae. Unlike the Orkésh or dryads, we more resembled wolves. Our history told the stories of how that all had come to be, but I was still trying to comprehend the bulk of it.

I turned around and peered out at the ocean through our circular window. Our dormitory was housed inside a high, majestic tower that rose out of the sea. A large stone bridge connected us to our master's house, House Frost, which also connected us to the rest of his estate. That included his daughter's chambers, whom my packmates and I were employed to protect.

We were protectorates. *Her* protectorates.

"I could use a reflection, Kovuco," Tam said from the washroom, grabbing my attention again.

"I gotta clean my teeth; I hope that doesn't interfere with what you need to do," I said as I turned away from the view of fierce, crashing waves below.

"Nah. Just a glance is helpful."

Völfien couldn't see their reflections. We could only see our *Rinkin* through anything that cast a reflection. The Rinkin was the closest to that of our human form. *Medzio* was the name of our völf form, and it also was our primary—the form we were born in.

Our Rinkin ability had been gifted to us by an ancient Aureate named Albean. Although it was supposed to link us to the humans, it was a complicated shift and rarely utilized within our race. Even the eldest and most masterful Völfien preferred to remain in their Medzio due to the complexities involved in the shifts.

I didn't understand why our kind had this ability. It was a lingering question that frustrated me. At the end of the day, we were taught that we were Völfien, not humans. Why try to connect with a race that saw us only as a threat, weapon, or, even more demoralizing, a *guard dog*?

Besides, even with our ability to shift, humans still thought we were frightening. Apparently, our mysteriously dark nature intimidates them.

Honestly, behind our muzzles layered in bone-crushing teeth, our towering forms, our flesh-ripping claws, and all the other arsenal of weapon-like physical traits we possessed, seeing the human in me was *far* more frightening than anything the humans chose to be afraid of.

Gooseflesh surfaced along my forearms at the thought.

I loathed the idea of facing my Rinkin. Harrowing events leading up to my adulthood had led me to despise facing my Rinkin or even pursuing the shift. Admitting I didn't want to make eye contact with my Rinkin form or even try to master the transition was taboo. It was a subject I suppressed and kept to myself.

I supposed I was afraid to face who I truly was beneath my Medzio, as well as how the humans wished to see me, not that they'd treat me, or my race, any differently.

"C'mon, Kovuco. I've got to get these vials ready," Tam urged.

How could I forget? What's the point of the ability if we rely on the consumption of human blood to stay civilized?

We needed it. According to the Pjauti—the wülkure's studies on Fae—it was written that healthy human blood helped to maintain our sophisticated nature and kept us from behaving like wild animals. It also kept the Commission off our backs.

A contradicting predicament, in my opinion.

I preferred the old saying, "An ounce of blood a day keeps the monster at bay." But we needed their crimson antidote. I guess one could say we are what we eat.

"Give me another minute," I called out to Tam.

Get out of your head, Kovuco. Focus.

Before heading to our washroom, I pulled out our low-sitting table folded beneath my bunk and lit the stove built into it. It was a round plate of iron with a central landing. On it, I placed our cast-iron kettle to heat water for tea, the preferred beverage in our Shaar'an city, Tsunetomo. I checked to make sure it was filled with water and grabbed my uniform for the day.

I then slipped on my pair of dark slacks. With our legs bent more in the manner of our ancestors, we needed a buckle fastened just above the knee and another buckle fastened below the knee. The design allowed full leg movement without pulling or stretching the fabric. I then tightened my leather belt, which held the pants to my hips, and sealed the carefully sewn pocket to allow my tail to hang freely. Next, I put on

House Frost's red ascot, an essential piece of our uniform. Finally, I put on my leather greaves and bracers, along with my pauldron harness. My packmates and I were all ambidextrous, except for my cousin Tam. Tam was our right-pawed völf and had higher leg armor. It was a combination of leather cuisses, which protected his upper legs, and leather poleyns, which protected his knees while still allowing for ease of movement. He often was our outgoing brute when we had armed assignments.

Finally, I meandered into the washroom and over to my sink that connected next to Tam's. The scents of our specialized soaps filled the tiled room. He faced me quickly to use my Medzio look, gestured for me to turn my head, and used my face as a makeshift reflection so he could assess the leftover food in his teeth as well as ask me if I noticed any leftover pieces.

"I'm good," he finally said, turning away.

I acknowledged him with a nod and resumed my morning routine. Behind me was Nav'i's sink, and next to his was Dancer's. Their stations were always clean and organized. Mine was, too, for the most part. I had a relatively linear routine that I frequently gave up on thanks to Tam's less favored approach to organizing. For Tam being a relative, we surely have our differences.

Using a long rag with particular bristled fabric, I went tooth by tooth, pressing my fingers against the white daggers and rubbing at the blackened gums conservatively before pinching down to the tips of each tooth. I rinsed and then brushed. I gargled the paste in the back of my throat, taking two six-ounce mouthfuls of water to finish the rinse.

Each time, I strategically avoided my reflection.

Finally, the rest of my packmates entered our dorm. Dancer entered first. I heard him setting the table and getting into the tea leaf canisters above his bunk.

Nav'i called out, "Breakfast time, beasts. We're already running behind. Ash will be back soon, if he isn't caught talking again."

"He'll be late," answered Dancer.

Tam laughed. "That old man's always late."

I left the washroom just in time to hear the poultry-laid embryos sizzling on the stovetop. It was the fourth day of the week, which meant the eggs had been recently laid and prepped. With all our meat regulations, eggs were the hero of the protectorate diet.

I glanced over at Nav'i, who was already engrossed in a book. We all actively read and occasionally partook in comic releases every other month, but Nav'i was our most avid and diverse reader. His demeanor was as dark as his fur; his green eyes always were glaring and scoffing at the incongruities of his surroundings. Since perfection was impossible, Nav'i scoffed at others often.

I sat opposite him and crossed my legs, carefully tucking my feet beneath the table's edge. I eagerly eyed Dancer's ingredients, realizing eggs weren't the only thing on the menu.

"Salmon's fresh too?" I asked as my ancestral instincts kicked in, causing my mouth to salivate.

Nav'i eyed me with botheration and then returned to his reading.

"Fresh as it gets. Caught them this morning with Ash," Dancer answered.

Thank Uridei, the fish were rarely regulated on the island, and the greatest of all fish was salmon. *At least I thought so. Better than the bland shit that's administered.*

Dancer grabbed my attention. His brown eyes widened as he impatiently held out an egg on his spatula. I lifted my rice bowl earnestly as the over-easy egg slipped onto the mountain of steaming white kernels. I reached for the finely chopped green onions and scattered them over the sleek protein.

I nodded at him as a thank-you as he turned back toward the hot stove. Dancer's actual name was Danflor, but he'd earned the nickname Dancer for his culinary abilities. He strategically bounced around our small dormitory kitchen and always was quick on his feet. Of the four of us, Dancer was the only one with an unfortunate past. He had been abused and trafficked for most of his life until he'd been liberated by the Religious Order when he was almost fourteen years old.

During that period, he'd assisted a lead chef who taught him his cooking expertise, all while being monitored under the Commission's watchful eye. Once rehabilitated, he had been gifted to our lady by the abbot of Rúnar on her sixteenth birthday. The dark völf remained lean and reserved but found solace through cooking; he executed his dishes well. He, like Nav'i, always looked intense, except he carried an inner peace about him that influenced others to stay grounded and calm.

Tam finally left the washroom just before Nav'i lost his patience. He was dressed in his uniform, which contrasted against his dark golden fur, now groomed for the day. He had a slightly lighter coloration around his left eye that softened his rigid Völfien grimace. Tam was always the most ornery and humorous among us, yet it never detracted from his duties, such as handling our blood doses. His glaring golden eyes fixated on the four vials of blood he carefully set out on the table, two ounces each—the vials ordered daily by Commission regulation.

Next to our tea glasses were lukewarm shots of rice liquor. We all gathered and raised our shots in unison with faith in Uridei and then recited the Order's prayer together:

> Oh, light of Uridei,
> merit me to your will.
> Grant me the hand to Purge, to cleanse, sanctify, and
> purify.
> Give me the courage to stand in the way.
> Forgive us our transgressions.
> Cast out the darkness; make way your fire.
> Speak, Uridei; your servant is listening.

Moments later, like clockwork, we finished at the same time. We uncorked the vials, spilled the blood into the lucent liquor, and shot it to the back of our throats.

I watched the ceiling, wide-eyed. My pupils dilated. My face tightened, locking in the sedative through my blood vessels and arteries. Like a drug, it excited my senses. My nostrils flared, and saliva spilled over my teeth. My chest vastly expanded as my fists clenched; claws dug into my palms, and my ears fell limp. All we could do was breathe through it—breathe till the spell set in, and we were granted one more day in human graces.

All of those sensations happened in a few quick moments. Outsiders would probably have thought they were watching a cult phenomenon—four armored völves sitting cross-legged and sharing a shuddering moment in unison.

Or just something else to add to the list of fears we raise in humans.

Once we were finished with our vials, we cleaned our muzzles and returned to the breakfast that fueled our daily duties. Dancer returned to the stove while Tam drizzled syrup over his bowl like the inner child he was. The rest of us, who had *normal* cravings, added a pinch of pink salt.

I began to eat quickly, retreating into my thoughts.

All my packmates were far darker-furred than I was; I was the rarity. The only coloration we had in common was in the bits of lighter fur extending from our mandibles down to our abdomens. We had been hand-picked because of this lighter throat coloration. It had become an unplanned trend of our lady's preference and had earned us the name *White Throats*.

Our lady seemed to think those lighter areas of fur were cute. The feather-like darker marks on either side of my neck were also cute to her, despite where they had come from. My packmates and I didn't prefer that word being associated with our characteristics, but we would never admit that to her; because of her role, she could say and do as she pleased.

Ameilja Rose Frost, practically royalty, was the lady of the Religious Order of Shaar, and the highly sought-after daughter of High Abbot András Frost.

Since day one, she had demanded we call her by her first name in her presence; personal recognition meant more to her than her title. Again, we acknowledged her requests.

"Do you think Ameilja will be training in our House temple today?" Tam asked Dancer as he took another heaping bite.

Hearing her name caught my attention.

Dancer shrugged, continuing to cook. Nav'i eyed them, took a bite, and then glanced back to his book. I, too, retreated back into my thoughts.

Völves were considered adults at the age of fourteen; however, the age to serve as a protectorate in the Commission was eighteen. I had just turned eighteen, already passed the Völfien rite of passage into adulthood, and applied for the protectorate calling in House Frost. A fresh start after my dispiriting, almost deadly trial.

All because of who I am.

I did not bear any of our race's typical colorations; I was platinum-furred. My fur was smooth like metal, devoid of pigment except for a gasp of blond that only the sun could uncover. I was extraordinary, wrapped from head to toe in this unusual coloration. I was the only duplicate of my father but far less legendary.

As if it wasn't enough to heighten my sense of mental leprosy, I possessed a unique set of eyes. Those who enamored them defined them as *"bright, burning diamonds."* Some even compared them to the ocean's icebergs, with frigid, dark unknowns hidden beneath their tips. There was a widespread idea in the Eastern Isles that Fae with blue eyes were cursed with demonic ancestry. Blue was regarded as the demon's color, and rumor had it that when an open flame met a demon's brimstone flesh, it illuminated blue.

My rare eyes and fur coloration were one of the reasons I'd had to face a deadly trial, but it had been primarily due to my father, the ancient, legendary Adémaro Blackstar. He was known to have survived many centuries, aided Albean during the war against the Näkk, and fought alongside the humans during the later years of the divisive Great War.

He, too, had faced a similar trial. It had been required that he establish with the human race, and by the will of Uridei, that he was not a demon and prove that his soul was not denounced. When he'd demonstrated his worth and won the trial, he had become one of the most powerful Völfien in the Eastern Isles, the first sworn Völfien paladin, and worked alongside the humans of the Religious Order. That had led to the rise of the Order of Völfien, who erected the Temple of Spears in honor of our race.

Those had been the days when the humans accepted us as allies, the gifted race from their savior Albean, and granted us the ability to live like paladins.

Those days had been short-lived.

When sworn in as a paladin, per implemented custom, you needed House approval before taking a wife or, in our case, a mate. My father's first mate, Rhúlain, had been killed during the war, leaving my two elder black-furred, dark-eyed brothers without their mother. My father had been stricken with grief for nearly a century until he met *my* mother.

I was a bastard born from a mother I'd never met. My father had taken a new mate without the blessing of the Order. Since my elder brothers were highly trusted and bore proper coloration, they were liberated from my father's forbidden actions. My unique appearance had delivered bad omens throughout the Religious Order, and my mother's unknowns had given many paladins great concern. They'd demanded my father reveal my mother's identity, but he'd refused. He immediately had been ex-communicated and demoted from paladin, leaving me to later face a trial that almost led to my demise.

I hadn't decided if I'd forgiven my father, although many Völfien still saw him as a legend. If they had their life dangling before their eyes as I had, I'd presume they'd feel differently, too.

Since after my father's fall, it seemed the Order of Völfien had fallen with him. A human now ran the Temple of Spears despite its representation of us. I utterly believe my father's forbidden actions had been the official excuse to keep our race under the Commission's thumb; since then, they had strictly silenced us and practically shackled us under their rules and regulations. The other Fae races, unfortunately, fell under similar treatment, but we were the focus.

However, despite my reservations about the human race, I will forever be grateful for my current position within House Frost. I felt accepted there.

Accepted by *her*.

It had been four years since I took the position, but I remembered that day as if it had been yesterday.

☆

I stood in the line of thirteen Völfien candidates, standing out like a sore thumb. At the time, I knew little of Lady Ameilja. I'd only seen a photo of her, but I knew she was twenty at the time.

When Ameilja entered the room, it was as if time itself stopped. Her long, flowing hair was down, red like a river of warm blood against her white uniform shirt. Unlike most women of the Order, who chose a formal dress, Ameilja wore dark pants with pockets, a Commission belt, and dark boots. Her leather corset hugged her curved waist perfectly, allowing bits of the shirt to flow freely with her gait. She had to pick two more völves to complete her Völfien protectorate, also called a Court of Völfien bodyguards.

At the time, she hadn't thought about her pattern of choosing White Throats. I watched her pick Nav'i first. He was in my graduating class and had also grown up with me during our training years in Kyottó. I assessed her in my peripheral vision as she twisted a few of his differently colored hairs before she approved him. She then proceeded until she got to me, pivoted to face me more directly, and eyed the darker marks on either side of my neck.

She then gingerly smiled at my lighter spots, admiring them as if they had been painted by an artist's fine brush, but instead, my large form was the canvas.

"May I?" she asked, holding out her dainty hands.

I was surprised she asked, but I nodded nervously and leaned forward so she could reach them better.

"These are cute," she said, smiling warmly at me. "What's your name, Blue Eyes?"

The wülkure in the chamber said, "His name is—"

She held up a hand to interrupt. "I asked the Völfien, not a wülkure."

I swallowed hard. "Kovuco, Lady Ameilja."

"Kovuco. You're Adémaro's son, aren't you?" she asked without hesitation.

I nodded and answered, "Yes, Lady Ameilja. Third-born son of Adémaro Blackstar."

Surnames were discouraged among völves, but it slipped out.

Ameilja smiled wider. "Kovuco Blackstar, you are perfect."

I trembled, trying to remain statuesque and proud.

"But is this a perfect match?" she added, tilting her head in question.

I shifted. "Lady Ameilja?"

"Ameilja," she corrected sharply. "Just call me Ameilja."

I nodded. "Ameilja. Apologies."

"What do you say? Do you want to be my fourth and final Völfien?"

I didn't understand. The choice wasn't mine to make. It was hers. "I, uh—"

"Kovuco, I want you, but you have to want me too. Otherwise, this will never work. So? What say you, blue-eyed Kovuco Blackstar of Adémaro? Do you want to be my final Völfien?"

Her glistening, fearless green eyes locked with mine. In that moment, I felt smaller. I stood two feet above her, but somehow, I felt minuscule. I felt safe in some strange sector of her world. Her dauntless eyes beckoned me to some distant place rich with her, a world far from here. Her smell I captured like a scent desiring to be discovered only by me—a scent to kill for.

She waited for my answer. If I said yes to her, it would be my oath, my sole purpose. I'd leave my father's side to serve the Commission and protect the daughter of High Abbot András Frost. I knew nothing of her and would only learn afterward. All I had was that moment; her every move was intoxicating. The way her eyes narrowed—she smirked at challenges and invited them like friends. Her blood-red hair—I was lost in its supernatural, otherworldly beauty.

Even scarier, that was the moment I realized my thoughts wandered to a place new, unfamiliar, and gravely forbidden.

Damn it.

I bowed low. "Yes, Ameilja Frost. I, Kovuco Blackstar, will be your final Völfien. My life for yours. My teeth and claws, my strength, and my thirst belong to you."

She crossed her chest with her right fist. "Light of Uridei, Kovuco Blackstar."

I reciprocated. "Light of Uridei, Ameilja." I smiled so vastly that it hurt. I didn't think I'd ever smiled so big.

For once, I felt accepted.

Accepted by her.

☆

"Are you done, Kovuco?" asked Tam, nudging me with his elbow.

I snapped back into reality and gazed down into my bowl, picking at an empty hollow. "Yeah, yeah, I'm finished."

"You still want your salmon, right?" asked Dancer, balancing a spatula toward me.

Nav'i glared at my empty bowl. "Eat with some dignity, Kovuco. No one's going to take it from you."

I cleared my throat. "Sorry. I was distracted."

"You're always distracted," Nav'i grumbled, adjusting his shoulders.

I offered my bowl, and the fillet of salmon spilled into the ceramic pit. Dancer smothered the fillet in cream cheese and layered slices of cucumber.

A knock sounded at the door.

Dancer remained attentive to the stovetop, and Nav'i continued reading; he grunted at his inability to volunteer, while Tam reached for a second helping of rice. I rose to answer.

"Mouth's full," Tam managed to say to excuse his inability to answer the door too.

"I've got it." I sighed.

I opened our dormitory door and was instantly met with our wülkure guardian, Ash.

Wülkure, members of the Commission's Sentry department, owned the roles of watching, hunting, and handling the Fae if they stepped out of line. That included us. Wülkure were known for their combat prowess. They also were masters at understanding and utilizing Fae magic, venom, or concocted emulsions to protect humanity in their everyday lives.

House Frost had to employ a team of wülkure because we völves were there.

"G'morning, Kovey. Did I miss breakfast?" Ash said in his usual chipper fashion. A slight twang coated his accent.

Dancer called out, "Always plenty."

"Just a joke, but I do smell that salmon. Have an extra?" he asked as he strutted in.

Unlike most of the wülkure, Ash was considerate and genuinely interested in us. Often, we had to remind him that we weren't his children. He was old enough to be our senior. Although he was twice the age of most wülkure, he had the energy of a young human adult.

"Age is a matter of the mind," he always reminded us. I found it funny since our race were practically immortal compared to his.

Over the years, he had lacked a proper shave, which made his goatee more prominent and added character to his rugged voice. As of the past year, his tiny-circled spectacles had become a transparent prescription. Behind his collar, he had a monocle he utilized to read. He'd hook it onto the lens over his right eye when needed. His hair was shoulder-length, maple blond fading into a white-ish gray, and typically bound by a red ribbon. A metal cross charm hung from the center knot.

He wore his usual trench coat, and his wide-brimmed hat and was armed with his father's gun, White Powder, a forty-five-caliber revolver with a red lens scope. The handle was etched with a thorn pattern. We each caught scent of the deadly féja and vilkanás wafting off of his form, but we trusted Ash entirely. As a wülkure, Ash had to carry those lethal vials and bullets to take advantage of our weak points if anything got out of control.

Féja powder was a sort of tranquilizer for members of the Fae, but it also was reasonably effective on members outside the Fae class. Vilkanás was specific to völves; it was our bane.

Ash sat at the head of the table and removed his hat. Dancer prepared him a bowl. "Egg?" Dancer asked.

Ash shook his head. "Nah, just the salmon, but spare not the rice. Gotta keep those calories up."

Dancer quickly prepared his rice bowl with the cream cheese salmon but omitted the cucumber, as he knew Ash loathed vegetables.

Nav'i wrinkled his muzzle and gave Ash a judgmental look, eyeing the wülkure's rounded abdomen. "Do you need the extra calories, Ash?"

"Thank you, Dancey!" He turned to Nav'i. "Naturally. How else would I keep this gut I have accumulated?"

Ash had a thing for nicknames. He was quite lax with them, as evidenced by his selection of Dancey and Kovey. Tam and Nav'i were fortunate in that their names were already brief.

"Always delicious when Dancey makes it. What's on the menu for dinner tonight?"

"You're already thinking about dinner?" Nav'i grimaced.

Tam held back a laugh.

"I premade gyoza," answered Dancer, still attending to his kitchen duties.

"Excellent! Anything ya want me to add?"

"Maybe some of those pickled bean sprouts?"

"How's about a dessert instead?"

We all shook our heads. Typical Ash.

Ash finished the last of his salmon and set the bowl on the table. He reached into his jacket and brought out a sack filled with coins for his contribution to the groceries. "Here—take this as my thank-you."

Dancer nodded.

Ash swiftly adjusted his hat back on his head and sighed deeply. "Well, let's get on with it, boys. I know Ameilja has a stacked day today." He clipped his monocle over his lens as he pulled out a small, wrinkled notepad from his jacket pocket, flipped it to a particular page, and scanned the notes. "And it's the type of day she may want to slack off on—or bite one of our heads off knowing what day tomorrow is … either way, today's training might be a long one." He sighed again as he raised his thick brows.

We quickly cleaned up and prepared our beds per our daily structured orders, followed by adding our harnesses, which sheathed our tonfa swords. Ameilja's Court of Völfien were known for twin tonfa swords, which were about the length of a human's forearm. With Tam's unruly nature, he called them our fish fins.

Per routine, we followed Ash down the spiral staircase to the large iron gate at our tower's base. Our freedom was through that gate. He retrieved a slightly rusted skeleton key from his jacket and unlocked it, shifting the spiraling metal into a screeching moan. We stepped forward onto the bridge, and a forceful coastal breeze swept over our forms as the salty air instantly hit our senses, diminishing the bitter scent from the iron gate.

The wind was harsh, especially for a human. The landscape below was even more arduous, as the aggressive waves crashed into the large, jagged rocks beneath us; the sound often created a whirling roar that echoed against our tower.

Walking, I could see the city's rooftops beyond the Frost estate due to the bridge's height. The silhouetted rooftops and ornately designed buildings glistened against the sun's morning rays, sometimes resembling specks of white marble. The Frost estate's architecture was intricate and constructed of the highest quality of stone and wood. When in season, thick green vines mixed with roses, clematises, and other flowers creep up its tan-colored stones. Ameilja's courtyard specifically included snowdrop flowers in the colder months; they stood for hope—signs of change for the better.

The entire House structure had a waving, layered roof guarded by wooden dragons carved by Shaar's most skilled dwarven carvers. House Frost's preferred artisan and blacksmith was an elderly dwarf. His hair was ivory white and worn in a taut bun on top of his head, while numerous braids filled his beard like a military vest. As a Fae, he respected us and remembered us by name, so we always remembered him: Master Galfnik Genzatsu.

We finally entered the landing that led into the private halls of the estate. We always took the same route to get to Ameilja's wing. Each step welcomed a familiar scent that told me we were getting closer to her; by then, I could have found her blindly.

House Frost's interior was comprised of an intriguing mix of ogive architecture and an edge of the Shaar'an design. It emanated the strength of our land and its people. Oak floors, standing for bravery, ran the length of the halls. Tall vases stood on either side of every other window. Each piece had beautiful depictions of creatures native to Shaar and overflowed with exotic, indoor flowers. Lining the windows were thick teal curtains embroidered with gold, which always were drawn to allow the sunlight or moonlight to pour in. At the ends of the hall were suits of armor once worn by Shaar'an warriors. A statue of Albean was also placed in each hall, with a memorial piece from the war.

Ameilja had a whole hall to herself. Sometimes we'd catch her out there, swinging her swords or a spear. Occasionally, if she was angry enough, we'd see her shooting arrows from the windows blindly in her rage. Her whimsically wild nature stood out among the other paladin women and their gentler customs, but Ameilja was no ordinary woman.

There she is.

Ameilja appeared, having just left her room, swinging her blood-red hair from her face and tossing on her red jacket. My heart jumped to my throat, my muscles tensed as my nerves sliced through my form. My tongue danced behind my teeth nervously, practically acting involuntarily. All I could do was bite down on the lapping muscle and attempt to breathe normally.

Fucking hell—act normal, Kovuco!

Time slowed as we made our way to her. Every time I saw that storm of autumn fire and breathed in her scent, the same uncontrollable feeling overtook me. My völf mind went places it shouldn't have.

Where has she been? What has she touched? How did she sleep? Did she dream? What did she wear while she slept?

I eyed her form, allowing my senses to absorb every part. She wore her usual attire: slim-fitted pants of a leaf-green color, a gold-studded leather belt, and cuffed combat boots with modest heels made of fine suede and leather. She wore an underbust corset over her black cashmere blouse—her favorite fabric. Her jewelry was light and intentional, especially the Commission necklace that hung above the curve of her breasts. It had been a gift from her mother, and she never took it off.

Now wait for it.

Her head turned, her lips lightly parted, and a sweet smile formed on those pink lips as her eyes briefly met mine.

There it is. There's the smile.

It drove me crazy to contain the joy I felt and the strength that rose within me just to have her eyes lock with mine.

We stopped in unison behind Ash when we met her and then saluted one another.

"Good morn'in, kid," Ash said, tipping his hat.

"Good morning, Ash. Good morning, my White Throats." Her soothing voice surfaced the space. She turned back to Ash. "Thank you, Ash. I can take it from here."

Ash turned to us and shifted his eyebrows. "Again, we break the rules, boys, to give you some freedom. Make it a good day."

Ameilja was required to be escorted by a wülkure and her protectorates at all times; however, she often insisted that Ash keep his distance. For the most part, he did.

As soon as Ash disappeared, she nodded. "Come on then. We have a long day ahead." She paused, adjusting her sleeve. *"But* I have a surprise in store." She then turned confidently to lead us away from her wing.

"Surprise?" asked Nav'i, alerted. "Or an escapade?"

Escapades are what Ameilja and her White Throats do.

Her smile tightened, and her pale cheeks warmed. "Both. But the surprise will come later—just a little pre-birthday ritual."

I wondered if it would follow suit with last year's.

Nav'i nodded and shot us each an intense look as we began our usual walk. Ameilja walked between Tam and me; Dancer followed behind, while Nav'i led—our usual arrangement. It was obvious our escapades and Ameilja's random surprises made Nav'i nervous, as he knew the boundaries crossed.

Ameilja swiftly leaned closer to Tam. "You smell quite handsome today, Tambor; is that the new cologne I had Father grant you?"

"I believe so. And handsome, you say?" He smirked, lifting his chin.

Ameilja smiled proudly. "If the rest of the human populace want to fear you, fine. Let them. Let's see their reactions when they catch *my* Court of Völfien smelling of *hair-raising* deep spice and smoky accents."

Tam chuckled under his breath.

She looked up at him, raised a thumb to his lip, and flicked a rice kernel. "Oh, but you missed one, you big oaf!"

Tam rolled his eyes, wincing at her mischievously. "Didn't even bother scraping my teeth either." He winked as he opened his jaws and exhaled his hot breath on her forehead like a dragon igniting a knight ablaze, with a bellowing growl included.

She laughed and swatted him away. "Ugh! Keep that stench to yourself!"

"By that smell, he's probably not lying about skipping out on the teeth cleaning," added Nav'i over his shoulder.

Tam shot Nav'i a glowering look. "It's just a joke, Nav'i—lighten up."

Nav'i grinned, keeping his stride forward.

Some strange insecurity in me reminded me to inspect my teeth quickly. Naturally, our shredding teeth tended to retain ribbons of whatever we ate, even after we cleaned them. I swallowed hard and began picking at my teeth with my tongue, ensuring I had cleared any breakfast debris. I crossed a remnant of egg between my lower premolars.

Shit, this is what I get for sleeping in.

I tried to free the egg remnant with my tongue but decided to address the shred with a pinkie claw quickly. Unfortunately, I wasn't inconspicuous enough.

Ameilja caught my quick gesture, and with a gentle pinch, she nicked the tip of my lip just shy of my nose. I felt a mild sting, but it was a gift for her to bestow me with physical contact. It felt intentional and random as if she wanted the wide-eyed shift in my gaze so I could see that sweet smile of hers. Ameilja always smiled around us, but I wanted to think this smile was just for me.

Maybe it's all in my head.

This specific smile wasn't the sharp and confident one she always put on for everyone else, even when she was teasing Tam. This smile was different, accompanied by a casual glance and a playful smirk, leaving me to guess what it meant. It was as if she were looking straight into my soul, reminding me that I have a purpose in an unfair world. It was the same glance she had given me when she asked me to be her final völf, and it had haunted me ever since. It was the smile that invited me to the sector of the world where only she existed. I didn't know if I'd ever know what it meant. All I could do was hope to serve in this position for the rest of my life, and maybe one day I would unfold what that smile meant.

Perhaps I'd also gain an understanding of the unheard-of emotions I harbored within.

All I know, as does everyone, is that humans do not give their hearts to beasts.

CHAPTER THREE

THE WAY OF THE WÜLKURE

Isarah
Demitori City, Brass District
Grande Mariner Apartment Complex, room 504
Aousti 9

"I LOOK LIKE SHIT," KIEFER MURMURED TO THE twenty-nine-year-old reflection of himself. He wiped away the steamy condensation buildup on the mirror and gazed into his sullen brown eyes.

Always tired.

He pulled back the curtain of black bangs that hung around his face, freeing his dark brows, wondering why he kept such a haircut. His physique was well-toned, but his self-care and grooming were lacking; his weighted wülkure position was his reason.

Rae stepped out of the tub, pulled the towel from around Kiefer's waist, and dried off. She backhanded his bare buttock playfully. "Get cleaned up. I've gotta get going."

Kiefer didn't comment, even after she brushed his dark bangs aside, kissed his stubbled cheek, and left him alone to bathe.

"What time will you be home tonight, Kief?" she called from his bedroom across the hall.

"Not sure." He replied, tightening his lips as he got into the claw-foot tub and gradually submerged himself in the water.

He flinched—he'd hoped the water would be a little less scalding.

Rae always took painfully hot baths and showers, and he could never join her immediately. Carefully, he leaned back against the circular wall of the tub. He outstretched his arms to keep himself from sinking deeper into the scalding water.

Rae returned moments later, dressed, and began to apply her makeup.

Rae Arow, a wächter within the Commission, wore a maroon skirt, knee-high combat boots, and a uniform jacket. She was the only woman in her unit confident enough to wear a skirt, although she was one of the few females in her department.

The wächters were the operators of the seas and skies and were trained to operate heavy weaponry, ships and aircraft. They often studied the dangers of the *blues*, what they called the ocean and sky, in contrast to the wülkure, who wielded their weapons from a grounded stance and acquired guidance from the Book of Pjauti: *Art of the Fae, Banes, and Venoms.* Together they formulated a powerful Sentry department against any race that tried to bring harm or divisive tactics against the humans.

"Well, whatever you're up to, I might not be coming back here tonight," Rae said as she began applying eyeliner to her mahogany-brown eyes.

"Oh?" Kiefer asked, scrubbing his hair with Rae's expensive shampoo she insisted on leaving in his apartment.

He recalled her exact words: "The least you could do is give me a tiny spot on your bathroom shelf." She wasn't wrong, and he didn't mind, especially since it meant he didn't have to shop for shampoo. The stuff Rae picked out was better on the scalp anyway. Kiefer had seen improvement after a few treatments; surprisingly, his dark hair was less dull.

"What do you have to do that's so pressing?" he huffed as he reached for the showerhead, but Rae snatched it first.

"Okay, grouch," she said as she turned on the stream and ran the water over his head to massage his scalp.

Thank Uridei, it wasn't scalding. She didn't even test it with her hands first!

"You know you're supposed to apply conditioner too, right?" she reminded.

"Sure," he said, inhaling deeply as the hypnotic massage began. He had completely lost his train of thought, allowing the scent of warm lavender and vanilla to fill his senses.

Of all the women he'd been with, Rae was the most affectionate, even if, at times, he wanted her to leave him be. She seemed to have taken a liking to caring for him, an intrigue, or so he thought. One morning, he'd woken up to find his fingernails and toenails had been filed and cleaned—an odd gesture in showing her affection. *Maybe that's what people in love do.*

He thought that since they both worked in the same line of work, maybe she found some solace in their relationship. Or she just enjoyed disassembling him slowly in his environment, like a parasite he would learn to love. *Whatever love means.*

Rae might have been a wächter but had larger aspirations and an intentional mission. She was currently in school, hoping to earn her way into the Academy Branch of the Commission as an alchemist. Along with her ambition of joining a new department, she'd even explored the idea of being a journalist. Rather than inviting her adherent liberal professors or conservative military upbringing to tell her how the world worked, she wanted to experience the world firsthand to formulate her own opinions. As for Kiefer's aspirations, he never veered from the wülkure department.

Rae's father, the former centurion of Demitori City, was the one who'd hired Kiefer as a wülkure. Had Rae's father known he was sleeping with his daughter regularly, it stood to question whether he'd still have made the cut.

Kiefer had rightfully earned his role and was damned good at his job. Within just two years of stepping into the position, Kiefer had been promoted to æsir, a team leader within the Commission. Since then, he had led a team of wülkure in the neighboring district for the last seven years. No one was more dedicated than Kiefer Yuska.

Rae guided Kiefer's now mellowed body out of the tub and onto his washroom stool. He sighed satisfyingly as she continued to massage his neck and shoulders.

Kiefer saw the Commission for what it was—a corporation—despite what its mission stated in regard to order and peace. It was a working system of three main departments—the Sentry, Academy, and Religious

Order—simultaneously working together like an engine's gears interlocking to keep moving forward. Kiefer was not the religious type, nor had he befriended any paladins, but he understood their role was essential. He called them "the Uridei followers," and they were the ones who could effectively handle the more ominous forces of darkness, such as demons or the Näkk. It was all because of their acquired Purge powers.

Since the Näkk's defeat centuries ago, speaking its name aloud had practically become intolerable. It was a bone-chilling subject; no one wished to speak about it or risk awakening such devastation back into existence. Although the paladins would primarily handle the Näkk, each sector of the Commission knew what to look out for when it came to any hint or trace of its insidious power.

Rae started to pat Kiefer's hair dry; the palpations urged him out of his thoughts. The bathwater was now almost drained. She slapped the towel onto his lap, intending to playfully create a sting on his tenders, and then kissed his cheek.

"I'll be back soon, okay? Be safe." She smirked and then turned to the sink for some last-minute touch-ups.

"Sure," Kiefer mumbled. "Wait! *Where* are you going?"

She laughed, knowing he'd let the conversation slip him easily due to the scalp massage. "I have exams today and tomorrow. But I'll be back in a couple of days or so."

"Why not just come back here? My place is nicer than that dormitory of yours."

"Maybe. I've got some studying before the exam, and *you* are a distraction. I'll be back; don't worry." She finished putting her brown hair in a ponytail, accentuating her heart-shaped face. "Nicer than that dormitory, huh?" she scoffed.

Kiefer snorted. "My king-sized bed, fine silk sheets, and high-end amenities versus those cotton drabs on your twin in a room you share with two other women? Yeah, my place is nicer."

She leaned backward, batting her bright brown eyes. "Didn't stop you from following me into those cotton drabs, did it?" Before he could comment, she turned the corner, calling after him, "I'm off! Bye!"

The door slammed behind her.

Once. I followed her there once.

He rose from his stool, tightened the towel around his waist, headed into the hall, and trekked into his bedroom to dress. Before putting on his black leather boots, he put on a white dress shirt, dark slacks, and socks. He tightened on his dual-buckled utility belt, which held a holster for his pistol, and a bushcraft knife sheathed on the back. The knife's sheath contained a flint for fires and waterproof matches.

Whenever Kiefer slipped into his wülkure jacket, it no longer was just a jacket but became an arsenal of tools and banes he utilized with professional efficiency. His wülkure jacket visually stated his role; it symbolized the hunter of the Commission and was always notable: a full-length coat made of durable black denim with splits in the lower back and sides for easy movement. While it was a tool, it was a stylish jacket with broad period cuffs, braids, and golden buttons adorning the sleeves. The laced double-collar could be worn down or up for disguise.

Wülkures wore additional custom belts and straps under their jackets so they could effectively unleash hell in their own customized approaches. The belts held pouches of vials filled with deadly cocktails, crafted emulsions, ammunition, and tools. All were used against the Fae.

His most valued possessions, his cigarettes and lighter, were kept in the tiny customized pocket sewn inside his jacket, just over his heart.

Before leaving his flat, he lit a cigarette. He then swiftly headed into his kitchen and grabbed his pocket watch off the table. As soon as the aroma reached his nostrils, he realized coffee had just been freshly brewed.

Another caring feature of Rae.

He filled his canteen with scalding black coffee and left for another full day of tedious investigative work.

Isarah
Demitori City, Brass District
Grande Mariner Apartment Complex
Aousti 9

Kiefer stepped out onto the bustling streets of the Brass District and stumbled over the first step. He nearly careened into a man in obvious business attire. The unknown man's eyes met his; in a quick moment of judgment, he eyed Kiefer as if he were some petulant drunk, despite his obvious wülkure attire.

Kiefer hadn't had a drop; he never drank. He hated being numb. He hated being out of control. He had plenty of coffee and one too many cigarettes, but Kiefer had never been a drunkard.

"Fucking prick!" Kiefer scoffed under his breath, causing his cigarette to bob between his lips.

The look the man had given him was a false accusation he didn't want to accept. Kiefer had no room to be slow and slurred. He always was alert and hyperactive.

Quick and vigilant. Coffee and cigarettes. Fighting and fucking.

He brushed it off, adjusted his jacket, and continued forward through the lively streets.

Demitori was the largest city in Isarah, constructed along the sea, and owned the largest ports on the continent. It was comprised of five districts, each named after a mineral, gem, or metal: Brass, Copper, Pearl, Obsidian, and Sapphire. The architecture was uniquely designed per district.

As the sun ascended, Brass's streets were still gaslit. Citizens were finishing their nightly rounds or starting their mornings, walking the streets constructed of copper, bronze, and steel. Towering sandstone structures reinforced with metal scaffolding displayed large circular or square windows with weblike panes, some in swirls or geometric designs.

Along with steam and smoke-filled skies, glistening metals, and hums of operating machinery, the blusters of the Brass District's populace filled the atmosphere with an array of sounds. Their heavy accessories clinked as they walked and varied from leather holsters to small purses hanging from thick belts. They typically wore earth-tone colors, such as brown and black jackets over cream or light green shirts. Striped and strap-latched jackets were popular, often adorned with intricate metal buttons. Buckled boots and thigh straps to carry knives were considered fashion statements. Sometimes there was a mix, depending on their primary districts.

The locals sought to boldly coordinate the city's architecture with the creativity of their attire. Overall, Kiefer blended well with this crowd.

As for Kiefer's residence, it was located along the less desirable border of Brass, but it brought convenience since he was stationed two alleys down in the Copper District; the corner of Demitori avoided by the human populace.

The Fae were the primary inhabitants of Copper. It was also known as the infamous, forgotten district out of the five. Faeries of all shapes and sizes walked fearlessly in broad daylight; even the dainty, flying Fae could rhythmically dance about the lights or flutter under the moon like whimsical moths with no judgment. Larger Fae races, such as minotaurs, the Völfien, and some of the Orkésh, also inhabited Copper and thrived effortlessly. Völves didn't have to worry about being feared by humans, and minotaurs could grow their horns as large as they pleased. Compared to the human-dominated areas and establishments, Copper's structural design had been constructed to house both large and small forms. It stood out compared to the districts around it, which continued to gentrify. Copper had remained a quaint, uncanny place nearly untouched by technological advances and mechanics. A large contributor was the fact that the völves deterred humans and their preferred advancements.

Copper was the exception, stranger than strange, hidden and dark.

"Here we go," Kiefer whispered under his breath as he entered his District.

He could already feel the weight of the day as he took a long drag from his cigarette, exhaling the smoke as two Völfien walked by. They dipped their heads with a slight nod and quickly moved forward. Kiefer took note of the packaged vials of blood both of them carried.

While some of the Fae were an ethereal, complex, and strangely beautiful race, they were known for their tactics. For the most part, they were nonaggressive. Due to that fact, Kiefer's expertise was in the Völfien race. He did not often run into issues with the Völfien, but with the constant nitpicking and stereotyping from the Commission, they were always under their radar more than any other Fae, even more so than the unruly orks. From Kiefer's perspective, the Völfien were an intelligent race but troublesome without ever having to be problematic. He believed they were not vain or cruel, but they looked like creatures from nightmares, especially during a defensive attack. For years, the human race had harbored a lingering fear against them. They were civilized as long as there was no looming threat; their young were left alone; and, most importantly, they kept up with their ordered blood doses.

The völves had a vice: they needed blood. As alcoholics poured themselves a drink to drown their demons, the völves poured a couple of ounces of blood to sustain their wild nature.

Wülkures were often the preferred employers of their blood stations. It was the Commission's way of keeping its finger on the pulse of the Völfien race, ensuring they didn't escalate into their more feral state. Without the daily blood doses, Völfien would have lost some of their civility but, controversially, not their abilities.

The Völfiens' gifted abilities are a subject that's vastly fascinated Kiefer for years. He had practically memorized the Pjauti. In the text, it described the Völfien scent as a vision. The world would ground to a halt, and they could see an almost ultraviolet spectrum in an echo chamber. It was understood that at times, they could even make out actions already committed, through a transcendent level of knowledge. Their tall ears would stand up like antlers, sensing their environment with immortal muster—a fascinating feat. Kiefer had also learned that the völves could smell prey more than two miles away; they only needed a little scent of blood, saliva, or skin. He didn't mind utilizing them for under-the-table pay if necessary. Once, he'd had a völf scratch an ork female "by accident" so he could track her down a week later for questioning.

Völfien were keen, loyal creatures who harbored vast strengths. Like sharks in grandiose oceans, they could smell, track, and pursue prey with a single drop of blood. That was why völves were employed and utilized. Although he was not the religious type, he agreed with Albean's decision.

In theory, everything about the Völfien, and all Fae, was engrossing.

"Morning." Kiefer subtly nodded as he passed familiar faces before nearing his building. Some faces knew him, and some didn't. Some faces disliked him. The sting of their magic and unique food spices hit his senses. Even their choice of perfumes and colognes was uncanny. He called few inhabitants of this district a friend, but it didn't matter; Copper was Kiefer's; it was all under his control and expertise.

He neared his office, which was immediately past the fish market on Stonemill Road, next to a construction firm owned and maintained by an old minotaur named Carsten Castorbold. Carsten employed a wide range of Fae, including Kiefer's tracking völf, Teo.

Carsten and Kiefer were on good terms. Kiefer could have called him a friend, or maybe a close acquaintance, but he merely utilized Carsten and his employees as an eager resource.

Another Fae Kiefer utilized was a unique ork by the name of Arvo Hellinski. Arvo was quiet and collected compared to his kind. He and his partners operated a legal firm on the fourth floor in the same building as Kiefer. Arvo was astute and fair, which had earned him the right to legally represent the Copper District's wülkure department. Arvo's approved representation was a shock to Kiefer, but accepted.

As for the Orkésh, they were the race that troubled Kiefer, and he was transparent about his opinion of them, even justified. The Commission struggled to micromanage the Orkésh. Their numbers were significant, and they bred like rabbits. Since the beginning of the Great War's divide, a large wave of orks had migrated to the uninhabited lands of Isarah and called their new settlement A'grommár, while others had dispersed throughout the Eastern Isles and other continents.

The orks were a prideful, unruly race that chose to remain polarizing. They were far more tedious and criminally involved than other Fae. Over the years, they had chosen the path of the pariah, smuggler, or assassin. Deadly gangs had risen due to their divide. One of their largest, deadliest gangs was said to linger across the Eastern Isles—an underground operation constantly stirring drama with little likelihood of unity.

Orks also, compared to the other races, loathed humans predominately. Even though their divisive tactics had been birthed when the Näkk took hold of the lands, thankfully—if one wanted to call it a positive—their violence primarily stayed among their own race. It was a shame they disliked the humans so much, because the Orkésh resembled the humans' biological makeup the most, even more than the Völfien's Rinkin, if mastered.

Despite Kiefer having two team members who specialized in orks, he kept his connections on the street. *Wülkure 101: Allies are always a wülkure's best asset.* Kiefer had them in spades: völves to sniff out suspects; dryads to identify the most minute details; and an ork gifted in legal aid who harbored minor gang knowledge from his youth. Each ally was a weapon that made Kiefer Yuska's job much more accessible and far more interesting than any wülkure had been able to cultivate. That was precisely why he was so damned good at his job.

"Morning," Kiefer greeted again, smoke spewing from his lips.

Carsten and Teo stood outside the construction firm as Kiefer approached. Carsten held a coffee mug in his hoofed hand, dressed in his administration attire, and the völf, Teo, was in slacks and a sleeveless collared construction shirt.

The völf cracked a smile. "How's it, Kiefer?"

Carsten nodded to Kiefer as he took another gulp from his extra large minotaur-sized mug, which was more like a chum bucket with a ceramic handle.

"Same shit, different day, gentlebeasts," muttered Kiefer as he passed them to walk to his building's entrance.

"Gentlebeasts!" Teo laughed. "There's that term again." He took a long drag off his cigar.

Kiefer looked at the völf. "Would you prefer I call you something else?"

"Technically, aren't you a *gentle* man," said Carsten sarcastically, his deep voice booming, as he delivered a quick nudge to the völf with his hoofed fist. Teo practically fell forward from the force. "Get it? Gentleman, 'cause he's a human." Carsten boisterously laughed at his own joke.

Teo rolled his eyes.

"Pfft. Fuck that!" exclaimed Kiefer, flicking the last bit of charring ash from his cigarette. "C'mon, you know *gentle* isn't even in my vocabulary."

"I'm sure your female companions agree?" Teo arched a brow.

Kiefer smirked and shot them a side-eye. "Don't mistake me as soft."

The völf and the minotaur both laughed. They always got a big kick out of Kiefer's dark sarcasm. Or at least they fed into his ego to stay on his good side.

"Did I miss a day? I didn't think it was the weekend yet. Don't you two assholes have a job to do?"

The laughter continued while Kiefer withdrew his pocket watch, revealing the time to be 9:47. "Jokes aside, have any of you seen Yegor this morning?"

Carsten scratched his head near the base of his massive left horn. "I didn't, no, but I got in just before eight, and this is my first break." He turned to the völf. "Teo?"

Teo shrugged, speaking with a mellow, drawling voice. "Nah. No sign of him or Szonja."

"Hm," Kiefer huffed. "Tomorrow's my early morning, so I'll be here for smokes. Unless boredom eats you both alive first." He reached for his key, unlocked the knotty alder door, and pressed his way into the building, leaving the laughing minotaur and völf behind.

He passed the reception; nodded at the elderly Fae receptionist, who resembled an amphibian; and climbed the stairway to the second level. He breached the Wülkure department space, and there sat four desks, all evenly spread from one another. In the back of the room was Kiefer's space. Despite the change in his rank, he would always be in the back to face the door; he leads from behind to empower his team of wülkures to soar ahead.

His most trusted wülkure, Szonja, was the first desk on the left, by the only empty desk, which happened to be Kiefer's space before his promotion to æsir. Their work relationship crossed professional boundaries; they had slept with each other during earlier years and still did on occasion. His wülkure Yegor's desk was in the right-hand corner, and the desk next to his was occupied by his other wülkure, Leifur. Each desk sat before a shelf overflowing with books specific to their role. Every wülkure read religiously and often referred to their books whenever they became stumped on a case or forms of Fae magic.

"Good morning, Leif." Kiefer nodded.

After adjusting his circular glasses on his nose, Leif nodded. "Morn'in."

"At least someone showed up for work today. Where the hell is everyone?"

Leif rose up from his seat and grabbed Szonja's logbook. "Let's see," he whizzed, shuffling through the pages.

He read aloud: "Case 9008-623: missing human, adolescent female. Case 9008-724: missing human, adolescent female. Case 9008-349: missing human, adolescent male. Note: Meet with Wülkure Emma Válcava at 10:00 a.m. Correlations found by Brass District disappearances with the following cases. Válcava believes that with evidence found on several cases within the Brass District, there may be a correlation between potential kidnappings made by Völfien thought to reside within the Copper District."

Kiefer sighed. *Always escalating. Always jumping to conclusions against the Völfien.*

He ventured toward Yegor's desk, unsure why he had not heard a single word from him. He checked the details of Yegor's notes written in his personal encrypted language. If someone ever disappeared and needed to be tracked down, only the wülkure of Kiefer's department could legibly understand it.

He opened a file and continued speaking with Leif. "What are your thoughts on those cases?"

"More than likely, these human children are runaways. It's not likely that Völfien would risk human kidnapping in a city rich with its notable wülkure presence. It's an odd assumption too. I think she's trying to appease Válcava, hoping for something bigger than it is."

"Or she's trying to sleep with her." Kiefer smirked.

Leif shot him a side-eye and retreated to his work.

Kiefer leaned in to snatch Yegor's more extensive logbook, noticing an old cup of coffee on the desk's corner and various files still out of place. Something sticky was spilt over some of the files.

"Damn it, Yegor." Kiefer shook his head.

Not surprising given Yegor's known habits, indiscreet behavior, and occasional drug usage. He'd also been involved in some regretful Orkésh affairs. Kiefer was aware that his longest-serving wülkure frequently fetishized Orkésh and indulged in strange, lustful fantasies in his spare time, but as long as those activities never impaired his judgment on the job, Kiefer kept it quiet. He put up with Yegor's disarray as long as he was efficient at his job and maintained his specialty on the orks.

He opened Yegor's logbook and found only the following for that day:

SUMMONS to CENTURION'S office: HENRIK

Note: Meet about the sunspire incident
Time: 10:00 a.m.

Kiefer flipped the logbook to the day before:

case 6004-157: Tree'veld informant
Note: Meet tomorrow near copper bay
docks for exchange and new info
Time: 10:00 a.m.

Kiefer slammed the logbook shut after fetching the matching case file. "Fucking dolt! He double-booked himself!"

Leif chuckled under his breath, not surprised.

Kiefer remembered discussing the Tree'veld case with Yegor a few weeks back, but he would still need to review it to recall the details. He sat down at Yegor's desk, pushing aside a pile of dated files, to read through the recap of case 6004-157.

The primary subject was Dal'ghan Tree'veld, known as the *Wanderer*.

Tree'veld was an ork informant and smuggler. He was called the Wanderer simply because he was known to be nomadic, never claiming a home or tribe. In any town he passed through, he pursued what criminals needed and was the one to deliver the goods—of course, at a price. Tree'veld would get his hands dirty in anything: drugs, alcohol, money, firearms, and women and children of any race. If the price was right, Tree'veld made it happen.

A few weeks ago, the Copper District had become Tree'veld's next stop. He had been hired by the fishing orks. Their target was a well-known minotaur diagnosed with a deadly and rare allergy to a tree-bearing flower known as the canary harpwillow. What made this case odd was that the fishing orks weren't known to be involved in criminal behavior; however, that particular minotaur had become their opponent.

This specific minotaur was well known because of his fishing-boat expertise; he constructed them. He had recently created an extraordinary patented design that would help improve the lives of all his fellow

Fae within the Copper District. This water vessel would bring aid to the community. The fishing orks disagreed with that plan. They selfishly wanted his new life-altering design all to themselves to operate the best of the best and to cut out the smaller businesses, even individual fisher Fae. Unity and aid evidently meant nothing to the fishing orks.

They'd presented the minotaur with a hefty price for his design, but he'd refused their offer. In his defiance against them, they had begun spreading rumors about his new ships to try to trample on his business, but his highly known reputation could not be quashed. During their tirade of revenge, karma had worked its bidding. It only heightened the minotaur's revenue, leading him to up the pay of his two builders and pour his energy into creating a larger competing company; this challenged the fishing orks' mockery even more.

The enraged orks fled to the underground gangs, where they discovered the Wanderer. The fishing orks had hired Tree'veld to retain the fatal knowledge needed from this gang. Once Tree'veld had learned of the minotaur's deadly allergy, the assassination attempt had commenced. Even better, the potent flower was in season.

The assassination had played out thusly: The minotaur had been bitten by a planted snake and rushed to the local doctor to remedy the bite. Another civilian visiting Copper, a human, incidentally, had been bitten just hours before the minotaur. Tree'veld had infiltrated the clinic with the harpwillow's colorless liquid and replaced the vial used to cure snakebites. He'd planted the poison specifically for the minotaur; however, the minotaur had not been the one to receive the mock elixir. Unfortunately, the human victim admitted before him had died of the snakebite, because rather than receiving the antivenom, he'd received a useless flower elixir meant to kill a minotaur. The mission had failed terribly.

Tree'veld had used a local perfumer to create the mock elixir. Yegor had tracked the lethal liquid purchase back to Tree'veld, which had led to his recent capture. He was now under the wülkure's department's thumb.

Kiefer skimmed over Yegor's notes again. "But where's the name of this gang?" he mumbled, realizing the notes lacked this information—likely a piece of evidence Yegor was planning to obtain from Tree'veld.

He displeasingly shook his head and slammed the file shut, not feeling the least bit surprised over the Orkésh mess. This was why he easily allowed Yegor and Szonja to deal with them.

"Time to meet this damned *Wanderer* for Yegor," Kiefer huffed, pulling his fingers through his dark hair. "I'll be back."

Leif lifted a hand to bid him goodbye with his gaze still fixed on his tasks. Kiefer lit a cigarette before exiting back into the Fae-filled streets of Copper.

☆

Isarah
Demitori City, Copper District
Copper Bay, Y pier of Tartarus and Crete
Aousti 9

Kiefer leaned against a large post that indicated the directions of the dock. To the right was the Tartarus dock, and to the left was the Crete dock.

Copper's ports had large networks of piers wide and sufficient enough to function as roads, supporting the largest of Fae, such as minotaurs, and the cargo they hauled by pulleys or by hand. A giant minotaur could easily weigh upward of eight hundred pounds, not including the weight from the shipment.

Kiefer inhaled his cigarette with a murmur of dismay. He hoped Tree'veld would stick around under the assumption that Yegor was late. Besides, Tree'veld was counting on his survival through the graces of the wülkure. He was no longer a wanderer but an offender. He was stuck in Copper until Kiefer's department was done with him.

Moments later, Tree'veld made his appearance. He wore typical Orkésh attire: a long jacket covered his worn leather slacks, and decorative tribal ropes and tassels hung from his utility belt. Straps of animal hide held sparse pieces of protective armor to his sleeves. He undoubtedly was armed with knives and flintlock-style revolvers, but he tried to play off as confidently as possible that he lacked this security.

Kiefer immediately noticed that Tree'veld was repeatedly looking over his shoulders; the movements were meant to come off smooth but seemed a bit jouncy, as though he were nervous.

Tree'veld cleared his throat and peered through thick, unkempt hair. A few strands dangled in front of his eyes while the rest of his hair was tucked behind his hood. He lacked the common braid that orks prided when apart of an Orkésh community.

Kiefer knew the ork was expecting his colleague, so he addressed him casually. "I'm here for Yegor. Don't look so skittish, Dal'ghan."

"You're late," said Tree'veld in a guttural, hardy voice.

Due to the tusks on orks' lower jaws, they struggled to speak without a robust and uncouth accent. Depending on the tusk's size, their words usually were followed by gritty-sounding, raspy grunts. Since most orks were a culture of rebellion and brutality, they had little desire to fashion a classier tongue.

"Yegor had other business to attend to. Do you have something for me, Wanderer? Let's not waste time." Kiefer pressed, raking him over.

His calling out the nickname made Tree'veld's nervousness heighten. "Hold your tongue, human. Your department promised to protect me should I cooperate!"

Kiefer flicked his unfinished cigarette into the ocean and stepped ominously close to the ork. "And your little stunt got a human killed, which should've earned you a walk to the gallows! You are *my* property, ork. Watch your insults; humans don't take kindly to Fae calling out men as *humans* in that tone."

"It's not the humans I worry about—"

He was cut off as a pair of dryads walked by. They paid little to no attention to the existence of Tree'veld, but Tree'veld acted as if they might have been undercover assassins.

"Ah," sneered Kiefer, "the harsh reality finally settles in. You fuck with the Fae, and the Fae fuck with you, eh?"

Tree'veld relaxed his pose. "Fuck with orks, fuck with humans, fuck with Fae—it doesn't matter which species, tribe, family, or religion. Offenses in blood will always be repaid in blood, but the Fae are smart bastards who know what to sniff around for. That couple walked too close for my comfort."

"Orks are predictable, and unfortunately, so are we humans, but

I can agree that the Fae have their tricks and tactics." Kiefer paused in thought before continuing. "Funny that you know the gruesome realities, yet you still decide to take the illegal deals. Has this cultivated any trustworthy allies from your underground gangs? Or those fishing ones?" He slyly edged in, scoping for information.

"No!" Tree'veld blurted. "I'd be asking for a death wish."

"How so?"

"They can't know the mistake of a human death led to my capture! I was hired to kill that minotaur and involved their expertise under sworn secrecy." He paused and grunted anxious breaths. "If I created allies with any of those gangs, I might as well end my life and be done with it. These orks are sharp, and they'd find out I'm working with you."

"Hm, interesting."

"You may think these orks are stupid brutes, but I don't think you realize how large this gang's operation is. They have eyes everywhere."

"Which gang?"

Tree'veld paused, stepped closer to Kiefer, and quietly grunted, "The Svarfætúr."

Ah, there's the name. "One of the worst, Tree'veld. You realize the Svarfætúr is said to be one of the fiercest gangs in the Eastern Isles, right? And their leader is Declan Chappequa, yes?"

"Of course I do; I wouldn't lie about this! Why the fuck don't you get that this is why I'm on edge?"

"Okay, okay," Kiefer said, throwing up his hands in a calming gesture. He lit up a new cigarette. "But I need to know. *Why* would fishing orks be involved with the Svarfætúr? Couldn't they have just roughed the minotaur up a bit and blacklisted his permits—something other than execution and gang involvement all over a fucking boat design?"

Tree'veld smirked, then sighed loudly. "I know how it sounds … but there's more to it."

"Which is?"

"Are you willing to listen?"

Kiefer arched a brow as if answering his rhetorical question.

Tree'veld paused briefly, looked over his shoulders, and released a quieted grunt. He leaned closer to Kiefer again, his tusks practically scraping his ear. "They are beginning their hunt for the Wöndin ork," he spoke in a barely audible voice.

"The who?" Kiefer urged, narrowing his eyes.

"Malbec Fallz'den," Tree'veld clarified. "The Wöndin."

Kiefer took a hasty step backward, rolling his eyes. "He's a myth! Not a proven fact."

"Yes, yes I know. I am an ork, after all," Tree'veld huffed, annoyance trailing his tone. "Speculation aside, allow me to finish."

Kiefer tightened his glare.

"Malbec Fallz'den," Tree'veld continued, "is an ancient ork believed to exist within the society of the Orkésh. The legend is that he— the Wöndin—wields elemental bending powers and influences unity among my race. Despite what the Commission thinks of us, there are many hopeful, less aggressive orks that cling to the Wöndin lore, hoping he *is* real. Belief in the Wöndin provides a path of purpose among my race and influences less division." Tree'veld paused and checked his surroundings before continuing. "While many believe in his existence, it's these gangs', like the Svarfætúr, that fight to keep control in their own hands and destroy any living evidence of him."

Kiefer stared at him, remaining silent.

Tree'veld relaxed his broad shoulders, preparing for what he would share next. "The minotaur who was to be assassinated is supposedly linked to the Wöndin. They believe Malbec's powers influenced the minotaur's unique boat material. Killing him was meant to stir and draw him out of hiding. An easy kill."

"If he's real," Kiefer scoffed.

"My race believes he is; keep it at that! We're standing here having this conversation for a reason, right?"

Kiefer's lips curled. "Don't play me as a fool, Tree'veld." He warned.

"Listen, they won't stop until they've found him. These deaths will continue; it'll get gruesome!"

Kiefer hesitated, acutely dissecting Tree'veld's body language. "Fine. I need more evidence to back this claim. We need a major lead if fishing orks are cutting deals with the Svarfætúr because they're trying to draw out this *fantastical* ork."

"Zara Doz'hura is our lead." Tree'veld immediately answered. "We collaborated about the perfumer. I will learn more if I get into her inner circle. It's a risk I'll take."

"So you're looking for permission?"

"Zara is one of Declan's most respected members. Getting close to her can get me dangerously close to their inside operation. I imagine I will begin to dirty my hands even more once I have carved myself in."

Kiefer took a moment to ponder before responding. He inhaled the coastal air, stretching his lungs to their fullest capacity, and stared out at the horizon. The sounds of ships docking and aircraft flying overhead echoed through the bay. He knew that taking the case as far as the Svarfætúr heightened the danger of the situation. He also knew he needed to consult with Yegor immediately, but time was of the essence. Tree'veld needed to start securing allies now, or no matter what transpired, the orks would grow suspicious and enact his imminent death. Tree'veld couldn't die, not now. They needed him alive.

"I will update Yegor on these details. Under the circumstances, permission granted."

"Before we part, you should know one more item, Wülkure."

"Yes?"

"I think the orks plan on killing your völf."

"My völf?" Kiefer exclaimed, quickly taking his last drag from his cigarette.

"Yes. His name is Teo."

"Teo? Why the hell would they want to kill Teo?"

"He was snooping around ork territory recently for Yegor and keeping the scent off you guys. The orks found out he was helping you. They see Teo as a rat—a risk of discovering information about their gang—rats get killed."

"Fucking hell! Any idea when this is going to happen?"

"Could be anytime, but I presumed you'd use your staffed völf; thought he was safe—"

"Staffed? Safe?" Kiefer cut in, raising his voice. "Are you fucking serious? Völves don't get employed with the Commission! You should know how their race is viewed; shit, ever heard of a völf as a wülkure? He's just a fucking construction worker!"

"They're likely giving the word soon! He might already be dead."

Kiefer quickly pushed past Tree'veld. He ran toward Tree'veld's motorcycle parked at the end of the dock. "Get the fuck off the street and go find our lead! I have to save Teo!"

Tree'veld raced for his cycle, realizing Kiefer had snatched his keys. "Fuck that! I won't have his blood on my hands!"

Kiefer quickly mounted the cycle, started it up, and sped down the road toward the firm. He couldn't have cared less that he left the fugitive ork behind.

CHAPTER FOUR

THE SEER

Shaar
Tsunetomo
House Frost
Aousti 9

DESPITE AMEILJA'S SELF-ASSURED ATTITUDE, I
could sense that she had begun to grow anxious. She's built a steep wall
of confidence; working effortlessly to be the veil of strength for others;
however, I saw through the barrier.

There had been increased pressure on her. She was burdened by the
profound expectancy that she needed to achieve complete control of her
Purge flames; it was dangerous, and only the most devout to its power
could master it.

Thankfully it was the fourth day of the week, which was her final
day of Purge practice. She had been used to practicing a couple of times
a week, but recently, her father had increased it to four. The final day
was always her most taxing. I'd gathered that her added studies made
it even more daunting.

"Today's training may be rough; bear with me on my emotional
state," she told us over her shoulder.

We didn't respond.

I watched as Ameilja started to walk ahead of us, her hair swaying in time
with her stride. When she is anxious, her pace will quicken with each nervous
thought. Every time it happens, I will watch her intently—hyper-fixating on
every little move she'd make, the changes in her aroma, and the sounds of her

breathing, as she would unknowingly advance ahead. She may never admit it, but she walks with a rushed intention, just like András.

Her father, András Frost, was Shaar's high abbot and a heroic paladin of the Commission. He once had led a Purge against a demonic occult tyranny in Shaar. Freeing the people from that reign was an accomplishment András had championed during the lingering aftermath of the Great War, which had made him a loved man of the Shaar'an people and a well-known Purge manipulator.

The story of Ameilja's grim entrance into the world had forever been imprinted in the hearts of their people. The tragic death of András's wife, Johanna, had been profoundly devastating, leaving him widowed, with two daughters to raise. A massive attack had fallen upon many houses of paladins during the tyranny, and Johanna had been forced into early labor. András, without aid, had ensured Ameilja was born unharmed amid the final hours of the attack. Johanna, unfortunately, had succumbed to the trauma, never having met her beautiful daughter.

András had stood over his wife's dead body, holding a bloody naked baby in his hands, as the horns of victory sounded. They had won, but at what cost?

András had stayed in Shaar, stepped away from his involvement with the prominent social elites, and solely focused on his rightfully earned abbot role and daughters. He'd felt that after his victory, the humbling coastal lands of Tsunetomo were a safe place to raise a family and build a reclusive community around his estate. After everything he had been through, he'd deserved the solitude.

In his younger years, András also had fought alongside my father. Although my father once had been a dear family friend to András Frost, his ex-communication from the Religious Order had left them with little communication. András had always lent a forgiving heart to my father, but with his being a high-ranked paladin, accountability regarding my father's actions had taken precedence.

András appreciated the Völfien but had never been able to liberate us from the fear-entwined humans. I assumed that having me around reminded him of his distant friend. It was funny—he couldn't serve me an ounce of steak, but I could lock my jaws around anyone threatening his daughter and be rewarded for it.

As we walked through András's halls, we crossed paths with him; his two protectorates, Lain and Shirou; and a couple of other familiar paladins.

"Morning, Father." Ameilja bowed.

"Morning, my rose," he said with a pleased, exulting smile. His low, beaming voice filled the space. "Make today's training an unforgettable one."

"Understood, Father."

We paused briefly in unison to bow before him and then moved onward.

Although András was known for his victorious capabilities, Ameilja carried a far more unique ability, a title higher than any paladin or follower of Uridei.

Ameilja was the third-born seer of the Eastern Isles.

Being a seer was a rare role one could not sign up for. Seers were born, not made. They were gifted with the ability to perceive pieces of the past and the future. I'd learned that visions flowed in and out of Ameilja's mental realm, mostly out of her control. Rarely did she share what she saw; it was as if she harbored her own dark secrets.

Her rare gift was held to a higher standard and indebted expectancy, not just because of the visions but because seers were known to naturally transmute the Purge flames. They channeled the white flames through emotion and fibrous, fascial connections of the heart and mind much deeper than any paladin would ever comprehend. A sworn-in paladin who had to learn to master the Purge at more superficial levels would never experience the same connection as a seer.

Historical events had also proven that the first natural-born seers had aided against the Näkk; the original demonstrators of their Purge mastery.

Still, the early seers had passed down their knowledge, teaching young and aspiring seers that they were the light in the world. Their visions and abilities were merely gifts of Uridei and were only granted if they chose the right path. Thus, seers could be corrupted through their abilities, and worse, forces like the Näkk could seduce them.

With every light, a shadow followed. Seers always had to be aware.

The *Näkk*, a term we used lightly, was an insidious infection that spread across the lands by an Aureate named Sabor. The power he'd wielded was an energy none of us wanted to fathom, as it undoubtedly led to death, toyed with necromancy, and reanimated humans to its will. The departments within the Commission ran like clockwork, consistently training and preparing for the possibility of the plague or any other dark force awakening, all while protecting the fragile human race. This only added to Ameilja's push to control her Purge. She was a great asset; some even said she was an elemental weapon.

Ameilja gradually fell back in line between Tam and me. My pack-mates all started conversing with her about tomorrow's events; typical back-and-forth banter.

I drowned out the small talk.

Suddenly, I felt Ameilja's hand gently graze the side of my arm.

"Kovuco?" she spoke up.

"Hm?" In my peripheral view, I noticed her looking up at me through her dark lashes.

"You seem distant today."

"Oh?"

"What's on your mind, Kovuco?"

You. "Today's agenda. The tasks at hand," I answered.

She looked away from me as we continued to walk. "You shouldn't lie to me. I know you better."

I inhaled. *Fine. I think of you night and day. I imagine what a life with you would be like. What it would be like to call you mine. Claim you as mine. Mine alone.*

"Quiet, are we?" She arched her brow.

I tensed and quickly suppressed the visceral thoughts. "Apologies. You're right. I have many things on my mind, Ameilja, with protecting you through today's practice being one."

"Okay then, Blackstar. I guess I can accept that as truth."

I looked down at her, but she didn't look back up.

Her worth was much more than how the world viewed her. She was not just a seer, the daughter of the high abbot, or the lady of Shaar; she was a force of reason. Ameilja fought endlessly against the Fae's unjust treatment. She was an advocate, just as Albean had once been for the humans. The Commission's mission statement to keep *order and peace* roiled her nerves. She recognized that the humans had taken the will to protect themselves too far. We'd been privy to some of her overheated spiels with her father: "It's hypocritical! Unfair! Albean's probably turning in his grave, Father! Peace is not making someone feel like a pariah!"

Despite her objections to the Commission's outlook on her Völfien, she had always taken her seer gift and training seriously. The more she grounded herself, the more she tuned into her calling and advocacy tactics. Her relationship with Uridei was also not taken lightly. Her call to accept everyone as equal was a direct result.

"If we want to grab coffee, we must hurry. You *know* how Oboro feels about punctuality ... and coffee," Ameilja reminded, sarcasm coating her tone as she picked up her pace again.

We followed suit, descending the final steps leading away from her estate, and joined in with the gently mannered streets of our village.

Tsunetomo was a quaint, ornate area built along the sea. Splashes of red and gold brightened its Shaar'an designs. Many inhabitants lived in lofty, crafted inns, intricately designed cottages, or small airships idling above. The climate was primarily cool, with long, frigid winters, but thankfully the positioning of the sun blessed us with a couple of fervid months.

The grounded homes were generally more prominent wooden buildings reinforced with brick and stone and situated on tall stilts to combat the potential flooding from the ocean. As for the fields and stone walls, they served as another further protective measure against the ocean tide. The hillsides were always covered in livestock; their farmers tended to them often. Fishermen were active along the shores, constantly supplying the buffets and markets.

This village contained approximately two thousand citizens, primarily the human race, with a few Fae. A quarter were völves, who served the Frost family, all thanks to the bold-hearted advocate at my side. For the most part, the area was a tight-knit community tucked away from the rush of life, which was what András preferred.

In my experience, being a part of a quaint community had both positive and negative aspects to it.

Despite the fact that I am proud to be Ameilja's defender, my reclusive nature apprehended the attention we received. Passers-by would always watch, exchange grins or backward glances as we traveled through the city. A human couple once asked Ameilja to kiss their newborn infant on the head, hoping it would grant them Uridei's blessings. Many people will pause and bow in front of Ameilja, sometimes too near for comfort.

The experiences trigger my protective instincts; however, if I'm being honest, how could they not admire her? With Ameilja's radiating influence, bowing before her is an easy deed. She had a grip on me, not because I was employed to protect her.

Ameilja was a light in a dark place. Her charm was like a healing presence over depressive unknowns; she always brought out the best in others. She carried the heart of a warrior and was an inspiration, even if she was defending beasts like me. I couldn't quite put my finger on it, but Ameilja had a way of comforting my internal struggles and mental solitude.

"Good day, Lady Frost," passers cheerfully said with subtle bows, immediately pulling me out of my thoughts.

The passers eyed my packmates and me.

There it is, that bite of introversion pulling at my chest.

I watched Ameilja share a confident smile as we carried on our usual way, pretending we were her crew rather than her protectorates. Her public treatment of us always crossed the Commission's boundaries and regulations, but that never faltered her opinions.

As protectorates, we had to accompany Ameilja on all travels. It had been a couple of weeks since our last expedition to any of Shaar's temples, aside from the one built into her estate, and Ameilja's adventurous heart had been aching to see their vast beauty.

We didn't mind it. The temple visits were an exhilarating pace change and got us away from the House grounds. Considering how busy the daily routine could become, maintaining a journal was my primary method for savoring the time spent with her. Similar to jotting down a desired dream as soon as you'd awaken; you don't want to forget.

The smell of the coffee shop instantly hit my senses as we rounded the corner. We approached Shaar Night Café, which was owned and operated by a young dwarf couple. Their front entrance was more suitable for human height, leading my packmates and me to duck as we entered.

Their artistic nature was evident in the exterior and interior design of the small shop. It was filled with watercolors of vines and stars swirling around the known rowan trees of the Fae. Ameilja said it was whimsical and comforting, a piece of the Fae culture implemented into Tsunetomo, which was precisely why she liked it.

"Well hello, Hilde and Päl." Ameilja greeted the owners with a warm smile.

"G'morning, Lady Frost! The usual again?" Hilde asked as she tucked a piece of thick brown hair behind her dainty ear.

"Yes, thank you."

Ameilja preferred an overly sweetened latte, to be exact, and she always granted us our choice of coffee.

She stepped back from the counter and waited, twirling a piece of her hair as she eyed the art along the walls, but I could tell her mind was elsewhere.

What are you thinking, Ameilja?

The small shop never slowed as customers swept in and out with their desired beverages, along with their specific scents. Each time the door swung open, a small brass bell rang, catching my attention. Hilde and Päl hustled, speaking in their Fae language, as they finally granted us our coffees so we could move forward.

Ameilja nodded, swiftly tossing a coin into their tip jar.

"*Byile!*" Päl thanked Ameilja in his Fae tongue; the pronunciation was soft and soothing to the mind.

From there, we made our way to the Okumura Temple for training, ensuring we finished our coffee before facing Oboro. She highly disregarded the acidic beverage, especially for Ameilja. She believed it disrupted the fascial connections to the heart, slowing her Purge control and inhibiting natural blood flow.

"Remember, keep your chins held high," Ameilja told us as we approached the vast structure.

Its height towered ahead of us, along with a grand bamboo staircase. The stacked, crescent-designed roof presented carved carp and suns. The tall wooden beams supporting the structure were etched with historical writing from the Book of Uridei.

Sister Oboro, Ameilja's master trainer, immediately appeared. Her austere figure stood at the top of the steps like a statue. Ameilja's demeanor shifted as soon as she was in sight.

Master Oboro was fifty-two but looked as young as Ameilja with her slender, willowy build and impeccable features. Her white hair was the only sign of her aging body but also a result of the constant use of her Purge—another effect of constantly being exposed to the incredible heat of the flames. Her wardrobe consisted primarily of short shorts and waist-cut robes in various colors, negating any type of footwear. She wore a colossal farmer hat and smoked a bamboo pipe daily, which caused her to smell like a mix of fine tobacco and floral perfumes.

Despite her outward appearance, she was a highly gifted swordswoman and a well-known Purge manipulator. She could walk into a room, flick her fingers, and light her pipe and a hundred candles all at once, as any master of the Purge could. She was also known for her stringent disciplinary techniques. Oboro was rather blunt. She spoke boldly, regardless of the topic. She never hesitated to point out others' flaws, even her superiors'. Ameilja seemed to like this transparency about her, not just because Oboro was harsh and cursed like a captain but because, in her words, she was authentic.

My packmates and I liked her because she served us raw chunks of meat if she needed us to assist with Ameilja's training. Those moments were rare. We knew the risks. So did Oboro. The Commission's laws were strictly against Völfien eating raw meat; another lingering defeat, as it made me feel controlled—just another justification for how we Völfien were treated. Despite my internal feelings, I still accepted Oboro's raw morsels obediently, as my packmates did, all while I focused on my priority: Ameilja.

We began the ascension of the steep steps up to the temple. By my fifth step, the smell of the lingering Purge burns stung my senses. Ameilja took off her jacket and handed it to Tam while we ascended. I glanced over at him and then at Ameilja. She kept her focus on her master.

As soon as we reached the top, Ameilja bowed and then walked to the center of the temple.

"I see you've left your wülkure behind again, hm?" Oboro sternly noted.

Ameilja didn't respond as she positioned herself. My packmates and

I habitually took our corners only a few yards from our lady. Not once did I take my eyes off her.

Ameilja lowered herself to her knees and began praying to Uridei in a meditating posture.

Oboro smoked her pipe, stepping to a tune in her head, humming through smoke clouds that passed through her lips and nose as she walked up to her dais.

"Are you ready, Ameilja?" Oboro asked in her Shaar'an tongue.

"Yes," Ameilja answered confidently.

"Well, time is of the essence!"

Oboro swiftly pulled a sharpened bamboo shoot from its woven basket and thrust it toward Ameilja like a spear.

My heart tensed, my eyes shut tightly, and I nearly snarled. The thought of harm coming to Ameilja was always unbearable, even when I knew it was in practice. Their sessions often ended with blood being shed, and we were forced to keep our distance as Oboro's students tended to her wounds. I hated it. I especially hated the confusion it roiled inside me at the fact that I felt these emotions, while my packmates never blinked an eye.

Ameilja held up a hand, and the shoot halted just a hair before her flesh as it suddenly burst into a bright white flame. Ameilja concentrated the Purge into existence.

As she drew back her hand, the bright fire formed into a spear shape, ready to ignite its next victim. Ameilja immediately hurled the missile toward Oboro. Oboro deflected its heated power with a short blade, slashing it. The Purge split into a multitude of swirling flames. Oboro whirled them into a giant fireball and thrust them back at Ameilja. I held my breath, feeling its heat from where I stood.

Ameilja shot up to her feet to stop the fiery sphere, which had now doubled in size. She slipped. My jaw tensed. A growl rose to my throat. She quickly managed to gain control and cease the motion of the flames.

Gracefully, like a painter adding strokes to a masterpiece, she slid her hands together, causing the fireball to separate into four smaller flames. With a flinch of her finger, she tossed them in a dancing motion toward Oboro. Oboro arched a brow as she stopped the Purge with a simple gesture, and they vanished.

"You faltered," Oboro snipped. Her eyes were closed as she sucked at the bamboo pipe.

"Just barely," Ameilja huffed.

Oboro snapped open her eyes, drew another shoot, and thrust it, not at Ameilja but at me.

Still focused on Ameilja, I hadn't enough time to dodge or consider any defense from the attack. With a quick reflex, Ameilja zeroed her attention on me. She snapped her fingers, creating a spark, and with a diving motion of her hand, the flame made instant contact with the shoot, shattering it into tiny shards like a bullet from a firearm.

It was not nearly as eloquent as her last deflection, and it was apparent she hadn't been prepared to defend us.

"What the hell was that?" Ameilja demanded. Her tone toward Oboro slipped before she had time to think.

Oboro had never used us as targets before, but she was known for surprises in her lessons, and I had just become a piece of the curriculum.

Oboro descended from her dais, dismissing Ameilja's question and tone. "Kovuco? Are we a tad distracted today, hm?" She questioned, narrowing her eyes on me.

I fell to my knees and apologized in my humblest Shaar'an tongue when she sharply interrupted me in ancient Völfien.

"Snählend?" she snapped. The Völfien word *snählend* meant "snarling."

Shit, she noticed.

"Aye, as per your usual, Kovuco." She grabbed a rice ball off the small serving table and tossed it in my direction.

Confused by the reward, I accepted, catching it in my teeth with a Völfien snapping reflex. I chewed and swallowed quickly to free my voice. "A reward, master?" I asked. *For what exactly?*

"Your job is to protect Ameilja," she said sharply, throwing rice balls to my packmates, who deserved them. "I often wonder why you can't seem to settle your nerves." She paused for a brief moment to process her thoughts. "Remember, young völf, when Ameilja takes full control of her Purge abilities, she *technically* won't need her protectorates."

Where is she going with this?

"*Mimir appu*," she added with an arched brow.

The phrase translated to "Prick up your ears." It was meant as a reminder that we should always be on high alert and ready should the Purge become too overwhelming during her training. There was no room for worries or emotions. Ameilja's training was our focus.

"A Völfien protectorate should not let his emotions get ahead of him. Stick to your duties." She tossed another rice ball my way. "You might be a little different after all, Kovuco, and hard to read. But you're sharp like your father, no doubt."

Thanks? I wonder if her comments are meant as subtle compliments or cynical criticisms. Not to mention if she is dissecting my thoughts.

She turned her attention to Ameilja. "I'm going to assume what clouds Kovuco's mind is his task, but I can't help but wonder ... what clouds your mind, Ameilja. Certainly not *your* task, hm?"

Ameilja turned away with shame shrouding her. She sharply inhaled, and returned to her knees with her eyes closed. Oboro took a few more puffs of her pipe as she began to slowly pace around Ameilja, assessing her.

"Coronation tomorrow? Yes?" Oboro said.

Ameilja nodded.

"You're usually such a social person at your soirées, but your attitude has been shifting. You have been held up in your estate for quite some time, training endlessly, hm? Is this what's distracting you?" Oboro stopped and snapped her gaze down at Ameilja, awaiting an answer.

Ameilja sighed. "Yes. The coronation is tomorrow. And *another* redundant birthday event." Her voice lulled.

"But there's more, so spill it," Oboro snipped, demanding transparency.

"Meanwhile, there is impactful work a seer should be doing! *I* should be aiding our brothers and sisters in the South. *I* should be spreading the word of Uridei, master!" Ameilja paused, caught her breath, and continued. "And as I sit here, training against a force that no longer exists, my völves stagnate under the strictest, most unfair conditions. Has our human race forgotten that we were victorious during the war because of them? A gift from our savior." She clenched her eyes tighter. "If this is the answer you're demanding from me, then yes, master, it has been distracting."

I could feel the frustration radiating off Ameilja's form from where I stood. The temple atmosphere fell silent.

Ameilja...

The House Frost soirée was a yearly event that lavishly celebrated the birth of Ameilja, her gifting, and the anniversary of the Great War's end. Attendees included select centurions, æsirs, high abbots, and other prominent people, such as suitors, within the Commission from around the Isles. The coronation; however, is far grander. Ameilja's ability to fully control her Purge was an essential piece of this year's event as she would be crowned as a high seer, a profound honor she had trained tirelessly for. The empress of the Eastern Isles, Sinnika, and her royal family, who were the head of the Commission affairs, would be attending.

Oboro took another deep drag from the bamboo pipe. "You have a whole lifetime to chart your purpose, love. Try not to spread your wings too thin."

"Yes, master."

"*But* I need to get my results concerning your progress before your twenty-fourth birthday, which is less than twelve hours. What's a coronation without a crown, hm?"

"Master?" Ameilja said, snapping her eyes open, as confusion spread across her features.

Oboro turned back to me, ignoring Ameilja's question again. "Kovuco, *stérgé*," (Kovuco, rise), she ordered.

I obeyed and turned to return to my post.

"*Viern!*" (Wait!). Oboro hurriedly snapped her fingers. "Come! I need you!"

I bowed. "Yes, master."

She turned and snapped at my packmates, "Now you all step away," swishing her hand for them to shoo backward.

My packmates stepped farther back, and I grew anxious.

"Kovuco, I have to make a rather difficult call today, but I anticipate it will end well for all of us, *you* especially."

"Master?" I questioned.

Oboro ignored me and threw a knife onto the floor approximately six feet before Ameilja. I presumed she wanted me to take a position at the blade, so I walked over to it, adjusted my shoulders, and then faced Ameilja.

I looked down at her pale, heart-shaped face neatly decorated with crimson hair. My chest grew tight. Ameilja broke her concentration and lifted her gentle green eyes to lock with mine. My chest relaxed. It was too late to break my stare, so I grinned and scratched the tuft of my neck. I swallowed once more and nodded to her, hoping it would break the awkward look I found myself saturated with.

"Ameilja!" snapped Oboro.

I expected her to close her eyes again, but our locked stare didn't falter. She answered, "Yes, master?"

"Stand!"

Ameilja stood.

Oboro walked toward the weapon rack and snapped her fingers. An assistant seized a crossbow and loaded a bolt into it. Oboro snatched the crossbow and walked behind me, putting ten yards between us.

"Ameilja," Oboro said, "now is the time to prove you can master the art of observation with your Purge. I need you to focus; I am going to shoot Kovuco."

"What!" Ameilja gasped, breaking eye contact with me.

Surprisingly, my gaze remained fixed on Ameilja at the unexpected news.

Oboro hesitated and began tampering with the trigger mechanism. "How the fuck do you—"

Suddenly, the bolt fired and struck a vase, smashing it to pieces. The sharp, unnerving sound echoed throughout the temple.

"Fuck!" Oboro cursed. She began to laugh, while the rest of us now felt uncomfortable. "Ah! Forgot the safety." She chuckled as she flicked the safety back on and tossed the crossbow back to her assistant. "Load it again!" she demanded.

Her assistant quickly threw in another load.

"As I said, I am going to shoot Kovuco. I will not assist you with the flames; I am done doing that with you. You must control the flames and stop the bolt, or else Kovuco here will continue *snarling* from a wheelchair for the rest of his days." She paused. "Or it will puncture his heart, and he'll die." She held up the loaded crossbow, overemphasized switching off the safety with a sarcastic smile, and then walked a few yards behind me.

I felt her determined glare burn between my shoulder blades.

"So what's it going to be, love?" she asked Ameilja as she aimed the weapon in my direction.

"But, master, I can't; you have Kovuco standing between us. I need to see the weapon! I must see it to focus the Purge!"

"Concentrate! Listen to the release! Hear the bolt; feel the shift in the air!"

"Master Oboro, please!" Ameilja took a step forward. "I can't do this!"

"Are you ready, Ameilja?"

"Master, no! Are you insane? I will speak with my father; he'll be satisfied with what I've accomplished. I can't! I—"

"Can." I interrupted, speaking only an octave loud enough for her to hear.

Ameilja's features sunk as she bit her bottom lip and looked deep into the strange specks of blue in my eyes. I hoped she could see how serious I was. I hoped she could see how much I believed in her. I hoped she knew how much I trusted her with my life.

I nodded. "You can do this, Ameilja." I could see the muscles in her neck tense, and her pupils dilated as she strategically processed the moment. *You can do this.*

"I can do this," she whispered, speaking low enough that only my Völfien senses could hear.

I watched her primal instinct to succeed solidify and start to reenergize her. She placed her fingers together, preparing for a snap.

"I—" She slowly inhaled. "I am ready, master."

There she is.

She took a final breath, and as if she were made of stone, all went still. The room fell silent.

It felt like an eternity, and I was unsure if I had even blinked. Suddenly, her hair rose briskly in a breeze that stirred up from her feet. Her eyes closed, granting me the freedom to absorb her. At least I would get to stare at her if this were my final moment.

Ameilja.

I heard the twang from the crossbow and an ear-piercing whistle as the bolt began its journey to its target: me.

Ameilja snapped her fingers, and her hands outstretched; her body began to levitate. Silent and in an epic radiance, the Purge flames illuminated and spurted from her entire form like a fountain of infernal horror, only it was a flame of holy light.

She pressed her palm forward, and a wall of white fire undulated toward me. Its intense heat pressed against me in what should have been an instant deflagration reducing me to ash. I embraced the flame, preparing for its biting rage, but instead, it passed over me like a rolling wave. I never blinked.

The bolt disintegrated instantly. The flame dissipated into wisps of embers, and I remained miraculously unharmed.

She did it!

Then she fell. Her body went limp.

I darted for her and caught her before she hit the bamboo floorboards. "Lady Ameilja? Lady Ameilja, are you all right?" I gasped, my heart lurched to my throat as I assessed her form. I stood up, cradling her small body in my arms. *Ameilja? Say something!*

I needed her to say something so I knew that she was okay and that she hadn't overdone herself in the act. The Purge was a weapon to Uridei's servants, but it was undoubtedly a force not to be reckoned with, and seers could, without careful practice, find themselves victim to their flame.

My heart raced at the possibility that I'd let my guard down in the same displacement of fear, accepting death by fire or crossbow bolt. Had Ameilja taken the same road? Had she obliterated everything in her to ensure I wasn't harmed?

Ameilja, please say something.

"Kovuco," she suddenly whispered.

"Yes! Yes, Lady Ameilja! Are you okay?"

She reached up weakly, tugged my right ear with one hand, and clutched my shoulder with the other to pull herself closer. "You know I hate to be called Lady."

CHAPTER FIVE
UNCONVENTIONAL

Isarah
Demitori City, Copper District
Stonemill Road
Aousti 9

KIEFER PULLED AROUND THE CORNER AND SAW what he had hoped for: a busy street and Teo standing right in the middle, alive, but an unknowing target.

A new shipment of building supplies was in. He was one of the suppliers' contracted loading crew.

"Of course in a time like this," Kiefer huffed.

Kiefer leaped off the bike and paused, assessing the surroundings. He watched the hustle of the bay.

Within minutes, Tree'veld showed up, winded and gruff. "Think it's okay to steal my bike, huh?" he snapped.

"Get outta here!" Kiefer demanded.

"I said no more blood on my hands!"

"If any of the orks see you, that will confirm the rumors that you're involved with us. You'll be dead within the hour."

"Perhaps," said Tree'veld with an edge of terror in his voice.

Kiefer turned back to the crowds, zeroing in on the scene around Teo. "The völf appears to be safe. I'll take it from here. Yegor will contact you as soon as I update him on today's meeting. Get the hell out of here while you still can."

Tree'veld nodded and started up his bike. He sped off within seconds.

Kiefer made his way down the sidewalk. He kept a sharp eye on the happy-go-lucky Teo. Kiefer noted how content he was, with a stupid grin on his face. *How is anyone that fucking happy? Stupid völf,* he thought, shaking his head dismissively.

Kiefer had to keep a file on Teo. Even though he kept his interactions with the völf to a minimum, he knew his background well. Teo was married to a mate he'd known since his early maturity. He had four young tykes, all females, with his same powder-blue coat. He lived with integrity and never bothered anyone. It would have been a tragedy to lose someone like Teo.

Just because Teo made an exceptional actor when Kiefer needed his Völfien senses didn't mean he needed to die. Kiefer questioned how it would look if an æsir's actions got an innocent völf killed. Surely that wouldn't go well with Yegor's last-minute meeting with their centurion, the head of their region's Sentry department.

Fuck! They would chastise me for sloppy work and hold me accountable for four tykes without a father!

Teo suddenly spotted Kiefer walking toward him. He smirked from ear to ear with a hand raised for a wave, giving away his position.

No, no—don't wave at me. Shit!

A cloaked figure emerged, spotted Teo's hand motion, and then pivoted back to Kiefer, quickly drawing a weapon from his cloak.

"Get down!" Kiefer screamed, drawing his pistol.

Kiefer aimed among the crowds of civilians and fired at the cloaked figure. The bullet found its mark below the belt, where the weapon was being pulled. Because the cloaked figure didn't budge, two more shots followed, making their destination through his gut.

Another cloaked figure quickly emerged with a shotgun. Because Teo had ducked, the shot was aimed at Kiefer. Kiefer took cover behind a wooden light post. Fortunately, due to his slim profile, the attempt missed him. Stray shrapnel from the light post shattered the glass in the shop windows surrounding him. Screams echoed from inside the building and poured out into the streets.

"Get outta here! Take cover!" Kiefer ordered.

He swiftly emerged from his cover and fired two more shots, piercing the second assailant's skull. Brain matter decorated bystanders.

The crowds panicked and cleared out, opening a clear path for Kiefer to charge for Teo. He shuffled him to his feet as soon as he reached him. Three more cloaks emerged.

"Damn it! We need to get you out of here—now!"

One of the figures rushed up to where Teo and Kiefer stood, drawing a pistol, but Kiefer kicked the butt of the gun, throwing off the figure's aim. Next, he forced his weight against the assailant's wrist, snapping it against the cargo's mass. The figure grunted in agony. Kiefer swiftly drew his knife and slashed the figure where their throat lay exposed; then, while making contact, he delivered two more stabs to the ribcage, and forcefully pierced the heart.

The next cloaked figure came up behind Kiefer, pulled out a dagger, and attempted to attack him. Kiefer reversed his grip, thrusting his knife into the assassin's forearm, between their ulna and radius. Kiefer clenched his teeth and twisted the blade, aggressively causing the bones to snap. The figure screamed and collapsed on his knees, wailing in agony. Kiefer seized the assailant's dagger and drove it up through their chin, breaking the point through the top of their skull. He then pulled it free and threw it with expert accuracy at the third cloaked figure headed for Teo.

"Perfection!" Kiefer proudly huffed as the blade locked onto the third attacker's upper thigh, causing them to prematurely fire their flintlock gun into midair.

The assailant corrected his aim and prepared to fire again, but Kiefer was too close; he pushed off the stacked cargo and vaulted over the figure. With a flurry of motion, Kiefer pulled out a stake hidden under his sleeve and drove it deep into the attacker's throat, spewing arterial blood everywhere. Kiefer's face was immediately drenched from the crimson spray.

"Damn, so much for that shower today," Kiefer sneered, wiping his eyes clean.

He knelt and pulled the hood away from the limp figure. It revealed the face of what he expected. *Ork!* Kiefer dropped the hood, pulled the dagger from their thigh, and looked up. The fight was over, but where was Teo? Teo was out of sight, as were many other Copper District civilians subjected to the violence.

"Teo?" he called, whipping his body around in search of him. "Teo?"

He was gone.

A gunshot echoed in the distance. Kiefer took off down the street, following the sound. He caught a glimpse of a trio of male orks in pursuit. None were cloaked.

Fucking hell, there's more?

Kiefer readied his pistol once more. Turning the corner into a dark alleyway, he faced the group of orks backing Teo against a dead end.

Teo held up his paws, trembling. He pleaded for mercy. He wasn't confused; he knew this attack had resulted from his assistance to the Commission. His fate now faced him, as he'd crossed those who would stop at nothing to silence their opponents.

"Hey there, Völfy," one of them taunted, clicking his tongue. "We'll make this quick."

The three orks raised weapons to the docile völf, thinking they had been granted an easy execution, but they had not picked up on the fact that Kiefer had tailed them.

Kiefer inhaled, absorbing the mildewy scent of the alley, and quickly calculated. He held his breath, then fired. The bullet split right through the center ork's head; the largest of the three. His towering body careened into the ork on the left; the force sending him up against the wall.

Kiefer exhaled as the ork on the right was forced to turn his weapon on him. He tossed the smaller blade aside and ominously drew a savage machete from his belt. He smirked as he took in the well-known wülkure standing before him.

"Kiefer Yuska!" The ork rasped. "I've been waiting for this day for far too long."

His machete blade was a fixed twelve inches, arched and robust. The other ork gathered himself off the wall, adjusted his protective goggles, and pulled a knife resembling a harpoon hook linked to a chain that spilled from his thick belt.

Could this day get any worse? Yegor, you owe me big-time.

It was time to concentrate. Should he go down, Teo was doomed to the orks, who would surely end him worse than they had initially planned. The völf backed against the wall and waited for the fight to conclude.

Kiefer watched the machete flash in the specks of light seeping through the alley while listening to the chain links clinking in a now swinging motion. The sounds ricocheted off the looming alley walls. Kiefer quietly reached for his knife and a scourge from his belt.

Scourges could be in the form of a bullwhip, or even a rope. Kiefer preferred the rope, as it could be used in tighter circumstances. The ork who wielded the machete flinched at the sight of the scourge, giving Kiefer the advantage that any action he took with the rope would be the most effective against him.

The ork with the machete roared aloud and swung for him with agitation. Kiefer snapped the rope, catching the machete's pakkawood handle and constricted the ork's hand around the blade. The second ork raced forward, swinging his harpoon at Kiefer. Kiefer pulled the machete-wielding ork's wrist forward at that precise moment, causing his body to deflect the swinging harpoon, which impaled its hook deep into the ork's upper arm.

From the piercing pain, he shouted, nearly fainting to the ground. Kiefer grunted aloud as he tightened the grip on his scourge, allowing the harpoon to pierce the ork's flesh even further. This compelled the other ork to relax his grip and release his wounded comrade.

Kiefer was now fighting against the final assailant. He inhaled, rapidly calculated, then rushed onto the adjacent wall without hesitation, landing his weight on the ork's back and pushing him to the gritty, cobblestone ground. He rushed for the ork's neck with his knife but missed as the ork unexpectedly rolled over, causing Kiefer to lose his balance. The ork groped for his shotgun, which was slung at his side, but wasn't quick enough. Kiefer anchored his stance and snapped the rope at the ork's face, lacerating his goggles instantly. He then gathered his scourge like nunchucks and delivered a final blow to the ork's skull.

The ork was instantly knocked out, but a cerebral hemorrhage could have occurred. Kiefer's focus was obtaining the völf; medical personnel would decide the ork's fate.

Kiefer turned to Teo, who, relieved, fell to his knees and said, "Thank Uridei you showed up, Kiefer. I thought my wife and tykes were without me!"

Kiefer nodded. "Let's go. We need to get you out of here."

The völf shook his head. "No! No, I can't! I can't—"

"Can't *what?*" Kiefer snapped.

"Go into Commission custody! I can't start over! I can't start a new life! I refuse. I helped you of my own volition, and I will protect myself from here on out."

Kiefer was surprised Teo had put the pieces together enough to know that an attack like this meant his department would ship him out for questioning and protection. Teo, of course, knew that refusing meant he would, at his own risk, be set up for another attack. The minotaur, from Yegor's case, who almost had been poisoned had been forced into hiding until the wülkure settled the matter. Teo did not want that same treatment for his family.

"You have to, Teo. If you don't, these gangs will come for you again."

"I understand." The völf stood up straight. "I understand the consequences should I decide—"

"You saw how this encounter went down! We're lucky no one else was killed in the crossfire. You have to go into protective custody. We will sit down and discuss—"

"I will turn to the Blue Coats. They will protect me," Teo said confidently, shifting his tone.

Kiefer shook his head as if he were going crazy. The Blue Coats were an underground syndicate run entirely by humans and Völfien. They did not correlate with the Commission and were highly elusive. They existed primarily within the Obsidian District and the Brass District, known simply for wearing blue coats adorned in natural, elemental patterns— intricate swirling vines, wavering oceans, or explosive fires. The Blue Coats also utilized antique revolvers engraved with designs illuminating the Völfien culture. They were led and organized by the infamous outlaw Zero. No one outside the syndicate had met this mysterious lead.

Since they existed outside the Commission, they acted as a sort of liberation crime syndicate bent on protecting members of the Fae when they fell victim to situations like Teo's. The Blue Coats were not allied to Kiefer or the Commission.

"The Blue Coats, eh? Criminals?" Kiefer sneered.

"No! They protect völves in the event their lives become threatened. Please, let me—"

"Teo! I have to take you into custody. There is no choice in the matter. I—"

Kiefer heard a sound, but there was no time to redirect his attention. Several barrels were aimed at him, and revolver hammers clicked in scattered unison. He knew there wasn't a moment to turn and take the upper hand.

Kiefer dropped his pistol and the scourge and raised his hands in surrender. *Who could this be? More orks? Those fucking Blue Coats?*

"Wülkure Kiefer Yuska," said a growling voice.

"Do I know you, völf?" Kiefer hissed.

"So sure I am a völf?"

"All of you must be völves. I didn't hear you till the hammers clicked. No man or ork can sneak up on me like that."

"And yet you specialize in managing us." The völf gruffly chuckled. "How must that feel to your expertise?"

"I trust my limitations."

"Fortunately for you, we völves aren't a violent race, despite what the humans think. We ensure our protection, which is all we are here for today, Wülkure. Now, step aside."

"Fair enough," Kiefer huffed.

Teo looked at Kiefer nervously. His dream appeared to be coming true. His anxiety about the situation proved he regretted the ominous presence of the Blue Coats, even though he was being liberated from Commission custody.

Kiefer nodded to Teo. "It's okay," he whispered.

"Don't worry, brother," the Blue Coat said in his Völfien tongue to Teo. Kiefer knew their language was used among völves to build trust.

"We are here to help you. We already secured your wife and tykes," the Blue Coat assured.

"My wife? My tykes? Why?" Teo said in Völfien.

The Blue Coat ceased speaking in Völfien, so Kiefer would understand Teo's safety. "While there is a looming threat, you cannot remain in Demitori City."

Teo shook his head. "We have a life here! Friends!"

"And one day you may return when the threat is lifted. But we cannot risk your or your family's safety. You must come with us."

Teo torpidly walked toward the voices. He stopped parallel to Kiefer's gaze. "I am sorry, Kiefer."

Kiefer shook his head. "No, Teo. I am the one who is sorry. I am sorry I got you caught up in all of this."

"I'd do it again for you, friend. I'd do it again."

Kiefer nodded. "Yeah. Go be with your family."

Teo looked up to the völves and returned to his Völfien tongue. "You won't hurt this wülkure! He is a good man."

Kiefer understood most of what Teo said, including *good man*. It bothered him to think he was a good man in Teo's eyes. He did not hear a response from the Blue Coat but saw relief in Teo, who nodded and walked into the shadows, where he joined a pattering of clawed feet.

Kiefer presumed all the völves had fled, until he heard the last völf press his padded feet into the stone pathway, closing in on him. The völf spoke again, pushing the double-barreled weapon against Kiefer's head: "Pleasure to meet you finally, Wülkure Yuska."

"Curious? You know my name; what is yours?"

"The name's Richter."

Kiefer sighed. "Ah, surname?"

"Indeed."

"Huh, something the world wishes you to be without, an identity to pass on to your offspring, yet you have one," Kiefer noted. "It's the perfect outcry for your syndicate. You are my first Blue Coat encounter; do you trust me with your surname?"

The revolver barrel pressed deeper against Kiefer's skull. "It is a name your colleagues would surely know well had you paid any attention, Wülkure. But I'm not worried. I don't believe you will come looking for me; your personal prejudice lies within your race, not my own."

Kiefer laughed. "Appears you know a lot about me. What else do they say?"

"Well, your record is certainly discussed. You're good at what you do and swim well beneath the wake of the wülkure's department. Fortunately, with that said, there's still much to learn. Perhaps we will meet again under less unfortunate circumstances. I suggest you don't put a völf in danger again. Next time, our graces won't be shared."

"Is that a threat—"

The pressure from the revolver fleetly disappeared, and like a gentle wind, the völf called Richter was gone.

☆

Shaar
Tsunetomo
Okumura Temple
Aousti 9

Ameilja recovered her balance as her protectorate gently set her down. She felt weakness in her limbs, but the adrenaline surpassed the sensation. She looked into her protectorate's eyes, which were keen yet gently collecting her.

"I did it?" she asked, touching Kovuco's cheek, confirming that he was standing there and that it wasn't just her imagination.

He smiled, sighing with relief, revealing every tooth in his mouth. "Yes."

Tam, Dancer, and Nav'i had taken to their lady by now. Oboro had tossed the crossbow to the assistant and made her way toward Ameilja. She lit the tip of her thumb in white flares and brought her pipe back to life, taking in the fine tobacco.

"Ameilja, fine job. I knew you could do it."

Ameilja gathered her balance and stood firm. "At the risk of my friend! How could you—"

Oboro snapped her hand, cutting Ameilja's speech. "*That* is how you succeed!"

"What are you talking about?"

"Uridei does not grant his Purge flame as a mere tool to fiddle and play with at any time. Sure, it is a massive weapon against the forces of darkness and can be enjoyable once mastered, *but*, as I've taught you, it's so much deeper than that and must be taken seriously. As a seer, Ameilja, your soul is the purest fuel the Purge has." Without giving Ameilja a moment to answer, Oboro turned to Kovuco and continued. "Tell me, Kovuco—do you love Ameilja?"

What?

"Sorry?" Kovuco asked.

"What do you and your close-knit pack feel for Ameilja?" she reiterated. "It's love. Love is the secret ingredient to succeed in this test. Do you love Ameilja?"

"I—of course *we* love Ameilja!" Kovuco answered hurriedly, shifting where he stood. "Ameilja has demonstrated love for us all simply in our enlistment to her side. She treats us fairly." *Keep it together, Kovuco.* He nodded to Dancer. "Dancer was once enslaved. Ameilja took him in, and look at him now." Kovuco turned to Tam. "Tam here is my cousin; my father's brother, Halbjörn, is Tam's father. He was raised in Kyottó, an area where völves enjoy a far greater degree of freedom. Why would Tam serve as a protectorate, when he could have been practically anything he wanted back in our homeland? Right?"

Nav'i nodded and stepped in, hearing Kovuco's voice falter with insecurity at speaking candidly. "It's true, master. Ameilja chose us but gave us a choice to serve her equally. She picked us uniquely, and as Kovuco demonstrated, we will stand before the flames of Uridei for her."

Oboro smiled. Smoke elegantly spewed from her lips. "Ah, it's love, Ameilja. Love conquers all, and you would have never rendered this test had I not placed before you someone whom you love and who truly loves you in return." She paused. "You have shown Uridei that your heart is ready for his flame. A lesson we often speak but rarely enact. I am proud of you, Ameilja."

Oboro folded her hands and, for the first time in all her years, bowed to Ameilja. It was a gesture of respect, one only an apprentice granted a master.

Ameilja stood there holding back a smile in her shock. Her eyes welled with tears. She gracefully bowed low. "Thank you, Master Oboro."

Oboro crossed her chest. "Light of Uridei, my apprentice." She took a puff of her pipe and lightly chuckled. "I wondered. The mysterious son of Adémaro, the same völf your father nearly gave his life for—would that völf's kin be the growing pain you needed? It turns out I was right." She raised a brow.

Oboro stepped even closer to Ameilja and her Court of Völfien. She scanned the group meticulously as she began to hum to a tune in her head.

They all stood in silence and respectfully waited while she assessed each of them.

Tam, the brave, enthusiastic, affable one, always was prepared to bring a smile to everyone he encountered. It was a wonder he'd chosen the life of a protectorate in a foreign land, when he could have had a comfortable Völfien life with his father's family in the South. Rather than selecting a comfortable occupation, he had chosen a life of servitude and service to the Order and had remained chipper in every circumstance.

Nav'i was intelligent, hardworking, loyal, and dedicated to the perfection of himself and those around him. He was a no-nonsense protectorate. She wondered what might have become of him had he not stepped into House Frost.

Dancer, the survivor, was damaged but sweet, loyal, and gentle. His genuine nature was a great asset. She'd heard his cooking skills were superb.

Then there was Kovuco Blackstar, the tense, loyal, and somewhat reclusive one who admitted his surname around his lady. Oboro had always thought that if he were to break from some of those awkward traits, he'd rise into a natural leader, a driven and dynamic force of energy. There always had been something mysterious and dark about him beyond his unique physical traits. Oboro could only presume from the fidgeting völf that perhaps the truth would be revealed one day, whatever that truth was.

Oboro finally spoke up, breaking from her thoughts. "And you, Court of Völfien. I am proud of you. Ameilja has accomplished much with you four. I cannot wait for her demonstration with her father. He will be proud that his daughter has followed closely in his footsteps and now beyond."

The four völves crossed their chests, standing tall and proud, blazoning their broad stance in front of Master Oboro. All said in unison, "Light of Uridei, master."

Isarah
Demitori City, Brass District
The Blind Tiger Pub
Aoustí 9

With the events of the day and with Rae gone, Kiefer needed to visit his favorite pub after a long week of work, which had ended in bloodshed and the disappearance of a völf deemed a close acquaintance.

He was not sure when he would see Teo again.

The Blind Tiger pub was close to home, just around the corner from his apartment in the Brass District. Kiefer didn't visit this pub to drink; no, Kiefer never drank. Kiefer hunted. The Blind Tiger was his favorite hunting ground, not for völves, minotaurs, or orks but for companionship—creature comforts, sins of the flesh.

Considering their age difference of five years and her life ahead, Kiefer assumed Rae was likely to leave him eventually. Everyone else had. Why would she be any different? Kiefer was far too damaged for long-term romances. He always had been alone.

Kiefer was born in Blackwater City. His father remained unknown, and his mother had been killed in an alchemical bombing. Kiefer was cut from his mother's corpse, and survived. Without ever meeting his parents or even knowing their names, he had been handed to a paladin sister who brought him to the Temple of Spears, located just outside of Demitori's city limits.

Kiefer had been raised in the temple orphanage, attended school, but dropped out when he was eighteen. He joined the Commission and quickly climbed the ranks until he made æsir at age twenty-two.

His permanent station had become the Copper District since he maintained a solid record in handling members of the Fae. Despite his professionalism, Kiefer had a knack for treating most humans with extreme prejudice. Being an orphan, he had always been independent and built a protective wall stacked with trust issues. Having been alone most of his life, he didn't follow anybody's moral rules but his own. He felt he'd eventually hurt Rae one way or another, but Kiefer felt immune to such pains.

"Let's make tonight memorable, Kiefer," he whispered to himself, adjusting his wardrobe.

The elaborate pub stood before him. A young, deep-pocketed crowd often visited the Blind Tiger. More often the elites.

The atmosphere of dark slate floors, mahogany furniture, and percussion accents was usually met with a more complex group, but Kiefer always welcomed the challenge. He knew what he was looking for, and was accustomed to the routine. The Blind Tiger always invited at least one patron who stood out to his liking, rarely a handful.

Kiefer scanned the crowd. Amid a band of bearded bureaucrats, lavishly dressed women, and a group of wächters celebrating a comrade's final night as a single man, there she was.

The intriguing woman wore knee-high leather boots and a blue dress embroidered with bouquets of wild white roses and luscious green leaves. The garment was cinched to her porcelain skin by a corset of brown suede. Her silky brown hair was bound in a tight, neat bun at the top of her head.

Kiefer continued to assess her form, watching her flawless movements.

With a gloved hand, she elegantly held a book, which her glass-framed eyes fixated on. She read between careful, graceful sips from the glass of red wine resting on the table. Kiefer continued to watch her. Before she took a drink from the glass, she would cock her head slightly to read the collection of droplets along its sides, measuring the density of the droplets. When she was satisfied, she took a slow sip and smiled heartily.

Kiefer rose to his feet, and cautiously stepped toward the woman's table. When he met her side, he addressed her with a clearing of his throat. That caught her attention, and she turned and smiled.

"Good evening, madam," Kiefer said.

"Evening to you, sir."

"Are you alone?"

"I am."

"I don't mean to intrude, but it's been a rather long day; I hoped to chat with someone. Do you mind if I join you?"

The woman set down her book, closing the pages over a blue velvet ribbon. She gestured to the spare chair. "Please. Have a seat."

Kiefer sat in the spare seat, and she flagged a waiter.

"A glass, sir?" the waiter said.

"No. Coffee."

The woman's eyes widened a bit, and she turned back to the attentive waiter. "I'll keep with my wine."

She turned to Kiefer, and he nodded and said, "Espresso. Double."

The waiter acknowledged Kiefer and rushed to the back of the pub.

The woman chuckled as she turned back to him. "Apologies. I didn't mean to laugh. I'm not used to a gentleman not drinking with me."

"Not much of a drinker, I'm afraid."

"I suppose it's not a bad thing. Such constraint. A scarce quality in a man."

You have no idea, madam. "That is certainly one way of putting it."

The mysterious woman lifted her napkin, gently patted her lips, and then held out a hand to Kiefer. "My apologies, sir. My name is Emilíana."

Kiefer took her hand. "Please don't apologize. My name is Kiefer, Emilíana. I frequent this establishment from time to time. You don't match the clientele, so I take it you're not a local here in the great city of Demitori?"

Emilíana blushed. "No. I am staying at the Valtari here in the Brass District."

"The Valtari. Now, that is a scene you do meet—elegance. In my opinion, the Valtari doesn't even belong in the Brass District, but it neighbors the Pearl District just a few blocks away, so it works." He paused. "What brings you here?"

"Work. I am a wine and spirits consultant for the Lodi label in De'licyymbol."

"Does the Blind Tiger pass?"

"Well, Demitori, as you said, is a great city, but accountability is essential to the Lodi label if we have a bar selling one of our finest wines and mistreating a valued contract."

"So this brew"—Kiefer gestured toward the bottle on the table—"sounds like an old friend rather than a new taste."

"Indeed. This bottle is approaching its thirtieth birthday."

"You seem rather dedicated to measuring those—what do you call them? Legs?"

"Ah yes, we do call them legs. Whether it's a new wine or even a lifetime favorite, a great wine should always provide evidence of its measure." She swirled her wine, about to catch the droplets once more. Kiefer watched her as intrigue lightened her brown eyes. "The denser the legs, the higher the alcohol content. The faster the tears flow, the dryer the taste."

"What if the legs were not substantial to your expectation?"

"I would request a new bottle."

Kiefer laughed. "Wouldn't even a taste be worthy?"

"No, sir. It must pass visual and aroma, or I refuse even a sip. I wouldn't want to spit it back out in the glass!"

"You could swallow." He narrowed his eyes.

Emilíana's eyes locked with his. "No. I love wine, and I know it very well. I have strict expectations regarding my wine choice. If I don't love it, I *don't* swallow."

Kiefer grinned seductively. "And if it faults once more?"

"Well, that is the end of my enjoyable experience, and I must do the rough part of my job."

"I see. The Lodi must value you greatly."

Emilíana laughed. "Well, I have been a consultant for some time. The Lodi does value its staff."

"Well, time to put Lodi to the test then." Kiefer reached for Emilíana's glass, closing the distance between them, and leaned inward, sniffing the cabernet wavering inside the hollow of the glass. Kiefer noticed she hadn't backed away. He sensed her heart rate rise in his concentration on the aroma; her breathing calmed as she tried to compose herself—the same tension a rabbit might have felt as a snake slithered by, rubbing the scales against its soft fur.

"Okay."

"Okay?" she asked, blinking twice, batting her lashes at him nervously.

"Tell me. Why would I choose such a wine? Given the occasion we were to have dinner, how would this pair with a fine cut of sirloin?" he asked.

"Well, I prefer a different wine for a fine cut."

"Oh?" He smirked.

"This cabernet features a dark fruit with a scent of—"

"Don't tell me. May I?"

She leaned close to Kiefer and swirled the red wine in the glass, allowing him to savor the fragrant notes again through his nostrils.

"I sense the fruit. The other? There is another. Vanilla?"

"Indeed," she answered softly, intrigued by his intelligence. "Sirloin deserves a zinfandel. We want those sweeter berry notes, and imagine those notes of leather, oak, and spice complementing the meat. Maybe some thyme and perhaps a creamy, buttery mushroom sauce." Her eyes shifted from the red wine to Kiefer's dark eyes. "How does that sound, Kiefer?"

Kiefer smiled. "I see why they need you, Emilíana."

She turned her head, resting a gloved hand over Kiefer's hand. "I wish you could experience the taste yourself, Kiefer. This is by far my favorite."

Without effort, Kiefer turned his head and pressed his lips to Emilíana's. She inhaled deeply at the shock of contact but quickly eased herself into it and let him inside her. His tongue met hers and melded into an embrace momentarily, leaving her aghast at the stranger she let in. She had never met a man as bold as Kiefer and never allowed a man to kiss her like this. She had always kissed first and made the first move.

Not this time. Not with Kiefer.

He tasted her mouth—the aftertaste of the wine lingered on her tongue—and then backed away slowly. He finally ran his tongue against her bold red lips before peering into her brown eyes. She tried to cover her nerves, but all she could do was stare back and, at that moment, hope he had the following words to say.

And he did. "The fruit is blackberry, with notes of vanilla and one more. Mocha? A wonderful, delicious structure indeed, Emilíana. Say," he whispered, running a hand beneath her dress, resting his fingers along her inner thigh, "what other sorts of meat would you pair with this cabernet?"

She swallowed hard, resting her hands on her book before her. "Um, I would consider...I mean, I—" She gasped suddenly as a heavy presence drew in behind Kiefer.

Kiefer turned, and a pair of wülkure stood behind him. "Wülkure Yuska?" said one of the men.

"Unfortunately," Kiefer answered in annoyance.

"We apologize for interrupting, but some urgent business requires your attention. It involves the centurion."

Kiefer sighed, slowly drawing his hand back from Emilíana's thigh, regretting that his desires would not be fulfilled. "Of course it does."

Kiefer rose to his feet, masking the erection that had begun to swell, and held out a hand to invite hers. "Madam?"

Emilíana raised a hand shakily and placed it in Kiefer's palm. He licked his lips before placing them against her hand gently. His eyes met hers.

Her pupils dilated, not from shock but from intrigue. Kiefer made her nervous in a new way. She felt fascinated by the unexpected reaction this stranger had pulled from her. His kiss had left a sting like novocaine. She knew about this dark and intimidating energy from books she'd read, but here the dark stood right before her, and rather than consuming her, it let her go.

"My apologies, Madam Emilíana. It seems my occupation calls."

"Perhaps another time. It was a pleasure, Kiefer." She cleared her throat and allowed her confidence to return. "A pleasure to meet you."

"The pleasure is all mine, Emilíana."

Shaar
Tsunetomo
The oceanfront outside the West Wing
Aousti 9

Ameilja's surprise came that same evening: no more practices, physical challenges, or avid reading but a calm evening with her Court of Völfien to watch the sunset. It was the gift she desired most the night before her birthday.

Ameilja was relieved that her training was complete for the week and advised Ash that she would not be finished with her völves until after midnight. This night was far more memorable. She wanted to usher in the next chapter of her life with her closest companions, who protected and loved her for who she was.

Ash did not object. Per usual, it would do him no good to try to control the lady of Shaar.

Dancer and Nav'i started a fire in the small hole they'd dug out in the sand, while Tam and Kovuco tended to the gyozas Dancer had prepared that morning. As the sun sank behind the endless sea, the five of them gathered around the fire, speaking softly.

Ameilja sat between Kovuco and Tam, huddled against a large piece of driftwood. The heat from their large forms kept her warm as the coastal chill set in. The cold, salty air nipped at her pale face as she huddled in close. She leaned her head back and gazed up at the stars.

Tam got caught up in conversation with Nav'i on the merits of appropriate reference to the nature of the sun while Dancer intermittently tended to the fire. Ameilja took that moment to squeeze Kovuco's thumb.

He turned to her. "Hm? Are you okay?" he asked softly.

She nodded, watching the stars. "She's right, you know."

"Who?"

"Master Oboro. I wouldn't have been able to do what I did today had it not been for my love for you guys."

Kovuco smiled and chuckled softly, unable to manage a comment.

She grinned; nestled her head against his broad, warm arm, and rested her eyes.

"Kovuco," she subtly whispered.

"Ameilja?"

"I love you." She barely answered, drifting away into slumber.

Kovuco didn't answer, worried what his reply might admit.

He looked up at the moon and wondered. *Would it sound normal, like what she actually meant?*

He knew what the love between them would always be. A love such as his would never be accepted. He forced himself to remember the truth: *I am a völf, a member of the Fae, a labeled beast, and Ameilja's a human.*

A shooting star skimmed overhead. Kovuco blinked, and it was gone.

He looked down at Ameilja's sleepy face. The coastal breeze blew through her crimson hair; he closed his eyes and inhaled. Ameilja's scent was unlike anything he'd ever encountered. It stood out compared to the bitter scents of the world. Her aroma would swell within the depths of his being, taking his mind to a euphoric place filled with pine forests, cool coastal nights, and nostalgic dreams. It's the type of scent he wished he could bottle for an eternity.

I want you, but I'm not supposed to.

Kovuco worried about why he felt these feelings that no Völfien had ever experienced toward a human. Ameilja was a mortal, while his world was endless in comparison. The threat of decrepitude was unknown to his kind.

He kept his eyes closed and imagined things vastly forbidden. No one could stop him at that moment as the lulling waves rolled in from the dark sea illuminated by the moon.

Ameilja never let loose of his thumb, but he didn't dare touch her back.

CHAPTER SIX

FOREVER HERS

Shaar
Tsunetomo
West Wing protectorate tower, second floor
Aoustí 10

"KOVUCO!" CALLED TAM.

"I'm up!" I called out, leaning against the windowsill with a book in hand.

Tam turned the corner from the washroom, still dripping wet from his shower. "Good. You're up."

He returned to the shower and turned off the running water. I could hear his furious shakes and the thick water droplets sloshing onto the ceramic tiles of our small bathing space.

He walked out, still dabbing at his body with a towel. "What are you doing?"

"Just some light reading," I casually responded.

"What are you reading?"

"Huh?" I asked.

"*What* are you reading?"

"Oh, um—" I quickly inspected the cover. "The, uh—" The book was upside down and reversed. Too much correction was needed for a lie. *I'm caught.* "Okay, I'm not reading," I huffed, tossing the book toward my bunk, and I returned my gaze to the circular window.

The problem with being around peers constantly and being bad at hiding taunting emotions was that I eventually had to talk about them.

Vulnerability could be complicated. I acted as if I had a heart of stone, when in reality, my heart felt as fragile as glass.

"I don't know why you even try to lie," Tam said as he quickly dressed.

I cleared my throat and inhaled sharply. "What do you think of what Master Oboro said yesterday?"

Tam cocked his head and started delving into his mind, looking distant.

"Specifically, the part about *loving* Ameilja," I added.

"Uh, I mean, it makes sense. Uridei calls us to love one another so much that we should even love the ones who loathe us, love Uridei before ourselves, and so on. Why?"

"I don't know. Just not sure what defines *love*, I guess."

"I think you're looking a bit too deeply, Kovuco," Tam said as he stretched his arms and flexed. "You're in your head again."

"Do you love Ameilja?" I tried to ask without blatant curiosity attached but didn't see any hesitation in his response.

"Of course. Everything you said to Oboro about us was true. What are you getting at, Kovuco?"

I'm trying to break down the walls that hold my emotions hostage.

"Why did you join the Völfien Enlistment Program?" I asked, blatantly ignoring his question.

"I started to get into combat as an outlet, and my father told me I should enlist. I leaped at the opportunity when I discovered the Frost family was looking for protectorates. I didn't realize the assignment was for his daughter, but by the time I did, it was too late to withdraw."

"Why would you have withdrawn?" I furrowed my brows.

"Because, I felt like an idiot. I thought I was applying to be one of András's protectorates. I knew I had miscalculated the offer when I saw Shirou and Lain beside him."

Shirou and Lain were András's protectorates. They were much older and had graduated with my two elder brothers. They also had experience in the Great War, which had made them highly intimidating to a young Tam who thought he was applying for a seat next to them.

Tam continued. "Out stepped redheaded Ameilja, and my reservations changed. I knew I was in the right place somehow. I didn't think

I'd be a protectorate for his daughter, but Ameilja has a way with first impressions. I think I instantly cared for her at that moment too. She's so accepting of us. Treats us fairly, ya know?"

"And that's *love*?" I asked cautiously.

"Yes—I mean, that might be an exaggeration, Kovuco. I got to know her over time. Remember, at first, it was just Dancer and me. Dancer was still pretty standoffish. It was up to me to bring a few laughs, and then I became her *puppy*—at least that was what some of the humans labeled me since I was the youngest in the manor." His face grimaced, recalling the memories. "Pricks! Can't say I agreed with the nickname, but Shirou started kicking my ass whenever he saw me acting up. What are you getting at? Why are you so curious about this stuff all of a sudden?"

"Because I enlisted to escape my father," I answered, my gaze locking on Tam. "After my trial I had to get away. It's difficult enough to look the way I do, with lighter fur and blue eyes, but being next to him makes it even harder to go unnoticed. His lingering excommunication made matters worse. I wanted to get away from him and start a new life."

"I get it. I mean, you are unique, Kovuco; you faced a near-death trial. I'm sure it's not easy from your perspective. Humans view you as a unique case or view you as a sign of dark times. Being compared to your father isn't helpful ... even though he is known as a legend to our race, even *more* so than my father."

I nodded. "You wouldn't even know they were brothers by looking at them." My head then dipped as I continued. "I was never close to my father, Tam. Not like you are with yours. After my trial, I told him I hated him. He's this big legend who was excommunicated, yet I am the one who faced the harsher trial. I escaped those parts of my life because my father was so broken. I always thought he resented me. Because of him, and because of my past, I thought I would never be able to love or understand the emotion of it."

A solemnity overcame Tam's features as he met my frustration. A brief silence coated the space.

"Don't worry, Kovuco," Tam spoke up. "Being a protectorate doesn't have to be your calling; you'll know love once you find a mate—"

"But then I laid eyes on Ameilja." I blurted.

Tam paused and looked at me. He furrowed his brows in question. "So, at that moment? You experienced those feelings at that moment?"

I didn't answer. *I've said too much.*

Tam shook his head and stood upright, processing our conversation. Suddenly, he snapped his attention back to me. "Wait a minute. Kovuco, are you saying you like Ameilja? You *like* her?" He swallowed uncomfortably. "Romantically?"

I shifted where I stood. My form tensed as sweat beaded along my temple.

"Don't get me wrong; she's cute for a human, but she's a human, Kovuco!" He took a large stride toward me. "It's forbidden! You could be killed for such—"

"I know!" I snipped, sighing under my breath. *Shit, I've said too much.*

Tam waited for a moment. I could tell he wanted more information—something else to go on before he assumed the worst of me and before he had to remind me of what I had already worked hard to convince myself of.

Loving Ameilja in the way I thought I loved her was wrong. Yet I'm burdened with the emotions of this.

Tam said, "I'm a little shocked. I've always thought you carried a distaste for the human race. I'm not saying you can't care for our lady, but I can't disagree with your frustrations toward our treatment." He shook his head, narrowing his eyes as he looked at me with concern. "You have to be realistic. One of our race with a human? I don't think it would even work. How would you even kiss? Have you ever seen a human's, uh—" He made a waving gesture with his pinkie as a smirk spread across his face.

I couldn't help but scoff and belt out a laugh. Tam's ornery nature brought levity to the awkward conversation. It somehow brought a new level of trust to the topic.

Tam laughed, not realizing how ridiculous he sounded. Like any comedian, he continued. "Pretty sure they are only this size too!" He raised a brow and emphasized his pinkie size again.

I laughed even more hysterically than before. It felt good to make fun of the measly human male.

"I guess there is our *Rinkin* form if you master it, but still," he added, "we are one race, while they are another. As I said, it's forbidden, Kovuco."

My Rinkin...

My insides instantly recoiled at the thought of facing my human form. I didn't even face my reflection.

Tam continued to chuckle until the door abruptly opened, and Nav'i entered. He was fully dressed for the coronation, glaring at us. "What are you idiots doing?"

Tam caught his breath. "Ah, nothing. We—"

Nav'i snapped, interrupting Tam. "Get dressed, and quit screwing around! Dancer and I have been helping with prep, and you're both laughing your tails off, not even ready for the day. You know how important today is for the Frost family. The final House airships have landed, including the empress's airship. Get on with it!"

I nodded, alert. "We're readying ourselves now!"

Nav'i seemed to be addressing Tam more directly; as he left, he shot me a somewhat intentional glare before slamming the door behind him.

What the hell did that mean?

Nav'i and I always had been unspoken rivals, although more so while growing up. I'd questioned if Nav'i disliked my presence. He also seemed hell-bent on harming me more than the others in free sparring, proving some unknown point. So far, the issue never had been addressed as our paths crossed in Shaar.

Tam cleared his throat and turned back to me. "Kovuco, can we talk about this later?"

I nodded, silent. He sounded genuine, and as much as I wanted it to go away, I knew the concern would resurface. I followed him into the washroom to finish getting ready. We wore the same dark slacks and button-up, collared white shirts of our typical uniform. I rolled the sleeves and fastened the buttons below my elbows before fitting on my ascot.

I slipped on my red jacket with a tessellated pattern. Such a jacket was tailored for each protectorate for this specific occasion. There were polished gold buttons, but a sash held it together against the waist. If we needed to reach for the tonfa swords, they were tucked into leather sheaths strapped to our backs. Lastly, we fastened our bracers and armored shin guards.

We headed out and met Nav'i and Dancer, who waited at the gate, where Ash met us again.

"Look'n good, boys!" Ash proudly grinned, fishing for the rusted key.

Old Ash looked good too.

He smelled like fresh leather and cedarwood. A red ribbon bound his light hair that was slicked back, and finally freed from his hat. The jacket he wore matched his usual attire in detail, but the color was bold vermillion to match some of the selected colors of the coronation. It also appeared he trimmed his goatee.

He quickly freed us from our tower, the gate screeching to a complete close. I could hear the distant hums from the airships as we crossed the bridge in quick strides; however, it felt as if the minutes dragged. New scents began to flood my sinuses as each step took us closer to her wing.

Ash led us through Ameilja's courtyard. The stone walls were laden with ivy, but the yard was mostly clear for Ameilja's physical exercises. On a patio overlooking the ocean, a table and furniture layered in pillows lay for visits and meetings. She ate and read there often. Ameilja preferred to exercise her mind, especially under the glowing golden tea lights hung from the upper areas.

We officially breached her space. I braced myself for her bedroom door at the end of the hall, but then she appeared. My breath caught in my throat.

There she is.

She turned toward us. There was always something wild to Ameilja, even on the most formal occasions. I could smell her from where I stood. She was wearing a form-fitting dress of shining gold and black. Its embroidery was filled with swirling, celestial designs accentuating her every curve. Her hair was tied into an elegant braided design, but just like Ameilja, her hair refused to be tamed; a few wisps had broken free to caress her shoulders. My eyes drifted to her necklace hanging elegantly around her neck and lying just a couple of inches above the curve of her breasts.

Oh...shit. She's beautiful.

How she looked in that moment raised deeper, darker desires— desires so intense they suffocated my gentle, reclusive self. My blood stirred in my veins; my heart raced. I could hear each beat in my ears.

I could claim her as my own without hesitation. Right here, right now.

With just a clip of my claw, that delicate-fibered dress would have fallen from her form easily and slowly like a feather. Just the thought urged Völfien instincts that should only have arisen from taking a mate.

Damn it, Ameilja.

I swallowed hard and immediately suppressed the thoughts, slowing my heart.

She's not mine to claim.

She shared her usual smile with us, placing her knuckles on her hips. "Gentlemen, my sister will absolutely shit herself when she sees whom I have brought to my coronation!"

Nav'i chuckled. "Protectorates, Ameilja. It's not like we're taking you as your escorts."

"Well, I need an escort." She answered quickly.

So she denied the offers?

No one answered. We snapped our attention to Ash, who we now thought was her escort.

Ash coughed nervously. "Um, escort? Wouldn't that be me?"

Ameilja scoffed. "I don't think so. No one takes a man old enough to be her father to the ball. At least not me. I get to choose my date." She eyed her Court of Völfien.

Ash smiled. "I couldn't agree more, but your father will not be pleased, nor will the watchful eyes of the Commission. I—"

"This is my plan, Ash. And that's an order."

She meant what she said, and she was right; Ameilja outranked him as a Commission member.

He nodded and cocked his head. "So, who will escort you tonight, *Lady* Ameilja?"

She narrowed her eyes on Ash, then pointed to me.

What. Why is she pointing at me? My entire form tensed again, this time more furiously than before.

She clutched her chin, eyeing me intensely, studying what she wanted to do with me. "Let's do a brooch, a longer ascot, or a tie."

"Brooch?" Ash asked.

"Yes," she answered with a wave. "I have that brooch for my cape. You know that silly velvet one I have to wear on the holidays."

"Yes, ma'am, I do."

She ran back into her room with excited determination while I stood there, frozen, not sure if my fear would start shaking through my knees.

Why am I like this?

She came out with the gold pendant and stuck it on my jacket's lapel with a red feather. I gazed down at the charm, tipping it slightly to see the emblem of the Commission etched in gold and enclosed with blackened diamonds. I looked like a sporting huntsman. *It's too much—too much for a völf!*

"Um, are you sure about this?" I asked nervously.

Ameilja gazed up at me with her chin dipping low. "Kovuco"— she held out a hand as if offering it to me—"will you take me to my coronation?"

She postured herself like a dame. Those gloves were going to her head.

Don't do that! Don't flirtatiously ask me to do this. Damn it. Yes! This is a mistake. This human woman is crazy.

"Judging by his shock, I'd assume it's a yes," Tam said, smirking.

If I had been in Rinkin form, my face would have been as red as her hair. I was embarrassed at my lack of speaking and ability to be confident. I closed my eyes and swallowed hard. "Lady—"

"Ameilja," she corrected sharply.

"Ameilja, I'm afraid this is not right."

Her hand remained looming in the air, waiting for me to take it, hanging beneath a void I believed I might slip into, never to be seen again.

She pressed the back of her hand to her forehead. "But there is no one else who can take me, good sir. You don't want me to go alone, do you?" she spoke theatrically like a damned damsel in distress. "I will look silly walking by myself."

Nav'i snorted. "I mean, there is Ash." He eyed me accusingly, waiting for my reply.

"Alone or with an old wülkure? Kovuco, you wouldn't allow a

woman to go alone, because surely she cannot take this dirty old man," she playfully spoke, winking at Ash.

Ash burst into laughter. "Indeed! Come on, Kovey! What do you say?"

I took her hand and bowed before her; I breathed deeply and swallowed again. My saliva felt like glass. I sighed and took a humble knee.

Her tiny hand suddenly turned from its dramatic pose into an open palm. I caught a glimpse of her eyes and saw there was no denying she meant for me to say yes.

She beckoned me to trust her, take her hand, and follow her like on the first day we'd met—the day she'd touched my discolored marks. She gave the same sweet smile, which was cuter than any mark I could have possessed. Her way was primal, enchanting, and radiating the eyes of a Völfien.

I felt my body stir again. A flutter and a smirk crumbled through my defenses, and suddenly, I was brave. I embraced the feeling of her touch reverberating through my nerve endings. I felt right. I felt unafraid. Somehow, she made me feel right in my skin. I was an individual—a Völfien. *It's like I belong—dare I say, a human deserving of this beauty on my arm.*

I'll do this for you, Ameilja.

I bowed as low as possible. "Ameilja Frost, I will be your chosen escort." *Could it hurt? I mean, it's just for her coronation, right?*

She smiled wide, and her green eyes lit up. "Come with me!"

Light of Uridei, help me to be brave.

Ameilja didn't release me as she suddenly ferried me from a grounded stance to practically tripping and nearly falling over the ample padding beneath my feet. I pivoted and allowed her to drag me toward her chamber door. It swung open, and she pulled me through. She closed the door behind us.

The smell of her room smacked into my senses. It overwhelmingly smelled like her, the same as the last time I had been in there, but it had been brief and quite some time ago. My packmates and Ash had also accompanied me.

Ameilja's room was like entering a portal doused in rich earth-toned colors and calming vibrations. It was the opposite of the other areas of the House, which were covered in rich reds, teals, and bold Shaar'an colors. Her space was vast, more significant than an apartment that housed four völves; the main space was nearly four times the size. There was an open sitting area, a library, an armory, a closet, and a full washroom. Stone tiles lined the floors with plush rugs scattered for comfort. A large arched doorway opened to a secondary balcony overseeing the ocean.

Her bed had a canopy that connected with the high ceiling, bordering a hanging emblem of the Order and the symbol of the Commission. Next to the living space was a painting of Mother Vhera, the first abbess of the Commission—the one whom all female paladins aspired after. She had many pictures hung of the famed sisters of the Religious Order. The Commission wasn't strictly linked to religious beliefs, but to become a paladin, faith in Uridei was a must to use the Purge.

Her room was adorned with shelves of books, along with swords, all customized to her colors. On the wall above her headboard hung an original paladin sword, a replica of one a paladin under Albean would have wielded during the earliest days of the War.

Ameilja's chambers strategically represented her beauty, strength, and intelligence.

"Come," she whispered.

She walked me alone to her closet, just the two of us, and invited me through. A bench stood in the middle with a belt that made me audibly gasp.

It's ancient—undeserving of my view.

It was a magnificent piece of armor, a utility belt used by the first paladins of the war. It was said that Albean had worn a similar belt with similar designs, ones that had influenced the design of the Commission emblem.

"What do you think? Isn't it beautiful?" She questioned softly, as if in awe.

Her approach was as if she were showing me a relic. The leather was black and hemmed in golden thread. The sigil was neatly etched into the leather on a shimmering gold plating. She reached into a drawer and revealed a sash of bright yellow and gold. She laid it next to the belt, just over the lower corner.

"*This* goes with it."

"The Aureate's gold," I said in shock. I just stared at the belt and nodded, acknowledging the wonder of what was before me. It made my eyes glisten as I absorbed its majesty.

I could smell the fine leather and the polished steel forged in fire. It fortified the core of its wearer. Three buckles fastened it. Some straps hung from the sides, at which the wearer could reinforce armor or scabbards for weapons. It was the only garment worth salvaging from any member.

"It's too bad I couldn't get the tunic," Ameilja said, "but I did get a pair of the wrist gauntlets."

She reached into another drawer and brought out a pair of leather gauntlets that matched the belt. They, too, were original pieces—gauntlets that the first paladins of the Order had worn.

Ameilja suddenly stepped closer to me, took my left wrist, broke down the jacket cuff, and folded back the sleeve to my elbow. Beneath were four buttons that allowed the long cuff to slide off. I looked down at her and watched as she fitted on the gauntlet, fastened it, and gently rubbed my palm with her fingers.

"Perfect," she said. "I knew it would fit you."

An uneasiness rose in me.

I looked over at the belt and thought, *It's rather large.* It would have fit a more prominent man but not little Ameilja. Plus, the seers wore unique belts just for them. This was indeed a belt she would not fit into.

What is her plan with that belt?

I looked back down at her nervously. In that moment, I suddenly realized I was a Völfien wearing a gauntlet of fine leather and golden plates. I was alone with one of the most powerful women of Shaar, in her closet, with no supervision, and within reach of an ancient belt meant for a human man.

She wants me dead. She wants me dead because they'll shoot me, and as they clean the mess, they'll consider shooting her next. She oversteps.

She overstepped often, but it was as if she'd forgotten I was hardly a human man. She didn't know I hadn't seen my Rinkin form in years, and that was only gazing upon my reflection once. She didn't know I had no desire to step into that form.

She doesn't know.

I didn't understand why she didn't try this with Ash or another paladin, who would have been happy to have her on his arm. Many men had tried courting her. But a völf? Her protectorate? A glorified guard *dog*? That was all we were. This would outwardly look abhorrent. It was the equivalent of a prince bringing a scullery maid to a soirée. Actually, worse.

She closed her eyes calmly as my breathing rose in comparison. I wasn't hiding it any longer. The ruse was up. She must have felt my muscles tense within the gauntlets. The air from my nostrils pierced the quiet loudly so as not to allow me to pass out from the stress. My pupils dilated, staring at the belt in terror. My eyes widened that way when I focused on a kill, an opponent. The belt had become my opponent.

Ameilja wrapped her tiny fingers around my paw; it reacted with a slight shiver, with the tremble reaching through my every tendon.

What's next, Ameilja? Just ask, so this suspense will end. Say it. Ask me, so I can say yes and know that I have lost the battle.

"Kovuco?" she said in a gentle whisper. It was playful but still radiated her fiery confidence. She spoke as if even the threat of death were a cheap bluff.

I nodded and met her gaze. My expression didn't change. "Yes, Ameilja?"

"I want you to wear this belt tonight."

I know you do. I nodded, silent.

I should tell her I trust her. I do, but what choice do I have? I trusted her yesterday with flames that would have incinerated me. I am her völf—no one else's.

I'd promised to protect her. To lay my life down in a moment without hesitation. Frost had enemies; she had them too. I had harmed others for her, ripped apart the bodies of opponents to protect her. I had been dripping in gore, carrying ribbons of offal, while pieces of flesh dangled from my teeth and claws, like a trophy—all for her.

She slowly untied my sash, and my coat hung loose again. She undid the holsters that held my tonfa swords. I didn't protest, but I had to be armed at all times, especially in such events.

I allowed her to continue. She took the process seriously, as if dressing a warrior for his final battle.

She pressed my jacket to my abdomen, laid the golden sash, neatly splayed it around my waist, and tied it in a delicate knot to keep it flat.

She then picked up the belt and laid my paw over the large buckle to keep it in place. She gracefully walked behind me with her dress trailing behind her and began fastening the belt.

It was heavy yet light for me. I could imagine a member of the Commission wearing the belt proudly and being more formidable at the same time.

Impoverished priests, brothers, and sisters of the Order were helping the weak and needy and never fearing death. They were known as expressionless against the threat of martyrdom, burning, and beheading. Men and women of faith, rising as paladins, marched on battlefields, purging evil in the name of the Light. It felt like a dream that I would be able to wear a piece of armor that had been worn for generations—a symbol of purity, bravery, and honor.

A solemnity overcame me, as if I were finally accomplishing something I'd thought impossible to claim.

Of all the things, I was questioning my rebellion. That rebellion bellowed in my chest, with my heart throbbing against it in an adrenaline-coaxed appetite. There was something else emerging within me. Something I imprisoned deep inside. Something more substantial and steadfast. Something primal that was only natural. Natural and maybe distinguished me from other völves.

I've hated who I am, the reflection of my father. However, I will bring purpose to what I hate most. I'll do it for something I love. More so, someone I love.

Ameilja unexpectedly grabbed the sides of my face and turned my gaze to the mirror; it caught me off guard.

No! I slammed my eyes closed.

"Will you not look?" she asked, confused.

She doesn't know. I can't answer. I cannot tell her.

I didn't answer. I dropped to my knees before her, keeping my face turned from the mirror. She didn't know my secret, my inner struggle. The atmosphere suddenly shifted; the space became eerily quiet—engulfed by an icy chill. I looked back up, and Ameilja was staring off, concentrating intensely.

"Ameilja?"

She didn't answer. Something was off.

She abruptly lost her balance, catching herself with her forearm against the wall to avoid falling.

"Ameilja! Are you all right?"

She rapidly blinked her eyes and nodded. "I'm sorry—I-I had a vision just now." She kept staring at her hands, looking dazed. "So sorry ..." She trailed off.

I quickly stood, lifted her, and carried her dainty form out of the closet. I held her close. She wrapped an arm around my neck and another about my shoulders. She began to run her fingers through the exposed fur at the nape of my neck, the exact location of the bits of discolored fur; caressing them as if she were ensuring I was real.

She'd often fiddled with something after her visions arrived. They overwhelmed her, leaving her disoriented and weak.

I wanted to explain my shame, but I couldn't. The words wouldn't escape—trapped in a void of cowardice. Since I had no courage to bear my secrets, I did not dare to ask her what clouded her mind when her visions arrived. When she's ready, she will share what she sees.

For now, I have to continue with the task at hand. "Ameilja," I said finally.

There was a pause. She stroked my neck several more times before answering. "Yes, Kovuco?"

"I need my weapons. I cannot be defenseless and leave everything to the others."

"Of course."

I gently put her down. She confidently gathered her footing. "I have your weapon. Come," she said, gesturing for me to follow.

I hadn't noticed, but a sword lay on her bed. It was a forty-two-inch weapon. The blade was nearly thirty-one inches of exposed white steel, unrivaled in sharpness and strength. It was forged of the hardest steels in the world. The handle and sheath were wrapped in white leather contrasting against the golden steel designs resembling the Commission's emblem, whimsical and sharp, like a rose wrapped in thorns.

That was her flower; a rose protected by thorns. *Ameilja Rose.*

"Do you know what this is?" she asked.

I nodded. "It's Red Fang. Your mother's sword."

Ameilja's mother had been a paladin, a skilled warrior who'd learned the ways of the sword. Her weapon was worthy of a name and indeed had one. It was a customized paladin sword, accented with deep vermillion. Vermillion was her mother's color; representing the bravery of those she fought for. Her strength was said to be like the dragons of the skies and seas and awe-inspiring like the summits of glacier-coated mountains. It had been a tragedy to the people when her mother died, but her memory and perseverance had been forged into Ameilja's soul.

"I want Red Fang to remind us of what we originally set out to do," Ameilja said as she picked up the alluring sword, delicately, as if it was an infant. "The Commission has forgotten what Albean set us out to do: destroy the forces of darkness together and bring balance to the world. My father and his close colleagues have blindly allowed the Commission to become a business. A corporation of members bent on conquest and profit rather than peace. We will remind them of our true purpose—*your* true purpose." She closed the distance between us, presenting Red Fang. "We will remind them tonight, Kovuco."

I stared into her warrior-coated eyes. Her green irises beamed with determination.

She was right. Völves once had been members of the Commission: the Order of Völfien. The humans had made a völf, my father, an abbot once after he was sworn in as a paladin. Now we were just *völves*. Bodyguards. Tools. There were no more paladins like those in the days of Albean, or later years of the Great War. Priests were now peons, caring for the people while the Commission's leadership built a foundation that made men like András lords, rather than the original intended design. I didn't believe András was evil, but he had lost his way.

"We will. We will remind them tonight." I told her, taking hold of Red Fang, feeling its weight beneath my grasp.

I wanted what Ameilja wanted. I wanted to be free. I wanted to serve the Commission under Ameilja, seer of Uridei's holy flame. Her birthday had become a festive banquet, when it should have been a movement, and Ameilja wanted that back. She wanted change.

Would she gain it tonight? Would she succeed in her goal?

It didn't matter. Whatever she wanted from this life, I would follow her.

At this point, I am forever hers.

C H A P T E R S E V E N
THE NÄKK

Isarah
Demitori City, Brass District
Okra's Commission vehicle
Aousti 9

"YOU KNOW I HATE IT WHEN YOU SMOKE IN THE car, Kiefer," said Okra Zeutzius from the driver's seat of the Commission-marked vehicle parked just outside the Blind Tiger.

"These are Tithe Nines, Okra. I'm not putting it out," Kiefer said as he took another defiant drag from his cigarette. "Care to tell me what this is all about?"

"Couldn't tell you. I was hoping you might have an idea. I was dispatched to get you since I was in the area."

"It's Brass District. Where's Stahl?"

"Stahl has been at the centurion's office all day."

Kiefer nodded. "Along with Yegor, I presume?"

"Not sure. Something big is happening, Yuska."

"I reviewed Yegor's log. What the fuck could be happening with the good ole science facility?"

Okra pulled his log, a small leather-bound journal, from his coat pocket. "As I said, I don't know. I was just ordered to pick you up. The centurion only wants select wülkure on the case. No need for the Religious Order; I think he wants to keep them out of this one."

"Gotcha. So he's doing something irrevocably blasphemous." Kiefer smirked.

Okra laughed at Kiefer's term. "Eh, I prefer *secular-driven*."

"That's one way of putting it. If *worldly* isn't our custom, then maybe I should swear off smoking and women and get a job within the Order."

☆

Isarah
Demitori City, Pearl District
Commission headquarters, centurion's office
Aoustí 9

Between the rushing mobs of traffic and the city's lively atmosphere during the evening hours, they managed to pull into the Pearl District, beyond the comfort of the humbler districts of Demitori City.

Pearl was where the centurion's office was located. It was also the district of the upper class and was inhabited by many well-endowed elites. There the colors lightened to white, yellow, and periwinkle blue. Its residents wore delicate dresses, silk jackets, and brightly colored vests. Nobles wore top hats decorated with vibrant feathers, craftsmen wore etched goggles, and businessmen wore colorful, tailored suits; all for a society with standards only a deep pocket could pamper. Kiefer knew he stood out.

He and Okra exited the vehicle. Their headquarters structure matched the district's elaborate architecture. They passed through the large double doors resembling the afterlife's pearly gates and into the grand lobby doused in white granite and golden colors. In unison, they strode for the front desk.

An endomorphic wächter sat at the desk, filling out papers and sending out dispatches through the radio console. "Wülkure Okra?" he said, making brief eye contact with Okra after silencing his last dispatch. His eyes fell back to his work.

Okra spoke up, "Yes. Myself and Wülkure Yuska."

"Ah yes, you're both here for the centurion," he spoke loudly with a slight rumble to his voice.

Okra nodded. "Yes."

The wächter confirmed the appointment over the radio and the names assigned. He also confirmed that Kiefer and Okra were recognizable faces within their department, checking their badges. With a final radio response, the wächter typed a few keys on the board to his right and gestured with his head for them to leave. They both boarded the elevator. Okra tapped the number twelve, and the clockwork mechanisms went to work ascending the platform to the upper levels of the building.

They remained mute while ascending in the brass chamber until they reached the twelfth floor. The doors opened to reveal a lobby with floral-like gilded designs on white carpet. The furniture, including the desk at the end of the passage where another wächter worked and guarded the centurion's office, was made of finely polished cherry. Wächters were typically stationed close to the centurion in case they needed to make a quick escape by flight.

Okra and Kiefer passed the wächter with slight nods and proceeded through the office door.

Henrik Böestrum, the centurion of Demitori City, awaited them while polishing the glass face of his pearl pocket watch. He'd been stewing with the two other wülkure who were already there. The atmosphere felt dense.

Kiefer surveyed the room, focusing his attention on Henrik.

Böestrum wasn't just the centurion; he was very wealthy and had some of his financial affairs mixed in with some of his social elitist posse. He was a unique character, a spoiled trust fund kid with a smooth-talking etiquette. At just thirty years old he owned many establishments throughout the Pearl and Sapphire Districts. His good looks only added to the attention he received.

He had inspired many; the youth of his class had followed his example. Kiefer often wondered how insecure their post-war generation must have been to follow after a man like Henrik Böestrum. But he supposed when it came to the youth, they didn't care about character as much as they admired the most confident guy in the room.

Böestrum had been a dynamic success. Whenever tears ran down the face of humanity, he miraculously would appear. He needed more room on his face for that ever-growing smile. It was all about power, pride and wealth.

Despite his being an idol to many and appearing perfect, his spoiled tantrums didn't hold him back. Anytime something went amiss, his dramatic yet boisterous affections for control were always spearheaded in a flurry of frustration.

Kiefer harbored many reservations against him.

"About time you arrived," Henrik jeered as he tossed a pile of papers across his desk toward Okra and Kiefer.

The headlines were filled with insults to Böestrum's reputation. With great accomplishment come those who still choose to oppose him. Henrik was accustomed to slander and defamation, particularly from underground media, but not from his mass following or close colleagues. The gossip and rumors distorted his role, making the Commission and his personal association with the elites appear to be an organization of violence and enforcement rather than peace and order. Typically, the Fae stirred up slander, which resulted in nothing but laughter and eye rolls. Henrik's pride effortlessly negated the opinions of the Fae.

Marius Beckmann, the æsir wülkure of Pearl District, and Ruprecht Stahl, the æsir wülkure of Brass District, promptly rose from their seats, punctual and collected, to join Kiefer and Okra.

"Have either of you heard what's happening?" Henrik fussed, causing his blond curls to bounce in front of his sharp, hazel eyes.

"With the media?" Okra asked, eyeing the stack of papers.

"Of course you've heard that!" Henrik whined, tipping back his head obnoxiously. "Look at the damned communication log!"

Okra stepped toward Henrik's desk and lifted the tightly bound papers placed in its center. He quickly whipped through a few pages, and read aloud: "Sunspire's cult breach?"

Henrik dramatically flopped down into his office chair and attempted to collect his thoughts before speaking. "Not exactly a cult breach. That's for the public to believe." He half rolled his eyes, swatting his hand as if to brush off what he'd said. He then leaned in, cutting a glance at each of the men standing before him. "A most trusted and esteemed colleague, alchemist Dr. Kristján Baadar, has unexpectedly terminated the entire facility. I understand he has also released ork prisoners and taken some of the staff hostage on the upper levels. Reason? No fucking clue." His lips drooped into an overstretched frown. "Ever since I was a young boy, I looked up to Kristján. Such a shame." He paused momentarily and rubbed his temples. *"But* the more imminent threat is not the orks or Baadar. The threat is a damned völf!"

Kiefer shifted where he stood, processing the news that had just been nonchalantly shared, trying to connect the pieces. "Wait. Ork prisoners—what?" Kiefer's expression twisted. "What the hell were the doctors working on?"

Henrik leaned forward, tapping a finger on his desk. His eyes veered upward through a dipped gaze and locked with Kiefer's. He collected himself as he pushed his wheat-colored hair away from his face, then cleared his throat. "We have stumbled upon traces of the Näkk."

Silence.

Insufferable silence collapsed the space.

Henrik's confession sent a bone-chilling flurry throughout the office. Gooseflesh surfaced Kiefer's forearms. He sighed aloud, shaking his head. *Fuck!*

The whole purpose of the Commission was to protect humanity, especially from forces like the Näkk. Now one of the most illustrious labs on the continent had it in its hands.

Fucking hell. "Please tell me this is some sick joke!" Kiefer gutturally urged, taking a stride forward.

"Control yourself!" Marius snipped, eyeing Kiefer.

Kiefer shot Marius and Stahl a look of disgust. It was evident they knew of this too.

"It's fine, Marius, let him process." Henrik slyly added, casually glancing at each of the men. "Allow me to explain. Nineteen years ago, there was a report that an attack occurred near Fjorthúr. A young ork was said to have journeyed deep within a cave and emerged infected by something. It was reported to the Commission, and was immediately investigated. The reports were correct; the ork was infected. They discovered it: the Näkk, in all its glory ..." Henrik lowered his gaze, and a mischievous grin stretched across his thin lips. "The Näkk circulated through the ork's body, just like history taught. Oh, what a phenomenal discovery."

"There is nothing phenomenal about this!" Okra scoffed, worry blanketing his tone.

Henrik shot Okra a pouty look but continued. "It was never supposed to get out of hand like this. They began investigating with a small, closed group under direct orders, keeping the news secret. When I stepped in as Demitori's centurion, I had to ensure the best of the best were involved. *I personally found someone in our ranks who knew of the* Näkk. He's an alchemist—"

"Let me guess. Frahm?" Kiefer interjected.

Henrik cut him a glance. "How do you know?"

"Trust me, I know." Kiefer arched a brow. "It's no secret he's well known for his knowledge of the Näkk. Besides, he has a residence in Copper, despite the Fae. I remember when his wife passed away; she was involved in one of the cult suicides against the Commission. It was unfortunate that she fell victim to their tactics, but I understand that the loss of his wife drove him away from the Religious Order, and their beliefs, with grief being his driving force. I've also learned that Frahm stepped up as a well-known alchemist within the Sunspire." Kiefer glared at Henrik. "I am correct, aren't I, Centurion?"

Henrik nodded, remaining composed. "Frahm confirmed that there was a source of the Näkk present and has worked closely with the other doctors. Over the years, they have enhanced the facility within its lower labs, testing on live subjects there—" he paused, chewing on his words. "Well, I might as well put my pride to the side and admit to you … the operation has escalated into an unethical testing ground resulting in bloodshed daily."

Silence blanketed the room, again.

Kiefer and Okra swallowed hard, keeping composed, as they eyed the man sitting before them: Henrik Böestrum, the superior of their department, one of the high-ranked centurions of their Commission, is a leader who'd devastatingly betrayed them all. He was no better than the one who'd brought the Näkk into existence. Henrik had taken an oath to build trust and protection over humanity, yet he had aided in an underground abomination, risking the very lives he'd sworn to protect.

Fucking traitor!

Anger roiled through Kiefer's veins. He'd wished this was all a dream, just a taunting nightmare he'd wake up from any moment.

The Näkk's history flashed through Kiefer's mental realm. *It had all come to be by an Aureate, a godlike being compared to regular humans. He had begun wreaking havoc on the early settlers of the Eastern Isles. It was Albean that ceased the infection. It was Albean who saved humanity. He saved the people. All of the people ... everyone ... Rae ...*

Visions of Rae's smiling face appeared. Kiefer blinked, then saw her face covered in blood, rotting from the inside out. *No!*

He retracted, curling his hands into fists as the outrage whipped through his form. "Who's *they*? Who the fuck is spearheading this operation? *Why* did you get involved?" The questions hurled out of Kiefer's throat like a crashing wave, abrupt and forceful.

As if Kiefer were stealing a toy from a young child, Henrik rapidly shook his head. "*That* information you are not privy to."

"Damn you!" Kiefer growled, taking a leaping stride forward. If it wasn't for the desk, Kiefer would have had his hands around his centurions's throat.

"Stay in your lane, Wülkure!" Henrik yelled, standing to his feet so forcefully his office chair fell backward.

Marius and Stahl both snapped a warning glare at Kiefer, preparing to defend their centurion.

"Has this news reached the Religious Order? The Empress?" Kiefer demanded.

"No!" exclaimed Henrik. "Frahm told me I shouldn't tell them."

"Naturally, an ex-member of the Order would suggest not telling the Order. We must report signs of the Näkk! The Religious Order should be on this, *not* me. Not any of us here."

"No! Frahm believes there is something we can continue to extract from the studies. Something even more life-changing we can harness—we'd be making a difference!"

What he means is a profit, no doubt. Sick fuck! Kiefer visibly gritted his teeth, abstaining from his wrath.

"Where is Frahm?" Okra interjected, ceasing Kiefer from losing his grip.

"Here. In Pearl," Wülkure Stahl said, stroking his black goatee. "To his luck, he had just taken a two-week leave before this mess went down. He is currently preparing to join a team of wächters who will accompany one of us to take back the Spire and capture the völf, and Baadar."

Henrik nodded. "Precisely. And this mission does not go public either, or all of your fates will be in *my* hands. Yes, that is a threat." He eyed

Kiefer specifically. "These wächters are a tight crew under my lead. They have been together for several years. Their æsir is Anton Rotenfeld."

Oh shit. Could this get any worse? Kiefer didn't say it aloud but knew that was a significant problem. Rotenfeld was Isabelle's brother, another hot-tempered individual. Rumor had it Rotenfeld wasn't too keen on his adulterous brother-in-law. Kiefer knew Rotenfeld would kill for the opportunity to skin Baadar alive should he get the chance. He'd also be willing to challenge any wülkure's authority should one attempt to stop him.

"Why the hell have you not involved the paladins to fix this?" Kiefer edged in again.

"I couldn't—I can't! I'm not the one in charge of this operation. Besides, I am a man of honor Kiefer; I will *not* betray them."

Kiefer scoffed. "How ironic. You're worried about your betrayal yet you've betrayed all of humanity."

"It's not what you think—"

"Enlighten me."

"Enough, Yuska!" Henrik warned. "You do not speak to your centurion with such—"

"Accountability. Truth."

Henrik's mouth dropped into another dramatic frown. The veins along his temple pulsated with each heartbeat.

"Tread lightly, wülkure," Marius warned, clicking his tongue steadily. "I'd watch what you say next."

"Or what?" Kiefer snapped his attention toward Marius. "You'll kill me?"

Marius and Stahl dipped their ominous gazes. The room grew hot; heated by their fuming forms. One wrong move or choice of words would lead to combustion.

Henrik broke the scorched silence. "Gentlemen, as I said. This will not go public." He paused again, calming his nerves. "Understand I did not call the Order because I knew they would seek to Purge and destroy what was found, and I can't call them in now. There's been a breach, and Baadar has shut it down for unknown reasons. Under direct orders, I need the best wülkure on this." Henrik bobbed his head to Kiefer. "You are the choice."

"You called me in because of the völf, didn't you?" Kiefer sneered.

"You're by far the best when it comes to dealing with those beasts. Stahl and Marius specialize in Orkésh, same with Okra, but my concern is Baadar's attack by the völf, and he has somehow survived it. It sounds like he might be held hostage by the creature. The völf very well may pose the largest threat to us all!" He solemnly shook his head. "Those dreaded fucking beasts."

Kiefer cleared his throat. "Seems you need to look in the mirror, Böestrum, and reevaluate who's the actual threat."

Henrik scowled at Kiefer. He stiffened his shoulders and drew his lips into a thin line, clearly offended by his comment. Kiefer was prepared for another childish tantrum or an added threat. He boldly continued. "Let's secure what we can, but since a völf is possibly working to manipulate Baadar, and since the Näkk *is* present, I anticipate we will find a reason to report this to the Order immediately. You'll need to prepare an explanation as to why you have neglected to report this, Henrik. As a centurion of the—"

"You leave that to me, Yuska!" Henrik hissed, pointing a finger directly at Kiefer's face.

"He's a feisty one, isn't he? He doesn't seem to know when to shut the fuck up!" Stahl jeered and reached for his weapon.

"Stand down." Henrik ordered Stahl. He wiped his curly hair away from his eyes and laid his palms on the table, his gaze fixed on Kiefer. His voice cut through the air as he spoke slowly and precisely. "The Order is unforgiving when it comes to the Näkk, but I don't believe in burning what you can control. Remember, Yuska, this mission to fix this is mine. Either you assist with Baadar's capture, or you die."

Isarah
Demitori City, Pearl District
Commission headquarters
Aousti 9

After hours of deliberating and processing arrangements to take over the Sunspire, they finally dispersed. Kiefer pushed Yegor's assignment pertaining to Tree'veld to the back of his mind. It felt pointless, knowing the Näkk was present.

Kiefer stepped into the elevator and tapped the lobby button. His head throbbed from the weighted news and from having to listen to his spoiled centurion's spiels. He was certain Henrik just loved the sound of his own voice.

I need a smoke or to imbed myself between the legs of a woman.

"Shit, this can't be happening," he grumbled aloud, leaning his head against the elevator wall. He wanted nothing to do with the mission or the burden of carrying this news.

The door was nearly shut, when Marius blocked the door and stepped into the elevator. He pushed back his long black hair and cracked his knuckles as the doors closed behind him. Kiefer eyed him, annoyed that he had breached his solitude.

Marius had porcelain-like features. He wore eyeliner to deepen his sadistic edge and to accompany his slick, snakelike mannerisms. He could easily make one feel uneasy, which worked well in his wülkure position.

"Know my desperate desire to remove you from this assignment entirely, Yuska. My apologies that you were insisted upon as the first choice," Marius taunted, his slithering voice grating against Kiefer's exhausted mind.

Kiefer smirked. "Oh? Am I not the best man? Strange. I never heard your objection."

"Oh, I did, but due to your expert dealings with Völfien, you're the closest to the centurion for the job. I also think you're a perfect match when it comes to dealing with women."

The elevator reached the lobby, and the doors opened.

"Walk with me. I have more to share," Marius said over his shoulder.

Kiefer, cockeyed, reeled over the suggestion that he was a "perfect match" when it came to "dealing with women."

"Women?" Kiefer asked.

"Yes, the völf is a female. At least judging by the report, I would presume so."

"I'm not going to ask the völf out for dinner in exchange for her cooperation, if that's what you think."

"With the Näkk involved, we have nothing to lose." Marius chuckled.

Kiefer followed Marius out of the building and onto the dimly lit streets of the Pearl District. The yellowish cobblestone streets were pristine, showing no signs of the bustling activities from the day. It was accented with exotic trees and large stone pots filled with bountiful flower arrangements. They were accompanied by tiny moths swirling about the lantern glow of the streetlights overhead.

Kiefer noted that the streets' quietness was unlike the Fae streets. Late-night taverns and social clubs were always open in Copper. Very few Pearl inhabitants found a purpose to wander their streets at night.

"Anton Rotenfeld, as you know, has a history with Baadar, yes?" Marius said.

"I am aware. Yes."

"Henrik is also aware. He knows of Baadar's affair; who doesn't? Rotenfeld will take any opportunity to kill Baadar and any witnesses involved to protect this secret mission." Marius paused momentarily as a man in a blue peacoat, and his family quickly walked by. Their children skipped alongside them, humming playful tunes. They nodded at Marius.

Marius casually tipped his hat to them, acting less intimidating. "Have a good night," he casually said to them, resuming his talk once they were out of earshot. "Baadar is your mission. After all this, I'd actually like to see him alive, not six feet under due to Rotenfeld's wrath."

"Why does the life of an unethical doctor mean anything to me?"

"Baadar is a better man than you think. There's a reason the völf didn't murder him. My gut instincts tell me that Baadar knows something." He reached into his jacket pocket and pulled a cigarette from a leather case, offering Kiefer one. Marius was a light smoker and harbored expensive tastes for his occasional habit. "Remember, Kiefer, that everything I am about to tell you is of grave importance. It could get us all killed if we're not careful."

Kiefer rolled his eyes. "Right. Now that I am officially involved."

"You may have noticed that Yegor was not involved in today's meeting. There's a reason for that too."

"What's the reason?"

Marius didn't respond rapidly. He led Kiefer to a bridge crossing over a small stream and paused at the railing. "I also heard that Tree'veld has gotten caught up with an ork gang. I'm going to assume it's the Svarfætúr based on what I know."

Kiefer took a long drag from his cigarette, eyeing him suspiciously. "How do you know about Yegor's investigation?"

"Yegor has his reasons to speak with me. Besides, I'm consistently buried in unresolved issues with the Orkésh shit show."

"What the hell does this have to do with Yegor's absence today?" Kiefer urged.

"Come on now, Yuska. You'll get your answers."

"Answer me, Marius!"

"Fine, fine." He chuckled tauntingly. "Do you know about the Wöndin ork, Malbec Fallz'den?"

Kiefer took a step back and sighed aloud, evidently irritated with Marius's lack of clear communication. "You're fucking kidding, right? I don't have time for this nonsense; Yegor's investigation wasn't mine to begin with. I—"

"I need you to listen!" Marius raised his voice. "There's a connecting piece." He lowered his voice again. He paused and leaned in close to Kiefer. Parts of his dark hair fell over his eyes. "The ork boy who was exposed to the Näkk is supposedly the Wöndin's son."

"What?"

"Yes." Another chuckle slithered from Marius's throat.

"I don't recall any of this shit being funny."

"No, no. You're taking me all wrong, Yuska. Listen, listen." Marius's voice lulled. "I'm just passing along some information, one wülkure to another." He took a brief moment to smoke his cigarette. "Malbec was once married to this ork boy's mother when he would still have been involved with his own gang. I guess his gang rivaled the Svarfætúr, which only adds to the issue. The word is that the ork boy's mother divorced Fallz'den, and married a rich ork from Fjorthúr. She brought their boy with her. That was when the boy became exposed to the Näkk somewhere in those mountains. Because of the Svarfætúr's hatred toward Malbec, I have reason to believe they also have involvement in the Sunspire's secret dealings. Nothing would bring them more pleasure than knowing the child of the infamous peacekeeper was being tortured and tested on."

Kiefer slightly shook his head. "Here we go with the nonsense again." He took another hit off his cigarette. "Are you sure it's not just a normal ork boy who got infected? Not the offspring of the infamous Wöndin? C'mon, Marius. Let's make sense of this. Do you think the Svarfætúr would risk jumping on every opportunity to draw out the Wöndin so much so that they would be involved with an underground lab that experiments with the Näkk? It's a bit far-fetched, don't you think?"

Marius's sly smile formed as smoke spewed from his thin, pale lips. "It makes perfect sense. For one, the Näkk desires powerful beings. I don't doubt the ork boy inherited Fallz'den's fantastical traits. And two, that wretched ork gang will do anything to take out the peace-keeping Wöndin. Their goal is to reign superior. That's their motive: to win. They live to quell competition from rising against them and their grudges run deep. Think about it, Yuska; it's the völf who doesn't make sense." He pulled his fingers through his shiny black hair, allow-ing his eyeliner-pasted eyes to breathe. "If you read through the logs, it is evident that the völf attacked within the same vicinity as Dr. Tiem. Tiem and Baadar would have been together at the time of his death. The report suggests Tiem's throat was slit, and several others were killed by knifepoint in the locker rooms. A breach took place and they were described to have been brutally dismembered by Völfien attacks. Funny how it all took place simultaneously, yet Baadar survived."

"So either Baadar escaped the völf, or—"

"The völf is his savior." Marius sadistically grinned.

Kiefer nodded, finished off his cigarette, and then flicked it over the bridge. "Okay, I'll keep my eye out. Let me process all of this."

"One more thing, Yuska. Keep your distance from Yegor. At least for now."

"You're asking me, an æsir, not to consult with *my* wülkure?"

"The less people know, the better. He doesn't know about Fallz'den being linked to the ork boy. He also doesn't know about Baadar or the völf. It's just a cult breach in his mind. Like I said, everything we know stays under the radar." Marius paused and absorbed the final bits of his cigarette. "And that's precisely why Yegor was not involved in our meeting."

"You think I'd dump this nonsense on Yegor?"

"Not a word, Yuska. You heard Henrik."

"I take it the empress doesn't know either, huh?"

"Can't answer that."

"Of course you can't."

Kiefer processed for a moment, considering Marius's proposal. As much as he wanted to disagree, he understood why he couldn't tell his team. He wouldn't put them at risk. The fact that the Näkk had resurged was a profound, life-altering threat. Its news would create mass hysteria. That knowledge could not get out or involve more people than necessary.

Fuck, this is a mess.

"I won't say a word. Until then, stay the fuck away from my team. Worry about your own district—got it?" Kiefer warned.

Marius laughed. "Try not to get eaten out there, Yuska."

CHAPTER EIGHT

THE HAND

Shaar
Tsunetomo
House Frost, the dining hall
Aoustí 10, the coronation of Lady Ameilja Frost

THERE WAS A GREAT CLAMORING OF VOICES AND
applause as the coronation began.

I stood behind a large red curtain with a confident Ameilja hanging on my arm. Her perfume lingered in my senses. Her eagerness radiated off her body. My chest rose and fell with each anxious breath. Surprisingly, no one had paid much attention to me, even as we waited in the line of other couples. Or they had and just kept my existence locked in their peripherals.

Time will tell.

The initial introductions included select high-ranked paladins, missionaries, and nobles from around the continent. Some names I recognized were colleagues of Ameilja's generation, all names of importance; however, the introduction itinerary was planned for Ameilja and her escort to be introduced last. We were the grand finale, the entire purpose of the event.

Soon Ameilja and I would stand before the primary leaders over Shaar: our centurion, Jakob Malkovich, our high abbot, András Frost, and most importantly, the empress of the Eastern Isles, Sinnika Wympriest.

No pressure at all.

Jakob Malkovich's voice boomed through our waiting space. He was not only our centurion, but also the high abbot of his temple, House Malkovich, on our neighboring isle, Rúnar.

The same House that held my near-death trial.

Jakob stood out amongst a crowd of leaders. He was well known for his stoic nature, advanced intellect, and penchant for politics, but he was also known for being the youngest abbot and centurion of the Isles, proudly holding two titles and deeply devout in the customs of being a follower of Uridei. Jakob consistently exhibited control, an imperious reminder of pride and power within the Commission. He always wore his armor of the modern-day paladin, layers of fabric and leather. While his wardrobe appeared formal, it was decorated with golden pauldrons adorned in gems of piercing green sapphire to match his House palette. He had blond hair and fierce green eyes, darker than Ameilja's. I'd noted that his age was the same as hers. Also, the way he looked at her.

Jakob eyed Ameilja with determination and desire.

Empress Sinnika, the ruler of the Eastern Isles, was the first woman to rule independently. She was known as an influential, eminent leader and had succeeded the throne from her valiant husband, Emperor Truvakken, who had been slain during the Great War. She often wore white dresses with a golden crown and armor of solid gold that radiantly complemented her tanned golden skin. Her black-as-night hair was always braided atop her head, centered elegantly within her crown. Although she was older, her beauty stood firm.

András was also lean and attractive for a man his age. He had a thick dark beard with a romantic handlebar-style mustache. He always looked jovial and usually was. Since his wife had passed away from bringing Ameilja into the world, he cared for his daughters as if they were the last two diamonds that ever existed. Tanja, Ameilja's older sister of four years, had married into the royal family a few years ago, to Sinnika's son, Atür, to keep their bloodlines strong.

The abrupt stop of the applause pulled me from my thoughts as Jakob began speaking again with astute charisma; his voice echoed through the great hall. "Today we come together to celebrate the birth of a special young woman. This woman is an influential example of being a devout follower of Uridei and a member of our great Commission. She was born to become one of the great symbols of the Light's unsurpassed watch over us, a rare gift to us all. Together we will celebrate our unity, strength, and the light of Uridei!"

Another round of roaring applause sounded.

I quickly looked down at Ameilja, hoping she'd reconsidered. Her eyes were still calm, her smile was confident, and her eloquence was intact.

This is happening. There's no going back.

Malkovich continued. "So I will ask this noble rarity to join us, and we will feast. We will dance. We will fellowship as one Commission, one great empire, under Uridei." There was a brief pause. "But first, may I welcome the daughter of the great empress of the Eastern Isles, and heir to the throne, Princess Maon Wympriest!"

Applause erupted throughout the dining hall again as she and her escort walked out, the curtain swiftly closing behind them.

Unlike the Frosts, who could trace their lineage back to Isarah across the Eastern Sea, Princess Maon was a native of Shaar. Despite her brother Atür's objections, she was Sinnika's firstborn and thus the rightful heir to the Eastern Isles's throne.

I'd met the princess informally a handful of times in the years I'd been Ameilja's protectorate. I was sure she'd also looked at me a handful of times but would still dismiss the fact that I was part of Ameilja's Court of Völfien. Despite the royal family's castle being located in De'licyymbol, a known area accustomed to Fae inhabitants, they were loyal to the Commission's regulations and viewed our race the same as the majority of the human populace did.

Jakob continued. "Finally, I ask the host of this event's celebration to rise and call his daughter to join us. The high abbot of Shaar's Religious Order, Father András Frost!"

More applause sounded, and András's resounding voice filled the space. "Thank you all for gathering here tonight to celebrate my beloved daughter, my rose. We have all been patiently anticipating this grand gathering, eagerly expecting the outcome of Ameilja's efforts. Ameilja Rose Frost, the recognized third seer of Shaar's Commission, has triumphantly mastered her Purge!"

Shouts of praise and applause echoed louder than before. The curtain began to move.

I shut my eyes. *Breathe.*

I inhaled a sharp breath before taking my first step. My first step with Ameilja.

I tensed as soon as the light blared from the curtainfall. The applause continued, even as my face was seen. I opened my eyes and forgot at that moment that my Völfien face was even a thing. I felt for a moment that all was well.

Even if it was just in my mind, I could imagine that Ameilja was mine. *I could die today, knowing I have this moment forever.*

Our three leaders sat side by side at their table, which resembled a throne. Their assessing glare locked on Ameilja. Then me. An aura of power and eminence radiated around their forms. The empress was centered between András and Jakob. Jakob sat to her left, while András sat to her right as the host of the coronation. Their bodyguards surrounded them; András was the only leader with Völfien protectorates.

I absorbed the great hall from that view; it was magnificently decorated in our Shaar'an designs. Two long tables extended the length of the two hundred guests there. András, Jakob, and the empress were seated at the head of the connecting tables to overlook the entire hall.

I waited for Ameilja's cue, but before we descended the grand steps, Ameilja raised a hand, and the applause instantly ceased. The entire hall fell silent. I had no idea what she was doing but watched her, instantly captivated. With a quick flick of her hand, all the candles lining the centers of the tables lit up in unison.

There was a brief silence, and then the applause roared back to life. András's face was beaming with pride. Some guests looked shocked, while some guests were brought to tears. Then there was Jakob, eyeing her with earnest intrigue.

The innate instinct to protect Ameilja crawled up my spine. My glare fixated on Jakob's hungry stare. His eyes bore into Ameilja, absorbing every piece of her.

If looks could kill, mine would have ripped him to shreds twice over, slicing his eyes from that thick, prideful skull. *Take your eyes off her.*

Maon's form appeared, and my glare snapped back; instantly settling.

Control yourself, Kovuco.

Maon stepped forward, behind her were two diens, one holding a red silk pillow with a crown sitting atop it. Its white and translucent jewels glistened against the gold plating that intricately swirled and intertwined into its curved shape. The princess turned and gracefully lifted the crown meant for Ameilja. Maon smiled and placed it on Ameilja's bowed head, her red hair enhanced the crown's radiance.

Maon leaned forward and kissed Ameilja's cheek. "Congrats, my friend," she whispered.

Ameilja stood tall, smiling brightly. I watched as her chest rose, inhaling that moment with accomplished pride.

She's radiant.

Maon shot an unreadable glance in my direction, then turned to face the audience. "As princess of the Eastern Isles, it is my deepest honor to announce Ameilja Rose Frost, high seer of the Eastern Isles!" She raised a henna-covered hand toward Ameilja, presenting her friend proudly to the entire hall.

The applause roared again as Maon returned to her escort.

Ameilja looked up at me and shared that smile I knew all too well, instantly redirecting my thoughts into her world.

There it is.

"Are you ready?" she whispered to me.

I nodded, and we descended the marble stairway to meet the awaiting couples below. The men wore their armor, all adorned in their family colors, layers of delicate fabric and leather, similar to the armor I was dressed in. The women all wore dresses designed similarly to Ameilja's.

Princess Maon stood next to us. Her sleeves were long, her dress was white, and a tunic hung from her right arm. Her black hair was long and held in a metal cuff, exposing the tan, shaved sides of her head. Her makeup was tribal and fierce, contrasting against her bright brown eyes and accentuating the intricate tattoos and henna on her body. It instilled the beauty of her culture. She was escorted by a massive bearded man; his scent was rich and earthly. Instead of a white or dark beard, his looked as if it had been dipped in rusty-red mud.

The woman who stood on the other side of Ameilja was also a close friend, more so than Princess Maon. Her name was Haruka Inari-Hu, and she was a member of House Malkovich and a ward to Jakob. Her father had been the prior high abbot of Rúnar but had succumbed to his injuries inflicted during the Great War, along with her family. Haruka was the sole survivor. Jakob had earned his title as the abbot, even at a young age, due to his position at the time of her father's death. House Malkovich's secrets now belonged to her.

Haruka's raven-black hair was short, cropped elegantly along her adornment of plush lapels, which she always sported in her fashion. Her eyes were always wide and bright; her gray-blue irises were gentle despite her cutting-edge attitude. Her cream-colored dress was cut in two places, showing off both legs. Large bracelets accented her necklace with emerald sapphires identical to those Jakob wore. She was escorted by Kärleiv, Malkovich's headman and one of his most trusted bodyguards. Due to his severely disfigured face, his true identity was unclear.

Kärleiv always wore a white porcelain mask and never disclosed his injuries. Ameilja once shared that many of House Malkovich's handmaidens referred to him as "the man in the mask" as a result of Haruka's keen hearing of idle gossip.

"Let us sit and enjoy a fine meal together!" Jakob announced, grabbing our attention.

All the couples, except for Ameilja and me, began their seating process. The men stepped forward in unison and pulled out the seats for their lady escorts. The women all stepped forward but did not take their seats until the men stood behind their chairs and waited for the toast to commence.

Ameilja whispered, "I'll squeeze your thumb, and you'll take me to my seat. When I sit, everyone sits. When ready, lift the glass placed closest to your seat, and raise it to Malkovich. The others will follow. When Malkovich drinks, we all drink. When he eats, we all eat. Okay?"

"Yes," I said through my teeth.

I wanted Kärleiv's mask; I wanted to hide my face. Maybe even oversized sleeves to cover my hand-like paws and clawed feet. *Get out of your head, Kovuco.*

Ameilja gently squeezed my thumb, and we were off. I shuddered as each clawed foot tapped the marble floor; my toes spread over the surface with each landing. I knew everyone was looking at me, watching me, wondering why a völf was escorting a noble lady. I felt their discomfort.

I pulled out Ameilja's chair and reached for her hand. I then tucked in her chair as she neatly rested on the cushion. Immediately following, all the women took their seats, and their male escorts pushed them in. I stood next to my chair and swiftly glanced across the tabletop of elegant dishware. A wineglass reinforced with stone-gray plating and beaded with red sapphires stared up at me with a liquid as dark as blood. It was wine. I had never tasted wine before; that night would be my first.

From what I'd read, wine was like our rice liquor but a tad more potent, with a berry-like finish, thus the color. This wine was probably worth more than a week's cost of my food. I prayed I wouldn't react to it unexpectedly or make a fool of myself.

I finally reached for the glass, carefully cradled it in my claws, and raised it to Malkovich, who was only yards from me.

I saw his confident smile and his sharp green eyes piercing the veil between us. He raised his glass in unison with every member of the room. Surely he knew about us völves. After all, my trial had been held in his House. He also had gifted Dancer to Ameilja years before, so he knew how we worked. Malkovich did not employ protectorates in his House. Fae were also not common inhabitants of his isle—a profound difference compared to Shaar.

Surely he knew I could feel him staring at me. Not at the crowd or at the food, but at me.

He was human but glowered with a carnivore's pride, yet he smiled, maintaining brilliant composure. Sure, he was a trained hunter with the disciplined nature and force of a paladin, but somehow, some disturbing insecurity in me told me he'd already found me out, and this was my warning. He seemed to disarm me and dissect me.

What is he dissecting? My blue eyes? My unique color? The fact that I'm at Lady Ameilja's side during her coronation, and he's not?

While I wanted to submit, I could not, not with Ameilja's hand resting over my thumb. She'd already taken the risk, and she wore it heavily on her shoulders, pridefully, so all I had to do was play my role and play it to her glory. I channeled her courage, swallowed hard, and joined his stare. He must've felt the intensity of my stare as it urged him to respond. He suddenly closed his eyes and began to pray the prayer of the Order aloud: "Oh, light of Uridei, merit us to your will. Grant us the hand to Purge, cleanse, sanctify, and purify. Give us the courage to stand in the way, and forgive us for our transgressions. Cast out the darkness; make way your fire."

Everyone then joined in unison with Malkovich: "Speak, Uridei; your servant is listening."

Then he drank, and we all drank. The wine poured down my throat. I needed the alcohol to shake the stare.

My senses kicked in. It was delicious, quintessential, and medium-bodied. Spicy, peppery notes of dark cherries, blood plums, and fresh raspberries sparked within my tastebuds. The red fruits added a sweet delight to the fine, velvety tannins, and a lingering secret was unlocked: a toasty chocolate finish lingered. It was the most elegant thing I could imagine tasting.

Malkovich sat as quickly as the wine was gone, and every man in the space took his seat next to his lady.

Attendants brought plates to every guest as quickly as he sat. Others refilled the glasses of wine and provided tumblers of water.

Each plate consisted of a glazed cod cut with lightly seasoned rice and fresh green vegetables. An edible flower sat between the cod and rice. The dish was Dancer-quality and Tsunetomo's finest, although he might have found the flower in bad taste. The dish looked pleasing and smelled exquisite. I was relieved that a cod steak was served, but I did wish for raw meat. Placed within reach were appetizers of squid, shark, and other shellfish with complementing sushi, garnishes, and sauces.

Do I deserve this?

"Try it, Kovuco. Eat as much as you like." Ameilja nudged me.

"I feel bad." I turned slightly to her.

"Why?"

"Because I'll be going back to the tower stuffed. What about—"

"Already got Ash on making their plates. Don't worry."

"Really? You won't be punished?"

"Kovuco, don't worry. Eat!"

I obeyed, digging into the dish. The cod's warm meat peeled off the bone and glistened like gold. The veggies melted at the slightest prick of my teeth. Every bite was like a new chapter I'd absorb and remember, like reading Uridei's scripture.

The entire dining hall broke into discussions as guests murmured among one another, enjoying their meal. I tried to pace myself, matching the speed of a select few guests, to ensure I didn't stand out even more than I already did. The hall had prominent Commission members from around the Eastern Empire. I was sure Ameilja's questioning would come later. I dared not stare into the crowd. *I shouldn't know which guests are staring at me.*

"So, Ameilja," said Haruka to my left, "who is your escort?"

"This is Kovuco, son of Adémaro Blackstar. You've seen him, yes?"

"Sure. Judging by that white throat, one of your protectorates, no doubt. You almost miss it with all that Blackstar-famous platinum."

Haruka looked at me with an intense side-eye stare and then turned to look at me; I tried to stare straight ahead at the floor between the guests, not making it obvious that I could see her. The awkward moment finally cracked when her lips formed into a gentle, curious smile. I smirked, trying to be polite.

"Don't think we don't see Red Fang hanging off his side," Maon added in after tapping her lips with a napkin. "I suppose for my birthday I should clad a minotaur?"

Ameilja set down her fork and looked at Maon, holding her composure. "If I survive till then, you both are welcome to my gesture."

"We aren't as bold as you, Ameilja. As nervous as your father must be about your feat, I guess it's appropriate, considering Frost's values and care toward the Völfien race."

Ameilja swallowed, keeping her shoulders relaxed from being caught off guard by her friend's accountable remarks. "Yes, Maon, I *do* care."

I felt her frustration. I sat there, unable to speak on my own behalf as they spoke openly about me as if I had no ears to hear.

The three of them fell silent.

I glanced at each of them. One by one.

I'd noticed that over recent years, the natural elegance of these women had begun to fade. I had been used to their vibrant confidence, but they seemed tired now, worn down from the redundancy of rules and such events. They were unfulfilled by a pretentious nature; it fueled their cynical appetite. I supposed I couldn't blame them. Maon, Haruka, and Ameilja had accomplished much in their young lives since entering the Commission. Yes, they were a princess, a paladin, and a seer, but their royal restrictions kept them from living up to their fullest potential. None of them deserved to live a mundane, deficient life.

Ameilja had read all Divinities of Light, every volume of alchemy, and even the darker books of witchcraft and demonic rituals. She was currently studying fictional tales and historic folklore from her childhood, recalling favorite passages from memory. Now she had pulled off an incredible feat with the Purge. Ameilja was not a creature to be caged; she was a wild, free spirit.

I wondered if Maon and Haruka shared Ameilja's same anxiety in their tasks. Maon appeared to be Ameilja's closest equal, compared to Haruka, although she was much more dedicated to the customs of Shaar. Every move Maon made was executed with precision, with a luster of perfection in everything she accomplished. People were either intimidated by the Princess or they were inspired by her. Thankfully, it never bothered Ameilja how much more attention Maon earned from fellow paladins or members of the Order. I wondered if Maon was so dedicated to her perfection that she harbored dark secrets, much like my infatuation for Ameilja.

Haruka, however, did not carry a royal connection but had upheld her inheritance pridefully, not backing down from her place, despite her family's unfortunate deaths. Some said she was spoiled, always delving into the secrets of House Malkovich, while some said she was rightfully privy to them.

Either way, both Maon and Haruka were fierce women of the Eastern Isles and good friends to Ameilja. I saw the way men looked at them: hungry to devour their intelligence and skill.

As we finished our meal, I paced myself, trying not to unveil noisy responses to each delectable bite. The attendants began collecting our plates, clearing the tables swiftly to keep them in a presentable state. We then stood up from our seats, and many paladins and guests began making their way to Ameilja, not only to wish her a happy birthday but also to congratulate her on mastering the Purge. I keenly watched every single person. I received some strange looks but was greeted with bows and addressed as Völfien Kovuco, a respectful response I didn't expect. Ameilja welcomed their praise humbly, navigating through the small talk effortlessly.

My focus was immediately diverted when I noticed a peculiar woman approaching us from across the dining hall. Her hips swayed sharply with her gait. She paused, turned, and raised her wineglass to András. I observed as András raised his glass in response, glaring sternly at her. She grinned slyly through her dark makeup.

The woman was pallid, and her as-dark-as-onyx-black hair was braided and secured in a large bun on top of her head. A spiky headpiece accentuated the radiance of her dark hair. She donned a form-fitting black dress with a bright orange, spider-like lapel. The low-cut dress exposed her back and nearly the entirety of her torso. The dress scarcely concealed her firm breasts, revealing her alluring form. Two younger women accompanied her, wearing similar dresses with ominous designs accentuating their sexuality in cruel, venomous detail. Their intense facial expressions emphasized their appearance. The three of them devoured your thoughts with just one look.

As the woman drew near, my senses picked up on something strangely familiar radiating off of her form. It bothered me that I couldn't place it.

She bowed low. "Good evening, girls," she said with a soft chuckle. "And happy birthday, sweet Ami." She purred.

Every motion and flare of her playful voice suggestively reached the ears of all around her. Her charisma was darkly apparent. She was unashamed, confident, and eerily beautiful in her movements. Even how she sipped the thick wine meant to stir desire. She made the air around us feel tight, and her perfume only added to the noir atmosphere she created, leading both young and elder Commission members to eye her lustfully.

"Well hello, Aunt Nathalii." Ameilja sighed.

How could I forget?

Nathalii was the great baroness of Isarah, a member of the royal family, and Ameilja's aunt; sister to her deceased mother, Johanna. While Johanna had an arranged marriage to András, Nathalii had an arranged marriage to the empress's brother, Chédomir. The marriages had combined the two great isles into Sinnika's empire and upheld their important bloodlines. Chédomir, like many, unfortunately, had been killed during the final days of the Great War. Nathalii had inherited all his fortune and influence, rightfully keeping her role; however, she had vastly distanced herself from family and solely focused on her involvement with her social elite posse—specifically the ones who made people feel like they could never be worthy enough to participate.

Haruka spoke up. "Nathalii, does the devil design your wardrobe? Surely someone who has been tortured thought of such a display for a celebration within the Order." She took a long sip of her wine while keeping her eyes locked on Nathalii.

Nathalii blew a kiss and then pursed her lips. "Thank you, love. So sweet," she sarcastically responded as her eyes narrowed into a gouging glare. The two younger women standing behind her remained silent.

As bold as Haruka came off, it brought an underlying joy to Nathalii. She liked the attention.

Nathalii's glare lifted and she turned back to Ameilja. "Ameilja, darling, you have certainly outdone yourself this evening, not only with the fantastic news that you've mastered your Purge but also by bringing this *fine* specimen with you. I couldn't help but watch your father's veins constrict when you came down those steps, smiling that *Ameiljaesque* smile."

Ameilja chuckled softly. "Thank you for noticing, but I'm afraid my father doesn't enjoy suffering, as you seem to acclaim so often."

"Shame, although you might be surprised what young András used to partake in. He still makes my mouth water at the slightest sight of chest hair. Oh, such a handsome man." She shifted, turning her gaze back to him, pressing her palms against her chest while making a shivering motion. "But I suppose you might be partaking in darker acts, as you came in with this völf here." She added, turning back to face us. She smiled mischievously and quickly reached for my chin. Her bony hand caressed my jaw; her fingernails felt like knives. I could feel the points tickle my flesh.

"His name is Kovuco," Ameilja said agitatedly.

Nathalii gasped as if in a performance. "Kovuco! Well, Kovuco, I hope to see more of you at such events. The Commission can be so boring, you know." She leaned in closer, and her seductive gaze locked with my eyes. Her dark red lips were just inches from mine as she whispered, "It's so formal and bland, you know. What a nice change of scenery to see you here."

My pupils dilated, assessing her. She continued to touch my face as if I were a puppet she could tauntingly manipulate. Something felt deeply wrong with her touch. I managed a fake grin out of respect, but it probably only worsened the situation, with my teeth peeking between massaged gums.

Ameilja tensed, gritting her teeth. "He's not a *pet*. Please stop."

"Well, I treat all pretty faces with such splendor—"

"Well, he's mine, not yours!" Ameilja's voice rose enough that the hall quieted briefly. "Do *not* touch him!"

Nathalii snapped her gaze toward Ameilja. She finally released me and leaned away. The guests respectfully resumed their conversations. "Sorry, love. I meant no disrespect. Hopefully, you and I can have that drink, Ami. You're always so—"

"Busy," Ameilja cut in, her words slicing the small talk. "Yes, very busy. Maybe in the next century, I won't be so preoccupied." Ameilja arched an eyebrow, evidently suggesting she was done with the conversation.

There looked to be some silent message between the two women. After a moment, Nathalii blew another kiss and walked off. "Enjoy that crown," she purred over her shoulder.

The tension instantly lifted as Nathalii and her two followers left. By then, guests were standing in circles, speaking quietly with their wine glasses in hand. The music heightened to encourage dancers to the main hall.

I wanted to ask about the exchange, but Ameilja quickly explained as I turned to her.

"Kovuco, I'm sure you know, but that's my aunt Nathalii. Let Nav'i, Dancer, and Tam know that if the opportunity arises, they should kill her on sight." She took a huge swig of her wine.

Maon laughed. "Don't eat her, though. The thought of what she might be carrying in her blood." She shuddered.

Haruka chuckled. "Venom and Wormwood."

A sly grin formed across Maon's lips.

It disturbed me somewhat that Ameilja would joke so openly about killing a relative, but I knew only superficial details about the baroness, and it was evident that Ameilja was not a fan. Perhaps that was the eerie feeling I felt.

I looked out at the crowd. As her mysterious aunt walked about, she addressed other guests with candor, lasciviously confident. Even if the opportunity presented itself, I would hesitate to harm her, just as a wolf would hesitate to attack a serpent.

The discomforting exchange became suppressed when Ameilja's focus was quickly swept up by other visitors. She was visited by Master Oboro, directly following, several other families also addressed us: prominent paladin Houses, approved dwarven carvers, and capitalists responsible for the Frost's incredible wealth, not to be confused with the insufferable elite crowd.

Ameilja's face grew tired, despite the smile on her lips. She sighed and withdrew. "Ladies, I think I'm going to have a dance."

"Go for it," said Haruka. "There are plenty of suitors here."

"Do any catch your attention?" Ameilja asked.

Haruka shrugged. "Hm. Still undecided."

"Same," Ameilja said. Suddenly, she flicked my shoulder. "Come on."

Surprised, I responded, "Huh? You and me?"

"Yes, you and me. Let's go!"

Haruka and Maon eyed her, silent.

Another nightmare was in progress. Ameilja seized my wrist, pulling me past the long table and onto the ballroom floor. Above us was a vaulted ceiling intricately painted like a clockwork design of Shaar's seasons surrounding a mural of Albean. The marble floor beneath us was laid out with the emblem of the Commission.

Ameilja took my paw in one hand and motioned for me to place the other at her side. I carefully clutched the fabric of her dress, careful not to snag the delicate fibers in my neatly filed claws. We began to dance, and I followed her lead cautiously, feeling the slow movements of her warm curves sway under my touch. Moments later, she beckoned me to twirl her around or try a new step to keep my mind focused on the task, not my apparent anxiety. At first, I thought she was performing a royal dance routine, but she was just having fun, keeping the mood light, as always.

I twirled her again, more confidently this time, and swept her back into my embrace. Our eyes locked.

"Kovuco?"

"Hm?"

"Thank you for doing this," she whispered to me.

"Of course," I said.

I wanted to say: *Of course, Ameilja. Anything for you. I am your shield. Speak anything, and this Völfien is yours. To watch you, Ameilja. To shield you. Kill on demand by the rising of your hand. Embrace your flames of Uridei in glorious battle should we be granted such an encore. I would follow you into any hell you needed me to.*

I wished to say her name as if repeating a wolf's song to the moon. *Could you howl such a name?* There was much weight in a name. A name was only a name until it resonated with meaning in the face behind it. My name was useless to her, nothing she should have had to regard. All she needed was my presence for the night.

My blood belonged to House Frost now, and no matter how hard I wished or prayed, my desires would forever be denied. The oath I vowed would make me stay, no matter where this beautiful woman was destined. I would always follow her, forever questioning why I was burdened with these emotions toward a human.

I stopped suddenly, and in synchrony, so did she. Her green eyes searched mine; her sweet smile beguiled my blind dedication. I pulled her closer to me, completely diminishing the leftover space between us. Her dainty body was flush against mine.

Say something, you idiot. Can you even manage that, Kovuco?

"Ameilja. I would do anything—"

A hand tapped my shoulder. "Pardon me, Master Völfien."

I turned, and a familiar face met mine: Kjartan Arnulf. His armor was that of a paladin but a darker shade of gold, and his fabric was deep violet. His pauldrons were of rams' heads.

"Sir Arnulf," I said, caught off guard, immediately loosening my grip on Ameilja. I bowed.

Arnulf returned the bow. "Kovuco, is it?"

I nodded. "Yes, sir."

"I was hoping I could ask your lady for a dance before my company departs."

I hesitated; however, the paladin had surrendered much of his authority in granting me a returned bow and the title of *master*. It would have been rude not to give him the respect to relinquish Ameilja for the pleasure of his dancing with her.

"If the lady would be so inclined," I said as I turned to her.

She rolled her eyes a bit, but there was a reuniting smile as she stepped between the space dividing us. "Just a quick one," she replied.

I stepped back and allowed Kjartan to take over. Her perfume lingered as I returned to the shadows between the dining hall and the ballroom. I secretly observed their dance. Out of respect, I tuned out my heightened hearing and refused to read their lips. I just watched.

I'd heard the two of them recently had a falling-out that divided the childhood friendship, but I knew that as children grew, especially humans, sexual tension always cut in. It appeared from the observed behavior that Kjartan was apologizing for something. He was playing it off in the same way I had observed. There was no such thing as being best friends with a female, not with humans. Eventually, one would want more, and the desire was either reciprocated or denied. Ameilja suddenly hugged Kjartan while continuing the dance. I caught her lips uttering, "Thank you."

Thank you? Thank you for what?

"Don't worry," said Haruka, emerging from the shadows.

"Lady Haruka—sorry. I didn't see you there."

She swiftly took my arm and guided me to the ballroom floor. We were approximately seven feet from where Ameilja and Kjartan danced. We started to sway, and Haruka caught her breath. "Is this a good distance?"

"Huh?" I asked. Haruka's bold move of taking a nonhuman onto the dance floor caught me off guard.

"Is this a good distance from your lady?" she repeated.

"Actually, yes. It's almost perfect. But I—"

Haruka laughed. "Relax, Kovuco. I know you more than you think. I see your hairs stand up every time Ameilja ventures too far from reach. You forget who my father was. I might study the Book of Light, but I am well aware of beastkind nature as well as any wülkure."

Great. Now she's analyzing me.

"Sorry. I guess I do get a bit overprotective."

"There is a strategy in that."

"Strategy?" I questioned.

"Sure. Consider your packmates. Nav'i appears good with distance but seems reactive to your impulses. Tam's been doing this too long, so his confidence is undeniable. Dancer is the hardest to grasp, but that's because he is more reserved compared to the rest of you. You're different. You're hard to read. It's best to keep you close."

"Why would Lady Ameilja want to keep me close?"

"Not sure yet? I spoke to Oboro earlier, and she told me about Ameilja's feat the other day. It seems you draw out a special strength in Ameilja."

I gazed over at Ameilja, who was still dancing with Kjartan. The two appeared to be having small talk, and there was some intermittent giggling between them. I was still unsure of his motives.

"So what is it, Kovuco?"

I didn't answer. An abrupt sound interrupted me, a sharp pitch halting my peaceful nature. The predator inside me was tapped.

"Kovuco?" she said. "Kovuco, are you—"

I placed a finger over Haruka's mouth and hushed her. My ears twitched, and the sound hit again. There were gaps of airflow that were trapped, different, as if locking into place. Metal rested; wood stretched and then snapped between thick twine.

No!

I drew Red Fang after quickly shoving Haruka aside, and I charged for Ameilja. I slid between her and Kjartan, scooped her up like an aimless child, and slid on the ball of my foot. My rump knocked Kjartan over. I made a complete circle. Then I saw it.

A bolt three feet in length spiraled toward us like a heat-seeking missile. Red Fang intercepted it, and the bolt propelled to my right. Nav'i caught it in the air, preventing it from hitting another guest.

Tam and Dancer formed a wall against the crowd, but round two had already sounded. It came from the opposite direction. Nav'i drew his tonfa sword and snapped it toward the second bolt. He cried out a roar as the suspense of missing it writhed in his chest.

All the guests gasped loudly in shock as their panic erupted.

Time seemed to stop, and I focused on my senses. The sounds. The smells. My eyes opened wide, and all was black. Bodies were made up of white chalk lines in my mind. They moved in solemn, static trips.

The bolts on the floor withered. Once a sharp pink color, now their lethality had been silenced. Four more bolts were fired almost at the exact same moment. We acted as if in a rehearsed performance, with Tam to the west and Nav'i to the east. Dancer was fixed on the south; the bolt from that direction reached us first. I quickly set Ameilja down and took off toward the north. I dived through the curtain, and my target turned to run, but I was upon him.

My nostrils had already seized the assassin and held him down in my keen world. A world I intended for him to die in.

I halted and bludgeoned him with a closed fist, and his helmet flew off his head violently. Dazed, he barely recovered before I produced a mighty kick, and he passed through the double doors of the North Wing. The wing stretched out toward a landing that overlooked the ocean. The coastal breeze smacked against my heated form.

The assassin rose, grasping his chest, and coughed blood onto the pavement. The kick had been enough to break a rib. He ran; he knew it was all he could do. It was all he had left. He ran to escape, but I was already between him and salvation.

I stood with my fingers outright like a web of knives dancing in the darkness. The assassin drew a blade, but before he could challenge me, I used Red Fang, slicing his hand away in a jet-like motion. He fell to his knees, squealing in pain—his blood showered against my face. I was soused in his red. My tongue lapped over my muzzle, which cracked into a smile of wrath. My eyes glazed over white, with no pupils to distinguish mercy of any kind, just predator and his prey.

You've made a grave mistake in attacking my lady!

He went for his second blade, but my jaw answered first, making its mark against his neck and then his torso. I clamped down, severing every tendon in his warm flesh.

Delicious.

With a pop, rip, and split, the blood, flesh, and gore pulsated against the walls of my mouth. I absorbed the flavor, and then I extracted it all away. A clavicle, bits of muscle, and tendons spilled onto the landing.

I lifted him and ripped him in two with all my rigor and strength. My predatory claws suspended him above the ground, waiting.

I dropped his lower half against the stone floor; it was splattered with his blood and offal, still steaming from its natural temperature. The ground turned into an abstract display sloshed in arterial spray bursting from open wounds. I let him continue to drain; he bayed and shrieked until no spirit was left.

The sharp, bitter scent of blood carried like steam into the bone-chilling coastal night air, along with the smell of urine, salty tears, and shit—the aroma of conquest.

The moon was my only witness.

I dropped him flat. As if he were nothing. He was nothing.

What terror he must have felt in that moment meant little to me when I suddenly saw a new specter—another man, a new body. He stood in the corner.

I stood tall, ready to leap, but his movements mirrored mine. I halted.

What the hell? What is this?

He mirrored me again.

I saw him—myself as a man.

No!

I was standing before a mirror. My Rinkin was covered in dark gore and blood; the eyes glistened with rage like a milky white shimmer.

I snapped my body away and fell to my knees, huffing loudly, but the image burned into my memory. After all this time, I had seen him.

No, no, no!

I remembered him, I was young, but he aged with me and continued my walk in life.

I looked down at the assassin and the severed halves of his body barely attached to an exposed spinal column. His remaining eye was frozen in fear.

Kovuco, you went too far...

My mental realm whirled.

Suddenly, I felt a strange pressure. I forced my eyes shut as the throbbing pain enveloped me.

What is happening?

It felt as if the atmosphere would implode at any moment. An intensified pounding thrummed against my skull. My ears began to ring.

The blood! The assassin's blood. It's been tainted—I've been poisoned!

The perfect trap for Ameilja's protectorate völves.

I stretched my paws out. "Poison! I—I've been poisoned!" I growled in pain.

I heard footsteps and then a man's voice: "Kovuco?"

I looked up through my blurred vision. It was Bernát, one of our on-site wülkure. He pointed a crossbow at me. "Kovuco, are you armed?"

It took me a minute, but I shook my head. "It's been poisoned! The blood!" I bellowed.

"Kovuco!" I heard her voice.

Ameilja!

"Stay back, Ameilja!" Bernát demanded. "He's ingested human meat! It's been poisoned!"

"Bernát, it's okay!"

"Take one more step, Ameilja, and I will have to kill him!"

"No!" She cried. "He won't hurt me!"

Does she not see? See the horror? See my platinum fur now a muddy dark red? Redder than her head of hair? The poison circulating through me, unleashing the demon inside?

"Bernát, please, no!" Ameilja wailed.

"Stay back!"

Haruka arrived and grabbed her shoulder as Ameilja began to sob. "It's okay, Ameilja," Haruka urged. "He could lash out at you! Bernát's right!"

I turned my gaze toward Ameilja; she was on her knees. Tears poured down her face. She said softly, "I'm sorry! I'm sorry, Kovuco! I am so sorry!"

I would kill anyone for you, Ameilja. No matter the sorrow it brought us. No matter the consequence. I should be proud. I have served my purpose, but the tears—oh, those sad tears.

Me too, Ameilja. I'm sorry too.

THE REFLECTION

Shaar
Tsunetomo
House Frost, North Wing landing
Aoustí 10

"DON'T TOUCH ME!" AMEILJA CRIED OUT AS SHE jerked herself free from Haruka's grip.

She made her way for Bernát. Haruka grabbed her arm again, coiling her fingers around her forearm. "Ameilja, stop!" She spoke in her Shaar'an tongue, hoping the intimacy of her mother tongue would garner some trust at that moment.

"Let me go!" Ameilja hissed, tensing her muscles beneath Haruka's steady hold. She refused to speak her tongue.

Kovuco gagged, pulling Ameilja's attention back to him. Two more wülkure ran past her to assist Bernát.

"Grab his arms; help him stand! He's not fighting back, but watch him!" Bernát sternly directed them.

Ameilja was well aware of the classic methods the wülkure used against a Völfien after it consumed an abundance of human meat, but these wülkure were on edge. There was an uneasiness cradling Bernát's tone.

"What's the poison?" One of the wülkure asked.

"Appears to be some sort of plant-based poison; possibly Datura." Bernát responded through thick, focused breaths.

"Shit. That's cruel." The wülkure huffed as he pulled a specific hydrostein from a satchel tucked within his jacket. "Who would've thought to poison a völf with the devil's trumpets?"

"Someone clever enough to know how." The other wülkure jeered, sounding heartless.

Bernát cut a glance at both wülkure. "Enough! Make sure the hydrostein takes full effect."

Both wülkure obeyed, stepping closer, preparing to subdue Kovuco if needed.

"Don't hurt him!" Ameilja cried out. "Kovuco is my völf! I am responsible for him!" She tried to step forward. "Please let me help him! I have to help him!"

Haruka tightened her grip. Witnessing Kovuco surrender to the poison was heart-wrenching; Ameilja knew Haruka was only trying to help, but her actions would mean facing Ameilja's immediate reprisal. "Forgive me, sister." Ameilja lifted her heel and stomped on Haruka's foot.

Haruka cried out in pain, dropping to her knee and releasing Ameilja's arm to embrace herself. Before she could attempt to recapture Ameilja, Haruka was forced to lift her arm in defense at the heel coming toward her torso. She blocked the blow and tried to grab Ameilja's ankle. Ameilja anticipated this and struck her against the brow with a chop of her hand, and Haruka fell to the ground, stunned.

Ameilja flipped around to face Bernát when Ash unexpectedly stood before her. "Ameilja," he said tenderly, but Ameilja had tired of being restrained.

Ameilja struck for his groin, thrusting her knee toward him, but he pivoted to the right and jabbed her beneath the ribs. He took the moment of vulnerability to seize her wrist and forced her back against his torso. She choked on the agony rising from the ache. Her rigid movements caused her crown to fall from her head and clamor to the stone tiles. The night air was penetrated by its sounds, accompanying Kovuco's wrenching moans.

Ash locked her in with his opposite arm, holding her in a gentler chokehold. He squeezed his bicep and forearm, closing her neck inward. He took a knee and bent his head against hers, pushing her head forward. She could not move without risking injury to her neck or wrist.

"I'm sorry to do this to you, kid, but you left me no choice," Ash said. "It's my duty to protect you too."

Ameilja surrendered. She watched as Kovuco choked on the hydrostein, a medicinal stone wülkure forced down the throats of völves in cases like these. It released a dense chemical compound that immediately caused the völves to heave their stomach contents.

"Take his suit! Get it off him!" Bernát ordered.

The wülkure stripped away Kovuco's red coat and tie. His shirt lay ripped open on his torso. The ancient belt and gauntlets he'd worn lay on the discarded fabric soaked in blood beside him. His body needed freedom from the pressure to breathe.

Kovuco's eyes rolled to the back of his head as he roared a horrid retch. His lips curled, baring his razor-sharp fangs, warning others of his feral intent. His tongue lapped slobber, bubbling blood remnants like a rabid beast.

Ameilja stared at him, wide-eyed, as tears continued to trickle down her flushed cheeks. Gooseflesh surfaced on her body. Seeing the terrible effects of the hydrostein transforming his peaceful expression into an afflicted monster overwhelmed her need to save him. A deluge of blood and offal spilled from his throat. It splashed against the stone floor like wet rags. He twisted in agony, with his white throat now soaked in earthy red.

An eye suddenly rolled from Kovuco's vomit and halted against Ameilja's knee. She looked down at it. The pupil stared up at her as the tip of a ring finger rolled after it. The thick, syrupy blood began to trickle toward them, slithering through the stone's cracks, eventually pooling around Ameilja's crown.

Ash tried to pivot away to shield Ameilja from the horror. She resisted, clenching her fists tightly, and then struggled with words. Ash loosened his grip enough to allow her to speak.

"Don't you dare turn me away!" she hissed.

"You shouldn't watch this, Ameilja!" Ash said, grimacing at the scene.

Ameilja inhaled deeply and forced herself to yell as loudly as she could from the back of her exhausted throat, "I did this to him! This is my punishment to bear!"

Haruka joined Ash's side and grabbed Ameilja's free hand. Ameilja received it, squeezing it tightly, as she watched her völf holler, retch, and repeat. Haruka's features twisted as she assessed the gory aftermath. It felt like an endless torment until Kovuco was fully drained. It was the worst thing Ameilja had ever had to see a völf endure, next to the dying of the vilkanás.

Kovuco collapsed to the ground like a dead weight. The wülkure tried everything to avoid the tremble to the floor, but the hydrostein was a harsh substance, and the body obeyed its rancorous command.

Bernát turned from Kovuco. His aging, bearded face was splashed with flecks of blood. Ameilja watched him as his eyes were filled with tears, scowling. She saw the torment in his eyes and knew he was as brokenhearted as she was. She knew because she'd grown up with Bernát being at her father's side. He was a hard man, strict, dutiful, and callous when necessary. His expression showed disdain for this duty. The glisten in his eyes told her all she needed to know. He too felt horrible that she had to witness this.

"I'm sorry, kid. This should never have transpired," Ash whispered to her.

A wülkure started checking Kovuco's vitals. "Should we prep him for questions?"

Bernát nodded his head. "Get him comfortable and stable. See if he gives you anything specific. I know some of these attackers and will report them to Frost. Not another word of this to anyone."

Ash released Ameilja, and Haruka cradled her in her arms. Ameilja was surprised Haruka was still present, even after being battered.

"Ash, is the hall cleared?" Bernát pressed.

He nodded. "Everyone is secured. The empress is safe. The armigers are securing the area." He paused before continuing. "We have made significant captures that will bring Frost great distress."

Kovuco let out a final quiet roar and coughed a final pint of blood and a blackened remainder of the hydrostein. It steamed like a hot coal, still bubbling its dissolvent coating.

Ash ran to his side and helped Kovuco to his knees. "You all right, Kovey?"

The hydrostein caused temporary blindness, along with fatigue.

Kovuco breathed hoarsely and answered with a weak nod. His eyes were closed. His Völfien strength was far away now from the significant trauma, but he could still respond to the familiar voice of someone he recognized.

"There you are. You're still in there, Kovey. Are you ready for a shower? Get cleaned up, eh?" Ash cautiously encouraged.

Kovuco nodded again, struggling to open his eyes. His nostrils were coated in crimson. Ameilja's sorrow increased as she believed her völf was oblivious to her presence.

Ash lifted Kovuco, who muttered hoarsely, "Ameilja? Is she—she okay?"

"She's safe, Kovey. No worries. You did your duty."

"Tell her—tell—I'm okay. T—tell not to worry," Kovuco forced the words out of his clenched chest.

"I'll tell her. Rest now," Ash said as he directed him to his feet.

Ameilja heard Ash continuing to talk to him as he guided him away, explaining his blindness, weakness, and poisoning, along with continued interruptions concerning Ameilja. A trail of blood followed. She closed her eyes, allowing a final tear to escape down her cheek, processing the tragic event. She received her crown, but at what cost? Something felt amiss.

Her eyes danced under her eyelids, searching for an answer—anything within reach. *My visions. Who attacked? Kovuco's demeanor …*

"Kovuco," she whispered.

She snapped open her eyes and looked over her left shoulder to see the large mirror that was decoratively hung beside the wing's entrance. It mirrored the white moon, which illuminated the horrible scene. Ameilja examined her flushed reflection, pondering the enigmatic piece of glass.

Kovuco?

Haruka stood up and tapped Ameilja's shoulder. "Are you ready?" she asked, offering her hand.

Ameilja swatted her away, picked up her bloodied crown, and rose to her feet. "I need to see my father, Haruka!"

"Ameilja, you need to—"

"No! I need to see my father. Now!"

⭐

Shaar
Tsunetomo
House Frost, András Frost's quarters
Aoustí 10

Despite Ameilja's demand to see her father, the security measures throughout the manor were too intense for her to get to the high abbot as quickly as she would have liked.

Her primary handmaiden stood by, along with the other armiger securing the area. Ameilja had not returned to her wing but instead grasped Red Fang and stood outside her father's quarters until she was finally granted his audience. She paced, talking to herself and replaying the entire scene with Kovuco in her mind. Finally, an armiger granted her access.

Ameilja entered his quarters on the top tier of the mansion. His fireplace was lit, and all guards had cleared, per his order. She waited for him among the walls of bookshelves filled with volumes upon volumes of text outlining the empire's vast history. His space smelled of him; his warm colognes had seeped within the walls and furniture of his chambers. She noticed his large desk was still cluttered with his studies and instruments, as it usually was, along with magnifiers and other crude analysis tools.

András finally entered the room; the light from the fireplace flickered against his sharp, romantic features. He wore his same pants and boots from the coronation but had removed his vest; he was still wearing the pieces of armor over his dark red shirt. The sword fastened to his belt never left him. He was a warrior and would always be dedicated to his vow as a paladin, remembering the pains they'd overcome.

Ameilja studied his distressed demeanor.

"Ameilja, my rose, are you all right?" He held out his calloused hands to her.

"I am fine, Father—what happened out there?"

András sighed. "We are still conducting our investigation. But luckily, my theory of the Völfien proved useful."

Ameilja dipped her head. "How?"

"You're alive, aren't you?"

"I was the target?" Ameilja took a step back.

"We believe so, yes."

Ameilja shook her head. "Who would have done this, Father?"

"I don't know. Have you seen your sister?"

"No," Ameilja answered, showing little emotion. "We did not speak tonight, but I am sure she and the royal family were all protected, even over you and Jakob Malkovich."

"Ameilja, you shouldn't speak so frankly about the royal family. They are our direct leadership, a standing—"

Ameilja held up a hand in protest. "I know, Father. Remember, Maon and I are friends, but please hear me! I loathe their laws and opinions of the Völfien, yet tonight all our assassinations were prevented by the Völfien. Did they not notice? And Kovuco was forced to take a hydrostein for his efforts. Even poisoned! He saved me, Father!"

"He wasn't forced, Ameilja. He had consumed poisoned blood. He would have ripped through any living thing in reach and died had he not taken the antidote. And of course, he saved you; that's what his training is for."

"I know, but—" Ameilja paused, taken aback by her father's blatancy. "I just hated seeing him so horrified. The wülkure wouldn't even give me a chance to comfort him. Poisoned or not, I just wanted to be there for him. It was like he'd seen a ghost after killing that man—something was different."

There was that mirror.

"I think I have noticed something, Father," she added. "Something I know Kovuco won't tell me."

András tensed his shoulders. "What is it, Ameilja?"

Before she answered him, she thought back to the moment in her closet—the mirror. She remembered a similar situation a month ago. She had been standing in front of a mirror with Haruka and Maon as she adjusted her mother's necklace. Kovuco had turned his face and closed his eyes before the mirror while she caressed the sacred piece of jewelry. She remembered asking him why he had turned away, but he never had answered. Ameilja recalled many other moments when he had been faced with mirrors, still water, or anything reflective; he would always look away, never giving an answer.

"Father?" Ameilja's bewildered stare met his. "Has Kovuco ever taken his Rinkin form?"

András sighed loudly and turned toward his desk, hesitant to say a word. The silence of the room felt suffocating; the only sounds were of the crackling fire warming the space. Ameilja waited patiently while he reached into a cabinet and pulled out a book in which he kept all his Völfien records. He pulled out a large leather folder from the book and placed it on his desk, motioning for her to join him.

Ameilja walked over as he untied the straps and handed her four folders, still silent. She read the top folder's cover:

Name: Nav'i Oakhardt
Gender: Male
Species: Völfien
Birth: Avithen 14
Blood Type: B

Ameilja opened the folder, and all his records were tucked inside. The most prominent were his photos. A photo like a mugshot was plastered on the top. Clipped behind it was a photo of his Rinkin face. He had thick black hair brushed back behind his ears, which were still curved like a völf's. He had a few piercings on his right ear and fur-like sideburns along the sides of his face. His incisors were still pointed. She could see it was him by his green eyes and his stern fighter's grimace. Nav'i's Rinkin looked like a blend of human and völf but was still an impressive transformation for his age.

Ameilja looked at her father, wondering if he was following her investigation.

"Check Tam's next." He nodded, motioning for her to turn to the following folder.

Ameilja closed Nav'i's record and turned to Tam's folder:

Name: Tambor Blackstar
Gender: Male
Species: Völfien
Birth: Aoustí 18
Blood Type: O

She inspected his folder, seeing a confirmed Rinkin picture of Tam. His dark hair barely hid the birthmark around his eye and that teasing smile. Other records included his family and extensive reviews of Tam's educational background, and questionable interest in joining the Commission as a protectorate of Shaar. Tam was less identifiable as a human in his Rinkin form, but those in his hometown were predominantly proud of their Völfien identity. They didn't regard the Rinkin concentration. His photo was proof enough.

Next, she turned to Dancer's file:

Name: Danflor Reguba
Gender: Male
Species: Völfien
Birth: Elftyr 25
Blood Type: B

His Rinkin photo was present. His brown eyes stood out, matching his dark hair and extra tufts of leftover fur. His Rinkin form was partially mastered like Nav'i's, but she could still point out his quirks and the calamity he carried. His file included a substantial amount of criminal records from his past, from when he had been trafficked. He'd been pardoned upon his recovery from Malkovich's sentry.

Getting frustrated, she finally turned to the file her father had placed on the bottom, Kovuco's file:

Name: Kovuco Blackstar
Gender: Male
Species: Völfien
Birth: Avithen 4
Blood Type: O

Ameilja opened the file, and she saw Kovuco. There was no question the photo was him, with his platinum fur on full display, but there was no picture of his Rinkin form.

Ameilja glanced up at her father, and he drew in another breath. Ameilja laid the other three files aside, set Kovuco's file down, and began rummaging through the papers. She inspected all his records, including family ties as a Blackstar and his trial, but there were no photos of his Rinkin form.

"Where is it?" she huffed. "There is a Rinkin face to each of my protectorates."

She reinspected the folders and began rifling through some others, profile after profile, a face of a near-human to every Völfien. Every last one in service to the Commission of House Frost had a face, except Kovuco.

He has no Rinkin photo?

Ameilja's gaze skipped, quickly studying the files now spread out across her father's large desk. She tried to make sense of this discovery.

The Rinkin form was sacred, constantly changing as völves mastered the transformation. It was known as the practice of becoming one with their human brothers and was part of their identity, the gift of human sentience and understanding from the holy Aureate Albean.

It all had started because of a female wolf named Fenris. Albean had chosen Fenris and blessed her womb beyond the ability of the wolf species. She had birthed the first Völfien.

Why would Kovuco not even try? Is he not proud?

"Father? What is this?" Ameilja finally asked, knowing now that she had found the proof.

"Kovuco refuses to take Rinkin form, Ameilja," he answered bluntly. "As you know, my rose, Völfien are born in their Medzio form and stay a Medzio until they learn how to shift. Kovuco was born in a strict Völfien society, so he never needed to change. When he faced his trial into adulthood, he saw his reflection, and *something* occurred— *something* that seemed to traumatize him."

"What happened?" Ameilja asked, bringing a hand to her chest. Her body tensed as she processed the fact that her father had known this about Kovuco and had said nothing to her.

"I'm afraid I don't have an answer for you. At the time, I was closer to his father, but even he could not account for what Kovuco saw. All we know is that he has never tried to shift into his Rinkin form or beyond the Kovuco we've known since you chose him. The only one who knows Kovuco's Rinkin—as a man—is Kovuco, and only through his reflection."

Ameilja gazed down at Kovuco's picture once more. *I can't compre-hend this information. Why would Kovuco resent his Rinkin form?*

"Ameilja," her father said, "I am showing you this so you will un-derstand my heart for Kovuco. I do love and appreciate our Völfien. It brings me great comfort that you chose him as your final protectorate. Many years ago, I fought with Kovuco's father during the end of the Great War; he saved my life numerous times, and I gained this." He pulled back his shirt to reveal a scar on his neck and shoulder. "A pain-ful reminder for saving his life in return, and I would do it again, given a second chance. But this world is not Uridei's anymore. It's no longer the world I raised you in, my rose; it's a mad place that fears its brother, conspires with the shadows, and strikes its tail when cornered." He tucked away the scar, looking dismayed.

He turned to where Shirou and Lain stood watching their mas-ter. He sighed. "The Völfien are my brothers and sisters. And I will encourage their equality till the day I die, but it's never that simple, my daughter. I desire nothing more than to make you happy, but some laws and boundaries still cannot be crossed. I must honor our laws with utmost loyalty. As high abbot, my leadership is held to a much higher standard. You as well, Ameilja. You must tread lightly. Your choice to have Kovuco escort you tonight was—"

A knock abruptly sounded at the door. András sighed loudly but squeezed his daughter's hand, imploring her patience. "Yes?" He spoke aloud, impatiently.

The door opened, and Bernát, Ash, and a third wülkure entered the chamber.

"Can this wait?" András eyed them.

Bernát shook his head. "My lord, it's about your other daughter."

"Tanja! Is she hurt?"

"No. She has fled."

"Fled?"

"We captured a bodyguard we have linked to her and Atür's staff. We believe they may have led the attack."

András's gaze grew ominous. "Bernát, are you telling me that my eldest daughter and the empress's son were behind this plot to assassi-nate Ameilja?"

Ameilja's jaw tightened. Her gaze locked with Bernát's concerned stare.

"We wish not to draw this conclusion, but we believe a full investigation will be required first and foremost. The empress is on her way to speak with you."

András nodded and looked to Ameilja with distressed concern. Ameilja shielded her impatient gaze, hoping it revealed that she didn't want to care. Tanja had always harbored a hatred for Ameilja and disrespected their father vehemently, yet he loved her the same way he loved Ameilja.

"Thank you, gentlemen. We can conclude these findings soon. If my daughter and her husband have gone rogue, we must fully heighten security. Every hall should be covered—a völf for every five armigers and two wülkure to ensure quality. Do I make myself clear?"

The three wülkure crossed their chests and said, "Light of Uridei, Father."

András crossed his chest. "Light of Uridei, brothers. Ash, wait outside, will you? I want you and Jayna to escort Ameilja back to her chamber."

Ash nodded and stepped out. Ameilja remained fixed on her father.

He met her with a solemn look and then reached out a hand to caress her flushed face. "My beautiful daughter, I see your mother's disappointment when you look at me like that. With the law set aside, I promise I will push to lighten the weapons of the wülkure and grasp on our Völfien. I will do my best. There is much to discuss."

"*And* my protectorates? Will they ever be our equals?"

He sighed. "I cannot promise that, Ameilja. The Völfien may always be treated this way. But that doesn't mean you can't be the voice of reason when I am gone. Especially if you are all I have left."

Ameilja laid a hand over his and kissed his signet ring. "Don't worry about Tanja, Father. Until we know the truth, we will take precautions."

"Indeed. I am sorry, my daughter."

She nodded. "Me too."

He kissed her forehead and whispered, "I love you, my rose."

"Love you too. Light of Uridei, Father."

Ameilja turned and left him in his study. She could feel his eyes on her back every step of the way. She entered the hall where Ash and Jayna were waiting. They immediately followed after her hurried stride.

"Close my wing of the mansion!" Ameilja ordered as Ash and Jayna caught up to her.

"Yes, at once." Ash and Jayna simultaneously responded.

Throughout the mansion, armigers were already setting up posts. Every member beat his chest and lent a bow to Ameilja as she passed. She acknowledged everyone, even as she fumed forward, highly agitated.

"Am I at least privileged to my Völfien protection?" she huffed over her shoulder.

"Kovuco is recovering. We'll be escorting him to the dorm for the night. Considering the attack, we should allow the elder völves to guard the estate, your wing included. For all we know, the numerous bolts were for your völves, not you."

Ameilja rolled her eyes. The idea made no sense to her, but she knew Kovuco could not serve that night, and if one of them came, they'd all come—her loyal Court of Völfien.

"Fine," she snipped.

Thoughts sped through Ameilja's head. With each hasty step, her mind was pummeled by another critical notion. They had been attacked, possibly by her sister. Her völf almost had died from poisoning. Her father wasn't pressing for change within the Commission. To top it off, she couldn't get over the missing photographs in Kovuco's file or rid her mind of the vomited gore and his drained body hitting the stone floor. Her father's loving words rang in her head, but they didn't clear the hedge of things that could not be changed.

Her thoughts were abruptly interrupted as a large group of imperial guards followed after Empress Sinnika. Maon accompanied her by her side.

Ameilja stopped along with Ash and Jayna, and each bowed to the empress. Expecting her to pass, Ameilja was surprised when Sinnika halted the guards: "Wait."

She turned to Ameilja. "Rise, Ameilja Frost," she said melodically.

Ameilja rose and looked into Sinnika's commanding eyes. "My empress?"

Empress Sinnika cleared her throat. "I am happy to see you are well."

"Yes. I owe my thanks to my protectorates."

She nodded. "As do I."

Ameilja nearly fainted at the confession. She'd made the statement while expecting it to come off as passive-aggressive, yet the empress met her appreciation.

"I am on my way to see your father. It wasn't until your father's Völfien responded that I believed I was out of harm's way. Six of my guards have been killed. The assassin was devoured by your escort tonight."

"Yes. Kovuco. The assassin's blood, unfortunately, poisoned him."

"Will he be all right?" The empress inquired genuinely.

Ameilja nodded. "Yes. He needs time to recover."

"Excellent. He is to be commended. He has taken out a very deadly enemy of the Commission."

"My empress, who?"

"Lazar Blóðsorg."

Ameilja's eyes widened. She was familiar with the name. He had been a renowned assailant of paladins, specializing in arranged assassinations. Someone had hired him to take them out. The fact that he was now dead, not just because of House Frost's security but because of her Völfien Kovuco, made her feel comforted.

"My empress, I hope you recognize Kovuco and all our Völfien as our brothers. They are not just our servants but our trusted brethren!"

Sinnika nodded. "I will discuss this matter further with your father. There are more important concerns for us to attend to currently."

"My empress, please, I—"

Sinnika held up a hand, and Ameilja fell silent. Ameilja knew this movement all too well. Sinnika began her usual formal deterrents and promises to speak on the matter later, merely words avoiding the true answer meant to shut down anyone with a heart to feel or a mind to think.

The empress's words grew silent in Ameilja's mind, droning into deadened whispers—the same ramblings she was used to hearing. Her thoughts wandered back to Kovuco's face dipping from his reflection and turning blindly to the image of himself as a human man.

Suddenly, she wondered if Kovuco's reflection reminded him of why she had lost so much hope in the Commission and even partially in her own race.

The Commission had been set to be the golden standard of humanity, but now she couldn't even recognize it from its glorious past.

Is Kovuco mindful of the truth I desperately fight to disband? Has he merely clung to this truth—is he right? Is humanity even worth facing?

Is a human reflection too abhorrent to bear?

CHAPTER TEN

TRANSGRESSIONS

Shaar
Tsunetomo
House Frost, North Wing, the wülkure's barracks
Aousti 10

I WAS NAKED, DRIPPING, AND FEELING DEEP RE-morse. The pale green tiles were tinged with brackish residue where they had been splashed with blood, sweat, and tears—the smells of anguish.

What a day, Kovuco.

How long you have avoided that damned mirror, the reflection you detest, and when you finally met that distant foe, you remained covered in gore.

Did you even know that Rinkin face? It's always covered in blood anytime you seem to fall upon it. Do you hate his face because he is human? Or because you know the völf inside?

Images of the assassin's body ripping in two flashed through my mind. The way his flesh had melded into my incisors and stretched away from the bone. Easy. Effortless.

Do you truly despise the human race? Or do you hate the way you've been judged harshly because of your father's sins? Do you hate them because they look down on the Völfien, labeling your kind as monstrous? Are we truly monstrous, or is it their way of projecting their own faults onto an innocent race?

Maybe you hate the fact that you continue to bow to mankind and loyally protect the ones who shackle and limit you. Even more, do you hate that your race possesses a unique gift linking you to the reflection you refuse to face?

Forgive me, Albean …

I inhaled deeply, expanding my lungs to their fullest capacity, before submerging my head under the hot water again.

What the hell do you want, Kovuco? You want nothing to do with your Rinkin, yet you diminish your Medzio characteristics daily.

No matter how hard I try, I can't seem to resign my stubbornness. I can't let it go. From this platinum coat, the chase of blue beneath a sheet of shattering ice in these eyes of mine, to my dismissive social behaviors. Maybe I am the problem.

Maybe it's the guilt I feel in pursuing a forbidden affair. Are my actions, my desires for a human, so detestable that perhaps I am a demon?

Why would I ever have hope that someone like Ameilja could love someone as broken and cursed as I?

I thought back to my trial in Rúnar. I knew that if Uridei willed it, I would win, and I did. I had to fight to prove my life was worth living.

During my trial, should I have died in combat? Should I even be in this world?

Is that too dark to ponder?

I remembered a paladin during the trial saying a prayer: "Uridei, Kovuco Blackstar was born outside the sanctity of marriage and bears a resemblance unnatural to his kind. By the authority of the Order, we ask today that should we find a demon, you will bless our weapons that we may purge this völf from this world. Should you find favor in his salvation, may he strike us down and rise victorious."

I memorized every word of his prayer. I didn't care about him, just like I didn't care about the assassin I had slain tonight. I'd never questioned who they were before I slaughtered them with my claws. I'd tasted their blood, earned it, and proven my worth with it, but all it did was keep my steps moving forward.

Did Uridei allow my salvation so I may be a test to his people? Is my purpose to be evil? To love? Or to kill?

The steaming water washed away every trace of the man I had taken from the world. I finally released my mind from my self-destructive thoughts. I needed a break from my psyche.

Two women from our tower arrived to clean me. They trusted me enough to remove the shackles that bound my wrists and feet. They lived a level above our dorm and were happy to help in my recovery. They'd aided Nav'i during his past two incidents.

As they soaped my body from head to toe, all I could smell were the fragrant hints to mask the evidence of the death. The relaxing, spiced scents quickly diluted the taunting smells beneath the hot water, disappearing into the drain I hovered over. I thanked them for their assistance.

After dabbing my fur dry, I rose, and two elder völves helped escort me to the tower. There Nav'i, Tam, and Dancer greeted me gingerly and guided me to my bunk, giving me peace to rest while dinner was prepared. The smell of Dancer's bone broth made my mouth water. I could hear him faintly talking with Nav'i about the nutritious vegetables he added and, in mine, a splash of blood to lull me back to the graces of civility. *A good little völf. Locked and loaded for the next threat.*

After such an event, the pack were expected to clothe in nothing made of natural leather or animal hide, especially since the hydrostein drove out so much blood. While we had to rebalance the blood intake into our systems, this helped völves tap into the civil state naturally against the primal nature each völf had. It was far more comforting than just being forced back into the state humans preferred us in.

After eating the contents of my soup and slurping down the broth, I insisted that my roommates return to normalcy. Tam objected, sharing that they all would be staying with me for the night; we were ordered to stay in our tower while Ameilja carried out responsibilities with the royal family.

Ash updated my packmates on the heightened security; in the upcoming week, he would be escorting Tam to Ameilja's wing to cover the night shift, while Nav'i and Dancer would guard her during the day. I stayed in bed, quiet, listening to their concerned banter until my exhausted body forced me into a deep slumber.

I just … need sleep …

I slept almost the entire weekend away. There were no dreams, only deep sleep—a mental emptiness.

Each time my packmates returned from a shift, they would fall into their bunk and drift to sleep, knowing there wouldn't be a day off ahead. Not once did they disturb me.

Due to my hydrostein, I was ordered to stay in the dorm until a week had passed.

I did my best to stay in my bunk but couldn't seem to relax. After two days the anxieties bit at my nerves. The day to celebrate the birth of my favorite human had tragically ended on a sour note, and I was doomed to quarantine by myself. Worse, I was forbidden to reunite with Ameilja during that time. I remembered her tears. Her repetitious apologies for something beyond her control repeated in my ears like a tormented clamor.

Despite the chemical taste the hydrostein left in my mouth, I was hungry now. My body felt hollow and completely famished. Fourteen pounds of meat and blood were regurgitated from my system—even the delicious cod and wine from that night, not to mention my breakfast and lunch. I needed a full stomach for my cooperation, and the leftover bone broth wasn't cutting it.

I got up and decided to prepare a large bowl of rice noodles. I seasoned the dish with vegetables and topped it with my usual egg.

Thank Uridei for eggs.

My thoughts bounced around again. *We still have half a dozen eggs to get us through the next few days. I can deny breakfast for myself. I can't punish my comrades for my late-night meal.*

I steadily ate the food, thinking about the next few days within these stone walls. The thoughts helped me to focus on something else— something other than Ameilja's tears, not to mention the reflection I had locked eyes with.

My thoughts eventually failed me.

They wandered to the fine details of my Rinkin.

His face—my face.

He was older now, but my youth was still preserved, mild-mannered, and somewhat docile, despite the enraged look at that moment. My hair was shorter and flaxen, with a slight shag. My eyes were intense, and still blue, even more so against a pale human face with contrasting dark brows. My jaw structure was strongly defined yet gently distinguished, matching my reclusive characteristics.

Interesting.

I was told there had been a total of six assailants. I'd killed the lead assassin. Armigers had killed four archers after my packmates slowed them down. Wülkure guarding the floor had secured one archer and also captured one more associated with the attack. Suspect number six had given a clue about the conspiracy. A woman from De'licyymbol. She was identified as a maiden of Tanja. Tanja and her husband, Atür, had vanished with the eruption of chaos; their questioning was still pending. The wülkure were presuming the worst. That was probably why the empress had kept busy with András and Ameilja. I also presumed it didn't help that her royal son was a suspect, a fact she would ruthlessly conceal from the public's ears.

This news didn't surprise me. Tanja had always cast hatred toward Ameilja; she envied everything she did. I was positive Ameilja's rare seer gift and Purge mastery added to the rivalry.

Tanja was beautiful all on her own, with high cheekbones, full lips, tall stature, and wavy blonde hair. She was cunning, ruthless, volatile, and emotionally driven rather than logical. She obsessed over retribution, and as a völf, I could feel her unrest and thirst for turmoil. Atür's energy mirrored hers. That unrest regarding Ameilja had lingered too long.

What was their motive?

Behind me, Nav'i stirred.

Rather than try to deceive me, he kicked back his shade and smelled the air.

I heard his stomach grumble as strands of noodles hung from my lips. I slurped them to the back of my throat and swallowed. "You want some?" I asked.

He crawled out from his bunk and sat cross-legged before the plate of noodles. "Don't cut the egg," he said quickly, knowing I would cut it in two to share. "You need it."

I gave him a chopstick, and with a claw, he wrapped noodles around the stick and then slurped the soy-fried noodles into his muzzle. He didn't typically say anything when he knew something was wrong, but that night was different. Nav'i sensed it.

"It's always us, isn't it?" He let out a guttural sigh.

I peered up at him. "Huh? You mean the, uh—" I gestured toward my throat, and he nodded. I returned the nod and slurped another claw of noodles. "I suppose."

"Dancer has a way of sniffing out the poison. He is so used to being drugged up he can tell. Tam has less opportunity because he usually inflicts less damage."

"I don't think Tam has ever consumed human."

"Wouldn't put it past him. But you and I—that's where it gets complicated."

"Complicated?"

Nav'i nodded. "You ever wonder why I have been poisoned twice, and you come into hydrostein number three?"

I thought for a second and then spun my chopstick with my claw, hoping I could come up with something clever as Nav'i stared intently. "No?"

"I compete. Compete with you, Kovuco."

"You compete with me?" I arched a brow.

He nodded. "Yes. Don't ask. It's just how it has been between us."

Nav'i and I had fought for most of our youth. We were both somewhat introverted and shy around crowds, except Nav'i was livelier and more gifted, with an analytical and deducting mind. I, as some put it, lacked simplicity. During our training years, when others spoke, I listened but constantly processed mistakes or noted questions to run by them once they were done instructing. It was as if every encounter were a constant test. I needed more depth to piece together my own understanding. Nav'i always saw me as a competitor, yet I measured down to avoid the conflict.

"I can't say I reciprocate, Nav'i."

"I recognize my foolishness in competing with you," he said. "Hell, it was only my second time dealing with hydrostein, and all I kept thinking about was you—and how *you* made me do it. By being the one Völfien in Ameilja's court who handled the drug the most, I would prove I was stronger than you—better than you. It's immature, I know. I see that now. I want to call it an old grudge between us. Let's put it in the past."

I nodded. I didn't argue. "Okay, Nav'i. Not another word of it." I sighed and took a few rushed bites of noodles.

He shook his head slowly. "You need to be more careful, Kovuco. Even with Master Oboro, you seem tense and ready to avenge Ameilja, even during just practice."

I laughed nervously. "Nav'i, it was just my sinuses. I wasn't snarling, as the master insisted."

"Then why didn't you correct her? Rather, you risked being annihilated in Purge flames."

"I mean, yes, what was I supposed to do? Correct Master Oboro?"

"Yes!" he huffed. "But since you didn't, you're a liar—you were snarling! You snarl weekly. Don't take me for a fool!"

I thought for a moment. I had been so blinded by ravenous energy that I remembered hardly anything at all. I remembered kicking the assassin through the double doors. Of course, I remembered the rest from there, but I hadn't considered why I had been left to my own devices for so long; otherwise, I might have spared the man. I'd moved like a swift wind; my passion for defending Ameilja had caused me to cast Haruka to the floor and even Kjartan. It had ended with me viciously killing the assassin. Had he needed to die such a brutal death?

Nav'i glared at me. His features shifted in the shadows cast from the circular window. "I recall a conversation about liking Ameilja."

I swallowed. "Look, I was conversing with Tam about the broader subject of love. We have familial relations, and as you know I drew back from my family. The concept of love just confused me. That's it—okay?"

"Not very convincing, Kovuco."

"I'm not sure what else you expect me to say."

"You're gonna tell me you didn't enjoy yourself that evening?"

"I mean, I got to eat cod and drink wine. I got to dance with Ameilja while you and the others kept watch. Yeah, I enjoyed myself."

Nav'i scooted the bowl, which now held only broth, toward me. "Finish it."

I lifted the bowl, and gulped the broth until the bowl was empty. I belched nervously, concealing it as best as I could, trying not to hurl my anxieties. "I'm not sure what answer you're expecting me to give, Nav—"

"You can start by telling me the truth!"

"I'm not saying you're wrong, but—"

"Who said I was wrong? I want the truth, Kovuco."

"I don't know," I snapped. "All I can say is that my purpose has made me second-guess my feelings. I come from a very rough beginning, you know this! I should've had a great beginning. Son of Adémaro. Son of a legend, but I was labeled an abomination. A bastard. A demon. My existence is the symbolic end of Adémaro of the Commission. I guess love is confusing—that's it." I paused, angered desperation rose out of my throat. "How do *you* feel about love, Nav'i? Give me your insight since you seem to grasp it all."

Nav'i responded to my hasty sarcasm. "Just because I have no brood doesn't mean I don't understand what it means to feel love for a fellow völf or even Lady Ameilja." He sighed and then scoffed, "but romantic love—that's the type of love that makes you do crazy things. Things that will even put *you* in danger." He paused and looked as if he wanted to say more, but he swallowed the words. He turned his gaze and tightly closed his eyes.

"Nav'i?" I urged.

He stood up. "You should get some sleep."

"Nav'i?"

He crawled into his bunk and pulled the shade.

What the hell?

I hated that I frustrated him, but I couldn't answer his question.

I did love Ameilja, but admitting that aloud would bring out the dangerous truth. Nav'i would kill me, if not, the Order would get to me first.

Shit.

Loving Ameilja is wrong. I needed to forget all of that. I needed to get my head on straight, focus, and regain my strength. I am a völf—a protectorate who took an oath.

I need to forget.

Forget that the ghost of a hidden truth haunts me.

CHAPTER ELEVEN
SUFFOCATION

Shaar
Tsunetomo
House Frost, West Wing
Aoustí 12

"WHERE IS ASH?" AMEILJA IMPATIENTLY HUFFED as she waited with Tam by the gate outside her wing.

She was exhausted from pacing all night; her worries had kept her from sleep. Armigers and a couple of other Völfien lining her wing were the only defense standing between them and any specters. Tam was relieved he could finally end his shift to go to sleep.

"You sure you have everything?" Ameilja asked for the fifth time.

Tam nodded. "Yes. All the food, the two books, and your letter. Yes, Ameilja, all those things. All you're missing is something to chew on."

Ameilja rolled her eyes. "Then tie up some socks, you idiot! Don't be crude!"

Your socks might be preferred … or any piece of clothing for that matter, he thought. "I am sure he's fine, Ameilja. Kovuco's been with Nav'i and Dancer. They are way more equipped for this kind of thing. Remember, Nav'i has been through this twice already this year."

"I know. Even then, I was a mess. But there's more to it this time, Tam."

More? he thought. "Like what?" he asked aloud.

"Just that—it's nothing I wish to speak on right now."

Tam thought back to the conversation with Kovuco before the coronation. He remembered it vividly. His thoughts wandered.

Ameilja caught the disturbing glint on his face and glared at him ominously. "What? What's with the face?"

"Nothing. I mean, yeah, just nothing," he reluctantly replied, trying to shrug the whole thing off.

"Tam?" she sternly urged.

"What do you mean by there is more to it now?"

Ameilja hesitated. "I have found some things out about Kovuco. I am just not sure it's appropriate to say."

"Appropriate?"

"Yes. It's not proper to discuss someone's secrets."

"Sure, I get it. Don't kiss and tell—whoa! I mean—"

Ameilja shot daggers at him. "What the hell is going on with you, Tambor?"

"That came out wrong!" He shook his head awkwardly.

Ash finally appeared at the gate. Nav'i and Dancer followed.

"Thank Uridei ..." Tam grumbled.

Ash smirked, displaying his cocky grin. "Whatever is the matter here?"

"Nothing!" snapped Ameilja. She crossed her arms and turned her gaze from the anxious völf.

Ash unlocked the gate and let Nav'i and Dancer join them on the other side.

Tam bowed. "I'm sorry, Ameilja. I truly am—"

Ameilja brought him in close and hugged him tightly. She refused to have him depart with any negativity. "No need to apologize, you brute. See you tonight, yes? Chalk it up to our obvious exhaustion."

Tam nodded and followed after Ash. The two walked away, and she quickly turned to her two remaining protectorates. "Well? How is he?"

Nav'i shrugged. "He's fine. Ashamed and glum, but that's to be expected."

Ameilja brought her hand to her mouth. "I'm so sorry, Nav'i! I am so sorry this has to happen every single time."

"It's fine. It sucks, but we are Völfien, and we are capable. Kovuco will be fine by the time this is all over. Trust me."

"I hope so. I hate that I have to wait an entire week. It just doesn't feel fair."

"Well, come see us this weekend. I'll make us food." Dancer added as he remained locked in meditation with his arms crossed tightly.

Ameilja nodded enthusiastically. "Yes—yes! That sounds perfect."

Nav'i nodded, giving Ameilja a slight grimace of discernment.

"What?" she asked.

"Nothing. Nothing at all."

"What the hell is going on with everyone today?" she huffed, throwing up her hands and walking off.

"What?" Nav'i said, shifting his gaze to Ameilja and then to the emotionless and unmoved Dancer. "I just got here."

Ameilja whipped back toward them with frustration radiating off her body. "You! Both you and Tam! You both saying, 'Oh, nothing.' It's very irritating!" As she was known to do in a mood, she turned away again and stalked off, expecting them to follow after. "Let us go then. Maon has agreed to go shooting rather than just sitting in a stuffy conference room, and I am very much looking forward to it."

Nav'i looked to Dancer. "Should've signed up for night shifts, eh?"

Dancer sniffed sharply and chuckled.

"Are you coming?" Ameilja snipped over her shoulder.

They both quickly followed after their moody Lady Ameilja.

Isarah
Demitori City, Brass District
Shallotte Pines, condo of Szonja Marésato
Aoustí 12

Kiefer knocked on the door of his wülkure associate Szonja Marésato.

Szonja was one of his three wülkure who oversaw the Copper district. He hoped she wasn't busy from the weekend necessities before her next shift. There were other tasks to contend with, but free time meant your purpose was stifled, especially as a wülkure. Most barely had time for their families or stepped down due to the weighted expectations and extensive hours.

It was a wülkure's greatest gift—possibly even their burden—that they never were satisfied with their accomplishments. There was always a new skill to learn: a new way to disarm an enemy, a new way to understand the Fae, or a new way to kill and keep order.

The door opened and a pair of familiar long legs greeted him. Szonja wore a silk robe, and her hair lay down like a waterfall of shiny black. She was a Shaar'an woman born and raised by her Shaar'an mother and former centurion father. Kiefer knew he had a knack for sleeping with centurions' daughters but not so much ones under his own æsir leadership. Szonja was the exception.

She had a nasty tendency and desire to kill—there was no excuse for those who went against the Commission. She saw the other races as pests, unworthy. Kiefer didn't necessarily agree with her viewpoint, but he was not there for emotional connection.

Typically, after a kill, she needed a release, such as sex. Rough sex, to be exact. Her place had always meant a good time, but Kiefer prepared to leave with welts and bruises. During this particular visit, Kiefer needed this infliction. He needed to forget the news he was currently burdened with.

Szonja stepped aside and let him into her condo. He offered her a smoke, but she refused, as she always did. Szonja's entire form was in top shape; she held a strict diet and regimen that never faltered. She viewed her body as a temple. Since her parents' sicknesses, she'd taken her strength, health, and defense capabilities seriously. She once had been a wächter but had made a linear move to wülkure. Fortunately, she had made it to Demitori City and had remained under Kiefer's team in Copper.

Szonja's condo was pristine, a high-dollar investment she intended to keep until she'd decided on her next goal. It was decorated with elements of her culture back in Shaar and integrated with influential pieces of Demitori.

Szonja sat down and pulled her long black hair to the side, revealing her neck, so she could speak to Kiefer through her periphery. "Sunspire, huh?"

Kiefer nodded. "How'd you know?"

"Yegor and I had drinks at the office before closing that evening. He shared that there was a gruesome cult breach, along with unknown issues with a head doctor there. Heard about your völf Teo too. We hoped you would return to the office, but we presumed you headed home."

If she only knew the cult wasn't the real issue. "Yeah, they found me at the Blind Tiger. It was a long evening."

"Damn. You must be exhausted. Even after the shooting incident at the bay. I mean, you could've come over here." She joked but knew his intentions were never innocent.

"I'm here now, aren't I?"

Szonja met Kiefer's hungry gaze, stood up, untied her robe, and let it slip down her bare shoulders. She revealed herself to him, a statuesque work of art. She had swirling tattoos of dragons and water-like flames along her back and arms to enhance her display.

Kiefer sighed, wanting more than anything to resist, but he never could. Rae was gone, and he needed this to numb the pain. Numb the desire to hurt someone unwilling and inexperienced to his unnatural anguish, someone who would enjoy what he had to offer, even if it hurt. That someone was Szonja.

"Come here." He growled as he grabbed her by the neck and pushed her through the double doors of her study. He forced her onto the couch and tore off his jacket.

"I heard something about orks too," she said in a seductive whisper, waiting for him.

"Völf," he admitted, unbuckling his pants and letting them fall to his ankles. He propped himself on the couch, and she unbuttoned his shirt.

"I see. Interesting. I haven't ever heard of a völf working with cults. Now I see why they asked you over me." She kissed his bare chest, but Kiefer was ready to go.

"No one wants me on the Sunspire case," he said as he sunk his erection between her legs. A hoarse moan spilled from the back of his throat.

"You're good at what you do," she whimpered as he forcefully thrust into her.

"Noted," he said, inserting himself deeper, forcing her bare back against the couch cushion.

Szonja arched her spine and dug her nails into his back, embedding marks into his warm skin; they ran along his existing collection of scars from the nature of his work. Even though it was technically a violent career, some scars were crafted by her.

He swiftly lifted her off the couch with one hand clutching her throat and the other grabbing her ass to levitate her just right as he continued slipping himself in and out of her.

Their gaze locked; pieces of his dark hair swayed with each thrust. She assessed him, hoping to see what she'd seen their first time together. Just a shred that maybe he was enjoying it. Maybe even romantically.

They had been just youthful teens once upon a time. He had trained in Shaar for a few months; he hadn't been a wülkure yet, nor had she been a wächter. Even then, when their hormones had driven their desires, it never had been for love. Szonja had known early on that it was just for recognition and understanding between the two. Their sexual acts were a mere acknowledgment of the nature of their job and an attempt to find solace in the chaos—someone to comfort him through the infliction of pain. It was a harsh reminder that this life promised more hurt but could also offer pleasure in case the next shift stole your last breath away.

Kiefer was an experienced lover, especially with Szonja. He knew how to get her off compared to her other lovers. She may have pursued something more profound with him, but she had found herself a mere sedative to numb his pain. They'd stuck to strictly being rough fuck-mates since she'd shown up in Demitori.

"Faster!" She cried out, digging her nails further into his shoulders.

Kiefer obeyed. He liked to choke her so she couldn't breathe—not in a playful manner but enough to rebuke her, enough that she would want to fight back, need to fight back to allow air into her lungs. She'd played the game many times and only continued because she couldn't imagine him finding the wrong partner who might drive him to the destination he morbidly craved.

Before he could aggravate her breathing, she wrapped his belt around his neck and pulled it tightly. She heard the gurgle in his throat, the rasp for air, and immediately felt him grow harder.

"That's right," she hissed. "You like it!"

He pressed deeper into her, quick and vigorous, thrilled to be co-itally paired. He bared his teeth from the pleasure coursing through his body. With both hands, he held her higher and carried her to climax, pulling out before he came, per his usual.

She quickly released the belt, and he fell back onto the floor, trying to catch his breath, coughing and drooling. Sweat beaded on their naked forms.

Szonja got up and inhaled to ensure her lungs were at total capacity. "That's more like it." She sighed, fitting on her robe. She then fetched a glass of water.

Swiping her silky hair behind her shoulders, she knelt beside Kiefer, assessed his physique, and then coaxed him to drink. Usually, she'd try to cover him up, but the humiliation of gasping for air, helpless and naked, was part of his ritual, the dance of hatred he danced all too often.

"Well, even if our centurion thinks you're the wrong guy, I want to lend you my sword. You're gonna need it."

Kiefer caught his breath finally, and he shook his head. "Szonja, I don't need it. You don't have to—"

"Piss off, Yuska. Just take the fucking sword, will you? Copper's been manageable, thanks to the team you've assembled. I want you to have it in case that völf gives you a hard time."

He agreed to take it, to appease her. "Thanks. I will return it in one piece."

She nodded. "I know. You can return it over dinner. What do you say you plan to hit me up once you're back?"

Fuck. Rae flashed through his mind. *That's another dinner I am expected to have upon my return.*

He hesitated. "Yeah. Sure."

"Good." She rose to her feet.

"What's the occasion for dinner? You planning on killing someone while I'm gone?" he chuckled.

She scoffed. "Who said I wanted to fuck you when you come back? Let's start with dinner, Kief. I think Yegor should come too."

He cocked his head in disbelief. "Don't get soft on me, Marésato."

"What's soft about a dinner with colleagues? Maybe I just want to talk."

"You aren't fucking Yegor too, are you?"

She sloshed the water into Kiefer's face. "I have before. Not that it's any of your business. But he's just as fucked up as you are. He has fewer standards, though; plus, he prefers Orkésh." She stood up and walked back to her kitchen.

Kiefer could still view her from the floor. "So you do know of his infatuations?"

"Yes. But he's also delving into the path of hallucinogens. If he's not careful, those drugs will get to him."

"Orks. You ever had an ork before?" he blurted.

She obnoxiously sighed. "Can you try to be more well-mannered, Kiefer?"

"Why? I thought we were supposed to talk."

"Yes, but does it have to be so barbaric?" She poured herself a mug of steaming tea from her iron kettle. The smell of spiced chai filled the space. "Maybe next time, we'll talk before the sex."

"Ugh. That would be dreadful," he teased. "Okay, let's talk for real, and I will be less brutal, yeah?"

Szonja nodded, motioning for Kiefer to follow her. "Cover yourself up, and come to bed. You need sleep first. Then we'll talk."

☆

Shaar
Tsunetomo
Frost Estate, beachfront facing west
Aoustí 12

"It was foolish, you know," said Maon, aiming the barrel of an Aritaka Z98 sniper rifle. She took a moment to assess the wind before taking the shot. When she did, it was a bulls-eye. From almost nine hundred yards, she hit the target. The sound echoed; music to Maon's ears.

Ash, who stood behind, let out a puff of smoke from his cigar. "Nice work, princess."

Maon inspected the rifle, delighted with her successful shot. "It's a fine piece of machinery, Mr. Ulrendt. Did you use one in the war?"

"I did. I've also asked why you continue calling me Mr. Ulrendt," he replied, intending to be facetious.

"Oh, I forgot. *Ashley.* Ashley, did you use it in the war? This fine piece of machinery?"

Ash laughed, tipping his hat, when he saw how unamused Ameilja became, not yet holding the Aritaka.

Haruka stood next to her, trying to block the icy winds that swept by them under the morning sun. She kept checking the glare on Ameilja's face.

Ameilja stepped forward, and Maon handed over the Aritaka Z98. She took the rifle and loaded a bullet into the chamber before allowing Maon to step aside.

Maintaining her confident posture, Maon took a step back.

Ameilja shouldered the rifle, adjusting the scope. She took a deep breath, exhaled, and pulled the trigger midway through her breath. Her shot landed almost dead center on Maon's shot.

"What's foolish, Maon?" Ameilja finally asked, still aiming down the scope.

"Why would you put a völf in that situation? You do know it was strange, right?"

"Strange?" Ameilja said, pulling the trigger once more, nailing the next target. "Tell me, why was it strange?"

"Ameilja, you realize you have turned down sixteen suitors. The public also hears of these rumors."

"Yes, and?" She released another shot, another bulls-eye.

"You do realize your marriage is essential to your commitment to the people of Shaar, right?" Maon pressed, annoyance coating her tone.

Ameilja took two more shots before turning to Maon. "Yes, Maon. I also don't see *your* union with any lands beyond the Eastern Isles. Or here for that matter."

Maon sighed respectfully. "I suppose you're right. None of us have exactly been prized-wife material, but do you think it helped to walk a völf before the Houses of the Isles? Abbots, prominent paladins, and even æsirs were all present; none of them even bothered to speak to us. Why do you think?"

Ameilja rolled her eyes. "I suppose you think that must be because of Kovuco."

"What will leadership translate that to?" Maon looked to Haruka. "Sister, any input?"

Haruka shrugged. "I understand what you're saying, but I certainly have no drive to improve. Maybe Ameilja's walking out with that völf caught us some attention."

"Caught attention?" Ameilja huffed. "You mean to say you think I used him?"

"Did you?" Maon asked, assessing her.

"You're not in a relationship with this völf, right?" added Haruka with concern blanketing her face.

"No!" Ameilja snipped. "But Kovuco is very dear to me. I was happy to be escorted by him, and I wouldn't have had it any other way. Don't blatantly say such things aloud!" She inconspicuously glanced over her shoulder at Ash and her two völves.

"What about him then?" Maon pointed to Nav'i. "Or him?" She pointed to Dancer. They stood behind the women, keeping watch of their surroundings. "Could they not have made a similar impact?"

Ameilja ensured Nav'i and Dancer remained composed before answering. She leaned in, lowering her voice. "I chose Kovuco."

"Right. Kovuco. The Blackstar son of Adémaro. Adémaro, the völf who slept with an unknown mate, bears the same platinum fur and blue eyes never seen in history and was excommunicated from the Order. Are you sure these two black-coated völves would have made the same impact?" She arched an eyebrow.

"I didn't use Kovuco, Maon!" Ameilja said with agitation crawling up her spine. Her fingers gripped the weapon.

"You sure? Kovuco is the offspring of the symbol of disobedience within the Commission, yet you employed him as your protectorate. Have you ever seen Adémaro? He's got a good gut now and a gruff beard. He supposedly refuses to take his Rinkin form. Remains in solitude. Alone in the mountains, doing who knows what."

Ameilja's demeanor shifted, and her eyes flared.

Haruka quickly stepped forward to step between them. "Now, Maon. Kovuco faced trial, and he was deemed—"

"What? Not a demon? The Commission will always find a way to grant mercy if approved, especially involving the Order's will of Uridei. But his actions with Ameilja on the night of the coronation resonate rebellion; he knew better, and so did you, Ameilja. I can't begin to imagine what rumors are being spewed. Is that the attention you wanted?"

"Why the hell are you questioning me right now, when your brother may have involvement with the attack? Have you forgotten we were almost killed that night?" Ameilja stepped toward Maon, their noses were practically touching.

Ash, Nav'i, and Dancer all turned their attention toward them but quickly redirected their ears to give the feuding women their space.

"*My* brother?" Maon scoffed. "Aren't you forgetting his wife, that bitch sister of yours?"

Haruka quickly placed a hand on a shoulder of each, making her presence known. "Both of you, enough! There is much we don't know right now about the attack. Let's drop the subjects altogether and enjoy this time of peace outside the walls we're constantly bored with."

Maon rolled her eyes and stepped back from Haruka's touch.

Ameilja stood her ground. "Maybe that's what was needed, Maon! Maybe how we see things about the Völfien, even the Fae, is all wrong. Maybe we should remember that Uridei calls us to accept imperfections, and Kovuco's attendance that night could remind us to forgive and let go. Maybe we even hope to love more openly outside our race."

As she said *love*, she'd gained Nav'i's attention; his gaze briefly locked onto her. Ameilja shared a faint smile with him, then snapped away from Haruka, flipped the switch on the Z98 to automatic, and opened fire toward the eastern side of the beach. As soon as she squeezed the trigger, the rifle amassed a hellish flash as a spray of lead littered the targets. She finished, ejected the magazine, and tossed the rifle to Ash.

"We're done for today. My friends here need to return to their routine." Ameilja directly informed Ash, cutting a sharp glance to Maon and Haruka. "Ash, do you remember what I requested? Did I make myself clear?"

Ash smirked and spat his cigar out after holstering the Z98 across his back. "Yes, ma'am." He turned and walked away, pacing himself, hoping to continue to hear Ameilja's uproar.

She looked to Nav'i and Dancer. "Go! Go with Ash; the day is yours! You're no longer under any regulations today."

Nav'i and Dancer looked at each other in disbelief but bowed and followed after Ash. Maon and Haruka both shifted where they stood. Their expressions portrayed their discontent.

Maon shook her head. "You can't make these types of calls! My mother—*your* empress will—"

Ameilja confidently whipped around to face Maon again. "The empress will do what exactly? I am no fool, Maon. I am sorry if you have ever felt forced to watch me as a sister, but you don't have to call me Sister. Let me go ahead and free you from my whims, but I will no longer suffocate. I will no longer sit back and be a coward to the injustice undoubtedly dividing our world. I will be a voice of change. Even if I must die in the process!"

Haruka lent a hand to Ameilja. "Ameilja, we didn't mean—"

"Then mean what you say!" Ameilja's voice rose an octave. "Wear your emblem of the Commission, and wear it proudly! We must be a catalyst for love—for change! Fight for what we were supposed to stand for since the beginning: unity! Fight for those who are weak. Fight for those without a voice. And serve Uridei with all your heart, mind, and soul!" Ameilja turned away from them and looked out at the sea; the clouds stretched beyond their horizon. In her mind, it stood as a strong representation that the future's possibilities could be endless. "The fight starts now!"

CHAPTER TWELVE
FORBIDDEN

Shaar
Tsunetomo
West Wing protectorate tower, second floor
Aousti 13

IT WAS THE FIRST DAY OF THE NEW WEEK; I prayed I would be allowed to work out with my packmates—anything to get me out of that damned tower.

I could hear everyone preparing for the day in the washroom; however, I had been awake since two o'clock in the morning. While I eagerly waited, I redundantly read over the words in Ameilja's letter. It was riddled with apologies and acceptance of fault for the acts at her coronation.

At first, I was upset that she took the blame for actions beyond her control, but I eventually allowed the thoughts to settle. Her emotions were who she was, and she gave them full-heartedly. They empowered her strength. I wished I could tell her, "It was my job. This is who I am. It's what I'm meant to do and was hired to do."

I will forever fall into the darkness for you, Ameilja.

I ate the food she sent back with Tam: salted almonds and cuts of aged cheese. I slowly sipped the tiny bottle of wine left over from the coronation dinner. As delicious as it was, I only took little sips. I told myself to forget that night—forget my feelings for her, but I can't. All it takes is a thought and the natural impulses stir—it is inevitable.

I replayed the memory of walking Ameilja, the lady of Shaar, *my* lady, to a table and being granted to eat close to her as her escort. I remember the way her warm body and gentle curves felt under my grasp and the determined look in her green eyes. I wanted to prolong the memory.

Can I call it a date?

Sure, it had been enacted in an agenda for the Commission, but I didn't care. It was a memory I would cherish for the rest of my days. It uplifted and inspired me. The tastes, the smells—they were a memorial to a reality I never had imagined possible.

I kept her letter close and tucked it safely under my pillow. I had never lain dormant in bed for so long. I absorbed every written word.

The peace was short-lived. It was a new day, and I needed answers. I needed a new direction—new scenery rather than a bland dormitory.

I kicked back the shade and rose from my bed. I heard Nav'i, Dancer, and Tam getting ready as quietly as possible. I knew they planned to sneak out while I slept, but I intended to march through that gate with them.

Nav'i snapped toward me with his right ear twitching. "Kovuco?"

"You're up?" Tam questioned, shocked.

"I can go with you if I am not around humans!" I hurled the words.

Nav'i tensed. "Right. Well—"

"And Ash will let me go! He's gotten away with everything Ameilja has pushed. I am convinced I'll even have a moment to see Ameilja to—"

"Oh, and do you think that's best for her?" Nav'i snipped.

I faltered in answering.

Dancer came out of the washroom, eyed Nav'i, and then looked to me. "Tell him, Nav'i. We have the day off."

"Day off?" I shot them a baffled look. I had never heard of such a thing in all my years as a protectorate, or ever, for that matter. We didn't get days off. "What is a day off?" I scratched the back of my skull.

My packmates, even Dancer, shrugged.

"I guess we do whatever we want," Dancer answered.

"Well, what were you going to do then?" I said.

"I was going to go to the library after our workout," Nav'i added.

Dancer nodded. "I was going to travel downtown to try the new curry shop. Been wanting to for a while. Might as well while I now have the chance."

"That sounds fine, right?" Tam said, feeling as lost as Kovuco on what to do.

"Maybe we should all stick together. To be safe," Nav'i added authoritatively. "I'm still processing that we have been granted this free time. You know damn well not everyone will agree."

I nodded to agree, eyeing the three of them, while my mind thought about Ameilja. My goal was to break off at some point. I needed to try to see her. I needed to know she was okay.

Nav'i turned to me again. "There is no reason to worry about Ash approving you."

"Why?" I asked.

"You'll see."

We finished getting ready for the day, grabbed our packs, and headed to the base of our tower. The gate doors were wide open. No lock. No wülkure. No rusted skeleton key.

"What is happening?" I whispered aloud, cautiously taking in the scene.

Nav'i shrugged. "I guess Ameilja had a significant breakdown regarding the treatment of us. Dancer and I were partly witnesses; she had a feud with Haruka and Maon. Be prepared, Kovuco; I think many significant changes will come. She even ordered you to be allowed to be with us today. No quarantine required."

"And András approved of this?"

"I don't have that answer," Nav'i admitted. "Knowing András, he granted Ameilja this temporarily. You know how he feels toward his daughters."

"It's as if he harbors a guilt," Tam cautiously added.

"Yes ... something." Nav'i's eyes shifted.

Is this real?

Silence briefly held our voices captive until Nav'i spoke up, "Let's go then. We'll walk the streets of Tsunetomo as free völves."

We all followed his lead.

With our schedules clear of Ameilja's duties, we lived an unnatural day. We stuck with the schedule we were familiar with, roaming the streets we had walked many times with Ameilja. We stopped by Shaar Night café and ordered coffee. Of course, Tam ordered food: a cup of udon, and a soft-boiled egg.

I nodded at the owners; they responded with subtle grins. I was certain they wondered why our lady was absent, but we ignored the awkward energy.

We sat outside along the establishment's wall, on an extended bench for customers to eat and drink. Guests would glance over at us but then continue forward. At one point, a young child stopped and waved. His silky black hair blew around his face as the coastal winds swept through the street. I smiled and made eye contact with his parents. They nodded hesitantly and quickly grabbed their child's arm, nearly dragging him away.

Have they heard rumors?

We finished quickly, feeling unsettled—like the feeling you carried if you'd left something behind, except this time, it was our entire role.

To avoid the crowds, we took the extended route to the Okumura Temple on a pebbled pathway tucked behind the residences. At the temple, we could safely lift weights in peace.

We entered through the back entrance of the training grounds, where the equipment was already grouped according to regiment and activity. We used the workouts to hone in on our natural strength and skill, enhancing what Albean had blessed our kind with. Tam kept spitting out absurd nicknames for each activity; we appreciated the laughs, especially on an unnerving day like today.

Not once did we discuss the coronation, the attack, or Ameilja. We focused on our day off and the freedom that awaited us. We embraced the uncertainty.

If it had been a typical day in our role as protectorates, we would have been working on the chest, back, and abs. Völfien bodies were usually focused on the arms, shoulders, and legs, but that was where our natural-born strength lay. I focused on arms, while Nav'i and Dancer focused on their abs. Tam had been working heavily on all of those areas recently, probably so he could measure up to Shirou and Lain. We Völfien were not naturally vain creatures, but when measuring up to counterparts in our trade, it was difficult not to feel inadequate next to our more significant, more developed peers.

Nav'i eventually checked the time and noted that we should move onward. We showered and headed to the beach, where we planned to continue our arduous activities.

By the time dinner rolled around, we had sat about the fire pit built in the sand and decided that with no one needing to check us in, we'd experience an early night on the beach under the full moon. The waves were harsh, rolling in quickly under her lunar influence. While my packmates discussed topics on Fae upbringing, I zoned out and looked up at the moon's vibrancy.

I gazed at her beauty, as our ancestors once had. She shone brightly and existed entirely as herself, confident, with nothing to tell her otherwise, while she prepared for a new phase.

The moon was our symbolic reminder that change was inevitable; each cycle welcomed growth.

"Are you in your head again, Kovuco?" Tam asked.

I snapped my attention to him. "Uh, yeah."

"He asked you a question," Nav'i pressed, his intense eyes beaming against the fire's light.

I took that as a hint to redirect my thoughts. I was instantly swept into their conversation.

After a couple of hours passed, we eventually returned to our tower. I waited in my bunk, staring at the wooden ceiling, as my thoughts raced. I debated my next move, but my heart already confirmed the answer.

After my packmates finally fell asleep, I slipped out of my prison and merged into the darkness of night.

I headed for the West Wing.

I headed for Ameilja.

Shaar
Tsunetomo
West Wing
Aoustí 14

It was midnight. Under the cover of darkness, I melded myself into the shadows cast by the moon.

Naturally, I could integrate into a darkened world better than most humans. The House was heavily guarded, which made sense, considering Tanja was still missing, and everyone feared another attack could be imminent. Armored senior völf protectorates were included in the strengthened security and could potentially sniff me out. At least I didn't have to worry about Tam, since he had been given the night off, another perk of our freedom that day.

Rather than going around the walls and outdoor passages of Frost Manor, I would need to enter through her balcony. I would also need to cover my scent.

I went to the shoreline, removed my clothes, laid them on the craggy rocks, and dove into the ocean. I soaked long enough to feel the minerals saturating the texture and volume of my fur. This would temporarily mask any scent from the day. I shook off what water I could from my body and peered across the bay. The full moon illuminated the balcony cliffs surrounding her wing. It was now, ironically, barred and gated off, unlike our tower.

I quickly dressed and ventured quietly toward the western wall, locking into all of my senses. The cool sand moved under my feet. The closer I became, the more her scents swept through me.

I looked up at her balcony door and noticed it was open. *She's awake.*

I saw her. The faint glow from her chamber lights highlighted her dainty silhouette against the night sky. I moved in closer, slow and cautious.

Ameilja?

I noticed her pretty face was strewn with tears. Her solemn features gave away that she had been lost in thought. I studied her; she was in a white silk robe. It blew gently from the cold coastal wind; her glistening green eyes stared out over the crashing waves. I cautiously made it the rest of the way and breached her wing, still hidden in the shadows, as she stood there peering out into the ocean's darkness.

Her eyes suddenly closed; she seemed lost in some grief that didn't belong to her. My gaze fell to her hands; there was a pistol in her right hand, with the trigger clutched.

What is this? What is she doing with a gun?

Having sworn off guns from my skill set, I knew little of the weapons, but I knew what clutching the trigger meant. I waited and watched her. She looked lost, frustrated, and somewhat defeated. It made no sense since she had just managed to get her way, ripping down the gates of her Court of Völfien, even against the order of the empress.

What's wrong, Ameilja?

I slowly crawled on all fours toward her, with each claw pushed to the floor, preparing to leap and jet for the weapon. The chill in the air caressed my face, reminding me to move slowly. Part of me wanted to reach out from the shadows and grab hold of her. I wanted to take all her pain away. Her essence needed comfort in this time of distress. *Maybe if I reach out, maybe if I caress her, my touch will be all she needs.*

I paused and closed my eyes briefly. I envisioned her smiling face during our dance, an uncomfortable chore I never had imagined I'd practice. I'd awkwardly moved and followed her lead, feeling her warm form beneath my touch. She had looked happy and carefree. I wondered if her happiness had been because of my holding her and her feeling safe in my arms, and maybe now I was the antidote to her discomfort.

Ameilja...

I snapped open my eyes and swiftly moved toward her. When her flesh crossed the sensors of my claws, my paw seized the barrel. Instantly, her fighter reflexes kicked in. She pivoted like a whip so quickly I was pressed against the exterior of the wing's landing. The gun fired.

I suddenly was covered in my blood as the bullet exploded through the tendons of my paw. I watched the bullet spiral toward my chest until it halted in my throat. I had no breath. My airway tightened around the metal that pulsated against it. I felt it drive deep into my throat, and burning pain immediately flashed through me.

Vilkanás!

My world suddenly went black. The last thing I saw was the look of surprise in Ameilja's wide eyes.

My life flashed before my eyes. Feeling alone, the little Völfien bastard of Adémaro, motherless demon, had been foolish enough to fall to the hand of the lady he'd been ordered to protect.

I wondered, *Should I tell her? Tell her I love her? Tell her I have found myself dangerously infatuated with her? Tell her all these forbidden secrets before I die?*

Maybe. But the words couldn't escape as I drifted deeper into the darkness.

☆

Unknown place
Unknown time

I drifted into the darkness; I found myself suspended in the null of moribundity. There was nothing—no breeze but those final breaths. Even the sensation of my being was of no use. No feeling. Thinking of it only created anxiety that there was nothing to feel anymore.

Am I dead?

I snapped my eyes open, and the space was white. I was no longer comatose to the flashing pain of the bullet driving itself deep into my throat.

I clutched my chest, noticing how luminescent my fur was against the coma-white surroundings. I looked around, shifting my gaze to the left. Nothing. I shifted to the right. Nothing.

Where am I?

I turned back to face front and center, and a female wolf sat approximately twelve feet before me. She was not a völf like me but a distant memorial of what we once had been.

She sat like a hound. Her tail curved around her flat front, rounded paws. She was beautiful, natural, and somewhat wild looking. Her seated posture was confident, like that of a four-legged deity. I assessed her tricolored fur of white, black, and gold.

Not once did she open her eyes while I took her in. She seemed to be meditating in this eerie space of nothingness. Keeping her in the nervous peripheral of my sight, I tried to see if any other creature occupied this space. To my horror, no. Just this relic of a wolf and I.

Her eyes suddenly snapped open as I studied her; her demeanor remained calm and serene.

"Hello, Kovuco Blackstar," she spoke, but her maw did not budge.

She spoke in telepathic whispers; they caressed my mind. Her voice shuddered through me and beckoned my fear, demanding my attention and respect.

I know who she is.

I quickly knelt and bowed before the mother of all Völfien. "Hello, Fenris."

"You know who I am, Völfien?" Her voice echoed.

"Yes, and I believe I have perished. What other creature would appear before me in this purgatory?"

"No, Kovuco, you are not in purgatory."

"Then where am I?"

"You are comatose, young Völfien, not dead. But I wonder: Should you be?"

"I made a foolish error, Fenris. The lady I protect—I startled her, and now the vilkanás poison courses within me."

Fenris laughed. Her laugh was like a cackle, unlike the glorious thing before me. I'd forgotten she was not an elegant being, as Albean had been. She once had been a wild animal and given birth to the first Völfien. She symbolized my existence, this creature worthy of being chosen by Albean.

"So sure that vilkanás will have its way?" she asked.

"Our ways are different now, Fenris. The humans work against us. They use us. The only hope is that this man-made poison is extracted from my body. I will need to consume fresh human blood. Too much blood will be needed for my survival. There is no hope, Fenris. I will die here tonight!"

Fenris caught her breath and cleared her throat. She swished her tail and stood up. The air around her moved like rippling water as she walked closer to me. She paused two feet from my gaze, close enough to latch her jaws about my throat if she chose to, yet her presence restored the serenity I needed.

"What of Lady Ameilja?"

"You know her name?"

"Do you not believe this human will see to your salvation?"

I thought for a moment. *Would Ameilja? She'd do everything and anything she could to wake me, protect me, and—*

Fenris interrupted my thoughts. "You know, don't you, Kovuco?"

"But—"

"The choice is yours. I am giving you that choice today."

"The choice to live?"

"The choice to fight!" She raised her melodic voice; it vibrated against my skull. "For too long, you have been a recluse and stepped away due to fear. Know who you are, Kovuco. Look within. I call you now to step into your purpose. See who you truly are! Find strength, and fight!"

"Why, Fenris? Why do you appear before me and plead with me to fight? Why is my purpose so worth your time?"

"We all have purposes, young Völfien. Perhaps mine has been to appear before you now and remind you to do what you know you must."

I dropped my head. "I am sorry, Fenris. I don't understand."

"What are you doing now, Kovuco? What purpose did you serve in coming here tonight? You placed your life in harm's way, and for what?"

Because I love a human.

I looked back at Fenris; she suddenly appeared to show signs that she was no wild animal. Her wolf face stretched into an unnatural, radiant smile, and I could see a resemblance in her, evidence that Albean's Aureate blood had lived through her, unfathomable and omniscient.

"Live your purpose, Kovuco," her voice melodically whispered. "Go!"

Unbearable pain smacked into my form.

A blinding deluge of cerulean blue thundered over her and then blistered against me, surging feeling and emotion back into all my senses.

I instantly felt pain and—

Shaar
Tsunetomo
West Wing
Aoustí 14

An orange glow bled through the milky screen of my blurred vision. Cold water splashed against my face, and the light returned. I felt delicate hands tug me across a cold tile floor.

"Kovuco! Don't you die on me, damn it!"

I tried to move or sway—anything—but all I could do was drunkenly manage words as well as possible. Inappropriate as it might have been, the pain was so severe that I wanted to laugh at the absurdity of my situation, especially after what I had just experienced a few days ago.

How the hell am I still alive?

As if I were a sick idiot, strange laughing noises escaped me. I tried to cope with the punishment of living with this pain while the vilkanás continued its assault on my system.

"Kovuco, you need blood! Now!" Ameilja exclaimed, panic rising from her chest.

"Ameilja, I need—" I was too weak to say any more. It hurt. The pain continued, burning, sweltering, and coursing through my veins like acid.

Why did she have a vilkanás bullet?

Völfien were fatally allergic to vilkanás. When we were exposed to its lethal sting, the reactants chemically blocked off blood vessels, instantly constricting them. The blue-violet vilkanás would instantly begin poisoning cells unless …

She ripped open my shirt to reveal my blood-soaked fur. I felt her small form straddle me as she pressed her lips against my wound and started to suck free the remnants of blood, spitting the vilkanás-soiled crimson to her left each time.

Splatters of my blood covered her mouth as she gagged from the taste. The vilkanás smelled rancid; I was surprised she didn't vomit from its pungent flavor. She finally stopped to dig her finger into the wound to find where the bullet lay. I grunted, baring my teeth. She continued to gag on my blood as she dug.

"Shit!" she hissed, wiping her mouth clean.

She shot up once more to shut her door. There was a pause, followed by voices.

"I was just testing out my handgun!" Ameilja's voice said. "Had to clean it and wanted to make sure it fired properly."

A smooth lie.

Another voice sounded, but I could not make out whose. I felt myself fading even more.

"Sure thing. I'll see you tomorrow morning. Good night!"

Ameilja rushed back inside, slamming the door behind her and locking it. I heard her toss the key into the corner of her room. Its clamor rang in my ears.

She attended my side again and positioned herself back over me, straddling me and holding my neck secure as she attempted to dig the bullet from my throat with a knife she at some point retrieved. She huffed heavily as she focused. Each breath pulsated against the thick air around us. Her body involuntarily trembled.

I retched, muzzling my face, wanting to cry out in pain, as the sharp edge dug at sensitive flesh exposed and burned from the pistol fire. She finally retrieved the bullet and tossed it aggressively into the far corner of her washroom.

"I got it!" she declared.

Without a second thought, she pressed her wrist over my lips and held the knife against it. In a sobering moment, I slapped the blade across the room. "N—No!" I stammered.

Is she crazy? Everyone will believe she's suicidal if she slits her wrists. Everyone will know she's been bitten if I leave bite marks. Worse, it could lead to a more serious issue—this cannot be done. I'm not going to consume her blood! I will not!

She had to accept that she'd removed the bullet and helped ease the pain and that the effects had ceased. I had to accept my fate and wait to die.

She grabbed my chin and forced my gaze to hers. "Look at me! You are going to die, Kovuco! You *have* to drink my blood, or you're going to die! Do you understand?"

She stood up; cast off her white robe, which was now covered in my blood; and slipped down her pants. She hurriedly pushed them down, revealing black silk panties. They matched her black under top. She lifted my head and forced my nose against her inner thigh. "Bite, Kovuco! Do it now!"

Through the bits of cognitive delusion I held on to, I realized what was happening, and I didn't want anything to do with this plan. Traditionally, a wülkure would have intervened, finished me off, and taken me to my grave. The deadly vilkanás toxin worked fast, and the best antidote was fresh blood. They couldn't supplement me with artificial reserves or stored blood. It had to be new, pumped directly from the heart. *But it can't be Ameilja's. It can't!*

I tried to jerk away, but I fell into her. I could smell the blood flowing through her veins. It knocked me into ecstasy. That flow of sweet red, even the smell of her femininity, enticed my male senses. What dark, lustful visions filled my mind in a moment surrounded by death. My pools of blood now surrounded us; Ameilja was defenseless and at my resolute mercy. She wanted me to do this.

Her flesh smelled so sweet. Oh, how human flesh cut so easily. A soft, dainty thigh like hers would be like a snack. The blood of a human dripped like dark tears. *So beautiful, so delicious, so—*

I seized her sides with my claws. Her body quivered in response to the daggers tapping against her flesh.

Tears filled my eyes weakly. "Ameilja, I can't." I inhaled heavily, begging. "I—I can't do this." The tears flowed down my face. "You have to kill me! Please! We can't. I can't control—"

I breathed deeply and dispelled the visions. I had to tell her the truth. Tell her before I died. Tell her so I could rest in knowing that the one thing I'd pursued in this tiny life was loving her, and being by her side as her protectorate. I could at least be proud that I had known her.

"Ameilja, before I die, I need to tell you I—"

Before I could finish, Ameilja clutched my ear and yanked it as hard as she could in an upward motion. I yelped, and she gagged me, jamming her thigh into my jaws. She grabbed my ears and twisted them, and my jaw locked down onto her smooth flesh.

"Drink, Kovuco!"

My eyes clenched shut, and my emotions drifted to a lull. I was aware only of the sweet crimson that flowed from soft muscle over the glacial whites of my jaw. Like a heavenly rainfall, the drops spilled against my tongue, exciting papillae—rivers of her life coursed down the incline of my mouth and seeped to the back of my throat. Her warm, fresh blood.

Ameilja...

My eyes clouded white and widened fully, becoming circles of visible intent. Sudden, innate surges bristled into my structure. My völf instincts took over. I forcefully hurled Ameilja onto her back. My legs kicked, and I rushed her against her floor until she slammed into her footboard; my jaws were still wrapped around her inner thigh.

She cursed loudly from the pain as I partially lifted and held her with nothing but my jaws. My claws clutched the footboard, and I squeezed tightly, holding on. The wood groaned under my grasp. I didn't want to touch her, afraid I might rip her apart.

I bit down again, and her fingers clenched tightly around her mouth. She threw back her head and screamed into her blood-covered palms, holding back the sound of terror she wished to echo through the corridors of her room—for help, for safety, to cease the pain.

I loosened my bite, and the drops became a steady flow. The bitter iron taste intoxicated me. My wounds began to close, as if the bullet were reversed through time, erasing the evidence of its ever having existed in the world. There would be a scar, but my fur would cover the secret.

I have to stop ... but she tastes so sweet ... the blood.

Her blood continued to fill my mouth.

I need to stop.

But the blood.

Stop!

In a quick motion I lifted her and stepped forward; we both collapsed onto her king-sized bed, slamming onto her pillowy mattress. Her leg quickly slipped away from my fangs, leaving behind fleshy scabbards.

I gasped for air and allowed the crimson to mesh with my system and heal and rejuvenate me. Ameilja maneuvered herself off the bed as her handmaiden began pounding on the door, calling for her.

How long has she been pounding on the door?

"Jayna! Hold on!" Ameilja called.

"Ameilja? I heard a noise. Open the door!"

She stammered an excuse. "I'm—I'm indecent, Jayna. Wait!"

If anyone had seen Ameilja naked, her handmaidens had. She knew she had to devise something clever and quickly. The pounding, thankfully, stopped. Ameilja began to wrap her wound with a bandage hurriedly. Her quick tourniquet did the job of ceasing the bleeding until she could cover the injury more securely. She tossed on a new robe and quickly tied it shut. She threw a sheet over me, and I heard her footsteps tap toward the door.

She opened it. "Jayna, I am fine!"

"Are you sure, Lady Ameilja? First the gunshots and now all the other noise. Are you sure you're all right?"

"Yes, of course. Tell the guards I am not allowing anyone into the wing. Tell me you understand!"

"Yes, Lady Ameilja. If you need anything—"

"Thank you, Jayna. No more gunfire—nothing. I promise. Stay in your chambers for the rest of the evening, okay? Good night. Tea tomorrow, okay?"

The door shut.

Ameilja made her way back to me and removed the sheet. She pulled me up and ripped my shirt more to avoid lifting me farther off the bed. She checked my neck, front, and back, and then my palm, where the shot first made contact.

"Like it never happened," she whispered to herself. "Truly amazing. Are you okay? Do you feel okay?"

I didn't answer.

She got up and started a bath. She came back moments later, slightly limping, and helped me to my feet. We walked into her washroom. She pulled my belt forcefully out of the belt loops, and before I could stop her, my slacks slipped to my ankles. Despite what I had just put her through, her petite body somehow managed to direct my body to do what she wanted.

"Get in," she said as she helped me into the tub, looking away.

With a boyish shame, I curled into the rising water. She averted her gaze and began wiping the blood from the floor.

She then left, only to return with a towel and a clean pair of slacks. I watched her as she zoned out with each task, solely focused on cleaning up the evidence of what had taken place. It was evident her mind was racing.

She then fled to the other end of the washroom, but I caught her reflection in the corner of the far mirror angled toward her. She quickly undressed and unraveled the gauze around her wound. After turning on the showerhead, she sat on a stool and began to rinse the bite marks I had left. Her naked back faced me. I quickly averted my stare and sank beneath the surface of the water.

It was difficult to resist as my curiosity amassed. It was not as if I'd already seen enough to dishonor our sense of purity. I rose out of the bathwater just enough to view her. Without paying attention to the blood, I took her in—her whole body. Her light skin moved fluidly around her bone structure. She had a taut back; thin limbs; wide hips for birthing; and soft, fair skin. She was gorgeous head to toe, and I, a völf, liked what I saw so much that I snapped my gaze away to avoid furthering my forbidden thoughts or urging blasphemous sensations.

I sank back into the water.

The vilkanás should have killed me or at least driven me mad. She'd saved me, but at what cost?

Does she know? Did *the* Lady Ameilja of Shaar know what we'd done?

Did she know that we'd committed a forbidden act—the act of bloodletting for only mates of my race—all to allow me to live another day.

Does she know …

Know that we are now bonded.

I resurfaced, and Ameilja's dressed back was turned to me. "Hurry and get dressed. We need to talk."

She left the washroom, and I prayed. Prayed for forgiveness. Prayed for mercy. Prayed that I was worthy of Uridei's light.

Her blood continued to repair my system and rehabilitate my breathing and vitals.

Ameilja had tried to clean up as much as she could, but the floor would require a more thorough cleaning to keep any other völves from noticing what had happened there. I cleaned myself as much as possible until all traces of her blood and my own were gone, spiraling down the drain. I continued to allow the hot water to flow from the spout, hoping no other völf could trace it. I dried off as diligently as possible and continued looking for blood traces.

Someone's going to know.

I put on the slacks she had given me. They were leaf green, with golden buttons. I wondered why she had them. I couldn't even think of where I would have found such a pair. Her scent lay dormant in the fibers' memory. She must have made them by hand.

I walked into Ameilja's room. She sat on the end of her bed, which now was covered in fresh linens, with her back to me.

My gaze settled upon the gun on her dresser closest to the washroom. It had been unloaded and dismantled to its most minor parts.

I cautiously meandered to the opposite side of her bed and sat down with my back facing hers.

There was silence. I couldn't think of what to say or how to say it. I was thankful for her actions to liberate us. I admired her courage in the face of the Commission and as a strong woman representing the Order. I had yet to meet anyone dedicated to the cause of Albean more than Ameilja. I knew because we'd accompanied her to prayer. She adorned her hands to Uridei, cleaned them in holy waters, communed with the Light, and endured sacraments daily.

I turned and observed her in my periphery. Her shoulders were slumped. She appeared defeated and lost for words. Her hair, still wet from her shower, lay like stringy twine down her back. She curled into herself; perhaps I invoked that upon her from the chill of near death. Or maybe she knew what we'd done.

She had a right to recover. Did I even have the right to ask for closure?

I wondered if I should leave and risk being caught on my way back to the beach. I assumed my fear of being discovered matched the fear Ameilja had faced in the moments before my near death. I deserved it after what had been committed; however, it would raise alarm and curiosity against her if I were found half naked, walking from her wing.

I swallowed the bit of saliva in my throat. I finally mustered the bravery to speak. "Ameilja?"

She didn't answer.

I tried again. "Ameilja? Do you want—"

"Stay. You must stay."

I nodded. "I am sorry."

I heard her sigh. I still was unsure what was running through her mind.

"Maybe you should get some rest," I said gently.

She still didn't answer.

I got up and walked to her bedside. I fluffed her pillow and pulled back the linens she recently had laid down. I approached her cautiously, and she allowed me to lift her. I placed her on the bed and covered her, tucking her in the best I could. I went to her closet, retrieved a large fur blanket, and spread it over the bed, ensuring it looked nice and would keep her warm. I started to walk away, and she grabbed my thumb. Still, she said not a word. She held it tightly, as if she'd fall into the darkness by herself if she let go.

"You're staying, right?" she whispered.

I knelt at her bedside and cradled her hand in mine. I carefully maneuvered my fingers, trying not to cut her skin. "Yes. I'm staying right here."

"You can sleep in my bed. It's fine."

I didn't argue. I crawled in beside her, laid my head next to her pillow, and closed my eyes. My energy flowed through her hand; I hoped it was enough to protect and secure her without her being clamped in my arms.

I want to hold you.

I felt her heart beat with mine. We were in sync. The bond of bloodletting was settling in. My veins swelled and pulsated as her saliva and blood circulated through them.

A tear formed in my eye and spilled over my cheek.

Forgive me, Uridei. What I have done is forbidden.

What I had done had never been done in the ways of Völfien. This was blasphemy. Völfien did not drink from humans, nor did humans drink from us. It'd have been absurd.

Bloodletting was an act meant for Völfien mates only—lovers.

It was not to be confused with the event of an attack or defense. We völves could bite, eat, or devour the meat and blood of any human, but the scent left. Even if the person died, the memory was entirely at our disposal. Through a bite or scratch, Völfien could track down comrades, family, lovers, and children through our gifted senses. We could even uncover pieces of their pasts, divulge secrets, and retrace steps; everything was at our mortal discretion. It was part of our duties. No in-depth connections, just tools to be utilized when needed. They were attacks, not bonds, as with the assassin on the landing. I hadn't even absorbed his name or his origin. Nothing. I'd just killed him, consumed him, and discarded him.

But when Völfien became lovers, they drank each other's blood, linking their lives together through the act we called bloodletting. Love and sacrifice were the ingredients. Their memories. Their experiences. Everything. Their lives became tied to each other, and the bond never left. It was a taste that left Völfien forever craving their mates, a never-ending need. Ameilja had saved me and sacrificed herself for me, and in the act, she had tasted my blood as she siphoned out the poison with her mouth. I then drank from her and tasted her to survive.

Such a dark reality. Intimately chaotic.

Ameilja was a human; she might never need me as much as I would need her, but our saliva now flowed intravenously; my blood flowed through her as much as hers flowed in me. The bond was set.

Did she know the risk?

Bloodletting was not an act between a human and a völf.

I prayed I would dream sweetly of Ameilja, but I knew I was bound to learn more about her than she would ever have hoped to share. I would know her more intimately than any of her suitors ever would; I would know her as intimately as a lover would. I would know her like our synchronized heartbeats. I would maul in her sadness, exalt in her joy, and fright in her terror as long as she breathed.

I was with her, and she was with me. Forever.

Light of Uridei, let me dream tonight. Forgive me of my transgressions. Oh, Kovuco, what the hell have you done?

CHAPTER THIRTEEN
VERITY

Isarah
Demitori City
Demitori Spaceport, Mach 7, terminal nine
Aoustí 13

KIEFER MET WITH ANTON ROTENFELD AT THE
terminal of the airship *Mach 7*, commonly known as the *Autumn Rooster*.
It was a large vessel with red and gold accents. A large, regal, masculine
rooster was painted on its side.

When Rotenfeld approached, he firmly shook Kiefer's hand. Anton
Rotenfeld was a tall, intimidating man with jagged blond hair and predatory brown eyes. His physique was a sculpted work of muscle and armor. Anton, like his sister, Isabelle, had a partially shaved head, except
his with tribal bands and scarring. The entire family would have been
better off putting their children in the hands of orks or völves. Maybe
then they would have been more endearing adults.

The family all resembled the rough appearance of the person who'd
trained them. There were alleged abuse rumors that circled the training, but no confirmation or denial was ever uttered. Whether there was
merit to the allegations or not, the effect of their training was evident
in combat. Kiefer never saw himself as a pocket of sunshine compared
to the Rotenfelds, but at least no one had trained him to be cruel. Over
time, their work could easily make any person cold, but the Rotenfelds
were born that way.

Behind Rotenfeld was his most trusted wächter, Ólafur Urs, who stood tall in a militaristic fashion. Next to him was Dr. Tobias Frahm. Kiefer recognized Frahm only by his black hair pulled in a low, taut bun, the same style he'd had the last time Kiefer ran into him. Ólafur Urs had a mohawk, a nose ring, and a loud personality. He went by Ólaf, and he was a Fjorthúr'an-born musician who'd left Fjorthúr to hone his talent until he'd realized the same gifted hands that flowed across the strings of an instrument could as skillfully wield a weapon. Being a wild card, Ólaf served his most important purpose in his ability to make rash decisions—the perfect aid in the Commission. Even more perfect for Anton.

"Pleasure to have you with us," Rotenfeld sardonically sneered, assessing Kiefer.

Kiefer nodded, displaying little respect. Rotenfeld's tone suggested he felt anything but pleased by his involvement; he desired more than anything to run the show, this show especially. Rotenfeld wanted Baadar.

The group proceeded onto the bridge that connected the scaffold to the entry of the *Autumn Rooster*. Its massive fans spurred the air with violent whips. Kiefer's long jacket picked up in the wind and lingered around his head until he breached the door.

They entered a private lounge. It was a small study laden with six red-cushioned wingback chairs, a couch with circular pillows, and a large coffee table. On the table sat three full decanters filled with scotch, whiskey, and red wine, each with an elegant seven imprinted on the crystal face.

Kiefer was not a fan of heights. He chose his seat in the farthest chair on the left and wearily looked out at the city. He did his best not to choke nervously as he realized how high the spaceport was.

The airship hung in the clouds by heavy hydrogen-powered balloons. Henrik and four other illustrious elite families had devised this process to create an ever-working station that could keep the flammable hydrogen gas away from the city but still run like a station on the sea, smooth and efficient.

Kiefer managed to study the landscape. The clump of trees centered in the main park between the Brass and Pearl districts had colors flowing to represent each city district, creating a mosaic masterpiece that could only be seen from the clouds. His stomach was in knots, but he continued to disguise his discomfort. His resolute demeanor had to shine if he were to instill confidence when dealing with a murderous völf. The völf and Rotenfeld, of course.

Drinks were poured, and waitresses came out to ensure everyone was seated comfortably. A waitress approached Kiefer for his food order. He shook his head to decline. She asked if he wanted a drink, to which he replied dully, "Coffee." He then unveiled a cigarette from his jacket pocket.

"Um, sir, there's no smoking on the airship. Hydrogen gas is highly flammable."

He ignored her. "Black."

"Excuse me?"

"The coffee. Black. No cream and no sugar."

She walked away, shaking her head.

Kiefer lit his cigarette, stripping away the napkin placed delicately in the glassware on the side table beside him. The empty glass became his makeshift ashtray.

The airship started to pull away from the scaffold to embark towards the coast. Once it was moving, the airship's churning sounds lulled to a light hum. With the windows shut, any passenger could easily have slept soundly on the aircraft.

Kiefer planned to sleep as soon as his coffee arrived and his cigarette was smoked, but Rotenfeld made his way over to Kiefer and sat in the wingback facing him. He glared at Kiefer with his thick, vein-protruding arms crossed tightly. He arched his tight brow with a smirk playing on his lips.

"Something troubling you, Æsir?" Kiefer asked, trying to come off as disinterested in Anton's belittling tactics.

"Pleasantries aside, I need you to understand one thing, Wülkure: Baadar is mine."

Kiefer huffed, biting his lower lip, as he stretched his neck, cracking it on either side. "Yes, I know he's not a favorite relative of yours. But to what extent?" Kiefer made eye contact with Rotenfeld, narrowing his eyes, waiting for his answer.

"None of your concern."

"Well, it is among some of my concerns. How bad do you distaste Baadar?"

"Bitterly."

"*Bitter* as in impairing his walk or *bitter* as in disfiguring his face? Or worse?"

"We'll see once we arrive. I have reviewed reports that are deeply disturbing. There are abominations there no man should ever have to see—results from the Näkk experiments, no doubt—and if he's unleashed them, we're in for a real horror show." He curled in his lips, disgusted. "Releasing those infected pukes upon a squad of wächters and a wülkure will undoubtedly result in execution. I'm sure you know what the loss of Isabelle meant for the Sentry. Wouldn't you like to see the man who stole her from us die at my hands rather than potentially walk in a measly trial?"

"Aha. So that's it. Trial means a fifty-fifty chance he walks away. Resigns and gets to live a life of leisure."

Anton's neck tensed. "As I said, my regards to Kristján are *bitter*. Men like him deserve the undersides of boots. Henrik stands to suffer greatly once the Order intervenes in what is going on. Baadar threatens that greatly; I'll protect our centurion any day over Isabelle's measly speck of a human she'd led into her bed."

"That's Henrik's problem. Henrik's sins will haunt him in their own time—and Baadar's. But I will allow you your taste for revenge. Just allow me the opportunity to clear my duties as the wülkure first. I need answers. I also must ensure the Näkk does not pose any future threat. As should you."

"Wülkure duties allow trial for captured Commission members. A fucking joke!"

"You're sure as hell set on putting Baadar down. Do you think Isabelle will follow him to his little island getaway after what's taken place?"

Anton shrugged. "Not likely. She's missing."

"Again?" Kiefer scoffed. "Ever think she's not the type who wants to be found?"

"She's a mother. She's not likely to vanish while her son is still on the radar."

"Hm. Where is little junior Baadar?"

"Sapphire. Supposedly works with the Blue Coat syndicate."

"Oh, he sure sounds like a delight. Why not manipulate that relationship then? Why do Baadar's sins have to be your bloodlust? If I were you, I wouldn't risk killing him in the Sunspire. Let him go to trial, and partner with your nephew to take him out. Who knows? Isabelle might show up and join you."

Kiefer's coffee arrived. The conversation ceased until the waitress walked away.

"Her son does not quarrel with Baadar. Baadar's the closest thing he has to a father, and Baadar respects the space he needs. Likely, he'll convince his mother to join Baadar and live peacefully so his work with the syndicate can continue without a mother's concern to falter his actions."

"I see your predicament."

There was silence, as if Anton were acknowledging Kiefer's lack of justice toward Kristján. Not that Kiefer cared if Baadar lived or died in the end. Still, with potentially infected orks running loose, a völf, and whatever horrors Anton seemed to think they would find, Rotenfeld might propose Baadar's assassination without his wülkure approval.

"How about a deal, Rotenfeld?"

"I'm listening."

"I know Henrik wants to keep Baadar alive, but if you help me secure the völf, I will make sure you, I, and Baadar are alone in a room. I get what I want from Baadar and the völf first; then I'll let you loose on him."

"Not happening."

"Why?"

"Baadar's fucking smart! He's hacked the Spire and who knows what else. We get in, and we get out."

He means without Baadar. "Just think about it, Anton." Kiefer took a long sip from his coffee after putting the cigarette in the glass beside him. "Loose. I set you loose. One hundred percent. Skin him, eat him, fuck him up—take your pick. As I see it, your brother-in-law will not give up the Spire. He'll make certain the Sunspire remains secured. I think he means it to be his grave. Therefore, you need to work with me to figure out what he's hiding there before you take him out. Can we agree on that?"

Anton's eyes never relaxed from their viper's stare. He clicked his tongue against his teeth, rose from his seat, and walked over to the couch he'd been sitting on prior to their conversation. Kiefer watched him settle into the cushions and then close his eyes to rest.

Kiefer could only presume he was satisfied with his offer. *A simple yes would have been sufficient. It would allow me less suspense about what's ahead of us.*

Part of him wanted Kristján to deserve Anton's wrath, leaving less for his discretion. Part of him didn't care, but whatever horror lay in the Sunspire, his answers lay somewhere in the connection between Kristján and the völf.

☆

Unknown location
Unknown date

Ameilja found herself in a strange trance.

She hovered over a familiar world. A young Kovuco took up a reed and drew in the sand. His slacks were too small for him. His red sweater was a size too large. The sleeves nearly covered his tiny yet intimidating claws. His fur was still bright platinum, a little longer in his cheeks and around his ears, which he hadn't grown into yet. His eyes were more prominent on his head, lacking his sharper adult features.

He couldn't have been a day over ten, or maybe he was younger, she thought.

She watched him observe the other young Völfien playing on the beach. Some human children splashed in the salty waters and chased squawking seagulls. Ameilja noticed he kept a safe distance between himself and the others.

Why is he so shy? Even with his kin?

Ameilja had interacted with a few young völves in Shaar and had read up on them in detail. The Völfien were highly protective of their young until they reached the age of fourteen when they expected them to become young adults. Once fourteen, völves stepped into their defining roles and became productive members of their packs.

Völfien parents also taught their young to be highly in tune with their Medzio and how to control their emotional strength. Völfien tykes were much stronger than they looked. The Commission's blood doses were not ordered till the age of fourteen, so if völf parents failed to implement the teachings, their tykes could react and lash out with deadly results should another small child tease or provoke them. It was in their nature to defend what was right. She questioned if that was why the young Kovuco was so introverted. *Is he nervous? Does he not trust himself?*

The Völfien were not as lenient in the past; they had been known to keep a controlled population and work in familial packs until they broke away with mates. An alpha, or lead völf, within a family would be the one to grant reproduction rights; thus, Kovuco's birth had been a mortal sin. Ameilja had learned from reading his profile that he had been born from his father fornicating with an unknown outsider. Adémaro had broken his vow with the Religious Order and his own Völfien bylaws.

Ameilja watched Kovuco as he flopped over onto his rear, reached into his backpack, pulled out a book, and pretended to be interested in its pages as he intermittently peered over the brim to study his surroundings. The book was way beyond his age level, but early mental development was common for their intelligent race, and he seemed familiar with it as if it were one he was used to reading. It was an epic tale wherein a slave picked up a sword and vanquished a tyrant to free himself and others who fell to the same fate. It contained stories of heroes freeing the oppressed from tyranny. Heroes who possessed weapons of legend and souls filled with fire.

Is this what raised my young Kovuco?

Curious of what other tomes peeked out from his pack, she read the title of a book on consciousness and another on the Fae calendar and folklore. She knew the Völfien strived to drive knowledge into their young. They were open-minded beings.

Ameilja noticed two Völfien with fur as dark as night come into view, standing near the edge of the sand. One of them asked the other, "Do you see him, Sangállo?"

"He should have met us at the steps. Call him, Désoto!"

Their deep voices carried in her trance's atmosphere, moving smoothly like a floating feather.

"Kovuco! Where are you, little völf?" The black völf, Désoto, called in an adolescent voice.

Both of them were fierce and broad-built. Their fur was cut in a classic warrior style. It matched the Völfien culture in Kyottó.

Kovuco shuffled his books into his bag, propped the straps over his shoulders, and walked toward the stairwell.

"There you are! You're supposed to meet us here, Kovuco," said Sangállo jeeringly.

Kovuco didn't answer, even after Sangállo gave a quick tug on his ear. Kovuco followed after and walked proudly between the two older Völfien. They began to speak to one another in their language, discussing content among themselves, while holding matching leather-bound books. Kovuco listened intently; his large, bat-like ears bobbed like the ocean's current while he absorbed their conversation—something, Ameilja observed, he never had grown out of. She smiled at the thought.

The air around Ameilja unexpectedly shifted.

Without a moment to process, she tumbled into another scene. A pebble was kicked forward, creating a tapping sound on the ground. Kovuco turned to the sound but appeared to look right through her at something behind her. Ameilja presumed she was not visible, as she could observe him without being spotted.

The two elder völves stopped and turned to him.

"Kovuco? Come! Let's go!" Sangállo called with an adjusted tone of protection.

Kovuco turned to catch back up with them. He never spoke; he just turned and walked toward the older völves.

A shiver ran down Ameilja's spine as the two elder völves stared right through her; their intense eyes focused until their little Kovuco safely walked between them again.

What is it, Kovuco? What did you see?

She noted that Kovuco had remained a quiet and curious soul, restrained and gentle, even into his adulthood. There had been something unique about him as a young völf, just as there was now.

Ameilja pivoted to see what was behind her. Before she could look, her world faded black.

☆

Fjorthúr
The Sunspire oceanfront
The Autumn Rooster
Aoustí 14

The *Autumn Rooster* closed in on the island, just over the shallows. The group prepared for the drop; the Sunspire lay ahead of them.

It wasn't an ideal landing zone, but they moved forward with Captain Marlya Bayde's authorization. They also hadn't anticipated the brigade of orks raiding the island, granting them no favor.

"Looks like some of the mainland orks have moved right in," Captain Bayde alerted.

"Explains why we didn't hear from the main bunker. Those fucking pests didn't hesitate to sail their asses in as soon as the Spire was shut down," Rotenfeld said, eyeing the orks from the airship window. His tongue swirled around his teeth, picking apart remnants left behind. His expression remained firm.

"Must they meddle in everything?" Kiefer sighed. It only added to his distaste for their race.

The orks gathered in scattered huddles along the shore, eyeing the airship. Their team would not only have to breach the Spire but also have to take out the invasive orks who stood in their way—an unexpected deterrent.

Captain Bayde had previously agreed to lend two of her crew for support, Klein and Toffel, both technical-trained wächters and excellent support for hacking the Spire's mechanisms and technological mainframe. With orks now posing an additional threat, she made a last-minute call to lend two more add-ons for physical fighting support: wächters Yeddi and Dom.

"We'll take those bastards out!" Yeddi assured as he opened the Sentry crate to get the weapons intended for the operation, the standard-issue weaponry with which every Sentry member trained.

The first were three long-range Arslan-18 PSR rifles: one for Kiefer, and the other two for Ólaf and Toffel. Dom packed the explosives as the rest of the crew used the Arslan-4 MG.

Kiefer examined the eighteen-inch barrel of his precision sniper rifle. The models received the name for their barrel length. Arslan rifles had black steel metalwork and wood stocks.

"Load up! The pods are ready!" Rotenfeld called out. "As soon as you exit your pod, get the hell out of the water—and that's an order!" He leaped into the circular cell. "Unless you want to be eaten alive by those prehistoric sea freaks." He warned, chuckling maniacally as he retreated into his pod.

Kiefer, forgetting about the predatory marine creatures below, swallowed through a tight throat. He would have denied it, but the ocean's unknowns terrified him.

Each member slipped into a pod as if resting in a dark coffin. In just a few moments, they would be dropped from the airship in the bullet-like tombs. The interior padding of the pods was intended to protect passengers from the impact, but it could also be dangerous. They had to land on soft surfaces, such as water, avoiding the rocks below, or the passengers could be seriously injured. The material was also pumped with gas to further protect someone from the fall. The same gas was then used to eject the escape door.

Kiefer closed his eyes, positioning himself into the claustrophobic-inducing space. He breathed slowly, with the aid of the breathing tube, and listened to the rotating rack shuffle the pods through the cabin. He could barely hear the hiss of the engines but could at least listen for the clip to release.

Three. Two. One.

The clip sounded, followed by the immediate sinking feeling of being dropped high above the ocean. The gas immediately filled the material in the pod, solidifying him in place.

Seconds passed, and then there was a violent jolt in the buoyant material of the pod. The gases that supplied the buoyancy burst from within the cavity cells, and the doors jettisoned from their place. Before Kiefer jumped out, he spat the breathing tube out, unfastened his belts, and shouldered his rifle, satisfied he had safely landed.

He emerged, and the island winds instantly beat against his face. A male ork was already two meters before him, hustling through the shallow waters toward his pod.

"Shit!" Kiefer yelled.

He aimed and fired as soon as his boots hit the water. It was a split second, but he knew his aim was accurate. The bullet pierced the ork's sternum and exited out of his back, slicing the ocean's surface. However, he didn't anticipate the two orks behind him. He heard the sound of sloshing water just in time to duck, avoiding a swing from one of the bulky humanoid-looking beings.

Orks from the North had a dull skin coloration, a natural teal blue with hints of grayish brown. Their hair was in shades of either black or dark brown. Kiefer's current assailant had brown, and the other had black.

The brown-haired ork swung a machete at his face. Kiefer dodged again, drew Szonja's sword, and sliced its whetted edge along the ork's outer oblique muscle. The ork roared and whipped around, intent on returning a vengeful blow when Kiefer's blade swiftly slashed his throat. He fell dead into the shallows. Kiefer turned to face the black-haired ork, readying his sword, but a bullet unexpectedly pierced the ork's chest.

"Ólaf!" Kiefer yelled, satisfied to see the high-strung wächter.

Ólaf was Rotenfeld's top shooter. Thankfully, he had survived the drop and was already returning fire for the others.

Kiefer pulled out his pistol and fired into the bleeding ork, just enough to ensure his end while his corpse bled out in the water. They could not risk any live stragglers. He then wiped the blood from Szonja's sword and gave the blade a quick kiss before sheathing it. "Beautiful weapon. Thanks, Szonja," he whispered.

Kiefer turned and assessed the landscape. More orks lingered close by, standing on the rocks and sandy dunes, watching him and the crew. The island's heat index was higher than a typical day in the north. The sun blazed, causing sweat to pour down his temples despite the coastal winds sweeping against his face.

Kiefer noted that the other pods had landed accordingly, except two: Frahm's and Klein's.

Frahm's pod had landed between rocks, causing it to burst, sending his body reeling to the ground. Unfortunately, Klein's pod had landed in the deeper waters. It breached a sinkhole inhabited by a nest of violent oceanic creatures and submerged fully into the virulent water. He began to soak as the water uncontrollably injected into the crevices of his pod. Without reaching for his weapons, he released the lock as the pod struggled to fight the waves and abuse of the water. The pressurized doors finally released, and he swam out, surfacing for air.

He fought ferociously as the mass of insect-like fish chewed with prejudice at Klein's unarmored, more vulnerable areas. He screamed in agony as the creatures of the dark sea pulled at his flesh. Unlike basic predatory fish, these sea creatures were intelligent and lethal, with the bloodlust of sharks, fueled by the temper of a piranha.

Once Klein officially breached the shallows, he managed to crawl to shore and out of reach of the sea assailants. He vomited violently, trying to brace his injuries. Blood poured from his wounds. Despite his trauma, he didn't start screaming again, until he felt a pair of hands clutch his face; they happened to belong to a broadly built ork female.

"Fuck!" Kiefer hissed, shouldering his weapon.

"Ólaf! Now!" Rotenfeld's bellowing voice filled the distance air as he witnessed Klein's attack.

The female ork headbutted Klein's face and tore off his ear with her barbaric strength. She delivered a punch so intense it dislocated his jaw. Klein tried to pry away from her enraged attack, but his fish wounds consumed most of his strength. Ólaf's shot pierced the air, taking a chunk of the ork's shoulder. She screamed in rage as two other ork females joined her, cheering in uproarious applause, until suddenly, a stick grenade landed next to the fervor. In mere seconds, it exploded, and all the bodies, including Klein's, were mutilated in the blast.

The wielder of the explosive was their new counterpart, Dom. He ran past the blackened massacre and turned his interest to Frahm.

"The doctor is down! Let's move!" Dom screamed.

Orks began to crowd around Frahm. He sluggishly rose from the ground and shouldered his rifle. He locked a magazine into the weapon when he noticed Ólaf's and Toffel's long-range rifles eliminating the nearing ork raiders from a short fifty yards west. They took them all out, freeing Frahm from the imminent attack.

"Move! Let's go!" Rotenfeld barked, his voice breaking through the force.

The crew, including Frahm, gathered together behind a cluster of boulders near the bunker, except for Ólaf, who was still a good twenty yards away covering fire from the shoreline.

Rotenfeld pointed to Kiefer. "I need you to protect Toffel. We lost Klein. If we lose Toffel, there's no chance of hacking the Spire. I'll take Frahm, Yeddi, and Dom to the next set of rocks. You keep us—"

"No." Kiefer interrupted. "You need a sharpshooter to take out the ork snipers in the bunker. That's me. Have Dom cover Toffel. Once I am close, I can cover you while you charge the bunker. Who knows how many orks are in there? Plus, there could be hostages, knowing how those bastards work."

Rotenfeld didn't object; he whipped around and ran toward the bunker. Kiefer and the others followed after him through the shallows while Ólaf continued to cover the shoreline. Both Rotenfeld and Frahm opened fire on the shores while they moved in; a spray of lead mowed down an ork who neglected to take cover.

They congregated behind another cluster of rocks, and Kiefer backed against a craggy boulder. Through strained eyes, he scanned the windows of the bunker. Rotenfeld's earlier observation was correct: the orks had completely taken over, which confirmed why communication had been lost.

The aged building contained an observatory at the core. Kiefer focused his attention there, where more obvious ork snipers lingered. He aimed, and then dropped two orks in the observatory and another in the upper left window. "All clear! Go!" he shouted, and the others charged.

Kiefer double-checked his surroundings before abandoning the rocks and then took off through the sand. Yeddi, Dom, Toffel, and Frahm circled the entire building from the outside, while Rotenfeld forcefully breached; he drew his sword as he entered, screaming profanities to make his presence known.

Kiefer swiftly followed, but Rotenfeld wasted no time; he had sliced through two ork females by the time Kiefer entered the bunker. One of the ork females was pinned to the wall with Rotenfeld's sword. She was unarmed, begging for her life. Her eyes were fear stricken, with tears streaking down her cheeks. The other was lying dead in a pool of her own blood. Both female orks were scantily clad; one was topless. It appeared they were there to add to the disarray, or to entertain the male orks that had taken over the bunker.

In another room, an ork's scream pierced the air, and then a muffled crash to the floor. Kiefer turned, scanning the space. The bunker had been completely ransacked. Bullet holes and burn marks were littered throughout the walls, floors, and furniture. The smell was putrid.

"Disgusting!" he heaved as he continued walking through the bunker's main entry and entered the master bedroom. A male ork, barely dressed, lay on the floor with his throat gashed. He was holding his throat, trying to stop the bleeding, choking on his blood. On the bed were two naked ork females; one was still alive. She breathed slowly, whimpering for help.

"Rotenfeld swept through you quick, eh?" Kiefer scoffed. *They won't have long.*

He then entered another bedroom. Drug paraphernalia, food scraps, bullet casings, lingerie, and other tattered clothing were scattered throughout the space. Kiefer's gaze abruptly locked on the other side of the bed, where a human woman lay. She was naked, and evidence of sexual assault was visible. Kiefer knelt down and checked her pulse, confirming she was deceased. Her wrists were bruised and raw from the cord that bound her hands. He grimaced; he couldn't help but think of Rae. This woman couldn't have been any older than she was, perhaps younger. It roiled a massive wave of anger through his core. He rose back up and snapped his gaze from the sight of the young woman. With two rushed strides, he breached the bathroom, where two more humans were dead. Both were men. One was in the tub filled with blood-stained water. The other, hog-tied, showed severe signs of torture and assault.

A female ork stood in the corner. She shrieked, "Please! Please don't kill me!"

Kiefer aimed the sniper rifle towards her. "Quiet!" he gutturally screamed; saliva sprayed from his mouth in response to the force on his throat. Flashes of Rae's innocent face smashed into his mental realm.

Rae...

He could not show mercy. The state of the human woman, raped and tortured on the ground, disgusted him. Rotenfeld certainly wasn't showing any restraint; why should he?

Kiefer caught the ork female looking toward the countertop, where a large knife sat beside a moldy sink.

Kiefer fired the PSR, and the bullet split through her stomach. The blast smashed the tile wall, sending smoky ceramic fragments flying. The female ork slid down the wall leaving a trail of her own blood.

Frahm suddenly entered the room and gasped at the terror around him.

"Why are you so fucking shocked?" Kiefer snapped. "Isn't seeing mutilated bodies a norm for you?"

Frahm swallowed, pulling his lips tight, keeping silent.

Kiefer wiped splatters of ork blood away from his forehead and shook his head. He pulled the strap from the PSR over his shoulder. "Are we secured?"

Frahm nodded. "Yes. We're secured."

Kiefer grabbed the knife off the counter and exited the bathroom. He leaned down by the naked woman. He cut her loose, allowing her hands to rest at her sides. "Rest in peace," he whispered. He then assessed a table set up in the corner of the room. Inside a bloody bowl were a human man's fingers, an ear, and what could only have been his testicles. Kiefer held back vomit, biting his bottom lip, and turned back to Frahm. "Toffel?"

"Alive."

"Get him started on hacking the Spire—now! We need to get off this fucking rock before I find more orks."

Kiefer stalked back through the master bedroom, where the male ork had given up on his gushing throat, subtly moaning. Kiefer eyed him, processing the scene. He then lifted his leg and covered the ork's eyes with the sole of his boot. Slowly, and with all his body weight, he smashed the ork's skull into the floor. His rage was satisfied by the elongated sound of the crunch. As he wiped the bottom of his boot against the floor, he looked over at the last living female ork; she leaned near the edge of the bed, clutching the metal frame, hoping to keep herself from falling.

Kiefer raised his PSR and aimed it at her head. Knowing her complicity, she recognized her fate and invited it; it was better than bleeding slowly. When Kiefer saw the peace in her eyes, he returned the PSR to his shoulder, denying her a chance at a quick death.

"Oh no, no, no," he clicked his tongue.

Several minutes passed; he fetched a cigarette from his jacket while he waited. Through the puffs of smoke and low, intermittent humming, he gave her no closure in his thought of her. No glare of hatred, no re-mission—nothing. He just watched her drain slowly and painfully until the inevitability of death released her from her suffering.

☆

Shaar
Tsunetomo
House Frost, West Wing
Aoustí 14

Ameilja stirred, turned, and woke from her trance, realizing it was only a vivid dream.

She turned back, and the young Kovuco she had seen in her sleep was back to his twenty-two-year-old self, with his adult chin sunken into the mattress. She wondered how he managed to sleep. She hoped he'd still be inebriated from her blood, which had successfully repaired the damage from the vilkanás.

She took that restful moment to study her Protectorate.

"Kovuco?" she whispered. He didn't stir.

She knew the vilkanás was a wrecking ball of terror for his kind. No one had yet tested the lasting effects of vilkanás on particular subjects, but Kovuco seemed to have a high tolerance for it, or he seemed to be able to resist the immediate reaction to it—death.

She calculated the timeframe of the shooting; she'd had enough time to cover her tracks and replenish him, while most völves were known to die within minutes of the poisoning.

Interesting.

Flashbacks of his canid, desperate jaw clasping around her naked flesh flashed through her mental realm like a fearsome dream. Tears pooled in her eyes. There was nothing she could do now to correct what had been done.

She grabbed his arms and coaxed his sleepy body onto the center of her bed. His legs did most of the work as he sluggishly buried his face into her silky sheets. Unintentionally, she had allowed him to overtake any potential space left, so she decided to get up. She needed time to ensure the room was void of evidence of last night's events.

A faint shiver instantly swept over her form as she walked to her closet. The tile ground nipped at her feet while the bite marks pulsated between her thighs, reminding her that she needed to heal. She carefully dressed for the day; her primary handmaiden had already planned a week's worth of outfits, but Ameilja added a comforting, wool sweater. The blood loss left her cold and weak.

Anxious thoughts pummeled her mind again; she recalled in the Pjauti text that the first twenty hours were the most vital; it was the time recommended for a völf to recover from a wound of this magnitude. It also dawned on her that Kovuco might need two to four ounces of blood every four hours that day. *Is that even possible for me?* She calculated further. *With an injury such as the one inflicted last night, to at least maintain his health, maybe just three to four ounces will get him through six hours as his body continues to heal. That should be enough. Is that realistic?*

"Shit! Think Ameilja—think!" She sighed aloud, exhausted. She knew it might be a fight to get him to drink from her again. Also, how would she manage that much blood? In her current state, she remained dizzy and nauseated from the previous night.

Ameilja closed the door to her washroom and inspected her wound, rebandaged it, and tried to conceal it more inconspicuously. Once done, she walked back into her bedroom to immediately be caught off guard by her primary handmaiden, Jayna, standing in her doorway.

Ameilja froze. The action of unlocking her chamber door a final time to peek at her surroundings smacked her memory. She had forgotten to lock it afterward.

Shit.

Jayna, old enough to be her mother, stood straight and tall with her hands folded before her. Her long, thick brown hair was in a tight bun, and she wore the everyday yellow dress with the handmaiden-designed flower-embroidered corset. Her eyes were laser-focused on Ameilja. She upheld her usual serious expression on her face.

Ameilja tried to repel her anxiety and make her response natural and relaxed. She was hopeful that Jayna didn't catch on to her distress, but if she did, Ameilja intended to play it off.

Sure, a völf is lying unconscious in my bed. Nothing strange here.

Ameilja then remembered her invitation last night as a manipulation tactic to convince Jayna to leave her be.

"Tea?" Ameilja casually asked.

Jayna sternly sighed. Her hands remained folded as her eyes shifted from Kovuco sleeping in the bed to the pile of bloody towels in a bag next to the closet door. Her gaze returned to Ameilja, and she collected her thoughts. "No," she replied.

"No?" Ameilja asked, swallowing nervously.

"Red meat," Jayna blurted out.

"Excuse me?"

"With leafy greens and dried apricots and peaches. The high bio-availability of iron from red meat makes it the best source for rebuilding red blood cells—hemoglobin will increase from the greens and iron from the dried fruits. We'll skip tea. Maybe some coconut water or orange juice. I insist, my lady."

Ameilja nearly fainted. "Uh, yes. But—"

"No coffee. It would be best if you reenergized yourself without the acidic drink. I will fetch food for you both right away, my lady." She bowed and then left.

Ameilja's chest tightened. *She knows.*

Ameilja tried to collect herself. Her body lightly trembled as she rushed out to her courtyard and decided to prepare the low-setting table for breakfast. She tried to do so quickly, keeping an eye out for other handmaidens to ensure they didn't enter her chamber. She set out her intricately designed pillows to form chair-like structures for three guests. She presumed it would just be the three of them until she saw Ash striding into her wing. One look at his grim face told her he knew what was happening.

Shit, shit, shit!

Without knocking, he breached her chamber. "Ameilja," he uneasily whispered as soon as he reached her.

She shot him a flustered look as he handed her some clothing.

"For Kovuco?" she asked as she lifted the shirt and saw he had brought an entire outfit: shirt, pants, undergarments, and belt. "Do you think I kept him here naked?" she snipped.

Ash shook his head and cleared his throat. "Did he come here na-ked?" He arched his brow. "This looks rather, um—"

"No! No—I mean— Ash, damn it! I'm just frustrated! I didn't want everyone involved—it was an accident, that's it—just an accident. I didn't even know he was here last night!"

Ameilja continued to prep the table for breakfast as she stammered; her nerves wreaked havoc on her mind. Her hands continued to tremble noticeably.

"I understand, but you shot him with a vilkanás-treated bullet? How did that even happen?"

"Who told you that?" Ameilja hissed, pausing to look at him. He looked just as confused and exhausted as she.

"Jayna. You know that vilkanás has a very distinct smell. And Jayna knows that smell."

Ameilja sighed. "Yes. I did shoot him with one. I hate those bul-lets, and since I sent my völves away for the night, I felt safe shooting them over the regular rounds. I wanted to be rid of them; it was just an accident—"

"An accident that almost got you both killed!" Ash's raspy voice rose in concern. "You're lucky he didn't die on the spot. He must have good genes that no doubt kept him alive. But you're lucky to be alive too, Ameilja; thank Uridei he had the sense to stop drinking from you! You do realize they typically drink to death, right? In his case, he needed your human blood to survive. His instincts could've sucked you down like a bottle of good scotch."

"Luckily, that's not in his nature."

Ash scoffed. "Oh, it's in his nature, Ameilja. Did you see him suck down that wine at your coronation? Völves are like dwarves for the drink, and Kovuco has Dancer training for taste."

Ameilja shook her head to dismiss his words. She turned to the table. "Then I guess we're just left with bloodletting then …"

Ash froze. "Excuse me?" He swallowed. "W-what did you just say?"

Ameilja ignored his question. "Are you joining us for breakfast?"

"Ameilja," he pushed, voice dipping, "what did you just say?"

"Breakfast? Yes or no?"

Ash's demeanor tensed.

"Yes or no, Ash? I demand an answer!" Ameilja's voice heightened.

He uncomfortably shifted where he stood, hesitating to answer her. The rolling waves crashed loudly beyond the courtyard, adding to the ominous moment.

"Sure ... for a bit. I need to return to your other völves." He finally answered, suppressing his questioning. "Jayna and I plan to ensure this whole incident doesn't become a problem. Fortunately for you, we can take advantage of your sister's little stunt in all this."

"What do you mean?" she asked, giving Ash her full attention.

Ash nodded. "We need to plan a trip. With your sister still missing and that defiant little leap of tearing down locks for your Völfien and such, we could play the 'Daddy, I need a vacation' card to get you out of here for a bit."

"Where will I go?"

"To Haruka's."

"Haruka? How is Rúnar any better than here?"

"You'll see. With Haruka being a ward to Jakob, her inheritance allows her to live a pretty normal life beyond the Commission's grasp."

"She's a dear friend, Ash, I know, but—"

"Haruka has a home off the coast. It used to belong to her parents. You'll be going there. It's safe and secluded. Besides, Jakob has a tight hold over Rúnar; your father will appreciate his close proximity to you."

Ameilja paused to process, wanting nothing more than to roll her eyes. *Of course he will.* "Okay. Fine. Fill me in; I need to know the plan."

"Of course, my lady."

She glared at him. As always, she corrected him and then motioned for him to sit next to her to discuss the imminent future.

TRANSCENDENCE

Shaar
Tsunetomo
West Wing, Ameilja's chamber
Aoustí 14

I WOKE UP IN AMEILJA'S BED. ALONE.

Her room smelled sanitized and clean, lacking evidence of any struggle from the night before. The sting of blood no longer lingered in my senses.

I struggled to find my footing and finally stood up, stretching slowly. My muscles protested due to the hypertensive state they had experienced just hours ago. Muffled voices drifted in from the courtyard. I followed the voices, cautiously pushed one of the curtained doors open, and immediately saw Ameilja, with Jayna sitting beside her.

"Kovuco," Ameilja subtly gasped as she rose to her feet.

I locked eyes with Ameilja briefly and then stared at my feet, sighing despairingly.

Jayna looked disgruntled and moved quickly to my side. I didn't turn my gaze. My eyes narrowed, and I locked my jaw tightly to avoid vocal, protective growling as she moved close.

"Kovuco?" Jayna asked cautiously.

My head remained lowered. I bowed in frustration, even if it was a shame that Ameilja and I shared.

Jayna reached for my chin with her hand, undoubtedly feeling the rumble of my nervous growling. With no fear, she lifted my face to hers.

"Let me see you," she insisted.

My eyes held disenchanted embarrassment, but I hoped she mistook it for exhaustion.

"There are those blue eyes," she said. "There is no need to fear me. Come on. We're gonna talk. You can trust me."

I nodded, and she guided me to the table. I saw the clothes neatly folded and quickly snatched up the shirt and slipped it on over my head. We were then seated in unison. Jayna must have thought low of me for parading shirtless in my lady's chambers.

I studied her features. This woman was made of stone; her expression never changed, and I often wondered if Ameilja feared her, as she never corrected her when she called her Lady Ameilja. Tam had heard rumors that she had a distraught past that had formed her into a formidable force. Her scarred hands displayed the wear and tear of her life's experiences.

I personally never interacted with Jayna, respectfully keeping my distance. I could never tell if she genuinely liked Ameilja's Court of Völfien.

I looked at the plate before me. A snap pea and spinach salad next to a rare cut of fillet stared up at me; the scent was a specter coaxing me to consume it with fury. My silverware sat next to a bowl of dried peaches and apricots and two drinking glasses, one filled with coconut water and the other with orange juice. Not to mention a vial of blood. It was larger than usual, and the scent was more appetizing than our typical morning dose.

"Kovuco," Jayna said sternly.

My eyes shifted to her.

"As you may know, my name is Jayna. I am Ameilja's head handmaiden. I know you have seen me from time to time."

I nodded. "I know you, miss."

"You are aware that the wülkure, such as Ash, use techniques derived from the Book of Pjauti, yes? Are you familiar with this book?"

"I am. Yes," I said, nodding to affirm my attention.

"Wülkure are the sole enforcement of the Fae. In Ash's case, you, a Völfien. Here in House Frost, their role is necessary in case something gets out of hand. Your actions last night were considered out of hand.

Majorly." She drew her lips into a thin line before continuing, locking her stern gaze with mine. "Kovuco, you have consumed live blood from a human. Not just any human, but Lady Ameilja, a prominent political figure in the Commission's survival. Thus, here in Shaar, you would have been executed last night."

I know. I tensed at the thought.

"Before you, I have made you a meal. I was trained to prepare this meal should I ever need to protect a Völfien from something like this."

"I am forbidden to eat this meat," I interjected, pointing at the plate.

Jayna acknowledged that but pressed on with a determined tone. "As was *your* act committed last night in the lady's quarters!"

My jaw clenched.

"Now, listen to me, Kovuco; your act has created a complicated cycle, which I will explain. Do I have your attention?" Her glare intensified, searching my face for the answer she expected.

"Yes."

"It was I who dissuaded the guards from entering Ameilja's wing last night, but I knew something amiss had occurred. I also heard the whole thing from outside Ameilja's door. You must understand that I will be sent to De'licyymbol for trial if they discover this has happened." She paused before continuing, taking a moment to think about her next words. "When I was young, Kovuco, I was abducted and sold into sex slavery. I was raped and tortured for three years until a wülkure liberated me from the man who'd sailed me here to Shaar. That wülkure was Ash."

My heart rate increased. I thought of old Ash—that smirking, stubbled face—and I couldn't imagine him fighting in struggles beyond his tumbler of bourbon.

"He brought me here and instituted me to the Commission's service. He has also taught me the ways of Pjauti. It is illegal for him to share this knowledge with a mere handmaiden, but he knew that teaching me would protect you and your packmates within these walls. Kovuco, because he did this, he will also face trial in De'licyymbol and face imprisonment ... or even execution—"

"Execution?" I turned to Ameilja and then back to Jayna. "How are you both to face execution? This is *my* sin, not yours."

Jayna caught her breath as if concealing her frustration with being interrupted. "This place, the Frost estate, is our sanctuary." She closed her eyes. The movement beneath her eyelids told me she was reliving memories, details, and events of her past that were difficult. Things I believed weren't sins but acts committed for the sake of others. The consequences likely overwhelmingly justified the means.

She opened her eyes. "This is what we must do, and if we don't"— she took another deep breath—"Ameilja could be sent to De'licyymbol, to the Temple of Songs, where she would likely never see her father again. Possibly even be excommunicated. Here's where it gets worse: you White Throats would need to disband. Tam would likely return to his family. Nav'i does not have kin, so he and Dancer would likely return to Rúnar and be at Malkovich's disposal to be placed in new protectorate positions, or whatever our centurion sees fit." She solemnly shook her head. "Don't you see, Kovuco? A lot rests on this secret, so we must act quickly, and you will do whatever is asked, or you will place all of us at risk!"

I couldn't bear the thought of those events happening. The idea of never seeing Ameilja again was even worse. It all weighed heavily upon me.

I bowed low. "I will eat the food. I understand. Thank you for doing all of this."

Jayna bowed. "Ash will be making arrangements for Tam, Dancer, and Nav'i to leave for Rúnar temporarily to aid Haruka. We have arranged for Ameilja to stay at Haruka's estate until things blow over with the investigation into Tanja. You are assigned to guard Ameilja on her trip to Rúnar, while the rest of the White Throats will secure other dwellings. I will act as Ameilja's decoy in case Tanja attempts to return here. This is a handmaiden credal agreement. Ash will be present, so I do not fear death." She got up from the table. "But time is of the essence, I need to leave. I have to begin preparations. Ash will be here any moment; he's working to arrange for us to get the right amount of blood to get you through the next twenty-four hours. Ash has connections to get exactly what you need and will have similar benefits to live blood. You've healed nicely, Kovuco; this new blood should do you just fine—"

"He can drink from me!" Ameilja abruptly spoke.

We snapped our attention to her.

Jayna dipped her gaze. "Lady Ameilja—"

"No! I insist. This is my fault. We will use my blood and *my* blood only—no one else's. However much is needed, ensure that Kovuco takes the right amount."

"Lady Ameilja, allow me to talk with Ash. We'll find blood that—"

"No! It *has* to be mine."

I shifted my attention to Jayna. She inhaled sharply, restraining herself from losing her patience with her lady.

"Lady Ameilja, forgive me, but that is absurd. I can—"

"Jayna—"

"My Lady, no—"

"We've bloodlet, Jayna!"

The atmosphere shifted, along with Ameilja's features.

"Kovuco and I ... w-we are bonded."

My entire body lulled into the sounds of our synced heartbeats.

She knew. She knew what we'd done.

"What?" The word slipped like a slow, dreadful whisper between Jayna's curled lips. Her face flushed. "H—how?" She turned away from us and placed her fingers along her forehead, processing. "Uridei be with us," I heard her mumble under her breath.

She whipped toward us again and focused on me, furrowing her brow. I took a step back from the intensity of her stare.

"Did you do anything to violate Lady Ameilja?" She snarled, pointing a finger in my face.

I swallowed sharply, shaking my head.

"No such thing happened!" Ameilja cut in, angry at Jayna's accusation. "I saved him! He would have died had I not taken these steps! I *chose* to allow him to drink from me, and in the process, I had to remove some of the poison, including the bullet."

"That explains the gagging and coughing I heard," Jayna whispered aloud. "You consumed his blood ..."

"Yes, Jayna. That's all it was. I knew what I was doing, I knew the risk, and it happened. There's no going back!" Ameilja turned toward me, her soft green eyes locked with mine. "We're bonded—till death do us part."

Ameilja ...

We all fell silent. The air felt thick in my lungs.

"And as your lady," Ameilja turned back to Jayna, using her authority, "I am forbidding you to speak another word of it."

Jayna reluctantly nodded. "My lady, before I vow silence, I must know this: How much?"

"How much?" Ameilja furrowed her brow.

Jayna nodded again. "Yes." She eyed me. "How much blood, approximately, was consumed?"

I grew anxious. Last night, in those moments, my cognitive control had been far from reach; I'd had to break through the temptation and convince myself to stop, taking into account what was happening. Jayna seemed to sense my frustration, hopefully understanding I was no scientist or mathematician to plainly state the exact amount I lustfully had slurped from Ameilja's wounds.

"How many shot glasses?"

I at first thought the suggestion was ridiculous, but I remembered our shot glasses, the ones we filled with rice liquor to chase the two ounces of blood.

"Maybe four," I answered.

Jayna gasped loudly. "That glass is three ounces! Which means you consumed almost a whole pint—this means you can only safely do four more ounces to ensure the vilkanás is completely distilled from your blood."

"I understand."

Jayna shook her head disapprovingly. "Because of the unique method in which you committed this healing, we need to look at the logistics of this. Lady Ameilja is human, and you, Kovuco, are a völf. Your bloodletting must continue in order to stabilize your bonded strengths. Kovuco, I fear that you will not drink appropriately from our lady while in Rúnar. There will be no one to monitor you."

Jayna's coloration turned pale. While she upheld a stern nature, her worry for her lady crept through the protective, emotionless walls she'd built around herself.

"I will consult with Ash on this." Jayna cleared her throat and looked up at me again. "Ash and I will ensure you drink the right amount from Lady Ameilja one final time so that you may return to your tower. After, we will arrange your departure to Rúnar." She turned her weary gaze to Ameilja. "I must caution you, Lady Ameilja. What you both are committing is very dangerous. After this blood draw, you are going to be very weak. If you are not careful, you could—"she paused—"die."

"No!" I said forcefully. It slipped.

Jayna and Ameilja snapped their attention to me, caught off guard by the guttural force in my voice.

"I won't let that happen. I won't lose you." I shifted my eyes to Ameilja as I said it.

Her features softened as she processed what I'd said.

"Good. You understand then," Jayna stated.

"Very well. I understand too," Ameilja said, holding her chin high. The dark circles under her eyes gave away the sacrifice she had committed. "I'll drink lots of water, have lots of chicken broth, and get restful naps. We have to make sure Kovuco doesn't expire, and we'll work out the future once we are in Rúnar."

"Uridei be with you if your father ever finds out," Jayna added.

"And he won't," Ameilja answered matter of fact. Her features betrayed her words, giving away the worry shading her eyes.

I took the opportunity to shift the conversation. "Who will take our place? Won't Tanja become suspicious when there are no more White Throats here in the West Wing?"

"Potentially. With some of the transfers we are making, we hope Tanja will assume we have heightened security, rather than Lady Ameilja keeping her Court of Völfien. She will not challenge Malkovich—that we are sure of. Or we will see another attack coming before any attempt is made. I've heard many rumors about the power of his fleet."

"That could lead to war," I stated.

Jayna didn't reply. A moment passed, and she cleared her throat. "I will leave you to your breakfast. Every bite, Kovuco. Ash and I will be back shortly, so you can drink. With your permission, Lady Ameilja, I'd like to share the bloodletting details with Ash."

"Yes, you may." Ameilja nodded. "I'm certain from our previous conversation he knows."

Jayna didn't hesitate to depart. She walked to the end of the wing and disappeared, along with her stringent presence.

I released a heavy, pent up sigh. *I cannot believe I didn't even receive a smack for—*

Suddenly, Ameilja backhanded me across the nose. Wide-eyed in terror, I looked at her. Her eyes were filled with tears.

"Do you know how devastated I would have been if you had died last night? What the hell were you thinking, Kovuco?"

"I wanted to see you, and I didn't want to scare you. I—"

"Failed on that one! You scared me, and you got shot!"

"I know. It was the gun. I wasn't sure why you had it—"

"What danger was I in with a gun present, Kovuco? *You* are a protectorate; seeing guns should be normal for you!"

"I don't know. I just—for a moment, I thought …"

Ameilja leaned in close and placed a hand on my knee. With a gentler tone, she spoke again, "You thought what exactly?"

I stared back into her curious eyes and lost my train of thought.

"What was going on in your head when you growled in my last session with Master Oboro? What was going on in your mind after you dismantled that assassin at the coronation? Kovuco, I could name a dozen more times this year alone when you lost your grip on reality, saw a danger that was not there, and took it too far."

I inhaled. "I agree. I've been off."

"Off? You got shot yesterday. Do you think it's time to get back on?"

I couldn't say it aloud, but I thought, *I couldn't live without you in this world, Ameilja. I will be your sword if anyone or anything comes between you and your existence. Therefore, I don't think I can ever control this.*

Unexpectedly, she leaned in fully and wrapped her arms around my torso. I held my arms out, unsure if I should receive her embrace.

"I am just so happy you're alive; that's all that matters. I don't know what I would have done if you had died. I—I love you, Kovuco!"

There it is again, that little phrase I second-guess. The phrase I can't wrap my head around.

I tenderly clutched her shoulders and coaxed her away from me, back to her seat. "I'm here, Ameilja. I'm alive, okay."

She nodded, reached for a napkin, and began drying her tears. "I care for you, all of my White Throats, so much."

I know you do. I changed the topic. "I, uh, should eat, yes?"

She nodded. "Yes, you need to. I'm sorry, please eat."

I looked at the meat. *Just stuff it down your throat as quickly as possible. Then it will be over, and you can—*

Ameilja sensed my urgency. She snatched the fork and knife, cut a small piece of the fillet, and raised it to my mouth. I nodded, playing it off as confidently as I could. I gently bit the meat and pulled it from the fork. At first, I gave Ameilja a curious, awkward look, until the taste of the meat melted in my mouth, and I relaxed into a deep nostalgia.

"Good?" she asked.

"It's perfect. It is the best thing I have ever tasted." *Besides your blood.*

She smiled and cut another piece.

I stopped her, placing my palm over her hand. "I'll do it."

I gave her a reassuring smile, took up the silverware, and began slicing. To show I meant what I said, I slowly cut a much larger piece than she had initially cut. Next, I stabbed a few greens with the fork to accompany the fillet.

She watched me as I indulged. I couldn't tell if she felt wonderment at my existence or if something was resting on her.

"Kovuco?"

"Hm?"

"Can I ask you something?"

I continued to eat my food. "Mhmm."

"Who's Désoto? And Sangállo?"

I stopped, set down my silverware, and took a long gulp of the orange juice. I set down the glass and relaxed my shoulders. "Where'd you hear those names?"

"I saw them. I saw you. You were little. You had these baggy clothes. You were playing on the beach, and they walked with you. I dreamed this, Kovuco. I am unsure if it was an effect of the bloodletting or a unique vision, but it was as if I stepped into your memories."

I nodded. "What else did you see?" I was curious to know just how much she had seen.

"Your red sweater. The elder völves were dark. Very dark-furred."

"What color were their eyes?"

"Sangállo's were nearly red; Désoto's were gold. Bright gold."

I subtly smiled. "I think your dream was spot-on, Ameilja. Perhaps you did, as you said, step into my memories. I've heard that when blood-letting sets in, we absorb each other's memories, emotions, sensations—you name it." I paused and looked at her. "I also dreamed of you. You were a little girl in Songs. I saw you dropping a basket of apples onto the steps. You were frustrated when Sister Nance came to help you."

Tears filled her eyes again. "You saw Sister Nance?"

I nodded. "She was your mentor within the Temple of Songs, right?"

"Yes." She quickly dried her tears. "She was like a mother to me. You know my mother died during childbirth, so Sister Nance was the one who taught me how to be a young girl. She taught me to sew, cook, and pray and even how to shoot the bow. She cherished my bold abilities. Sister Nance was even by my side when I experienced my first vision. Oh, Kovuco, she was everything to me. I miss her!"

"Well, I am sure you can now see some of my memories. But Désoto and Sangállo are my elder brothers. You've probably heard that my father was a great warrior during the war. His wife, Rhúlain, was too. She was killed, and he fell into a deep depression, partly due to losing the bond with his mate. Losing a bond slows you down as your body recovers from the disconnect. Bloodletting is not taken lightly within my race."

Ameilja shifted slightly after I shared those words.

"After the war, he took a lover. My unknown mother gave me up, and I was delivered to him at the Temple of Spears in Demitori. He wasn't around me much. My elder brothers practically raised me until my trial at eighteen. Then I met you and became a White Throat."

"I had no idea you had brothers. You were raised primarily by male figures, your father and brothers. You didn't have a mother?"

I shook my head. "No. No, mother."

"Just like I didn't have a mother. We both have dutiful fathers. We are both products of the Great War." Concern filled her words. "I hope that doesn't bother you."

"Not at all," I said. "It's a bit enlightening to know our paths are so similar. Kinda gives me hope that it'll be okay."

"Do you miss them?"

I nodded. "Yes." I couldn't help but smile at her innocent attempts to learn from me, not just my written information. "My father's first wife was from Shaar, so Désoto and Sangállo are both black-furred. What else did you pick up from them?"

"Désoto must be protective. Sangállo is strict."

I nodded again; my smile was becoming more prominent the more we talked, and the more she revealed about my family through the shared memory. "Yes. Désoto tutored me for most of my childhood. He taught me to read and write. Survival skills. How to heal my wounds. How to start fires. Sangállo taught me the tonfa sword. I have him to thank for my ambidexterity. He taught me to shoot a bow, crack a whip, and toss a spear. They both taught me everything."

There was a silence, and solemnity returned. I realized I only said those things aloud because I knew she might see them one day. I knew she would discover them without my permission. *Better I tell the truth than lie, even if the truth is about the darker secrets I hold.*

She grabbed my thumb and squeezed it. "It's okay. Your secrets are safe with me."

I smiled at her. She slowly tucked a piece of her hair behind her ear. Her gentle smile lit up her tired, wavering complexion. Her breathing was slow, and her demeanor was weak.

"Ameilja?"

"Yes?"

"Why did you insist on letting me drink from you? Why did you take the risk?"

She inhaled slowly and dropped her gaze to the floor. "I didn't want to lose you. Plus, it was my fault you were shot, whether you snuck up on me or not."

I could tell she was frustrated. She felt I was the victim, but it was my poor choices that had led me to be shot. I honestly hoped it derailed her from digging deeper into why I earnestly made risky choices for her. It would hopefully keep her off the trail of my true feelings.

I took a moment to absorb her words, understand them, and interpret them. She truly wanted the best for me, even if it meant her life. *This experience may break me. It may make me stronger. Time will tell.*

"Kovuco?"

"Hm?"

"Do our actions dishonor you?"

"Dishonor me? I get to live because of your decision, Ameilja."

"I know, but I can't help but feel I have taken your chance to synchronize with someone willingly."

You have no idea, Ameilja. No idea.

"As protectorates of the Order, you all are virgins, chaste, and committed to Uridei. I feel this took away an opportunity for you to connect with someone, intimately love someone, and be bonded to someone deserving, especially since you'll always crave and need my blood. I feel I have violated you, Kovuco." Her eyes sorrowfully widened.

She thought she had saved me and damned me in the process. I was certain that one day soon, when a suitor came along whom Ameilja liked, I would have to determine how any of this would work. We had yet to know what this bond would look like for us.

"I do want us always to stay close, Kovuco. I want you by my side; I want to change the ways of the Order and the Commission, and I will! I will fight for the freedoms and fairness of your race—of all races. And I want you at my side every step of the way. I can't say what we did was the best decision or circumstance for our futures, but I was not ready to lose you. Your life is worth more. You reminded me that life is too precious to end. I'm sorry for the chaos. I'm sorry, Kovuco. I hope you can forgive me for what I have done."

I want to hold you, embrace you, and tell you that you are the one most deserving. You Ameilja, only you. I leaned toward her, locking my eyes with hers. Her tender face was inches from mine. I paused, and suppressed the urge. "Ameilja?"

"Yes?"

"I am honored to be your protectorate. What is chaotic to one person may be normal to another; I am honored to be bonded to you. I don't know where we go from here, but we'll figure it out together." I took her hand in mine. "We will."

She hesitantly nodded. "For being a rare seer, you would have thought I would have seen this coming." She bit her bottom lip. "How did I not know?"

She's feeling useless. This isn't her fault. She should not diminish her gifting. I wanted to ask her about her visions, but I hesitated.

"Kovuco, I need to speak candidly with you." She paused, collecting her words. "Understand, I will not allow anyone to define me." She brought her hand to her chest and clenched her sweater. "But I have always had this lingering parasite that gnaws at my chest and tells me I should care what others think of me. It's such an aggravating place to be in—stuck between confidence and uncertainty. If I have ever failed you, Kovuco, please hear me when I tell you I had never intended to." Her light skin flushed again as she desperately held back more tears. "I'm trying to understand my own demons while also protecting and fighting off others.' I just wanted House Frost, *my* House, to be a safe haven for Fae while the rest of our world has grown selfishly unfair."

I know. Every single one of her words palpated my mind. The urge to hold her resurfaced.

She looked relieved to share her heart, but the brokenness lingered. She ceased the weighted silence by gulping her coconut water, gagging on it as it went down. "Awful stuff when it's raw!"

I laughed at her and poured half her orange juice into the space of the coconut water. "That'll help give it some extra flavor," I smirked.

She turned back to me. "Kovuco, I've been a member of the Order since I was five. I never carried shame that I killed my mother or was the cause, but I knew my father's heart was broken. Growing up, I accomplished so much, always striving to make him proud and show him and my mother that I would live my life purposefully. As you know, I was born into this role. I've mastered all the divinities and skills, but we have yet to reclaim Albean's vision, because we have distracted ourselves with other priorities. I vowed to myself that I would be like Albean. I vowed to Uridei to become the next advocate for the Eastern Isles, crushing evil as he had and stopping injustice. I was just a little girl, but I took that vow seriously."

I watched as her gaze shifted to her crown, placed elegantly on its red pillow atop her dresser.

"I need to tell you something. The night of my coronation, when I saw you on the ledge with Bernát, covered in gore and despair, I thought my vow may never come true."

"Why? What do you mean?" I urged.

"I know about your reflection, Kovuco." Her words washed over me like burning acid. "I understand why you froze so often, noticing your disdain for mirrors."

The truth grated against my skull. I swallowed, holding back the food I had just consumed, and shifted uncomfortably, wondering where she was going to go with this.

"I don't judge you, Kovuco." She leaned in closer to me, speaking tenderly. "Somehow, seeing you there on that ledge, I saw my own reflection too, my suppressed purpose, and grew nauseous, as you have done with yours. That night was a representation, a recoiling reminder of how badly our world has fallen."

I wanted to recoil—to elude the topic, but she continued.

"Is *nausea* how you would describe your trauma?" she asked me cautiously with the utmost respect.

I sighed, hesitating before answering her. I dolefully dipped my gaze. "When I saw my reflection, I saw the human who was me ... I was splattered in blood, dripping in offal, with a human grimace and rage, and in that moment, I grew hatred for humanity."

"Oh, Kovuco," Ameilja wispily sighed.

"Why would I want anything to do with that?" I said with affliction rising in my tone. "My Rinkin form. Why did humans cast us out? Cast us as monsters and treat us as such? That day, I learned one thing about myself: I would have to learn to love humanity. It would be my greatest challenge. I guess avoiding my reflection denies the rage I hide in my heart. Nothing has urged me to want to take my Rinkin or even try to master its complexities. Why the hell would I?"

Ameilja didn't answer; she didn't know how to. This was my trauma to bear.

"Has it helped?" She moved a hand up to my forearm and caressed it soothingly. "Do you feel less angry toward humans by avoiding your reflection?"

I looked at her and smiled. "Well, I managed to like you somewhat, right?" I winked.

She chuckled, lifting the daunting moment as silence settled over us.

I urgently changed the topic. "Bernát—is he something significant to you?"

She grinned. "Yes. Bernát mentored me. He challenged me and wasn't afraid to kick me down, wallop me, or push me beyond my own ability. It's not common for a lady paladin to learn the roles of men, but

I demanded more. Bernát understood. He taught me that failure is part of life but that I should always fail forward, not backward. Bernát taught me to get back up on my feet and stand tall. He's a wülkure like Ash, who sometimes treats me like his child; he cares."

I felt an appreciation for Bernát grow in my chest.

"What I don't understand is how the Commission, even the Empress, doesn't see what this operation has turned into. Are they blind? The Commission has capped us and stripped us of our dreams and vows. Why serve Uridei if it is only to an end that man decides? Then whom do we worship?"

"Ourselves."

She snapped her gaze toward me, and her weary green eyes met mine. The only sound cushioning our thoughts was the wind and lulling waves; nature's whispers was the only remedy to our current anxieties.

I understand how far our world has fallen. I feel even more justified in the profound truth I harbor against my reflection. Even more now that Ameilja understands.

I studied her heart-shaped face. Her dark hair contrasted against its porcelain glow more deeply than before. A thought dawned on me: What did Ameilja see in her reflection? Did she see her crimson red hair the way I saw it, as a representation of blood and power? Blood represented the deep, regretful sorrow and hatred inflicted on the Fae—all of us. The power represented her influence and the fight for the unity we once had shared in the earlier days of the world.

She wears so much on her shoulders; a constant veil of protection for others.

Ameilja peered into my ice-blue eyes, and I felt she understood. I hadn't thought I could love her any deeper until that moment. She'd shown me that I could turn my wounds into wisdom and embrace the völf I was destined to be.

We must change; a revival is in order. We must transform our pain into power. Albean's efforts, and even the Commission's true mission, will remain a deadened memory, and who knows what evils will creep back in, if we don't fight for change.

When there is no light, darkness remains.

CHAPTER FIFTEEN

THE SIEGE

Fjorthúr
The Sunspire
The bunker
Aoustí 14

FORTY-FIVE MINUTES HAD PASSED, AND TOFFEL still hadn't hacked through the mainframe.

They stood in the rancid bunker, keeping watch, anxious to move on from its looming walls. Toffel knew that any likely survivors would be on the upper levels.

The clockwork mechanisms within the Sunspire were designed only to be traced while inside the facility. Still, if someone infiltrated the Spire from the inside, it would have been insanity not to create a workaround to reverse the control from the outside.

Suddenly, a voice sounded through the communication unit. "Hello?"

"This is Wächter Toffel. I am with the Demitori Sentry. Do you read?"

"Yes! This is Rikard. Do you copy?"

"Copy that! Who is with you?"

"Copy. My security crew: lead Matthäus Brand and Kaja Liudae. We have gathered a few Spire members along with two other wächters."

"Brilliant! Perhaps your team can assist me in getting you guys out of there, yes?"

"Whatever you need, just get us the hell out of here!"

Kiefer turned to Rotenfeld. "This is good news. With inside

wächters and Toffel at the bunker controls, we shouldn't have a problem in getting those doors open, eh?"

"I told you: Baadar is better than any wächter the Sentry's got. He's a smart fucker."

"But not smarter than me," added Toffel. He adjusted his spectacles on his nose. "He may have knowledge about the Spire, but I was born in Blackwater City, the technical capital of the continent. I'll be inside in less than ten minutes. So if you're expecting company on the other side of those doors, you'd better suit up now, 'cause once I am in, we'll only have moments before Baadar can reclaim control and seal it again."

"Too bad we lost Klein," Frahm sighed. "We don't have his knowledge to bypass internal controls."

Toffel shot him a look. "Then you'd better get in, accomplish your mission, and get out."

They didn't hesitate; the crew moved out, taking to the sands before the large steel, entrance door of the Sunspire.

Kiefer stood next to Rotenfeld. Standing to the right of Rotenfeld were Frahm and Dom. Ólaf and Yeddi were standing to the left, next to Kiefer. Ólaf had found a lightweight battle-ax, which now was sheathed to his pack. Yeddi fixed a bayonet on his Arslan-4 MG.

Minutes ticked away as Dom called the time from his pocket watch. The minutes felt drawn out, until he called out, "Two minutes!"

Inhale.

Kiefer loaded a bullet into the chamber of his PSR and steadied his rifle toward the door.

Exhale.

"One minute, thirty seconds, shitheads! Look sharp!"

Kiefer's heart raced; adrenaline pumped through his veins. By now, every weapon was locked and loaded and set for the door.

"Thirty seconds!"

The door clicked and echoed through the coastal cliffs.

"One second!"

It slowly began dragging open.

An ominous black hole lay before them. A gust of chilled air escaped and sinisterly whispered past their forms. There was silence.

They waited.

Torpidly and sullenly, the sounds of muffled and gargled moans emerged. Sluggish scrapes followed the sounds. A mixed group of orks and humans breached the sun's light. Their forms were all naked, and most of them were viciously disfigured. Open chest cavities and intestines hung from stomachs like tentacle-like living organisms. Empty eye sockets, lips, and cheeks were cut away; some revealed entire mandibles of exposed teeth. The teeth were sharp, and lizard-like tongues hung out, unable to fully retract into the mouths.

The humans among them must've been bystanders who had not reached the upper levels before the plagued orks took over. The vile smell of rotting flesh, gore, and shit only added to the horror that befell them. They moaned as if sleepy, moving like slow, nightmarish silhouettes in a fragile trudge.

The crew hesitated to collect the horror. They were processing the truth before their eyes.

"Uridei, be with us all!" Kiefer desperately whispered, giving the unfathomable moment to a Creator he didn't believe in.

It was just like the stories they had been told. The undead walked the lands, consumed by the Näkk's insidious power.

The first shot sounded through the air, piercing Kiefer's ears. Ólaf fired again. The bullet made its mark against the upper pectoral of a mutilated male ork. He was thrown back, with his arm severed by the blast, but he kept walking.

"The head. Try the head!" Kiefer anxiously yelled.

Kiefer aimed at another ork. He focused on the flailing tongue. In between breaths, he took the shot, hitting his target. The top half of the skull evaporated in a mist of red, and the ork fell to its knees and hit the sand, dead.

The infected mass picked up speed, now hustling for the crew.

Rotenfeld screamed, "Open fire!" The machine guns all began spraying bullets upon the mutilated beings.

Dom cast a stick grenade, and the blast rent five or so to pieces. The others kept firing. Even when the plagued beings were shot multiple times, it was not enough. They kept charging, feeling no pain or fear. Only an unquenched hunger guided them.

They closed in dangerously close. Kiefer dropped his PSR, along with Ólaf, and they drew their bladed weapons.

Ólaf's ax winded the revenants almost to the point that some forgot they were pursuing the living. Kiefer concentrated his swings to disarm some more, enough to allow him to behead them, draw his pistol, and point-blank put them out with a quick shot to the brain.

Yeddi charged an ork, bellowing loudly in rage. He swung the butt of his rifle against a human's skull while he ran and then attacked the ork with his bayonet, pressing it into the abdominal cavity of offal that suddenly sprang to life. Mouths of teeth lashed out for his flesh, emerging from the ork's intestines. Yeddi hollered and quickly jerked away, but his rifle was lodged in the ork's gut. Another ork swooped in next to Yeddi, and its mutated arms reached for his backside. The layers of teeth ripped clothing, while the mutated arms tore his armor to get to exposed skin.

Ólaf and Kiefer tried to reach him, but by the time they got close enough, the orks had already begun feeding on his open flesh, ripping limbs and tendons. One ork's mutated intestines coursed into Yeddi's open wounds, while the other ork tore his wounded skin. The agony and slurping sounds urged Yeddi into shock as he fell into a seizure, with blood spilling from his ears and mouth, while the ork's intestines intertwined in and out of his body. He was now nothing but a rag of flesh.

Kiefer turned as vomit boiled up in his throat. An ork suddenly redirected his attention as it sent its infected intestines toward him. He acted quickly; in an upward slice, the blade severed most that leered for him. Dom initiated two more explosions that gave Kiefer enough of a lead to cut off the skull of the assailing ork corpse.

Toffel jumped in and began returning fire from the bunker, giving his comrades the headway.

The doors will shut—we only have so much time! Kiefer called out, "Anton! We need to get inside!"

Dom created a suitable path.

"Move forward! Go!" Rotenfeld ordered. "Now!"

Kiefer quickly beheaded the next offending undead. This left seven remaining outside the Sunspire's doors. Frahm and Rotenfeld mowed down three more, and the crew sprinted for the doors.

Toffel will have the whole beach. Indeed, he can take out four of these things from his position.

They breached the facility. Ólaf turned and loaded his PSR to put down two more before the doors came together, trapping them inside the darkness.

They were trapped with the corpses.

Trapped with the völf.

Trapped with Baadar, who perhaps was worse than any monster they had yet to face.

☆

Shaar
Tsunetomo
West Wing protectorate tower, second floor
Aoustí 14

Nav'i brought the coffee mug to his lips and gulped down the robust coffee. He had hoped it would bring him peace, but his nerves were shot; he wondered where Kovuco had gone all night. On cup number four, he was only feeding the anxiety.

Tam wrote out yesterday's experiences in one of his large leather-bound journals. Nav'i wondered if Tam had been involved, since he continuously peeked over the binding, catching glances, and then returned to his quill.

Völfien used to write via claw because of their large, awkward hand-like paws. Their elongated fingers weren't capable of handling human-sized devices. They eventually had adopted quills, which allowed them to practice proper penmanship like their human comrades.

Dancer, unbothered, per usual, meditated near their open window, allowing the coastal breeze to permeate the space.

Nav'i suddenly broke the silence by sighing loudly to display his discontent. He sat huddled in Kovuco's usual corner, wondering what trouble Kovuco had found himself in. When he had asked Ash earlier that morning where Kovuco was, Ash hadn't answered and only had advised Nav'i to stay with Tam and Dancer—a grave hint that something was amiss.

"He came back to the tower with us last night. We all fell asleep here. Where the hell did he go?" Nav'i finally blurted out.

He was done waiting. He rose to his feet and seized his coat from the corner.

"Where are you going?" Tam asked.

"I need to figure out what's going on, and I am not going to sit here waiting on them."

"But Ash said we should wait. We can't—"

"Ameilja freed us. Tore down the gate. Will let us leave on our own accord now until she states otherwise."

"That was just for the day." Tam urged.

Nav'i cut a sharp gaze over to Dancer. "Dancer?"

Dancer's eyes snapped open.

"Care to tell Tam what you purchased for dinner tonight?"

"Beef skewers. Shark," answered the Zen völf.

Tam snapped to attention. "How? How did you—"

"Regulations have been lifting," Nav'i said as he slipped on his jacket. "Things will be changing here, thanks to Ameilja. Word is spreading in some of the establishments. So I can leave this tower and demand our packmate."

Nav'i slammed the door behind him.

Tam leaped from his bunk, tossed his journal to the side, and grabbed his jacket. "I'm, uh, gonna go too," he said.

Dancer nodded. "I'll stay. Go."

Fjorthúr
The Sunspire
The foyer
Aoustí 14

A cold sweat beaded Kiefer's forehead.

The humidity dissipated once the doors were sealed shut, but there was a new condition they would need to adjust to: he and his comrades were stepping in puddles of blood.

Sloshes of liquid and soft chunks layered a cold metal floor, splashing against their boots. Dom lit a flare, and a red glare lit the truth of the senses: bodies. Human remains and gore. Limbs chewed down to the bone. Weapons lay about the human victims, showing they had done what they could to defend themselves from an onslaught of undead orks. The sight was horrendous, and the smell was even worse.

Unimaginable horror.

The entry to the Sunspire was a large foyer centered around a circular elevator. The foyer forked into different halls leading to the cafeteria, kitchen, gym, pool, and showers. It was also the level known as the bridge level because it bridged the gap between the lower and upper levels of the Spire.

The entire bridge level was dark; the security backup lights were all that offered light, creating an eerie orange glow on the crew's surroundings. Thankfully, the lower levels were sealed, containing the other unknown horrors.

All five crew members gathered near the elevator; its emergency gaslights were also activated, lighting the area and their distraught faces in a warm glow. The clockwork mechanisms began to rattle as the elevator lifted and steadied itself into place, following the sound of Toffel's voice through Dom's communication unit: "Dom. Can you hear me?"

Dom pressed the radio function to allow a free discussion to the group as he walked over to Rotenfeld. "We can hear you, Toffel. There are five of us here; we lost Yeddi. Is that you activating the elevator?"

"Yes. It's all me. Good news: I have taken the Spire. Baadar will try to take it back, but fortunately, I have broken through the Spire's defense mechanisms. It will need to be repaired from here for the Spire ever to work properly again; Baadar got his hands in deep."

Kiefer smirked. "You realize that breaking a Sentry security system is an act of treason, right?"

Toffel laughed. "I'll see you at the gallows, Wülkure."

Captain Bayde's men showed much more liking to Kiefer than Rotenfeld. The envious Rotenfeld sensed this semblance and snapped, "Brief us, Toffel. We need to get a move on!" He then shot Kiefer a warning glare.

"Yes, sir." His tone changed under the direct order of his æsir. "You are currently on the ground level, the bridge. The Spire has six levels total: three above you in the tower and two below. Those lower basement levels are the labs built into the ocean's depth. That's where those fuckers on the beach came from, but keep watch; from what I've gathered, there aren't any more of them hanging out on your level, but that's no promise. Oh, and it looks like the labs are flooded."

"Flooded?" exclaimed Ólaf. "Sounds like there's something we need to investigate."

Kiefer shook his head. "We'll deal with it after we get to Baadar. Toffel, where is he? Where is the völf?"

"According to the logs, he appears to remain in the control room, T3."

Rotenfeld grumbled, "Makes sense. Wouldn't want to risk having someone retake control."

Ólaf nodded. "There's no way he has enough supplies to sustain himself there. He's gotta be exhausted."

"Unless the völf is making runs for him. Remember, it's likely the two are working together," Rotenfeld hastily added.

Dom lit another flare. "Which means that fucking beast could be anywhere in this place!"

Rotenfeld continued. "Break down the facility. Give us eyes, Toffel. We have six total, but what about the others?"

"Yes, sir. The bridge is where Baadar was attacked. That includes the showers, cafeteria, fitness, and such. Above you is T1, the suites. That's where the security lead, Matthäus, and the survivors should be secured. T2 should be clear. T3 is your destination. Like I said, the lower labs are closed and secured."

Rotenfeld turned to the crew. "Once we get to Matthäus and his team, we'll finalize the rest of our plans." He turned to his comm unit. "Toffel, let Matthäus know we are on our way."

They boarded the elevator, and it began ascending slowly through Toffel's control up to the suites. Kiefer glanced at Rotenfeld, making sure he appeared composed. It was evident he was jonesing for his revenge, but Kiefer hoped he still afforded him the respect to deal with Baadar.

The doors opened, and faces matching the names of the security team immediately poured into the elevator shaft. The doors closed behind Matthäus, Rikard, and Kaja. Two additional wächter survivors, Albrecht and Vali, were with them.

Kiefer nodded, raking over each of them. All were in good health, with no infection in sight.

They all were armed with their standard-issue Arslan-5 MPs, tight weapons that could be held comfortably with one hand. They also carried batons the length of tomahawks, which could emit up to 7,700 watts of attacker-stopping power when utilized.

They saluted Rotenfeld. "Thank you for coming to our aid, Æsir," said Matthäus.

Rotenfeld nodded, assessing Matthäus. For him being a broad-built man who'd seen a lot in his day, he looked as if he'd been through hell, witnessing horrors never thought of. The odors wafting from his body was evident enough.

"The current survivors are secured in a doctor's suite. Nothing's getting in; however, the level hasn't been fully searched. We can't get them out of here safely until the other levels are clear. What news do you have for us?" Matthäus urged, wiping sweat from his brow.

"We are taking back the Spire," Rotenfeld stated, studying the added crew members. "No one's getting out of this shit show until that psycho doctor and völf are in our control." He adjusted his weapons and locked his stern gaze on the team. "Kaja, Rikard, I need you two to remain here on T1 with my wächter Ólaf. Kaja, direct him to the survivors, and keep them secured. Let's get you back off this elevator and in action." He dispatched Toffel and had him open the doors again before ascending up to T3. "Wächter Albrecht, you protect Frahm at all costs. Dom, Matthäus, and Vali, I'd rather have you help Kiefer and me with Baadar. Especially you, Dom."

No one said a word.

"Are we clear?"

"Yes, sir!" The team responded in unison, besides Kiefer.

Kiefer eyed Dom and then turned to Rotenfeld. "Why Dom?"

"We're dealing with a völf. If you decide to get diplomatic with it, Dom is a cutting-edge negotiator and is not afraid of friendly fire. Even if that means taking out Baadar. You see the explosives he wields."

Anger built in Kiefer's core as he drew his pistol and loaded it. "I thought we had an understanding, Anton."

The others loaded and readied their weapons while Rotenfeld intentionally refused to answer Kiefer.

Kiefer started to speak up as they were nearing T3, when the elevator doors unexpectedly opened sooner than they should have. A large dark-cloaked figure sprang into the elevator, catching them all off guard.

The figure flipped past Rotenfeld and Kiefer. It leveraged its form and stood tall, quickly delivering a brutal kick to Dom, who had turned to face the assailant but fell and hit the ground, cracking his head open. The fall instantly knocked him unconscious.

Albrecht immediately stepped in front of Frahm to protect him, aiming his weapon. Being in a smaller space, they had to use their weapons strategically.

The figure, armed with two knives, swiftly slit Vali's throat. His blood sprayed onto the wall just as Kiefer aimed his pistol. The assailant deflected him, forwarding the aim for Rotenfeld. Expertly, Kiefer released the trigger and returned a kick to the figure's gut, throwing the assailant off balance. The figure smacked the wall, throwing off Matthäus's readied aim. He, however, had squeezed the trigger, and his weapon rapid-fired a spray of deadly lead into Vali's corpse. Pieces of intestines splattered the floor.

Anton roared in anger as he quickly grounded his footing.

The figure looked to the crew and slowly drew back the hood, revealing a muzzle full of bared fangs. The attacker growled at them beneath the hood's shadows.

"The fucking völf!" Rotenfeld bellowed.

Rotenfeld drew his sword and swung for the völf with a vengeance. She caught the sword's weight with her knife and returned another kick to Rotenfeld, sending him into the hallway through the open door at the T3. Frahm and Albrecht leaped out of the elevator to take cover; they took off somewhere safe and far away from the massive beast.

Dom gained consciousness and dizzily rose to his feet, aimed his shotgun at the völf, and fired. The blast caught her right arm, peeling her sleeve and ripping flesh. She snarled loudly, shockingly still holding her knife, which she cast at Dom. The knife violently bounced off the barrel of his shotgun, emitting sparks, and the blade met its mark through his left eye. He hit the ground, dead.

Matthäus screamed as he reloaded, ducked and rolled out of the elevator.

Kiefer drew his blade and swung for the völf. She caught the attack with her remaining knife; Kiefer drew a stake from his boot and stabbed her through the leg. She yelped, limping, and shoved Kiefer against the wall. She swung for his throat with her claws, but he ducked only to fall out of the elevator and onto the floor.

While the völf and Kiefer remained in combat, Rotenfeld dragged Dom's body partially out of the elevator and quickly pulled a pin from his vest. He then forcefully pushed his dead comrade back into the elevator. Kiefer caught the quick action and, with all his human strength, kicked the völf. She held up her arms, but due to her leg wound, she lost her balance and stumbled back into the elevator shaft.

Rotenfeld screamed into his communication unit, "Toffel! Shut the doors! Now!"

The elevator descended just in time before the blast sounded behind its closed doors. They didn't break their stare until a brief flash of fire and a surge of smoke slipped through the cracks of the elevator, hoping the völf had been killed.

Kiefer whipped toward Anton, gritting his teeth as he drew his pistol, and immediately pointed it at him.

"You dare point that pistol at me, Yuska?" snapped Rotenfeld, catching his breath. He wiped away a piece of gore from his temple.

"You and I had a deal!"

Another unexpected sound came from Kiefer's right. He turned, and Baadar stood with an MP aimed at his head. "Don't move!" Baadar threatened.

Kiefer obeyed, dropped his pistol, and raised his hands.

"You too! Drop it; all of you!" Baadar demanded, eyeing the disgruntled crew.

Matthäus threw down his weapon, then held up his hands.

Rotenfeld hesitantly tossed his weapons to the ground in frustration. "That völf just took out my men, you fucking idiot!"

"She's not going to hurt you!" Baadar urged.

Anton took a step forward, ready to take down Baadar with his bare hands.

Baadar swiftly took a step back and tightened his grip on the MP, turning it on his brother-in-law. "It's Isabelle!" He desperately blurted.

"Isabelle?" Rotenfeld scoffed.

"Yes! The völf—it's Isabelle!"

They all fell silent.

"Come with me—now!" Baadar demanded.

He nudged the crew toward the workspace center of the control room, keeping the MP aimed. Kiefer noticed the edginess in Kristján's grip, which gave away his lack of skill to fight. Kiefer shot Rotenfeld a side-eye, affirming this fact and assessing the current situation.

"Put your swords on the table," Baadar directed, and Kiefer and Rotenfeld took off their swords, set them on the table, and returned to the far side of the control room. Matthäus was ordered to stand near a panel, arms held high.

Rotenfeld shook his head. "Siding with a fucking völf. How far you've fallen."

"I am telling you, Anton. It's Isabelle. She *is* the völf!"

"Impossible! Have you lost your fucking mind? My sister and I both entered this world from a human's womb!"

"Did you not just witness an attack similar to your own tactics?"

Rotenfeld shook his head, again. "Others can learn the same fighting style. We teach—"

"Then why aren't you dead? Don't you think she could have eliminated you? Answer me that," Kristján huffed, wiping sweat from his brow. "You are her brother, *but* I am married to her. I've never witnessed anything so bizarre, but she's changed since she returned years ago. It's why she has been so distant!"

Kiefer grew impatient and interjected. "Baadar, what's going on? If the völf is Isabelle, then what does she want here? Why did she attack you?"

"She wanted me to see the truth." He paused momentarily.

Kiefer eyed Rotenfeld and could see him fuming in disbelief. He wanted answers just as much as Kiefer did.

"After her disappearance, Isabelle changed. I saw it in her eyes; I felt it in her touch. Even in her older age, she somehow looked younger, and stronger. Listen to me. She wanted me to learn the truth about this place—she found out about my contract—she had to stop us from making a huge mistake!" Baadar stepped toward them with the pistol still focused in their direction. "You two don't deserve to know the full truth, nor can I tell you, but believe this: Isabelle became a völf when she disappeared."

"So was my sister captured or not?" Rotenfeld urged.

Kristján bit his tongue, refusing to answer that question.

"Answer me, you fucking puke!"

"No fucking questions! Nothing!" Kristján screamed, gripping the pistol as his spit spewed against Rotenfeld's face.

Kiefer and Rotenfeld stared at the doctor, mentally questioning his sanity.

"Don't look at me like that! I'm not fucking crazy! I'm not the bad guy here! Just listen to me. She absorbed the memories of the völf who changed her. These memories unlocked a knowledge we humans don't understand ..." He paused and swallowed hard. It was evident he was chewing on what pieces of truth he wanted to share. "The Näkk is here, and if it gets into the wrong hands, it will unleash not only the plague once more but also Sabor's power to wield it. A fucking death sentence for all of us; the end of the world as we know it!"

"This is preposterous shit! My sister wasn't changed into a damned beast!" Rotenfeld yelled.

"I said no speaking!" Baadar screamed. "Listen! I thought the same. I thought it was impossible, but she is a völf! She and her child—m—my boy." His voice lulled into a saddened whimper. "She told me unfathomable things."

"I've had enough of this fantasy-land bullshit," Rotenfeld huffed. "Either shoot me or fucking let us go!"

Kiefer took a deep breath, retreating into his thoughts while the brotherly feud continued.

He'd never paid much attention to the details of the paladins and their ways under Albean. Those were all stories in the Book of Light, the religion he'd pushed to the side and never followed. Naturally, though, tales of Albean and his Völfien creation had been riddled into the purpose and history of the Commission. All things have a beginning. *The beginning of the Völfien ... the mother of all Völfien ...*

"Is this related to Fenris?" Kiefer spoke up.

Baadar's eyes widened. "Yes! Yes!" He lowered his trembling pistol enough to relax his posture. He knew he had gained Kiefer's attention. "You know the tale, yes?"

Kiefer subtly nodded. "Somewhat."

"We don't acknowledge this story much, do we, Wülkure?" Kristján laughed ironically and proceeded to speak slowly. "How could we? Expect a völf to be responsible for the annihilation of something so dreadful as the undead? But Albean knew what he was doing. He rose his beloved race and designed them after the creature known for loyalty and protection—incorruptible by the world's ways and the infectious Näkk." Kristján's eyes darted around the room as he recollected the knowledge. "She was just a regular wolf. Just a four-legged dog of the forest, pregnant. Did you know that Albean had Fenris drink his blood? *His* blood, the pure and powerful Aureate blood. You see, this bloodletting act transformed her womb, leading to the birth of the first Völfien. Per Albean's order, the other wolves in Fenris's pack drank from her, which led them to transform into the Völfien we know today."

Kristján had gained Anton and Kiefer's full attention.

"You know, Wülkure, despite what we humans may think, the Völfien will never rise to destroy humans out of cruelty, yet we fear them as if they will." Kristján chuckled again. "They'll rise to stop destruction but will always be bound to Albean's holy imprint."

Kristján then fell silent, staring at the two men.

Kiefer's shoulders slumped. He assessed Kristján's perplexed and unhinged expression. It was evident he wore the troubling guilt of all he'd betrayed and the implausible knowledge he was burdened with.

"Please, help me to understand further." Kiefer cautiously urged, hoping to earn a false trust with the doctor.

"I can't give you all the details—you heard me!" Kristján rose his voice again, gripping his pistol.

"Because he's fucking lying!" Rotenfeld snapped, evidently vexed, breaking the brief solemnity. "He's gone mad—fucking insane!"

"I am no liar, Anton! I've made mistakes—there's no denying that—but I am no liar!"

Kiefer threw up his hands. "Both of you, stop! Speak, Kristján. At least give us something else; we don't have much time!"

"We fucked up! Not them. We did—the humans. We've really fucked up!" He paused to catch his breath. A nervous sweat continued to bead along his hairline. Under the strain of his mania, the lines on his forehead deepened. "I know how this plague works from being part of this operation. The Näkk moves quickly; it's like an evolving entity. It doesn't just kill and reanimate mindless corpses; it belongs to a host, a beholder of its power. It doesn't stop."

A shiver crawled up Kiefer's spine.

"The Näkk *wants* to be found; it *needs* to be used by a powerful being so it can consume all in its path—unless ..." He paused. "Unless ..." He paused again.

"Unless what? Just say it!" Kiefer demanded.

"Unless the Völfien born of Fenris stop it."

"What do you mean?" Rotenfeld pressed. "I thought it was the Purge that stopped the Näkk."

"Yes, but so did the Völfien—specifically the ones ..." he paused. "It's in the blood—only theirs. The leader of this operation thinks he can control what is here, he thinks he's unstoppable, but he's forgetting a key issue: there is no control of the Näkk, not without killing ..."

"Killing who?" Kiefer urged.

"I can't tell you!"

"This still doesn't answer how Isabelle was changed," Kiefer edged in.

"Stop! I've already shared too much! Just take what I've told you—"

"No! We need to know! Does this bloodline still exist?"

Kristján gulped down the salvia building up from his spiel. "No more questions; that's it!"

A sudden gunshot blast sounded from behind Kiefer and Anton. Kristján's hand exploded as a bullet met his knuckles. His pistol dropped among the sloshes of fingers, bone, and blood.

"Fuck!" Kristján wailed.

Kiefer took that moment to jump over the control desk and reach for the swords. Seizing the handles, he slung one of the blades in the shooter's direction. The shooter was Albrecht. He dodged the sword and went to fire again when Kiefer tossed Szonja's sword next. The blade plunged through Albrecht's shoulder. He dropped the gun and fell into the hallway. Kiefer charged for him, when Frahm pointed an MP at his head. "Stop right there, Yuska!"

Rotenfeld's boots clapped against the tiles as he approached Kiefer, leaving Baadar bleeding on the floor. "I'll take my sword back, Wülkure," he huffed, snatching it from Kiefer's grasp.

He struck Kiefer's jaw with the pommel of the handle. The blow cut his lip. Anton then lifted his comm unit. "Ólaf, get Kaja up here now! Albrecht is wounded."

"I was saving your life, Kiefer!" Albrecht snapped. "Baadar had his gun aimed right at you!"

"I need Baadar alive, you fucks!" Kiefer growled.

Rotenfeld strapped his scabbard back to his belt, sheathed his sword, and straightened his sleeves. "The Spire is ours now. But I need someone to get on that control panel and get Toffel to empty those lower labs."

Frahm pushed past Kiefer and began working with the controls, speaking to Toffel. Moments later, Ólaf and Kaja breached T3. They guided Baadar into the hall and propped him against the wall. As soon as Albrecht's wound was attended to, Kaja addressed Baadar.

Kiefer assessed the situation. Guns were focused in his direction. He had weapons concealed within his jacket, but he knew that using them would not proffer success. He too was directed to sit next to Baadar like a prisoner. He cut Kristján a glance; he sat there, looking dismayed.

Kiefer tilted his head back, pulling his hands through his hair. Ólaf stood nearby with his PSR ready. Kiefer could see him in his peripheral; he tried not to harbor resentment for the wächter; he knew he was following orders. He then tilted his head toward Matthäus, who continued to stand back, looking confused. Matthäus knew something was wrong, evidently not connecting to the bigger picture.

Rotenfeld suddenly appeared. "Ready to go, Yuska?" he sneered.

Kiefer didn't answer.

Baadar spoke suddenly, "Anton. Please! You must believe me, brother!"

Anton glared at Kristján Baadar with a dark hatred that chilled

Kiefer to the bone. Anton pulled out his pistol and pointed it at Kristján's head. Kristján remained emotionless and closed his eyes.

"You killed her!" Anton hissed. "You killed my sister!" He trembled with angst as he clutched the trigger. "As far as I'm concerned, she's dead to me."

Kristján pleaded, "Anton …"

Kiefer closed his eyes, and a shot pierced the silence.

CHAPTER SIXTEEN
BLOODLUST

Shaar
Tsunetomo
West Wing, Ameilja's chamber
Aousti 14

I RELIVED HER TASTE, WHICH WAS SWEETER AND far more potent than the finest of wines. I relived her smell, an aroma that elevated the human condition to unimaginable heights. I relived the moment in ecstasy when my teeth made their way into Ameilja's naked flesh. Ash and Jayna were in the room, but I only needed to wish them out of my mind.

I couldn't touch her, but something in the intent of biting down on Ameilja's right thigh was different from before. It was consensual now, intimate, and somehow felt like less of an ambuscade upon her. My survival depended on this act, and permission was granted. I, of course, felt Ameilja's discomfort but only because she was aware of the observers in the room.

I dug my claws into the bedsheets and, one by one, allowed my teeth to breach and settle into her flesh. My tongue lathered the open wounds as the sweet blood poured into the vacuum of my toiling throat muscles, coursing the life stream down my gullet. I loosened my jaw and then lightly applied new pressure around the wounds to encourage the blood to flow, gentle and slow.

At the coronation, in a furious rage, I had ripped flesh and consumed vast swaths of gore into my system, but this was different. Knowing I was still hurting her and causing her harm slowed me down. This was deeper. I was connected to her willingness, her desire to see me thrive, as I swallowed her lifeblood, restoring my strength.

If only I could claim her as my own.

I nipped her again, her muscles twitched, and my hypnotic trance ended once I'd had my fill. I released her. My eyes closed, and I averted my nose toward her ankle, away from the open wounds. I didn't want to look.

Ash patted me on the shoulder. "You okay?"

I breathed deeply, gave a quick nod, and attempted to stand. Ash quickly removed his coat and laid it over my shoulders. I glanced at Ameilja, who appeared to be meditating through the process. She lifted herself and locked eyes with me briefly. I absorbed her face in a new way. My attraction to her pulsated as a unique strength was revitalized through her eyes. It urged a new enticement through me, especially with her blood on my lips.

"He doesn't need more?" Jayna asked.

"Nah, he's good," Ash said quickly.

"He's—"

"Yes, sister. He's had enough. Tend to Ameilja. I've got Kovuco." Ash pointed toward Ameilja's desk, where his blood-drawing equipment was still set up. "Be sure to get that blood processed properly," he ordered her.

I grew concerned since Ash had referred to me as Kovuco, not Kovey. A serious urgency blanketed his tone. Also, he was intent on rushing me away quickly. He must have been ashamed of my actions and what we'd committed. Or maybe I had done something wrong.

Is Ameilja okay? Did I unknowingly do something to her?

Ash guided me out of Ameilja's chambers, and I slowly licked away the little bits of her, savoring what might be my last time to drink of her in such a manner as this.

He then rushed me to the gate at her entryway and retrieved a key from his pocket, but paused, not allowing me out.

I placed a palm on the ledge, leaning against the column. "Is everything okay?"

Ash nodded. "Yep. You?"

His tone was casual and collected, so I tried to match it. "Yeah, I am good! I feel terrific, actually."

"I can see that," he said, clearing his throat.

I shot him a confused look. "What do you mean?"

Ash's eyes shifted toward the ground, or what appeared to be my feet. I turned my attention toward the floor and was immediately alerted to the cue. The arch in my hips brought attention to my arousal.

"What the hell?" I huffed under my breath. I cradled Ash's jacket in front of me, covering my groin quickly, hoping that somehow eliminated the evidence.

"All good. Whenever you are ready—"

"Did I do anything inappropriate? I got so lost in there," I blurted. *How is this even happening?*

"You're fine! It's natural," Ash reassured me.

"Natural? How the hell is this natural, Ash?"

"For *you*, it's natural. Trust me. And give it a rest, will ya? Just ignore it!"

"She undressed me and put me in her bath! What if I—"

"Kovey, listen! Don't make this moment any stranger than it already is. Accept that whatever Ameilja saw, she would do this again if it meant saving your life. I got you out because you're in working shape when this kind of thing happens. Remember, you're bonded. There will be urges."

I nodded, swallowing an anxious breath, trying to accept Ash's condolence.

I remained against the column until I'd finally begun calming down emotionally and physically, when Nav'i and Tam breached the entryway to Ameilja's wing. Tam looked a bit bewildered, perhaps at the idea of freely passing from our tower to Ameilja's wing without a wülkure escort.

Ash retrieved his jacket, handed me my protectorate gear, turned to the gate, and unlocked it. I found my harness, twin tonfa swords, and a black sash. I fitted them with my coat as Nav'i and Tam approached.

"Time to call it a night, eh, Kovey? I think we've pretty much covered our shift."

I caught the cue. "Yeah. Tired," I added.

Ash turned to Nav'i and Tam, who pushed past him and took my side.

"I'm fine," I said. "I—"

"I need a drink," Ash interjected. "What about you three? Drinks?"

"What the hell is going on, Ash?" Nav'i urged, raking me over.

Tam took a sniff and turned toward Ameilja's room. "Ameilja? She's hurt?"

"Just a cut," said Ash, breaching the gate outside the wing. "But she'll—"

"She's been bitten," Nav'i sneered, taking in the air with his nostrils. "By?"

Both völves turned to me. They knew. They could smell my saliva and the traces of her left on my lips.

Oh fuck.

"Drinks!" shouted Ash. "Hundred-proof whiskey? How about a cabernet? I don't care, but let's have it, eh?"

☆

Shaar
Tsunetomo
West Wing protectorate tower
Aoustí 14

I focused on the swirling amber-colored bourbon in my glass, followed by the sphere of slow-melting ice within the warm liquid; it wasn't enough to distract the tension I felt.

Nav'i's disappointed stare bore into me. Even Tam, always forgiving and understanding, looked at me with evident disappointment. Both stood before me with arms crossed, glaring. Their stares locked on to me, waiting for answers, but Ash was still distributing glasses of bourbon from a decanter.

We stood on the public porch built into our yard, facing the ocean. It was also a decent distance from the tower, so none of the residents could listen to our conversation unless we spoke at high volume. Ash had chosen this place for that reason. The breeze from the sea acted as a stream to carry words away, even from the sharpest of senses. A fire was lit in the outdoor stone fireplace; the wind teased its flames.

Ash finally sat in the wooden chair with his back to the wind to avoid the smoke bellowing into his sensitive, aged eyes. He pulled a cigar from his jacket and handed it to Tam. Tam snapped out of his furious glare and poked a claw into the cigar end, creating a perfect punch for the smoke to travel through.

Ash nodded. "Thank you, sir!" He lit the cigar, taking a few puffs to ignite the ashes. After allowing a cloud to spill from his lips, he scanned the scene, examining the energy from all three of us. "So can everyone take a drink, please?"

Tam and Nav'i, in unison, gulped down the glasses of bourbon as if they were shots—amounts that should have been nursed slowly.

I sighed and followed suit. I then walked over to the decanter and filled my glass once more. I turned to my packmates and offered to fill their glasses. "I know you're upset, but you can't be more upset than I already am at myself."

"What is going on, Kovuco?" Nav'i pressed.

I returned the decanter to the table and took a sip of the bourbon, this time experiencing the nutty aroma from the curved vessel.

"You left us last night. Carefully enough to slip our detection," Tam said. "Where did you go?"

"I went to see Ameilja," I answered.

Nav'i approached hostilely. He clutched my shirt and drew me close to his gaze. "And?"

"I wanted to see her." *I needed to see her.*

"Have anything to do with this *love* business?" growled the dark völf. His fierce stare cut through my thoughts.

I sensed Tam's tension, guilt, and perhaps even fear, knowing that Nav'i had been listening in on our conversation the night of the coronation.

"Yes, I suppose it does." I tried to break free from Nav'i's hold, but that only caused him to tighten his grip.

"Suppose?" Nav'i snarled as he forcefully pushed me away, and my bourbon spilled onto my arms.

Instinctively, I growled. "Don't touch me!" I said stiffly, bracing myself for Nav'i's retribution, with my lips curled back to expose bared teeth.

"You touched Lady Ameilja! I can touch you as much as I want—eat you should I decide to!"

He wasn't wrong. I had violated Ameilja. I'd attacked her, even if it hadn't been malicious. I calmed my growl, and my ears lay back in submission.

"She shot me, Nav'i. She used vilkanás. It wasn't her fault; I startled her."

His tensed form relaxed. "Then you drank from her," he regrettably acknowledged. A terror crept into his throat. "I—I can smell your bond."

I looked up at his concerned gaze. I nodded. "I know it's wrong. I am sure you're both shocked."

Tam inhaled gruffly. "Either that, or you'd be dead."

Nav'i looked at Tam. "Dead? Ameilja could have been killed. You know the consequences of bloodletting." He turned back to me. "So now you're bound to her? Our lady?"

"I didn't do this on purpose; I tried to repel her, but I was weak. She—" I turned my gaze, trying to resist the tears that filled my eyes, but I couldn't. I did my best to stand tall despite my shame. I couldn't blame Ameilja. I owed my life to her, but I would have chosen death over this path and the dangers it put her in.

Nav'i batted my jaw with two clawed fingers. "Kovuco?"

I opened my eyes and looked at him.

Nav'i's eyes softened, but his grimace did not. "Do you love her?"

I didn't like the idea of answering. Answering meant it was the truth. Answering meant it was out in the ether and made our act even deadlier than before.

Tam stepped in. "Kovuco? How does it feel to be bound to her? A human?"

I hesitated to answer. "It's strange. But I know so much now. I feel her energy. Sometimes I feel like I am reading, but it's just downloading into my memories."

"And Ameilja?" he asked.

"I mean, she's okay for now—exhausted. Supportive as always. Placing everyone above herself."

"What will become of you two? What does this mean for the future of a human and a völf?" he curiously asked.

I shrugged. "I'm not sure. I don't think this will disrupt our futures. I've sensed that Ameilja doesn't plan to marry soon, but that could change. I don't think our bond will hurt her relationship if she does. I don't have an answer right now. It's a lot to take in … I hope I do right by her."

"And right by you," added Nav'i.

"By me?" I asked, perplexed.

"Yes. Are we just going to stand here and pretend this isn't a destiny situation for you?"

"Destiny?" My voice broke.

"Come on, Kovuco! Don't play dumb. You've made Ameilja a devotional. You're gone half the time, lost somewhere mentally; we merely mention her name, and you wake up. You love Ameilja, don't you? Just say it!"

"I am a protectorate. Ameilja has always been someone special to me. There's no disputing that, but our love is friendly, not—"

"A devotion? What's wrong with a devotion?"

"Enough! I'm a völf; Ameilja is a human! I don't know how this is going to play out. Should it begin to cause harm to Ameilja, I will gladly take my own life. She deserves that. I can't possibly—"

"Why the hell do you choose to dip deeper into darkness? The older you get, the darker your path becomes," Nav'i stewed.

"Why would getting older mean the road got less dark?"

"As you get older, you should grow stronger! Live for something better!"

"I guess we don't always lock on to a road to happiness right away. Sometimes we get stronger so we can face things waiting for us in the darkness. I can only hope and pray I end up somewhere on the other side one day."

"So answer the question," Tam pressed.

I shook my head. "What?"

"You've already practically said it, but say it aloud. Do you love Ameilja?" Nav'i urged, growing impatient. "Since I met you, Kovuco, there's always been something off about you. Let's be honest; you're a bit different. And here it is: Ameilja's the missing link. The link to your—"

"Darkness." Tam finished. "Answer the question, Kovuco. Do you love her?"

I swallowed hard and let my arms fall to my sides; the final bits of bourbon from my glass splashed at my feet. "Yes," I said. "I love her. Always have. Always will." I looked over at Tam, whose expression, like Nav'i's, remained unchanged. "Ever since I laid eyes on her. Every day I find a reason to resent it, but it grows every waking moment. I know it's wrong. I know it doesn't make sense. I thought we were wired to only desire our kind, but I am learning to deal with it."

I stood tall, masking the trembles writhing through my form, and bracing myself for the impact if Nav'i struck me. "So now what?" I asked. "I said it. Happy?"

Nav'i laid his paws on my shoulders. I closed my eyes tightly, but rather than being hit, I felt his claws clench my shoulders. I opened my eyes and met his glare. His nostrils flared, and his teeth clenched, as if he were trying to chew on what he really wanted to do, but something inside restrained him, and he reconsidered his initial response.

I swallowed sharply, and then, to my surprise, Nav'i pulled me in. For the first time in all the years I had known Nav'i, he hugged me. His grip caused my spine to crack.

He released me and stared dagger-like eyes at me, and a slight smirk formed on his face. He nodded and huffed, "We'll get through this, Kovuco. We're a pack—the White Throats."

I nodded, acknowledging his assurances but still unsure if he was past his desire to throttle me.

Ash let out a relieved laugh. "Anyone want a cigar?"

Nav'i adjusted his shoulders. "What's next?" he asked, ignoring Ash's offer.

Ash took another concentrated drag. "We need to get Ameilja somewhere where we don't have a bunch of supersensory völves lingering about, and we need to conceal her wound until it heals. Only one handmaiden knows, and she is one hundred percent trustworthy. We cannot risk the suspicion of all the other handmaidens being pushed away."

"We could use the assassination attempt to persuade András to allow us to travel," Tam spoke.

"Bingo!" Ash snapped his fingers and pointed to Tam. "That is the easy get-the-hell-outa-Shaar ticket! With a homicidal sister, Ameilja could go anywhere on the coastline should her little heart contend. Even better, András has already approved this temporary move."

I took a moment to jump in. "Is it confirmed that Tanja made this attempt?"

"We don't know that for sure yet. But all this said, considering our present circumstances and Tanja's potentially being the assailant, Ameilja needs the change of scenery. Plus, I am still unsure how Ameilja will respond to the bloodletting. This presents our next concern: How will Ameilja respond in training? She made a breakthrough with her Purge flames, and now she has this new condition to which she will need to adjust."

"Do you know how this will affect her?" I asked, concerned.

"No, Kovey, I have no idea. She is a seer; she will survive, I am sure. She may just not be as sharp."

"What do you mean *sharp?*"

"Well, she's going to channel you for a bit. She's going to be picking up on your memories and who knows what other effects she might have? There is little wülkure know about what mates share in this act. It's very intimate. But between a völf and a seer, this is far more complex. Think of yourself as a first case study, Kovey. Rúnar is a good location to get you out of here. You can focus on this new condition. Together."

"Rúnar? How is that any safer?" Tam interjected. "Especially with Jakob's hands on everything. It's evident he has his mind set on Ameilja."

Hearing Tam voice what I had already noticed sent a burning wave of protective jealously throughout my form. My fists clenched.

"Haruka," answered Ash. "She is a trusted sister; you know she is a close friend to Ameilja. She has a secluded manor; it's the perfect hiding spot, a safer location to assess where her powers and union will lie."

I nodded. "This seems best for us. All of us."

"Jayna will act as Ameilja's decoy if Tanja returns and tries to assassinate her. I will be here, resuming my responsibilities as a wülkure. András is ordering two more wülkure that are to be assigned to protect Jayna, along with a couple additional völves who are almost twice your age. Haruka will be taking Nav'i, Tam, and Dancer separately. Kovuco, you will join Ameilja on a personal voyage within a couple days, after the rest of you secure Haruka's dwelling or whatever plans she has in store for you."

"So will the others be in danger if we are discovered?" I asked.

Ash shook his head. "We can't worry about that now, Kovey. We have to secure our location first."

"We cannot put anyone else in danger! Bad enough that you and Jayna are playing decoy with Tanja out there!"

"Kovey, you are the target. You are the one who bloodlet with a crowned seer, not to mention an abbot's daughter."

Ash's blatancy snatched my words. I fell silent.

Nav'i shook his head. "Don't worry about us, Kovuco. We all made an oath to protect Ameilja."

"Speaking of an oath, we need to get back to the tower and brief Dancer." Ash added as he took his final drag off his cigar.

"Fine," I replied. I eyed each of them.

I had a deep fear for the future.

I was exposed, acknowledged, and accepted. Still, exposure meant trial and tribulation that could and would likely continue to end in bloodshed—all the while, we were hoping to hide a secret that could undoubtedly change the course of our existence forever.

☆

Shaar
Tsunetomo
West Wing protectorate tower, second floor
Aoustí 15

The White Throat protectorates sat about our table, perhaps for the last time. It was a bit early to celebrate Tam's birthday, but we'd be apart with the upcoming events. We would be broken up for the first time since becoming Ameilja's Court of Völfien.

Dancer made Tsunetomo desserts: sweet rice and a sake cocktail. The sweet rice was topped with chestnuts, dried jujubes, and pine nuts. It was Tam's favorite, and we enjoyed it every year. Tam still chose to add syrup. *Typical.*

"Hope you're hungry," said Dancer, proudly laying down the two dishes.

Tam grinned, eyeing the cuisine.

I scanned the faces of my packmates as we enjoyed our last meal together.

Tam raised his glass. "Here's to us!"

Dancer reached for his glass and raised it. Finally, Nav'i and I joined.

"And till our next Dancer feast together!" added Nav'i.

We shot the cocktails and returned to the rice dish.

There was silence again.

I finally continued the discussion, breaking the silence. "When does the airship leave?"

Nav'i chimed in. "Early. We have to leave here in approximately"—he gazed at a pocket watch—"thirty minutes. Lady Haruka is stopping by to pick us up."

Dancer tapped Kovuco's wrist. "Did you officially meet Haruka at the coronation?"

"Yeah. I kinda tossed her onto the ground during our dance. I hope she doesn't hold a grudge."

Nav'i laughed. "Well, good thing you won't be traveling with her over the ocean."

I took a long bite, hoping to remove that moment from my mind.

"Kovuco?" Nav'i asked.

I looked up at him.

"Are you going to be okay?"

I managed a smile and a reassuring nod. "Yeah. I'm going to be okay."

A knock sounded at the door. Everyone quickly finished eating, while Dancer began clearing the table. I stood up, brushed off the crumbs from my lap, and headed for the door.

There stood Lady Haruka, resplendent in her floor-length velvet coat with its voluminous, puffy lapel. There was a narrow gap between her black hair and the fur of her coat. Her crisp, floral fragrance surrounded her, complementing her refined manner.

She shared an authoritative smile. "Good morning, Kovuco."

I stepped away and bowed, as did my packmates behind me. "Morning, Lady Haruka," I said.

"It's Haruka to you, Kovuco."

"Yes, of course. Haruka." *Another first-name basis. This is promising.*

"Well, I am afraid we need to get going. There's been a change in plans, so we must leave quickly. Are you packed and ready?"

My packmates quickly grabbed their packs and helped to pack away the table.

I cleared my throat. "Haruka, about the other night, when I tossed you—"

Haruka let out a boisterous laugh. "Think nothing of apologizing, Kovuco. Ameilja stomped on my ankle shortly after, when I tried to keep her from you. Let bygones be bygones, yes?"

I nodded. "Of course."

Tam was the first at the door, tapping my shoulder. He gave me a hug, then pounded his chest. "Light of Uridei, Cousin."

"Light of Uridei," I repeated the gesture.

Dancer bowed and followed after Tam. Dancer didn't like to be touched. Nav'i stood before me, with Haruka standing just to his left shoulder. He gave me a cold stare, sighed, and gave in with giving me a hug. He then brushed past Haruka, giving her a quick bow.

Haruka smiled at me again. "See you soon, Blackstar," she said slyly over her shoulder as she turned away.

I closed the door, leaned against it, and slid to the floor. I rested my arms on my knees, collecting the empty dorm. The years we had spent in that room felt distant now. Everything would change in the coming days. No more Dancer-quality breakfasts and dinners. No more having reading binges, enjoying Tam's ridiculous jokes, or divulging into the merits of our lands.

All I could do was stir alone in the emptiness. Alone and hollow.

I doubted I would get any sleep that night, but it would give me a chance to meditate on the new feelings I had adopted. *Ameilja.*

I could feel her steady breaths. The feeling of her heart beating in synchrony with mine. Her healing wounds were on my account. If I lived, these events would guarantee I could serve a greater purpose. Maybe I could even try to be happy, as Nav'i hoped for me.

All I know is that my life is hers now. More than ever before. Not as her lover. Not even as her protectorate. I am bound to her as her völf ... just a völf.

CHAPTER SEVENTEEN
DEFENDER

Shaar
Tsunetomo
West Wing
Aoustí 15

AMEILJA WOKE ABRUPTLY, JERKING AWAY FROM her desk as an uncontrollable gasp gushed from the depths of her chest. The amount of blood loss and the events of the last week, even the previous twenty-four hours, had begun to take a toll.

What's the time?

She quickly peered around her room, realizing she had dozed off while trying to preoccupy her mind with her studies. After all she had been through since her coronation, her body had forced her to rest.

She checked the time and sighed, relieved she hadn't slept past the time to see her völves depart. Her tired gaze then drifted down at her books.

Ameilja recalled a conversation she had with Haruka prior to her studies. She had asked Haruka to join her, particularly following the final encounter with Kovuco. Her goal was to become momentarily distracted by Haruka's presence, but this had inevitably led to her feeling apprehensive. While they'd only spoken of the forthcoming plans and unknowns regarding Tanja, Ameilja's thoughts whirled around her bond with Kovuco.

She had begun to sense her protectorate's heartbeats synchronized with her own, as well as his movements and essence. It was mentally consuming. A distraction.

Ash had instructed Ameilja to keep Haruka in the dark regarding their actions. Ameilja had known Haruka to be a trustworthy friend; she was effective at providing support, even if she was unaware of the specifics; however, Ameilja knew she could not tell her. She was aware that Haruka would be incapable of comprehending the actions she and Kovuco committed.

She wished she could tap into Haruka's wisdom or even Maon's and ask what they would have done in her position. Would they have allowed Kovuco to die there on the floor? Could they have let someone they cared for die?

Even more disheartening, Ameilja already knew the answer, especially when it came to a völf. She quickly disbanded the thoughts. There was too much at hand she needed to attend to.

Ameilja rose from her desk and meandered over to her armoire. Without the help of her handmaiden, she dressed in her typical attire: dark pants and combat boots. She wore a long-sleeved white blouse and a buttoned-up dark vest to offset the white. It matched her long black trench coat with gold buckles and dark fur lapels. She left her room, greeting handmaidens in passing, and quickly continued down the hallway, exiting her wing.

To her surprise, Bernát stood just outside the gate. She wished to show resentment, thinking back on the night of her coronation, but she wrapped her arms around him before he could even utter a word.

"Well, I wasn't expecting that," he said with surprise. "You've barely made eye contact with me the last week."

Ameilja chuckled.

"You okay, kid?" he asked cordially.

She nodded. "I think so."

"You look tired. It's a shame this attack occurred, but I hope you've been getting rest. Where are you headed?"

"Well, Haruka is taking my völves to Rúnar today. I have a few affairs I need to wrap up before I follow after. It will be safe for me there."

"Only three of your völves are leaving? Any reason why?"

"With the uncertainty of Tanja, we felt it was the best strategy that I travel with a single völf rather than all three."

"Hm." He paused.

"Yes?"

"That wasn't a rhetorical question."

"Well, that was a refutation if I ever heard one. Go ahead and be honest, Bernát. Just tell me." She pressed, having no patience to give.

"I know you have your secrets, Ameilja. I hope you know you can always trust me if you need my guidance."

"Of course. I do have my secrets, Bernát, but the right time will come, and you'll know soon enough. Please just trust me."

"Fair enough." He motioned a punch, pressing it gently against her chin.

Ameilja relaxed into a subtle grin. Bernát treated Ameilja like his son more so than the woman she had become, because he knew it made her feel like herself and appreciated. More often than not, it worked to uplift her strong spirit. "You know I hate emotions, but you remind me that we wülkure indeed have hearts. I am sorry you had to witness the hydrostein effects with your protectorate Kovuco."

"It's okay, Bernát. Thank you for your efforts. I get protective when it comes to my völves. I am their greatest defender. At least I feel like I am. I know Ash cares for them, and Father cares for them too, in his own way, but I am the one who stands up for them. Me."

Bernát shook his head. "That's always been your biggest problem, kid; you always have a cause, even if it burns you out. Some days I swear you make me look at them differently, self-reflecting on my outlooks and judgments, despite what we're taught."

"Someone has to stand up for the truth. I am strong enough to bear the arrows."

Bernát smirked. "You've always been strong, Ameilja. Don't ever adjust to the world; the world will adjust to you."

Ameilja smiled, visibly loosening her tensed shoulders.

"Well, I need to move forward; duty calls." Bernát insisted. "You'd better hurry too. You gotta see those völves out of here."

Ameilja realized time was ticking. She quickly gave Bernát a peck on the cheek and hurried off. She fled through the vast estate and rushed to the primary courtyard. She needed to catch them before they left the grounds.

The cold, morning winds stirred as she prepared to receive her

White Throats. Ameilja absorbed the atmosphere: the smells, the scenery, and the way the sun pierced the clouds just enough to warm her cold cheeks. She wanted that moment to become a core memory. It would be the last time she saw her Court of Völfien for a while, a lot longer than she was used to when separating from them, but even then, they were just a tower's glance away. Now they would be a whole ocean away.

Finally, she saw them breach the top of the stairway. *There're my guys.*

A warm tear formed in the corner of her eye, instantly chilling against her cool skin.

Led by Nav'i, her Völfien made their way into the courtyard. She felt confident there wouldn't be more tears, until Tam approached first and locked his broad arms around her. She could sense a slight awkwardness in his hug.

Kovuco must've told them everything. Or Ash.

It didn't matter; she locked her arms around Tam's firm body and kissed his cheek. "I'll miss you, Tam! You know I'll see you soon, right?" Her green eyes studied his.

He nodded, sharing his famous ornery grin. His golden eyes glistened, holding back the emotion in that moment. He stepped aside, and Nav'i locked on to her next. He lifted her from the ground, squeezing his lady tightly.

She kissed his cheek. "Be strong, as you always are!"

"I will!" he said.

"Got your books?"

"Of course I have my books. I am eager to delve into the halls of Haruka's library."

She laughed, kissed him again, and let go to quickly wrangle in the least affectionate of her White Throats, Dancer. "Don't think I won't take advantage of exceptional circumstances, Danflor!" she teased, calling him by his given name.

Dancer hugged her back and let her kiss him on his cheek.

Ameilja turned, and Haruka stood before her. Haruka looked upon her dear friend and said, "I wish you were coming with us, Ameilja. My heart aches in knowing we aren't making this trip together."

"I know. But I have to settle a few things before I leave. You understand, don't you?"

She nodded. "I know. That's always been our problem: we think with our hearts rather than our minds. Especially you." She winked.

"It's why Maon constantly rolls her eyes at us." Ameilja chuckled.

They shared a final laugh, and many old memories swept through Ameilja. She always had appreciated that distance never faltered their friendship. They'd see each other briefly and then go weeks without seeing each other, but then pick up right where they'd left off, no matter how long it had been. A genuine friendship. Ameilja hugged her tightly, and Haruka returned the energy.

"Be careful! Take care of them, okay?" Ameilja whispered with an emotional quiver.

With a soft smile, Haruka replied, "Please be watchful; so many unknowns are looming. And you take care of *him*."

Ameilja knew Haruka meant Kovuco. "Of course I will. We are grateful to have you open your manor for us to stay during these pertinent times."

She wiped a tear from Ameilja's eye. "Always. But I've noticed something about Kovuco. There's something special there. Maybe it's the platinum fur; maybe it's Adémaro. But something is there. It's good he's watching out for you."

Ameilja smiled faintly, unsure how to respond. Her intuitive friend might have been on to something, but she held her tongue from sharing anything further.

Haruka turned and left Ameilja in the courtyard, taking three of her White Throats with her. They were met at the gate by the caravan escorting them to their airship.

"I'll see you soon," she wearily whispered into the cold air.

Then they were gone.

Ameilja released the pent up breath she had been unconsciously holding. Her thoughts drifted to her final protectorate. *Kovuco* ...

Ameilja whipped around and headed toward the protectorate tower. She quickly took the stairs to the wall surrounding Frost Manor and treaded along the stone wall's walkway. The harsh winds near the bridge instantly picked up.

"Shit!" she cursed aloud as the icy wind beat against her tender face. Wisps of her red hair tangled around her eyes.

It frustrated her that she had repeatedly protested that they should build the völves, Ash, and her handmaidens dorms directly in her wing.

"But then you wouldn't have the luxury of having your own space," she'd been told many times.

She found the upper class's fascination with exclusivity and ego exhausting. She'd do anything to be close to those she regarded as her friends.

The winds picked up heavily, sweeping up her long black coat. All she could do was fold her arms tightly to deflect the whipping and thrashing fabric. The fur lapels helped some, but the bridge's roaring winds was often too much for humans to bear.

A large gust rolled in, and she was nearly lifted. Ameilja gasped and stumbled toward the edge of the wall until she unexpectedly fell into a set of warm arms. She quickly lifted her gaze to find that Kovuco had collected her.

"Kovuco," she gasped.

"It's cold, Ameilja. You should be inside," he spoke softly in her ear, using his body as a shield to protect her from the winds.

"I wanted to see you, but I—wait. What are you doing outside?"

"I felt your distress. I was compelled to come to you."

Oh.

He looked out into the ocean.

"Kovuco?" she said.

He snapped from his thought. "Sorry. You were coming to see me?"

"Yes, but what are you—" She was interrupted as he rapidly scooped her into his arms.

"You shouldn't be in this cold!" He insisted as he leaped onto the ledge of the stone wall. Before she could protest, he jumped again and descended to the beach below.

His form landed with force, but he absorbed the shock in his legs, harboring her from the velocity of the drop. He pivoted against the grains and sprinted along the chilled sand.

At first, Ameilja felt the rush of the wind, then nothing. She couldn't help but revel in the balance and power that rang through Kovuco's limbs and the smooth, flush stride transported through his massive being. He moved with such deft.

Although the Völfien were linked to the human race because they could shift into a near-human form, they also met the qualities of the Fae. There was something mystical and mysterious about them that could only be experienced in their skin. Only the Völfien understood.

Am I experiencing this? she wondered. Being in his arms, she could no longer feel the cold gusts of wind. She felt warm and somehow more vital. She felt his energy pumping through her veins.

Is this the bond?

She loosened her grip and laid a hand against his chest, feeling his heartbeat. Her heart beat with his. She felt his lungs inhale and exhale, wishing she could run miles alongside him. Whether from the saliva that had met with her blood or from those teeth that would surely leave a scar, she felt different now, somehow stronger than she had been before yesterday. Ameilja felt as if she were weightless now, like air joined with a mystic force that had become one with him.

She pulled her hand from his chest and leaned her head against him. With each heartbeat, lulling pulsations followed.

She felt unmistakably new. An intimate warmth filled her. With steady breaths, she inhaled his scent.

Kovuco … There was an unexpected, unfamiliar shift in her emotions, one she didn't dare to nurture further. Ameilja felt the shift for a split second, and then immediately suppressed it knowing such a thought could not go further.

She closed her eyes and inhaled, easing her thoughts.

Kovuco closed in on the western shore, Ameilja's little section of the beach that her wing overlooked. Kovuco leaped onto a rock and then another, and then, with a final lunge, his clawed feet clutched a misplaced block, and he launched to the ledge of her wing.

Even on the edge of a high drop, she felt safe. She looked up at her protectorate; his eyes were closed. His eyes moved under his eyelids, searching. Images seared through his mind; she knew because she felt them through his heaving chest. He clutched her tightly yet gently in his dissevering claws. She wanted to stop him but decided not to. As lost as he was in this moment, she wanted to lose herself and maybe find him there, to understand.

I can either resist or submit.

Ameilja chose submission. Submission into the mysterious völf.

Kovuco often was feared and misjudged by others, but he was the same shy and docile völf she had chosen all those years ago. Despite what made him frightening and enigmatic, she was glad she was synchronized not with just any völf but with someone she trusted.

Of all possibilities, she was thankful it was him.

☆

Fjorthúr
The Sunspire
Lab 2
Aoustí 14

"Load up!" Rotenfeld barked, eyeing his dispirited crew as he stepped into the elevator.

Matthäus, Ólaf, Albrecht, Frahm, and Kiefer followed while Kaja stayed behind. The pungent smell of the charred elevator swept through their nostrils as they took in the scene. The explosion from Dom's corpse was apparent on the elevator's floor and walls.

No one bothered to wipe Baadar's blood from Kiefer's face. He wore it like a mark of shame.

Rotenfeld stood next to Kiefer and smirked. "You permitted me. Don't get soft for that fucking whelp. He deserves the void."

Kiefer scoffed. "I also made a deal with you, and you certainly went back on that."

Rotenfeld scanned the elevator shaft with an unmistakable flair. "Well, I am no splatter expert, but this doesn't look like three bodies. Perhaps I'll still have a völf for you."

Kiefer shook his head. "Yeah, gathered that. Not sure I can negotiate with a völf with my hands bound."

Rotenfeld didn't answer. He turned to his comm unit. "Toffel, we're headed to Lab 2; ensure this elevator is still operating."

"All clear. The panels should be running."

The elevator shifted, then moaned into its descent, finally stopping on the deepest level beneath the bridge. The men readied their weapons, preparing for more undead orks. They exited the shaft, except for Ólaf, who was ordered to stay behind to secure the elevator if the völf made an appearance.

They reluctantly entered the open lab, where everything was soaked in salt water. Large open cages lined some of the walls. Rancid chemical smells lingered. Bloody instruments and discerning equipment lay scattered about the darkened space. In the center of the room near an upper landing was what appeared to be a cross-like restraint, where a blackened, scorched body was suspended with wires and breathing tubes hanging out of multiple orifices. It was the body of a young ork.

The ork was wearing a crude, blotchy patch that looked to be sealing a gouged eye and holding the creature's head together. His body was emaciated, deeply mangled, and covered in stitched incisions and grisly wounds that appeared to have been self-inflicted bite marks.

Along the upper landing of the lab were more suspended bodies of orks and men. The bodies were hairless and bizarrely blackened, like that of the ork in the center of the room.

"What the hell is this?" exclaimed Albrecht.

Frahm chuckled. A prideful smirk tilted his lips. "The hosts."

"Hosts?" Rotenfeld snapped. "You mean all that shit about bringing back the dead?"

Matthäus looked around the lab in disgust and horror. The reality of what had been taking place down there weighed him down. All that time, he'd been patrolling a facility that harbored one of humanity's greatest threats.

Frahm ignored Rotenfeld's angered banter. "Bring Yuska here," he spoke up, walking up to the upper landing.

They all hesitated to respond.

"Now!" Frahm demanded.

Matthäus escorted Kiefer up toward Frahm, sloshing through the leftover briny water, and then pushing him near a panel where the mutilated ork hung. The others cautiously followed.

"Very good." Frahm cooed as he revealed a vial of yellow liquid. He lifted it above him, cocking his head while admiring the emulsion. He then turned to Kiefer and sliced his cheek with a scalpel. "Don't move!" he ordered. He allowed Kiefer's blood to pool on the blade and then dipped it into the vial. He turned to the panel and injected the liquid into a tube protruding from the platform. Frahm eagerly assessed the movement of the fluid through the tube, then quickly began adjusting some controls. Each movement displayed his familiarity with the mechanisms, like a pianist expertly maneuvering across the keys.

Once finished, he pointed to the young ork. "Meet Dakka Fallz'den, Wülkure Yuska," Frahm spoke with prized amazement. "The Wöndin's son."

Kiefer's eyes widened; his lips parted with disbelief.

The corpse of the ork began to breathe heavily, twitching and roaring through his mask. Kiefer and the others watched in repulsed shock as the ork's belly inhaled and exhaled rapidly. Moments later, the ork's fingers started to writhe violently, and his veins pulsated out from his charred flesh. A terrible strength took over, animating the entire corpse. It became undeniably apparent why such significant restraints were required.

Suddenly, the ork snapped its attention toward Kiefer. He began reaching furiously toward the group, shrilling and thrashing as if trying to escape. Before anyone could think to raise a weapon to the revenant ork, Frahm spoke up. "Hold your weapons—watch! Matthäus, release Yuska."

Matthäus obeyed, stepping away from Kiefer. Instantly, the braying ork ceased his hollering, relieved that Kiefer was no longer restrained. The ork eyed Kiefer. He had a longing in his gaze, as if he were waiting for Kiefer to command his next move.

"What the fuck is this?" Rotenfeld urged.

"It's what we've been working on. This is how we've learned to control—"

An enraged, piercing scream erupted. A woman suddenly appeared, charging the group from behind. She wielded a Völfien scythe; the points were inverted, creating a double-ended weapon.

Her presence caught the entire group off guard.

With inhuman speed and strength, she hit Albrecht with the blunt end of the scythe so that he was thrown from the landing onto the lower level. Matthäus pivoted the aim of his MP toward her. In a quick slash, she severed Matthäus's arm from his body and kicked him to the lower level. Blood sloshed out of his arm like a fountain while he descended over the platform; the red crimson showered her face and hair.

Rotenfeld went to draw his sword when the woman expertly pivoted around Kiefer, noticing his wrists were bound, and pierced the scythe through Rotenfeld's forearm, pinning it to his gut so that he could no longer draw his sword. Rotenfeld cursed, and stumbled backward.

The woman then drew a pair of spring-loaded shuriken from her coat and cast them at the reanimated ork. The bladed discs found their marks on either side of its chest.

"No!" Frahm bellowed, reaching for the ork as if he could somehow save him.

The ork squealed a garbling roar, vomiting the yellow liquid pumping through him, until the shuriken's secondary mechanism was triggered and each one exploded, sending chunks of the ork's body about the space.

Frahm, still in shock, lost his footing due to the explosion and cascaded onto a lab table of glass beakers and other supplies.

The woman sensed a nearing presence. She drew her knife, whipped around, and plunged the blade into Rotenfeld's heart right as he approached her.

Anton fell to his knees. With terrible sadness, he looked upon his sister's face. "Isabelle!" he cried out.

She narrowed her fierce gaze on her brother. "You killed my husband, Anton!" she snarled, drawing a revolver from her belt. "You took him from us!"

Anton shook his head. "Isabelle, don't—"

Isabelle bared her teeth, vengeance fueling her next move. She pulled the trigger and a bullet pierced his skull, silencing him.

"Go to hell!" she hissed, then shoved Rotenfeld with her foot, watching him fall from the landing next to Albrecht's unconscious body.

Isabelle turned once more and aimed her revolver at Frahm, the next bullet was set on her final target. Frahm, currently unarmed and wearily standing to his feet, raised his hands in surrender. Before she could consider killing him, Kiefer inconspicuously pulled a dart from his coat pocket, with four of his unbound fingers he expertly fit the dart into a tube he pulled from his belt; he blew through his pipe, and the tranquilizer struck her shoulder, plunging the contents from the needle tip into her bloodstream.

The sting caused her to fire the shot, missing Frahm completely. She turned to the wülkure, who now used a piece of shattered glass to slice open his restraints. She staggered toward him, staring straight into his eyes. "Find my son. Only he can stop this ... he-h—" She fell unconscious into Kiefer's arms, sliding to the ground.

Kiefer collected her and released a withheld, troubled sigh. "Fucking hell."

He knew he needed to send a distress signal immediately, especially before the others learned of their æsir's fate. Instead, he paused, taking a brief moment to rest. He rested there with the unconscious Isabelle, the völf, in his arms.

Ólaf suddenly entered from behind with his PSR set for Kiefer's back, knowing he held Isabelle.

"Wülkure Yuska? Is she—"

"Secured. She's out."

Kiefer waited for a moment, expecting Ólaf to take the shot or hit him with the rifle, but instead, Ólaf stepped up to the control panel, where Frahm had inserted the vial earlier. He connected to the communication unit and made contact with the upper level.

"Kaja? You there?"

"This is Kaja. Is everything all right down there? Over."

Ólaf cleared his throat. "Not quite. This is Ólaf. We have secured the völf. Put out an SOS to the centurion's office in Demitori immediately!"

Kiefer let out another suppressed sigh. Cautiously, he lowered Isabelle to the ground, then eyed the wrecked laboratory space. His eyes darted to the dead body of Anton Rotenfeld, then to the distressed Doctor Frahm gathering his whits as he tried to wake Albrecht. Matthäus was currently wrapping his severed arm, wincing and cursing loudly due to the pain. This entire mission had gone in a completely different direction than Kiefer could have anticipated, but he'd survived. He survived the unthinkable.

His thoughts bounced back to a bothersome detail Frahm had mentioned earlier: that he would stay in the Sunspire to continue work.

What work exactly? Are all these people fucking insane?

How much of this would come to pass would depend on the test of time and who officially stopped it. Kiefer knew he was no longer in control; there was nothing he could do to safely stop this operation. Kiefer Yuska was just a piece in their sick game.

CHAPTER EIGHTEEN
FATHER

Shaar
Tsunetomo
West Wing protectorate tower, second floor
Aousti 16

I RETURNED TO OUR TOWER, FEELING AMEILJA'S lingering touch against my chest, to find that one of my White Throat comrades had set a cleverly placed trap for me upon leaving. A handwritten note stated, "Your father will be here at 4:00 a.m."

Tam's handwriting. Of course.

The news coiled my stomach, instantly pulling my thoughts from Ameilja. Something had been off with Tam earlier; he had been quieter and less humored than usual. On any other day, I would have been fiercely angry, but I thought this might be the best way to face my father, especially now.

I checked my watch: it was 1:25 a.m. I had time to walk to the train station but felt I should catch two hours of sleep before then.

Can't. Too much on my mind.

I decided to take a shower—anything to try to shake the senses around Ameilja. I felt her and her responses like ghostly breezes. It hit at random, out of my control. I desperately needed that day to go smoothly without these alerting distractions.

I cleaned my teeth. I pinched an incisor, gliding down to the sharp tip, and felt a sudden ecstasy of Ameilja's skin wash over me.

Her smooth legs.

I tried to clean my ears and pulled back one ear. I sensed her long blood-red hair.

It caressed the curve of her hips.

I shook my head and splashed hot water against my face; I began tasting her again.

Warm, sweet, savory blood.

"Damn it!" I bit my wrist out of some strange frustration.

I felt her in everything I did; every motion festered within me. It was pointless to try to mask it; this was the bond. I cursed more and decided just to get dressed. My nerves were already shot as I prepared to meet with my father.

It had been four years since I had even spoken to him. I realized our last conversation had been harsh. I'd told him I hated him, hated what he was, and hated what he had done to me. He'd broken his vow to the Order and impregnated someone, making me a bastard. I still didn't even know who my mother was.

As much as I held on to that resentment, I realized those were cruel things to say, especially to a völf as powerful as he. Who was I to judge him? He'd lost the love of his life, his bonded mate. His wife, Rhúlain, had been brutally killed in the war. He had been with her for decades. Back in his time, he had married when he was my age. I was sure he felt alone and broken and wanted companionship again.

Now here I was, bound to someone I couldn't have, still a virgin, trying to figure out what it meant to be Kovuco, the unique, motherless blue-eyed beast I was. I certainly didn't have a clue, and as my understanding of my father's situation weighed in, I didn't have the right to judge him as harshly as I did.

Shaar
Tsunetomo
Tsuno oceanfront terminal
Aoustí 16

It was my first meeting in a long while, so I had struggled to make myself up as decently as possible. I wore a formal black shirt and black slacks.

My jacket was blue, bound by a white-and-black sash. Since my black scarf had been discarded after the landing slaughter, I had difficulty in deciding on red versus green. I decided on the green, questioning why I was worried about it to begin with.

I stood close to the center of the main concourse, where an ample, towering fountain stood. Water poured from a concrete figure's mouth and eyes, representing the tears and outcry during the war. Another taller figure was built next to it, representing Albean. I eyed it, pondering briefly, and then turned my gaze. People hustled around me, thankfully not paying me much attention. They had places to be and work to attend to, even during the early hours. The moon's glow barely added to the brightly lit area.

The concourse ran underground, which was more efficient for speed and travel. I walked to the podium and read the incoming logs filled with departure and arrival times. My father would be offloaded from the west balcony at any moment.

I walked in that direction, until I was caught off guard by a large, bearded völf standing on the top stair, looking around. I felt the stinging tug in my heart, like an inner punch. He had a sack slung over his shoulder and a long green jacket. I looked just like him. My features were closely aligned with his—the rare crystalline eyes and platinum fur. He was undeniably my father, but he seemed more rugged than the last time I had seen him.

My father's snout was bulkier, and he had more fur on his chin, chest, and back. It was long enough around his head and beard that it was tied into thick braids two feet long. He spotted me waiting for him. I inhaled, and the breath caught in my throat, turning into an uncomfortable swallow. I stood still and awaited him to stand before me. His magnificence was unlike that of any other Völfien I would ever know.

I bowed low to him. "Hello, Father. Welcome to Tsunetomo."

A slight smirk played on his lips, but I wondered if I imagined it, until it melted into a large grin. Catching me off guard, he grabbed hold of me and squeezed me tightly in his arms. I felt big, warm tears soaking into my neck. When I thought the moment would end, his grip tightened, with the squeeze increasing until I could barely breathe. A few bones in my spine cracked. I finally returned the hug, thinking it might be my last opportunity to hug this ancient beast I called Father. I clutched him tightly, wanting him to recognize I had become stronger while away, even if he didn't say it aloud.

"I have prayed every night that you might look upon me again," he said, his deep, enigmatic voice filling the space. "How I have missed you, little Kovu."

"I've missed you too, Father."

It was the truth. I had.

☆

Shaar
Tsunetomo
Shaar'an shoreline
Aoustí 16

I took my father to the shore as the sun rose over the horizon. We could see my tower from where we walked.

Other völves of Shaar had assembled there to see my father, shocked to see his presence. He was still a celebrity among many Völfien. He shared gentle smiles as they passed, watching some of them whisper to one another in awe, but they kept their distance respectfully.

"How are Désoto and Sangállo?" I eagerly asked after informing him of the recent updates on the coronation attack.

"They are both well, Kovuco; both are working within the Temple of Spears. Surprisingly, Désoto is stepping in as the Völfien steward for High Abbot Connor Úlfur while he is away temporarily. He highly trusts Désoto, despite what the Commission states. Sangállo accepted a position as Connor's protectorate shortly after Lady Frost accepted you as hers."

"Ameilja," I corrected. I stopped in my tracks, realizing how out of line I was. I'd corrected my father as Ameilja would have corrected me. "Sorry." I shrugged, scratching my neck awkwardly. "She hates being called Lady. Now it's become habitual to bring correction."

My father bowed his head. "No need to apologize, son. I suppose she adopted her father's boldness. András is a good man."

"He is," I agreed.

"You know, I met him during the war." He started to ramble. "He's a phenomenal paladin, a good man with a good heart. He doesn't like to fight but can fight with fury. He was raised at sea and fought like a man at sea. Surely pirates feared the blade of Frost."

My mind wandered. I decided to change the motion of our conversation. Now that we were on the subject of Ameilja, I was afraid I would appear to be hiding something. I was concerned he hadn't picked up the bonded scent yet, but I could not deceive him. Perhaps my White Throat comrades had told him I was in peril. As much as I didn't want to admit it, I needed his guidance more than ever.

"I need to talk to you about Ameilja, Father." I cut in.

"What about?" His voice was gruff but still pleasant.

"I have done something I shouldn't have. I've—" My knees felt weak, and I dropped my head. "There was an accident; I was shot with a vilkanás-treated bullet. Ameilja did it, not on purpose. She tried to revive me. She ingested some of my blood as she siphoned out the poison; she wanted to save me—willingly." I paused briefly, allowing the salty wind to brush against my face. "I then drank from her, Father."

He stood still, unmoving. He appeared collected, but I knew better. Before stepping closer, he looked around to ensure no one was within earshot.

He pulled me toward him, leaning close. "Who knows of your actions, Kovuco?" he asked gravely, a guttural growl roiled in his chest. "You realize what you've both committed, yes?"

"Yes! And only trusted sources, Father! My comrades know and Ameilja's handmaiden. And my wülkure also knows."

"You mean Ash?"

"Yes. Only Ash. No one else. They are sending us away amid this attack on the family to Rúnar until things blow over. Oddly enough, this attack is aiding in the secret of this forbidden act." I paused again and looked at him. He appeared deep in thought. "I am sure you're furious with me."

"I can't say I'm overjoyed," he huffed. "I have questions. What opportunity was presented that Ameilja needed to use a vilkanás-treated bullet on you? And why did you get shot with it? Does she understand what's happening between you two?"

I was hesitant, but I continued. "I thought she—well, I don't know. Foolishly, I snuck up on her. I made a terrible call in judgment. I grabbed the gun, thinking she was going to harm herself. She turned on me and caught me off guard, and I was shot."

"I see."

"She knows. She knew the risk," I added.

His stern gaze locked with mine. "She knew the risk, yet she still saved you?"

I nodded.

"Interesting."

I eyed him questionably.

"You can trust Ash. He will guide you in the right direction," he said.

I lowered my gaze, staring at the sand coating my feet. "It's challenging. I always imagined sharing this bond with a mate, not someone I vowed to protect."

He tugged on my ear, which was still dipped in shame. "How do you feel, Kovuco? You also understand that this is not a mating arrangement. You must be careful that other Völfien don't sniff this out!"

His directness seized me. "I mean, well, she—"

"Kovuco!" My father snapped. "If you're going to talk to me, you must stop this stammering. I know your heart, and I am only here to guide you. I am apprehensive for you, but you must be strong. If you wish to stay in the Order, you must be vigilant!"

I sharply inhaled.

"You could be excommunicated. Or, worse, killed, Kovuco!"

I exhaled. "I know. The whiff of death has lingered; I have been on edge. I'm supposed to protect her. It's my job, Father. But I do care for her. I'm confused. I know it's forbidden, but—"

"But what?"

My chest tensed. "To love a human." I apprehensively blurted.

"You *love* her?" He stared at me as if he had something more to say, but paused. His ancient, fierce eyes bore into mine.

"I don't understand how this is even possible." I shamefully shook my head.

My father cleared his throat. He looked out at the crashing waves again, pondering. "Well, Kovuco." He paused again. "My son, you are *technically* part human."

My body shifted from the blatancy of his truth.

Part?

Not once had Völfien been compared to a human with such certainty. Our race had been taught to stay within our race; embrace our true form, the Medzio; and be of aid to humans. Nothing more.

"Then why do we call ourselves Rinkin, not human? That doesn't sound *human* to me." I sighed aloud, pressing for answers.

"Rinkin means brother to man. Völfien bear Uridei's image in the same respect as any human would. It's meant to be this way since Albean's gift to us, all to protect the humans during the war."

"I still have questions; something feels off." I turned from him, flustered at the notion. I had been reminded how I should feel all too often, but my heart could not be persuaded. "The love between a human and a völf would be complicated, Father."

"Yes, just because you can learn to master shifting doesn't make it any easier to fall for a human." He fell silent again and then sighed. "Kovuco, I know I haven't been a good father to you. I hope you'll understand one day why there are many things I cannot share at this time, but you must abandon this depredation from your past. There are things you need not worry about now or try to understand."

"I don't know if I can. I'm tired of feeling lost!"

There was an even more resounding, almost darker silence shared between us.

He's holding back. I clenched my claws and looked to the horizon as the sun's red glare embraced us.

"Kovuco?"

I turned to face him.

"This will not be easy. When you drink the blood of a mate—well, in this case, a human—it heightens you. You must also be aware it can weaken you, especially if you do not continue to bloodlet with her. You will need her more than she will need you. As you know, Kovuco, humans do not need blood like our kind."

"I understand, Father."

"I am not finished speaking. Listen. It is instilled within you to crave her now. With this bond, you must be prepared; you will feel her constantly. Every step. Every heartbeat. If she sneezes, you'll catch the sensation in your nostrils; if she becomes agitated, you'll feel her blood pressure change. If she calls out to you, you may hear or feel her needs. You are hers, and she is yours. You share a rare bond. Powerful. Beautiful. Unexplainable. I pray to Uridei that he alone will guide your path, and you will listen. She as well."

"Thank you. But, Father?"

"Yes, my son?"

"I want to beg for your forgiveness. I have spoken cruelly to you. I know you have suffered in this life, but everything I have is because of you. My brothers, the Order—all of it! It's all because I was born to you. This platinum fur, these blue eyes, and even the unanswered questions that linger. They are gifts. Gifts that have given me experience. Challenge."

I locked my gaze with him again, and he looked at me not with his rested glance but with a smile of admiration.

"I love you, Father. And I will always live to honor you, as Uridei would want."

He bowed. "You still have much to learn, young Kovuco, and much more to endure. Never stop learning. Never stop growing. Your gift is not a curse. Your suffering is not for nothing. You'll see."

I nodded as we both turned to view the rolling sea.

CHAPTER NINETEEN

REDEEMER

Shaar
Tsunetomo
West Wing
Aoustí 16

AMEILJA AWOKE, UNAWARE THAT HER EXPERI-
ence with Kovuco returning her to her wing had lulled her into another
deep sleep.

She'd dreamt wildly. She'd dreamt about his mysterious strength
and warmth, as well as his being connected to her. She recalled a pulling
sensation throughout her body as sounds of pulsating fluids melodically
filled her mental space. Blurred images of Kovuco's past swept through
her memory as the abstract dream twisted into a whirling world of red
waves.

Kovuco had laid her in her bed and tucked her in. It was the second
night she had been tucked into bed by a völf, only this time, it had been
peaceful.

Ameilja hustled out of bed and headed to her washroom. She was
still wearing her previous day's clothes and needed to urgently change.
She'd slept in and hadn't had a ton of visitation with Kovuco like she had
originally planned. She decided a late breakfast was in order. There was
much to arrange that day, realizing she still must make confirmations
for their pertinent flight to Rúnar.

Ameilja stood before the mirror, assessing her reflection. Although
the weariness lingered, the energetic effects of the bond pushed her

forward. Her skin looked healthy and nourished. There weren't any signs of discoloration or puffiness under her eyes from lack of sleep. She pulled a strand of her hair toward her nose and inhaled. Her scent seemed slightly different too—calming.

"Fascinating," she whispered.

It then dawned on her that Kovuco had removed her coat and vest. She appreciated it, as she would have been vastly uncomfortable otherwise. Gently, she placed a hand along her upper abdomen, feeling where he would have touched to unbutton her vest. His touch still lingered there.

Her chamber door suddenly opened, snatching her from her thoughts. She looked toward the sound and saw Jayna, who began setting her table.

"Well hello, Jayna. I am going to have breakfast with Kovuco."

"Oh?" she said. "Should I prepare for two then?"

"Oh no, that's not needed; I'm going to take him out."

"Out?"

"Yes. In the next town. There's a restaurant I have been dying to take my White Throats to, and now I can."

"Are you sure that's a good idea, Lady Ameilja? With all that is going on?"

Ameilja took another glance in the mirror to check her face. She took one final moment to absorb the new Ameilja who stared back—a new Ameilja had been born. Even more so than yesterday, she was more confident, resilient, and steadfast.

She turned to Jayna. "Yes. It will be fine. Kovuco will be with me."

Unexpectedly, Jayna smiled.

Ameilja felt perplexed by the smile. Jayna had always been stringent, but now there was a new energy to her that probed Ameilja's curiosities.

"What's with the smile, Jayna?"

"Nothing, Lady Ameilja. I am glad to see you so happy for once. You look well."

Happy? Am I really happy? Happier than yesterday with this new-found curse lingering over me?

Jayna turned from the table and began making her lady's bed. Ameilja joined her, hoping to assist.

"Are you ready then, Lady Ameilja? Does Kovuco know you are coming for him?"

"No, not yet. We were supposed to talk yesterday, but I more or less fell asleep after—well, after Haruka and the others left."

Another big smile emerged from Jayna.

"Jayna, you're making me dreadfully nervous. What are you hiding?"

"Nothing, Lady—"

"For once, I am going to correct you, Jayna. Don't call me *Lady*. Now you must tell me, what are you hiding?"

Jayna stood upright, pulled a chair from the table, and gestured for her to sit. Ameilja took the seat opposite, insisting on helping herself. Jayna took the chair she'd intended for Ameilja and gave her a mischievous look, as she knew her smiling was unnatural to her personality.

Ameilja braced herself. "So?" she asked.

"Lady Ameilja, I have always been fond of you. Ever since I took this post. Do you remember? You had barely graduated at the time."

"I was sixteen. You matched Dancer's quiet yet gloomy persona."

Jayna blushed. "Yes. Dancer and I took our roles seriously, you see. Ameilja, you remember what I shared with you and Kovuco, right?"

"About your past?"

"Yes. It was such a dark time. I have lived a very tumultuous life that I would never wish on anyone. I am grateful Ash brought me here to serve your family. Your family has been a tremendous blessing. It's as if my dark past has been erased, and I can retire in a trusted community. But, Ameilja, if I may be honest, you have always left me wondering."

"Wondering?" Ameilja furrowed her brow.

"Wondering why you wanted out so badly. You have the opportunity to live a life of leisure; politics may be your roughest area, but even then, you've strived to be a beacon of hope to the people. But then I pitied you, thinking of this mundane fate for you. You've strived to leave these city walls to the farthest reaches of the land. I mean, what girl would want to go to A'grommár? I dreaded every time we traveled south, yet your heart leaped at what Uridei called you to. I guess I have a confession …"

Ameilja leaned forward, and her smile drifted off as the conversation grew more serious.

"The night of the bloodletting, I heard the gunshot. It shocked me, but I quickly took measures to prevent anyone else from entering the wing. All along, I've had a key, Ameilja. When I returned to your door, I cracked it open to see that Kovuco and you were gone. I was armed, ready to take matters into my hands, because I knew if you were to hate anyone, it should be me, not any of the wülkure, but I stopped. I stopped, and I listened—halting the shuttering breaths coursing through my chest. I heard you plead with Kovuco and heard the desperation in your voice. Every part of my inner being said, *Rush through those doors! Don't allow this; you must kill this völf* ... But I refrained."

Jayna appeared to lose herself, quickly turning from Ameilja to focus on something else to keep tears from falling.

Ameilja spoke gently, "It's okay, Jayna. Why did you refrain?"

Jayna took a deep breath and continued, shaking her head. "I knew Kovuco was trouble the moment you picked him. I approved of your other Völfien selections; however, I prayed you wouldn't pick Kovuco. As soon as you reached for his marks, I knew at that moment everything would change."

"Is it because of his father?"

"Yes. Of course. But it wasn't his fault. He was innocent, but I knew his familial past would eventually come back to haunt him. I remember Adémaro from my past. He is magnificent, but a völf's past will always follow his offspring. But that all changed that night. You see, when I heard you plead with Kovuco to drink from you, my worries told me it would destroy you, but I refrained because in my heart ... I knew ..."

"Knew what?"

"That instead it would save you."

"Save me? How?"

"Kovuco has so much to learn about himself. Both of you do. You're so special Ameilja, and so is he." Jayna smiled again. "There is so much potential to tap into, and now that you will share parts of him—"

The two were startled when a hurried knock rapped against the door.

Jayna collected herself, embarrassed that even she was caught off guard by such emotions. She rose from her seat. "My goodness! Pardon me, Lady Ameilja."

Ameilja smiled tenderly as Jayna headed for the chamber door. She would never have imagined her trusted handmaiden would allow such a thing. Looking back on that night, she remembered that she had never had a chance to secure or check beyond the door. Were there traces of Kovuco's blood, fur, or prints left to be discovered? Had Jayna cleaned all the evidence and aided in hiding the secret? *All must be true.*

Ameilja's gaze drifted to the center of the table to see a small bouquet she hadn't noticed earlier.

"What's this?" She quietly questioned, reaching for the floral bundle.

Bound by a bright red band was a mix of Oleander, Lavender, Foxglove, and Begonia. The combination smelled lovely, but also had a hint of familiarity.

"Oleander? Foxglove?" Ameilja whispered, thinking back to one of her studies. "Foxglove is for secrecy. Oleander is for warning ... why—" A gasp leaped from Ameilja's throat as soon as the realization swept over her; a warning bouquet had been strategically placed.

Jayna opened Ameilja's chamber door. "Yes?"

There was no answer. No one awaited her. She pushed open the door farther, peering outside, and saw another handmaiden dead on the floor just as Ameilja fearfully yelled, "Jayna! Wait!"

Jayna instinctively pulled the door shut, when a booted foot forcefully kicked it open, causing her to stumble backward. A white, porcelain-masked figure sprang into the room.

"Ameilja!" Jayna bellowed.

Ameilja rose to her feet, but the assailant moved first. He delivered a brutal kick, throwing her against the wall. Jayna drew a knife from her bodice and delivered several slashes toward the assailant.

The masked figure deflected the blows with wrist blades, swooped in, and clutched Jayna's wrist. He seized the moment and quickly drove his second pair of blades through Jayna's stomach. She promptly broke free from the assailant's grasp, and the blades were pulled from her abdomen. She stumbled, falling harshly against the stone floor, gasping from the pain, with blood pouring from her wounds.

Ameilja, unable to check on her beloved handmaiden, charged for Red Fang on the far wall. The masked figure drew a sword from his back and stopped her, holding the blade steadily against her throat. "Don't even think about it, Lady Frost," he said with a cold, deathly declaration.

Ameilja instantly collected a full glimpse of the masked man. "Kärleiv! What is this?" she rasped as her shocked gaze dropped down to Jayna.

Tears pooled in her eyes as she stared into Jayna's open eyes, which were frozen in a death stare.

Oh, Jayna …

Kärleiv, Jakob Malkovich's trusted bodyguard, stood in the pool of Jayna's blood, which began spreading farther along the floor. He remained silent.

"Answer me!" Ameilja hissed.

As soon as she turned her gaze back to him, he struck her against the temple with the pommel of his sword. She hit the floor as her world began shifting into an agonizing stupor.

Kovuco.

She looked up through a morphed vision and saw Kärleiv's menacing mask cocked to one side, staring down at her curiously, just before she lost consciousness.

C H A P T E R   T W E N T Y

WITHOUT HER

Shaar
Tsunetomo
West Wing protectorate tower, second floor
Aoustí 16

I WALKED BACK HOME TO MY DORM ALONE. MY
father had said he would be in Tsunetomo for two more days. I'd agreed
to see him soon.

I would be alone again for now—something I was not used to.

With Ameilja reverberating through my senses, the solitude would
be more insufferable. I already missed the simple things. I'd gotten so
used to Tam dragging me out of bed that I wondered if I would even
wake without him there. No more having reading binges with Nav'i or
arguing the merits of his books. Would I lose weight without Dancer
there to facilitate consistent meals?

As soon as I entered my dormitory, I meandered to the washroom.
I used the toilet and walked over to the sink. The large mirror loomed
before me, but I dipped my head.

I paused and took a deep breath. I thought back to my father's words:
"You are part human, Kovuco."

But I am a völf. Can I face my Rinkin, my human form not yet
mastered?

I inhaled and held my breath.

Can I face him?

Can I face the human I've despised all this time?

I exhaled.

I hesitantly lifted my gaze toward my reflection. Slowly, my eyes glided upward—my stomach knotted. I could see the stranger standing before me in my peripheral vision, unmoving.

He waited.

Look at him! Look, Kovuco.

Do it!

I clenched my teeth; my jaw tightened. *Do it!*

I winced aloud. *Do it!*

I snapped my focus to the mirror. I locked eyes with my Rinkin. Inhale.

Exhale.

Similar, piercing blue eyes stared back. "Well, hello, distant friend."

My Rinkin looked sleepy, like I presently felt. His eyes were sullen, blue like mine, and relaxed under dark brows. His hair was a light, silver-like blond, almost matching my fur. His skin was slightly pale, but it wasn't covered in blood. No rage, no bared teeth, and no gore. He was human and was calm, but wasn't at peace either. A mysteriousness lingered. Strangely enough, he was me.

I tilted my head, and he followed. I stretched open my jaw, and he copied.

A defined, human face stared back. *This reflection is undeniably me. Are we really all that different?*

A sharp ache whipped through my chest. I tensed and dropped my head from my reflection as an image crashed through my mental realm. A blade was drawn; flesh was pierced. Blood rippled over stone tiles. Ameilja darted, running for a sword. She stopped.

What are you doing, Ameilja?

I listened, focusing on her mind and her movements. She spoke: "What is this?" Salty tears filled her eyes.

Blood. *I smell blood.* I licked my lips. It was not Ameilja's blood. *But whose?*

Suddenly, a violent jolt shifted my head. I roared, baring my teeth from the pain, as I smashed my fist against the mirror, catching myself as I did. The mirror cracked as I lost focus and nearly tripped and fell over myself, knocking contents to the ground. The glass then shattered into tiny pieces, while simultaneously, a bright flash erupted, and I was forcefully cast toward our living space, along with stone debris and remnants of the washroom.

The images shifted and rattled until I regained my focus and saw a large hole before me, from an explosion against the wall of our tower. *We've been bombed!*

The deafening sound of the blast left a lingering ringing in my ears. The smell of scorched rock swelled within my sinuses. I clenched my fists and slowly stood, gaining my balance. Smoke swept into my lungs and burned my eyes.

Our dorm was on one of three levels, but each level had two dormitories. Luckily, I wasn't hurt badly. The wounds I had sustained were minor. I had hit my head on the doorjamb when I was thrown. I lowered myself again, rolled toward the rupture of our washroom, and looked toward the next dorm. I could see our neighbors' washroom; it was in much worse shape than mine.

The explosion had hit the neighboring unit much more heavily. I scanned the area and saw that most of the level was demolished. I prayed no one was home. Survival was unlikely. Before I could investigate further, I heard a piercing squeal from an airship overhead. I realized it was sending another bomb to our tower.

"Get down!" Someone bellowed from behind, grabbing me by the shoulder.

The blast hit below us, sending rubble, dust, and fire embers all about the washroom. I turned, and it was Tam.

"What are you doing here?" I spoke loudly, surprised.

"Let's get out of here, and I'll explain!"

I nodded. "What if there are survivors?"

"The lower level was just hit, but I'll take it. You take the upper level?"

I nodded. "Make it quick!"

We stormed into the hall, and I began my ascent, while Tam descended to the lower level.

When I reached the top, a pair of handmaidens were in the hallway. They were dusty, with minor wounds.

"Are you two all right?" I asked.

They both nodded amid tears, and one said, "Yes, Kovuco. What's happening?"

"Can you walk?" I asked.

"I can," answered one. The other handmaiden's legs looked bruised and bloodied.

I turned to the able-bodied handmaiden. "Can you help her down the stairs to the yard?"

She nodded. "I'll do my best."

"Keep each other safe, and we'll help you once you get to the grass. Stay out of sight! There's an airship out there."

I reached the upper level and pounded on Ash's door. "Ash?" I knocked twice more. "Ash?"

Like a jackrabbit, I lifted my foot and smashed my heel against the door, blistering it in two. Ash's room was demolished, opened to the outside world. His tools were scattered, with papers flying about the room as the ocean breeze carried them. I stepped in warily, as I knew vilkanás and other poisons, such as féja, had been released into the air.

"Ash? Ash! Answer me!"

I heard him groaning. "Kovey?"

"Where are you, Ash?"

I turned the corner, and Ash lay on the ground. His white shirt was torn, bloodied, and slightly charred. He pointed to his living space. "Get my pop's gun. Get it, or I fucking stay in this tower!"

I ran to his nightstand and saw his father's gun, White Powder, in its holster. I lifted it carefully by the leather and brought it to him. He strapped it to his belt like a drunken idiot trying to zip his pants.

I lifted and cradled him. "Ready, ya old slag?"

"Onward, Kovey."

Quickly and carefully, we made our way down the stairs, and Tam met me by our dorm. "Is Ash okay?" He urged.

"As he'll ever be; let's hurry. There's a handmaiden who will need to be carried."

We raced down the stairs, and just outside the door were the hand-maidens. Tam lifted the wounded one, and we sprinted across the bridge toward the House, when another series of blasts flew in our direction.

"No!" Tam hollered as a bellowing growl escaped his chest.

Our bridge was pulverized. The explosion was so intense that we each lost our footing and tumbled to the ground. I was ironically grateful, as a few more steps would have meant a watery grave below.

The second wave of missiles whistled overhead; both penetrated the base of the tower, breaking the foundation. It fell in a colossal decimation into the ocean. It was hard to believe the place where we had slept was now a ruin, and we had been in it just moments ago.

"We need to go!" Tam yelled.

We focused on the twelve-foot gap looming before us. Tam looked at me and nodded. He charged, not alerting the handmaiden in his arms of his plan. He leaped and cleared the landing. He turned to me, expecting me to make the next call.

"Ash, ladies first," I told him as I set him down gently.

"Naturally. Good boy, Kovey!"

I gestured for the handmaiden to come to me. She looked terrified but closed her eyes and buried her face in my chest as I scooped her up. I took a deep breath and made the jump. A brick fell when I hit the other side, and I nearly fell through. We lost two more feet. I set the handmaiden down, and she joined Tam.

"I am going back for Ash!"

"No!" yelled Ash from across the divide.

Torpidly, he stood. As he did, I heard the landing crack ominously along its frame. We lost another foot of the landing on his side.

"Too risky. You have to wait for help, boys!"

I shook my head and sprinted for the jump. I cleared it but just barely. I recovered my footing and was met with the end of White Powder's barrel touching my nose.

"Curse it, Kovey!" he said sternly. "You shouldn't have done that!"

"Ash, no messing around. It's time to go!"

He swatted White Powder at me. "You barely made that jump! You'll never make it with me in your arms! Go back! Now!"

"No! I am not leaving you, Ash! Quit acting like an idiot. Let's go!"

"Fucking hell!" He pulled the hammer back on White Powder and centered the barrel against my nose. "Go back, Kovuco!"

Ash had never spoken so harshly to me. He talked through gritted teeth, but he might've done so from the pain of his wounds.

"What are you gonna do? Shoot me?"

"Fuck you! Go back! I'll not lose you for my old ass; I've lived my life!"

With another crack, the landing shifted. I kept my footing as Ash leaned against the baluster of the landing with White Powder still pointing for me. "Kovuco, I mean it! You have to go back!"

"I am not leaving you on this landing. And you're not going to shoot me; so quit screwing around!" I held out a paw for him to join me, slightly afraid of the consequences of testing the revolver aimed at me.

"You're right, Kovey. You're not going to leave me on this landing." He nodded to the other side. "But it is time." He glanced over the edge to the wild, crashing waters below. "Yep. It's time."

"Ash?"

He leered at me with his sleepy, studious eyes. His scraggly blond hair blew in the wind. He holstered White Powder and locked it in place. "You know I had a wife, right, Kovey? Did I ever tell you about her?" He looked over toward Tam and called out, "Tam, you remember?"

Tam nodded. "Yeah, Ash. I remember, but—"

"What was her name, Tam?"

"What?"

"Her fucking name! What was her fucking name, Tambor?"

"How could I forget? Carleigh. Her name was Carleigh!"

Ash looked back at me. "Carleigh. The most beautiful creature Uridei ever created, all for me. Do you believe Uridei created you, Kovuco?"

I looked at him, confused. With another crack, the landing leaned more. "Ash! Really? Can we—"

"Answer me, Kovey! Answer!"

"Of course! Of course he created me. What are you getting at, Ash? This can't wait till later?"

"Created me? Created Carleigh? Created us for each other?"

"Yes! All those things! Can we go now?"

"Whom did Uridei create you for?"

I paused.

The world slowed. I instantly forgot the danger. I didn't feel the chill of the wind anymore. The adrenaline and noise ceased to exist around me. My first thought screaming across my mind was the redheaded beauty I called my lady. Was it strange my answer was Ameilja?

"Ash, I—"

"What about her?"

"Who?" I asked.

"Whom did Uridei create Ameilja for?"

I felt as if he were a wizard reading my mind and manipulating my thoughts to hypnotize me.

"Goodbye, Tam!" He looked at me again. "Goodbye, Kovuco Blackstar."

I broke from my thoughts and reached for Ash, but he slipped away and fell to the water below. I dove forward and reached over the edge for him. "Ash!" I roared, but there was no answer.

I didn't even see him hit the water.

"Ash!" I cried out again. I watched the tossing, violent waves crashing against the jagged rocks and debris below. Salty tears spilled from my eyes like an open wound as his memories flashed through my mind.

I'd never again sit beside him for breakfast. I'd never again hear his nicknames, obnoxious jokes, or profanities. I'd never feel his presence again, hear the sound of his rugged voice, or his fatherly ways as he refrained from constantly watching us escort Ameilja. Never again ...

He was gone.

I sharply snapped from my sadness and made the jump back to Tam. Two more völves met us on the landing and grabbed me as I barely made the jump from the crumbling structure.

We urgently evacuated the area and breached the gates to the manor. As soon as the gates slammed shut, the remainder of the bridge tipped—moaning the song of demise—then violently crashed into the ocean.

"Goodbye, Ash," I whispered. *Goodbye, my friend. My brother. Uridei awaits you in the Vale of Heroes.*

Tam joined me and handed me a tonfa sword. "Kovuco, we have to hurry!"

I nodded, feeling my chest tighten, and nearly fell to my knees.

Tam secured me from falling. "Kovuco? What's wrong?"

"It's Ameilja!"

"What about her?"

"She's in danger!"

⭐

Shaar
Tsunetomo
House Frost, southern landing
Aoustí 16

I sensed her. All of her.

We charged through the double doors of the main hall out to the landing where I had killed the assassin. There we saw two large ships; they were docked. One, of wood and antique bronze and teal with spike-like scaffolds, was preparing to disembark. It wasn't a familiar-looking ship, but it resembled the vessel that had devastated our tower.

She's on that airship. Against her will. She's unconscious.

At the foot of the airship was a familiar masked face. "Kärleiv," I said aloud. *Malkovich's bodyguard.*

I felt this was a good sign until I noticed the bloody bodies of armigers, all fallen at his feet. He had two battle knives at his hip. His bronze, black, and emerald armor emblazoned his sinister notoriety, a chastisement to our will against him.

What the hell is he doing?

Tam and I wielded tonfa swords. The other two völves wielded scythes. We felt the urgency to hurry as we absorbed the scene.

"Lady Frost is in there!" I yelled to the völves. "She's in danger!"

Two of them pounded their chests, ready to take charge. We all ran toward the vessel.

Kärleiv casually drew his knives and cocked his head, clearly not intimidated by our approach. The first völf swung for him, but Kärleiv's blade deflected the first and second swings. Like a demonic whisper, Kärleiv slashed the völf across his chest and then dealt a finishing blow to the back of his neck. It snapped, and the völf fell, dead.

Kärleiv then pivoted and met my tonfa sword. He parried my first swing and then dodged the next völf's scythe. Expertly, he flipped between swings that should have pulverized him in a single blow, but he breezed past with ease. He delivered a swift thrust with both blades, injuring the other völf. Kärleiv leaped over him, using his body as a lift, and then stabbed him through the neck. The völf gargled through the blood filling his throat; vilkanás hissed against his flesh. He then collapsed.

Kärleiv pulled the knife from the völf's throat and twirled to deflect another blow from Tam and me.

We were down to just the two of us. Disbelief swept over me witnessing the two völves he put down with ease. For as agile as Kärleiv was, his blows were fierce and deadly accurate.

Tam charged, then dropped to his knees, sliding toward Kärleiv's ankles. Kärleiv leaped backward over him and then somersaulted toward me. I dodged him, hoping to propel him to the edge.

Tam, fuming with rage, swung for Kärleiv. Kärleiv acted fast; he inhumanly leaped over Tam's shoulders and slashed his throat with the vilkanás-infused blade.

"No!" I devastatingly roared.

I came at Kärleiv with a fury. Both his swords artistically deflected my tonfa sword.

Tam, holding his throat, still came to my aid, but Kärleiv maneuvered quick, catching us both off guard. He kicked Tam's shin, throwing him off balance. Tam fell, and Kärleiv slashed toward him again. Tam ducked, but the blade cut him across his back and upper arm; he rolled on the ground as his wounds sizzled from the slash.

I looked at Tam in horror—the horror that he might've been slain.

I picked up Tam's tonfa sword and held both in the White Throat stance we had strategically adopted. This masked human needed to die!

Kärleiv cackled beneath his mask. "Foolish völf. Do you think you have the grit to rise before me?"

A growl brewed through the depths of my core.

The airship suddenly began to pull away from the landing. In a stressed attempt, I tried to run for it, but Kärleiv leaped before me and, with a wild kick, sent me flying in the opposite direction.

I was winded, terrified that a human man could kick me with such force. *Who is he?*

He charged me once more, and all I could do was summon what speed I could manage to deflect the furious blows. Sparks flew from my tonfa's blade as I desperately deflected the impacts. The song of steel clashing echoed throughout the atmosphere like a hurried melody. I resumed a defensive position as the clashes continued.

Despite the massive change in his strength, he was still nimble and weightless, securing powerfully predacious blows at me, barely breathing with every strike I managed to deflect. I rasped and grunted with each movement, while he was silent in comparison.

Watch him, Kovuco! Get a hold of yourself!

I deflected another whispering slash, countering his furious blows to my advantage. I eyed him, tapping into my predatory state—the gift of Albean. I slowed down time as he moved, fueling my instincts to see his every vibrational move. When he thrust forward once more, I captured him like a photo, pausing him in place, then struck him with all my strength against his mask. The white porcelain shattered against his face, but he didn't even flinch.

I leaped from his swinging blade and stood tall, grounding my form and gazing upon the face of this unnatural human—the so-called trusted bodyguard of our centurion, Abbot Jakob Malkovich.

My pupils dilated, taking in his detail. His flesh was a withered gray, but from his forehead to his lower jaw, ear to ear was a skeletal, decayed amaranth of fungal green bone. I stared into his glowering eyes, which were luminescent and diabolical; bits of greenish flames intertwined in and out of the empty eye sockets. I stared at the horror.

No man could have moved the way Kärleiv moved; with each movement, he filled me with terror. Fighting human Kärleiv, with his mask, had given me the confidence that he could be wounded or killed, defeated in some way, but now, for the first time in my lifetime, I stared upon what appeared to be a member of the undead.

He's reanimated from the power of the Näkk! It can't be! How is this possible? How is this undead body functioning like an average human? Speaking like one? Fighting like one?

Memories flashed before my subconscious: Kärleiv walking among the living, a paladin member of House Malkovich and a trusted member for Jakob, all beneath a ceramic mask. All this time, he had hidden among us.

How?

There's no way I can manage to destroy him, not without—

I heard Ameilja's voice whisper in my mind as if she were standing there with me. I froze and listened as my gaze locked on Tam dragging himself toward a scythe, behind Kärleiv.

Kovuco. Her voice glided. *Use the purge …*

I shook my head. *Völfien can't Purge. I can't! A völf can't!*

There was no time to think. Once Tam reached the scythe, I charged Kärleiv, creating a barrage with my tonfa swords, countering his attacks with even more powerful slashes. I pushed him back, and Tam lifted the scythe and plunged the anchor-like blade into Kärleiv's back. I dropped a tonfa, leaped upward, and spun my form while grasping the other tonfa. My claws extended, time slowed, and I closed my eyes and prayed to Uridei: *Light of Uridei, please grant me a hand to Purge …*

My right arm hairs lifted, a supernatural heat spread through my veins, and my entire arm lit on fire. A white flame burst from my skin in a white-hot aura. My claws clutched Kärleiv's decaying face, and a holy combustion emitted from my palm so fiercely an uncontrollable roar burst from my throat as the fire doused him, caustically emblazoning his entire being to ash.

Tam ducked out of the way, leaving the scythe protruding from Kärleiv's back. My eyes spurted wisps of Uridei's light as I roared a mouth full of teeth. We hit the ground, I landed on my feet, and Kärleiv was all but hot, ashen debris caught in the wind like a lost memory.

The Purge settled and flickered away. My arm was badly burned, and my hair was singed away, leaving exposed skin, naked and charred.

Tam lunged for me and quickly began wrapping my arm in a bandage from his pack. "Oh shit! Kovuco, that was incredible!" he rasped in shock. "Where did you learn to Purge?" he asked as he continued to secure my arm with the cloth.

"I—I don't know." I shook my head, just as shocked, eyeing my arm disbelievingly. *It all happened so fast.*

I lunged back up and looked at the airship, which was now nearly ten miles away. I saw two other ships join it, escaping out to the Eastern Sea. Anger exploded inside my chest—burning, engulfing rage. I released a growl so intense I had no air left to give from my depleted lungs. *It's carrying away my Ameilja!*

I inhaled rapidly, filling my lungs back to their fullest capacity, locked and loaded for my next move. I turned to Tam. "Are you okay?" I urged through thick breaths.

He nodded. "I'll be okay. Don't worry; my first touch of vilkanás hurts like hell, but I'm lucky he didn't get me deep. I'm alive, aren't I?"

"Yea, you're lucky!" I nodded as relief replaced my feelings of shock.

I walked toward the edge of the landing and took a deep breath.

"Kovuco?" Tam called.

I turned toward him.

"What are you going to do?"

"I have to go after her!"

He hesitated, then nodded to me. "I'll see you soon."

There was so much I needed to ask him, but I had no time. Across the way, I saw a mass of Frost's armigers and wülkure charging toward the landing. I could not be captured for questioning. I needed to get to her.

I returned the nod and crossed my chest with my bandaged right arm, still steaming from Uridei's light.

He returned the gesture. "Light of Uridei, brother."

"Light of Uridei," I said.

I closed my eyes and leaned back, and I fell limp, submitting to the deafening exhaustion my body begged of me. I soared below to the frigid ocean and prayed for my survival. I had to survive.

I am coming, Ameilja! By Uridei, I will find you! I failed to protect you, but I will save you!

As I fell to the watery depths, I felt her heartbeat. We were still in sync. We were still together. We were still one.

Without her, I am nothing.

ARC TWO

CURSES

CHAPTER TWENTY-ONE

CALLOUS

Fjorthúr
The Sunspire
The beachfront
Aoustí 15

THE SMELL OF DEATH SCORCHED THE AIR. ALL the bodies and gore remnants were quickly recovered and burned outside the Sunspire. There could be no risk of the infection leaving the island or of the news of the Näkk getting out.

Two of the recovered bodies included Æsir Anton Rotenfeld and Dr. Kristján Baadar. Quiet funeral arrangements would be planned accordingly, still recognizing them with honors.

Members under Henrik's leadership were immediately sent to aid in stripping the Sunspire of the horrific crimes committed within the bunker and the halls of the Spire. They also aided the few survivors that were under Rikard's watch.

Henrik had been granted permission to arrange for the current security team to take on new positions; large sums of hush money were the influencing factor.

A new team would be assembled to replace the Commission members who had fallen, along with cleverly orchestrated lies to comfort the families of the deceased. A broad news blast regarding the cult massacre as the cause was a perfect coverup.

Despite everything that had happened, Sunspire would continue to progress, and its secrets would remain within its walls. Frahm's determination hinted that the Näkk studies needed to continue under his lead and knowledge. Security lead Matthäus Brand would be scheduled to return to Fjorthúr's governing city, Dubrojavík. Henrik was covering the costs for him to see Blackwater City's head surgeons specializing in cybernetic biology and biomechatronic body parts, to replace his severed arm. Cybernetic body parts were not uncommon and only elaborated on the ever-growing innovation in Isarah.

The tranquilizer Kiefer had shot into Isabelle was merely a hallucinogenic to a human but highly incapacitating to a völf. She was now heavily sedated in a coma-like state. The current plan was that she would return to Demitori with Kiefer to be admitted into Duskwell Hospital.

Kiefer stood on the roof balcony, awaiting clearance to return to the airship headed for Demitori. Wächter Ólafur Urs accessed the balcony and ventured toward Kiefer. He held a handkerchief to his nose, blocking the putrid smell of burning bodies, and leaned against the parapet. He gestured for a cigarette.

Kiefer pulled one from his pocket and held it out to him. Ólafur went for it, but just before he took it, Kiefer pinched it, ground the tobacco from the white paper, and flicked it from the balcony onto the sand below.

Ólafur stepped back and gave Kiefer a dissatisfied look. "You think I agreed with all that shit back there, don't you?"

"Nothing personal. You were following orders, but understand the wülkure aren't in the forgiving business," Kiefer sneered.

A wächter approached from behind Ólafur. "Wülkure Yuska, you're accompanying Ms. Baadar, correct?"

Kiefer nodded, putting out his cigarette, and followed after the man.

Ólafur didn't move, but as the unforgiving wülkure turned his back to him, he shouted, "Good luck, Yuska!"

Kiefer sighed irritably. "You too, Urs."

Kiefer didn't mean to criticize the wächter with such a vituperative attack, but Rotenfeld's ability to command a unit against him was a betrayal he would never forget. The whole matter had left a bitter taste in his mouth. Any allies he'd thought he had within this Commission department were now opponents and perhaps conspirators in an even darker plot.

He passed Frahm on the stairs and offered no parting words for the doctor. The doctor, however, grinned menacingly at Kiefer, who walked away unscathed from the encounter.

Who would have thought that Tobias Frahm, a former armiger, would stray so far from the divine path that he'd become a doctor and fully embrace the Näkk? *Guess that's why he didn't notice his cult-following wife until it was too late. He deserved it.*

Kiefer boarded the airship, one much smaller than the one he had come in on. As the vessel ascended above the Sunspire, he noted it was the most terrifying place he had experienced, and he was looking forward to seeing it as a distant memory. But knowing what he knew now, that might not be the case. The nightmare might find him sooner rather than later.

He turned to Isabelle in her bed. Thick leather straps secured her down. Her stunning features lightened from the sunlight streaming in through the window, and her blonde hair lay loosely around her shoulders. The once-shaved sides of her head were now covered in long, thick hair. Even though she was older, she looked youthful and flawless. He wondered if the völf transformation influenced her youthful appearance, knowing their lifespan longevity.

Would it impact a human the same?

Kiefer also thought it strange to see her strapped down like a dangerous nonhuman suspect. Her stance was one hundred percent plantigrade, but her ears were still slightly shaped like those of the völf.

Kiefer gently lifted her upper lip and noticed sharp Völfien incisors on top and bottom. He assessed her, noting that she was normal, healthy, and complete, despite the lingering transformation. She now intimidated even the likes of him; this was no ordinary female.

What had happened to her? How had a human transformed into a völf?

"What is the meaning of all this?" Kiefer whispered to her, continuing to study her form.

He knew he'd have to find out soon enough, on top of keeping her safe.

☆

The Eastern Sea
The Renouncer
Aoustí 16

"Kovuco!" Ameilja screamed, waking abruptly in a deep sweat.

Her eyes darted around an unfamiliar room. She felt nauseated. Her head throbbed. She quickly rolled out of the bed she lay on and stumbled onto a shaggy dark gray rug. Preparing to defend herself, she huddled in the corner, eyes locked ahead of her.

She was alone.

Kovuco? Please hear me, sense me—anything.

Ameilja pressed her hands down into the soft rug. It reminded her of her protectorate's fur. For a moment, she could also smell his scent as if he were there.

Her Court of Völfien were supplied with a wood-based wash that the Frost House diens prepared for them specifically. She could smell the individual notes caressing her senses.

Bergamot, pineapple, and coriander. Something fruity, earthy. A spice, or maybe it just finished that way.

"How can I smell these things?" she asked herself. *Did we really include pineapple in our fragrance for the Völfien?* "Are our senses in sync too?"

Everything had happened so quickly that she barely recalled Kärleiv's mask as her vision faded. Her frontal lobe continued to ache from his harsh blow. Now she was locked in a small, luxuriously decorated room, but one she knew she could not easily escape from. Her anxieties heightened as her emotions roiled.

"Focus!" She snapped at herself.

The room had only a large, canopied bed in the center, no other furniture. The walls were painted a heavy gray with vintage-styled decor hung throughout. Nothing brightened the unknown space.

Where am I?

She assessed her surroundings again before crawling over to the door. She found comfort only in knowing Kovuco was there in some bonded way—at least she hoped. If Kovuco was there, Ameilja knew her mighty protectorate could free her from her captors, whoever they were.

Ameilja, whispered Kovuco's voice in her mind.

"Kovuco!" she gasped aloud. Her heart quickened.

She waited, but there was no reply. That was all she needed to prompt her next step and attempt an escape. She knew she could do it; a surge of self-assurance fueled her form.

Ameilja quickly tucked her ruffled hair into a top knot, freeing her face, and then pressed her ear to the wooden door. The cool wood nipped at her flushed cheeks.

She heard footsteps.

Lend me your ears, Kovuco …

It took her ten or fifteen minutes to track the movements before she realized she could hear sounds that were beyond human perception.

The weight of the weapons. Rifles? Ammunition is approximately sixty-five grains, thirty-magazine capacity. Maybe a knife. It's in the left boot—no, the right! The hallway is approximately five feet wide; the guards are spaced ten feet apart—no, fifteen. One is walking in the opposite direction. He's guarding the hallway entrance. He must be overseeing the piloting bay.

Ameilja shifted her ear toward the other side of the door.

I can hear more. There is a guard near my door, but he's also walking away. I must be careful; I cannot alert him. I have to wait for an opportune moment …

Okay, I am ready.

"Holy shit, this is awesome!" Ameilja huffed.

She snapped her attention to the walls of the room, searching.

"I need … I need something …" She clicked her tongue. "Perfect!" she stated, grabbing one of the intricately crafted art pieces off of the wall.

She set the picture on the ground and placed her knee on the edge of the frame. With a quick tug with both of her hands, the frame cracked, loosening the smaller pieces of metal entwined within its design. Then, cautiously, Ameilja tampered with the door's lock mechanism with one of the shards, listening for the release. With each twist, she extended her acquired auditory skills to where the guards paced. Their footing gave away their distancing; the perfect opportunity to time her next move.

The lock clicked. The moment was presented. She paused briefly, then sprinted from the opened door and down the hall.

Forgive me, Uridei, for today I'll be taking lives!

Ameilja rolled behind a guard, apprehending a knife from his boot, and sliced his ankle at the tendon; he took a knee. Before he could scream, Ameilja covered his mouth and stabbed the blade through his throat. She waited for his life to slip away, concealing his scream within the wound as his warm blood drenched her hands.

The second guard turned, but before he could even process what had happened, she took the knife from the guard's neck and threw it at his face. The blade embedded deep into his eye socket, killing him instantly.

"Yes!" Ameilja hissed victoriously.

She urgently dragged the two bodies to her room and shut the door. Sweat coated her form as she assessed their weapons: Arslan-4 MGs with suppressors attached. "You're coming with me," she heavily huffed, claiming one.

Ameilja keenly reviewed her skill with the weapon and then embarked. She didn't get far as she instantly picked up on the other guards headed toward her. That led to her quick decision to trek back the other direction.

She breached an open area and observed an elevator toward the back, but there was no way to know where it would take her or if a wächter could stop her from inside. Too risky.

A door suddenly opened down the way, and a woman breached the space and spotted Ameilja. That left her no choice; she turned the weapon on the unknown woman, fired two shots, and then charged the room where the woman had exited. Ameilja was abruptly stopped by another woman inside. The woman reached for a pistol sitting on a nearby table, but with another quick pull of the trigger, Ameilja killed her.

After securing the room, Ameilja breached the hallway and searched for any control panels, but a door directly across opened. Ameilja inhaled as a shirtless man appeared. Again, she opened fire and put him down. That was when an unexpected, yet familiar voice called out to her ...

"Ameilja?" The voice questioned.

Ameilja's eyes widened as shock swept over her. *Nathalii?*

"You kept giving me excuses for not spending time together, so I thought I'd pull you away from all those mundane engagements. Now we can *finally* have that girl time we've always talked about, yes?" her voice cooed.

"Nathalii!" Ameilja gasped. "Do you know what kind of trouble you are in? This is treason! Kidnapping? The Commission—*my* father—will have your head!"

"Better to ask for forgiveness, sweetness. Being told no is so droll."

Ameilja paused. Her pupils skipped side to side as she processed. *What is she doing? Why is she doing this?*

"Come out, Ameilja. We need to talk. Talk to me, or I'm afraid Völfy here dies."

"Völf?" Ameilja's heart leaped to her throat.

"Yes, dear. But not your platinum-furred friend; it's the far darker, golden-looking one, whatever his name is. Kärleiv killed a few other völves in pursuit of this very vessel. It seems this one here was the sole survivor."

No!

Ameilja's heart sunk. She swallowed, gripped her rifle, and cautiously peered around the corner. "Tam," she whimpered.

Tam was kneeling, stripped down to his slacks, bound, collared, and muzzled by one of Nathalii's lascivious guards. Another had a crossbow aimed at his head.

Anger sliced through Ameilja's veins to see him in that state. *How is he even here? What about Nav'i and Dancer? What about Kovuco? He can't be dead, can he?*

Ameilja gathered her wits and turned the corner, aiming the rifle down the hall. Nathalii stood there, wearing another one of her devilish outfits: tall boots, a leather corset, and a frilly black blouse. She looked confident and comfortable, even with an angry and armed Ameilja staring back at her from down the hall.

Ameilja gripped the metal weapon to the point that her knuckles turned white. Pieces of her hair stuck to the sweat beading along her forehead. She considered shooting her, but she knew it would have meant Tam's demise.

"If you hurt him, I will kill everyone on this ship!" Ameilja snapped; her warning was so grave that it caused her voice to crack.

"Of course, baby! I can't have you killing everyone on the airship. We won't make it to Isarah with those odds," Nathalli stated, locking her eyes with Ameilja's scowl. "But you need to give us your weapon."

"Unbind him! Now!"

Behind Nathalii, a man with a mustache said, "Milady, we cannot—"

Nathalii held up a hand. "Sh!" She turned back to Ameilja. "First, hand over your weapon. Then, I want you to order this völf to take his Rinkin form. If I unbind him, you promise he'll be a good boy? I can also give him a special little collar, mkay?"

Bitch!

"He must remain unharmed!" Ameilja insisted.

"Of course, Ami, dear. But he needs this collar, and then I am perfectly compliant."

Untrusting of Nathalii's true motivations, Ameilja apprehensively tossed the rifle to the ground to reassure the guards that she posed no threat. Just as one of the guards picked up the rifle, she darted down the hallway and knelt by Tam. She raked over his face and body, making sure he hadn't been harmed.

"Tam?" she tenderly whispered to him. "Tam, are you okay?"

Before Tam reassured her, he obeyed orders. "Step back." He gruffly insisted as he shuffled around, gathering his balance.

"Tam …"

The atmosphere shifted. Tam's entire form immediately began to tremble. His muscles violently twitched—stretching and shifting—as his Völfien face began collapsing inward. Tam fiercely grasped the muzzle that bound him and tore it away.

Ameilja instinctively scooted back, bringing her hands to her mouth; she watched in horror as Tam's fur started to slip from his flesh. Large pieces of his völf skin shriveled and peeled away, slapping the ground like thick, bloodied rags. His bones cracked and moaned as his body molded into its new form; the new Rinkin skin dripped thick sweat droplets due to the struggle. His slacks tore away; the ropes that bound him shredded into nothing but small hair-like fibers.

Tam bared his teeth from the pain but eerily didn't make a sound. With one final breath, the transformation was finalized.

The transition left him weak, hot, and spastic, covered in pieces of his discarded fur and blood.

"Well done!" Nathalii's voice sliced the silence. She childishly giggled, clapping her hands as her guards silently stood by, discomforted by the scene.

Changing into a völf was said to be easy, but changing into Rinkin was discomforting and even a bit traumatic to the body. It took some recovery after it was accomplished.

Ameilja's eyes searched Tam; her mental realm skipped from thought to thought as she witnessed a völf transition into Rinkin form for the first time. She shuffled back over to him and cradled his head in her lap. He looked dazed; his golden eyes stared off into nothing.

"Tam?" she asked, her lips quivering.

Her stomach knotted from the sight of his painful transition. She questioned why völves' link to humanity had to be so taxing. Shifting to a full human was impossible for their race, but it could be learned profoundly close. When a Völfien transformed, parts of the Medzio form lingered, such as pointed ears, excessive hair, incisor-like teeth, oddly shaped extremities, or claws. It varied for each Völfien.

Ameilja remembered Tam's file, but his current Medzio hints were only his pointed ears, claws, and bits of fur on his lower legs. His feet also still slightly resembled a völf's.

Ameilja pulled him close, trying to cradle his entire body in her arms, shielding his naked form from everyone. "Back away! Get him some clothes! Now!"

Nathalii snapped her fingers. "As the lady asked. Ensure she and the völf are properly taken care of—" she suddenly paused.

Nathalii's guards stepped forward, staring at Tam as she too bent down and examined his features. "Interesting," she purred, arching a brow.

"What?" Ameilja shot daggers at her.

"I'm examining him."

"Why?"

"Don't you see?" Nathalii urged.

Ameilja pulled Tam closer. "Leave him alone! He's fine!"

But Ameilja knew just as well as Nathalii did. Tam's transformation continued. He shifted until he showed no evidence of his Völfien identity. None. From head to toe, Tam turned entirely human.

CHAPTER TWENTY-TWO
SHIROU

Unknown location
Unknown date

I STRUCK THE ICE.

I had been born around the water, and had always been a swimmer, even in the colder months; however, I didn't anticipate smashing through a thick layer of ice.

My tensed form broke through it like a stone shattering against glass. Jagged edges cut through my fur, releasing clouds of crimson into the icy blue.

I sank deep into the depths of a cold black abyss. It took me a few moments to shake the dazed, amnesiac feeling ringing throughout my body. I began struggling to breach the surface for air; the current pulled me farther out to sea. The stinging cold bit at my muscles.

I couldn't even remember resurfacing. All I remembered was a pitch-black cloud blanketing around me, with a fading dark blue above me.

Now I was warm, tucked into a twin-sized bed by a fire. I was in the top of what appeared to be a lighthouse. Where the rotating light beacon should have been was a makeshift fireplace.

Where am I?

I took a moment to thank Uridei for the miracle of this salvation. A desperate measure had led to what could've been a disgraceful death, not that I'd had many options. I only hoped I hadn't left Tam to chastisement. It was still a mystery that he'd shown up unannounced as he had. He should've been on his way to Rúnar with Haruka. He'd be punished for abandoning his duty.

Had something happened? Were Nav'i and Dancer safe?

My clothes hung near the fire in the center of the small room. I had been dressed in furs that helped further stave off the cold. My arm had been rewrapped in bandages thoroughly; it felt cooler, as if it were healing. I checked beneath the bandages; dark orange and purple leaves I didn't recognize had been laid strategically against my scorched flesh.

I got up and inspected what I presumed would be my new clothing. It was the garb of the Order: a monk robe of sun-bleached leather, and an extra layer to block the cold, equipped with fur and hide. I was still surveying myself, wondering how I'd gotten in my current state, when I sensed someone approach. I hadn't even begun to absorb my surroundings. I could hear the heavy coastal winds beating against the structure and not much else.

A völf entered the room. He dropped a pack onto the floor and hung his jacket on a random coat rack in the corner by the door. He still wore a cowl, but I recognized his scent.

"Shirou?" I spoke.

The towering völf ignored me. I knew him. Shirou was one of András's protectorates.

"Your clothes won't be suitable any longer, so those are yours," he said gruffly, pointing out the clothes I had inspected. "I am sure you're hungry."

I didn't answer. His voice was as big as his figure.

Shirou was a massive völf, two feet taller than I, with scars on his mellow face. He had dark fur and a broader, scruffier build than the clean-cut regime I was used to maintaining. He adjusted his wardrobe casually before seating himself by the fire. The wooden floor moaned under his weight as he reached for a pan that hung over the fire and retrieved two bowls on a counter next to where he sat.

"Shirou? Where are we?" My voice filled the tight space.

"You are in Paskalis. We're staying here in the old watchtower that overlooks the oceanfront. It extends to Tsunetomo's shores."

I wanted to ask him how he broke away from András, but he continued. "You put on quite a fight with Kärleiv before taking that plunge. I insist you eat. Eating is essential for your next steps, 'cause it might be a while until your next meal, unless you feel like eating a human being."

He motioned for me to grab the bowl next to him. Against my distrust of a familiar protectorate who should have killed me for leaving my post at the same time their lady disappeared, I decided to follow his order.

He began eating from his bowl. He swallowed quickly and spoke again, motioning to my arm. "Pay attention to how I bandaged your wound. Notice the fingers are still accessible. You can still use sparks this way. Just—" He snapped his fingers. "You can snap, right?"

I nodded, snapped my fingers, and noticed a puff of smoke whirl from the gruff skin of my fingertips. My anxiety grew. I had not realized I could summon the white flames this way; however, Shirou appeared to ignore the phenomenon.

"Purge doesn't just mean you get to obliterate someone anytime you decide. It is a holy endowed tool. Use it wisely, Kovuco."

I cleared my throat and mustered my deeper voice. "You know I used the Purge?"

"Yes. Saw you on that landing."

"I didn't know I could. Any völf could."

"The question is, how did a young völf like you learn it?"

I tensed. I dared not answer, worried that the intense Shirou might compel me to admit my bloodletting with a human. He stared at me, waiting for an answer. He must have sensed my unease.

He finally broke the silence and continued. "Don't worry. I wish not to dig for the truth of such a matter. My task is to make sure you are safe."

He's keeping me safe then. I looked down at the leaves woven into my bandages.

"They are rowan tree leaves. Your birth tree, Kovuco. It grows within the mountains of Isarah and has an ashen appearance. As you can see, the leaves are dark; they turn purple and orange in the changing seasons. In the spring, tiny white flowers bloom, followed by bright red fruit—all remedies to your wounds. I recommend you study the Fae mythos. The Völfien may be their own race, but Albean linked us to the Fae. We rely upon nature's bounty for our success."

I'd never really paid much attention to my birth tree. I remembered the Shaar Night Café's rowan tree painting back home, but I'd never realized it was *my* birth tree. I nodded and returned my focus to my bowl.

Shirou spoke again. "Per instruction of Wülkure Ashley Ulrendt, I have recourses that will guide your next steps."

"Ash?" I asked, alert.

"Ash gave me instructions, a backup plan if you will, in the event plans didn't go accordingly for you. I wasn't expecting to fish you out of the ocean, but be happy I had a good rapport with the old wülkure. Eat first; we will discuss those plans afterward."

Thank you, Ash.

We began eating the soup in silence. Only the crackling fire and hissing winds could be heard in the space. The soup he'd made was plentiful in veggies, with thick chunks of beef. I watched him add the raw chunks to the stew after he removed it from the flame. This marked my second meal with raw meat in the same week. As always, it was wonderful down to the last bite.

"You must lie low. Specific members of the Order who know Ash will disguise you with natural methods once you reach Isarah. I'd take you myself, but I must return to Father András soon. With Kärleiv's betrayal, I feel a deeper conspiracy will soon surface."

Respectfully, I pushed the subject. "I had seen the ships depart North; Isarah would be farther off track."

Shirou shook his head. "You would think, but no. Those ships turned for Isarah. Nathalii's fleet captured her. She's headed west, Kovuco."

Nathalii? I paused in thought. "I understand."

A brief silence blanketed the small space again.

"Too bad I can't go with you. I'd love to see your brother again. It's been too long." Shirou spoke up.

"My brother?"

"Yes. Sangállo." He slurped another spoonful of stew. "And Désoto. We grew up together. When we were very young I trained under Rhúlain, your father's prior mate, alongside your brothers. Back when we were known as the Order of the Völfien. I also saw you as a newborn tyke. You were in a sling across your father's chest. He wore a shield over you until the war was over. You never cried. I thought maybe you were dead, and your father couldn't bury you. We feared he may have lost his mind, but each night, Sangállo and Désoto took turns keeping watch. Your father barely allowed you to leave his grasp."

The story brought me more comfort after my last visit with my father, to know he'd cared for me as a mother should have.

"During the days of the Order of Völfien, your brother and I were summoned to lead an army of Völfien and paladins against the remaining followers of Sabor—cultists. After we'd won, it was shortly after that your father's excommunication commenced. We naturally resumed a position of humility within the Order as protectorates. As you see, I was over Abbot András Frost and your brother had stepped in to protect Abbot Father Connor Úlfur of the Temple of Spears."

"I had no idea you fought alongside one another."

Shirou sighed. "If you don't mind, I'll leave that tale for another time. You take a hundred lives in a single battle—it's not exactly something you wish to recall."

A hundred lives to save a thousand.

I closed my eyes and took a deep breath. I pressed my right palm against my chest, feeling the steady thumps reverberate collectively.

She is resting—maybe even sleeping. She's anxious, but at least she's safe. I'm coming, Ameilja.

"Eat, Kovuco." Shirou urged.

I gulped down the soup obediently.

"There's only one way off this rock, and that's by airship. You'll take a train to Nomad's Landing, a small outpost outside the perimeter of Frost's reach. Get on an airship once you arrive; then you'll cross the ocean to Isarah, and you can continue pursuing Ameilja. Are you following?"

I nodded.

Shirou continued. "All airships cross into Isarah via Blackwater City. Once you have landed, proceed to the Vaterlünd Temple. Hopefully, word will have reached our brothers there, and you will be secured and safe."

"Sounds solid," I said.

"Not quite, Kovuco. You should also know the empress has assigned her judge to find you."

Oh shit. I swallowed hard. "Empress Sinnika ordered her death reaper after me?"

The snarling winds beat louder against the tower. Shirou's glare tightened.

"Technically, you shouldn't have left the Frost estate; it looks bad. It will be assumed that your disappearance is linked to Ameilja's capture. Dependent on what public news is shared in regards to Ameilja, you'll need to be careful in crossing the ocean. The world is very different in Isarah. Even more so than here in Shaar. From here on out, the world will be different from what you know under the protection of House Frost. Many odds will be against you, Kovuco, with the worst being the judge." He sighed heavily. "Any more questions?"

"What about Ash?"

Shirou dropped his head. "We will continuously work to recover his body. I do have something for you." He reached into his pack, brought out a leather wallet, and tossed it to me. There was a letter addressed to me and a skeleton key bearing the Order's emblem inside.

I broke the wax seal, opened the letter and read Ash's scribbled cursive, which was surprisingly more eloquent than he ever had revealed himself to be.

Dear Kovuco,

If you're reading this, it might be because you're without me now. I want you to know that I never wanted Shaar to be your life. You and your comrades were made for so much more.

The Order needs you. Uridei needs you! Ameilja has big ideas that may change the course of the Order forever. She will need you; with that, you will need my inheritance.

You should head to the Vaterlünd temple when you cross the ocean. You're looking for a man there named Brother Rui. Give him my father's code: "White Powder has fallen." Everything he gives you I pass on to you.

Lastly, don't be afraid to live, Kovey! Remember what the Book of Uridei says about suffering. The suffering we face will make us stronger, but suffering does not conquer. You win!

You Persevere! You are the light! The suffering of present times is nothing compared to what the Light offers us in the Vale of Heroes. If Uridei is for us, nothing will stand against us.
Be happy, my friend.
Find peace.
Find redemption.
Find love.

Ash

My eyes pressed shut, and a tear spilled out. It hadn't sunk in that he was gone.

I pressed the letter to my forehead and then cast it into the fire. I watched his final words char and blacken in the flames.

I will, Ash. I'll find a way to be happy.

☆

Shaar
Paskalis
The old watchtower
Aousti 17

Like clockwork, Shirou woke me the following morning. It was so early that the stars still blanketed the shifting sky.

Shirou prepared a bag and handed it to me before we left.

"It's quite a journey across the ocean, so I packed you enough to keep you content until you get to Isarah. I packed you a loaf of bread, a small bottle of wine, water, a fresh slice of gouda, and an apple. Plus a medical pack, gauze, and preserved rowan leaves. Be sure to wash the oil off before applying. I packed you a knife, lantern, rope, and flint for fires."

"I thought you said last night was my final meal for a while," I said as we trekked down the spiraled staircase of the lighthouse.

Shirou shrugged. "How else was I going to get you to eat?"

Shirou led me through open woodlands and into an active town square. He took me to a stand where he filled a thermos full of coffee. He called it a parting gift before my journey.

He indicated that I should put on my hood. I did so, and we made our way through the crowd.

We got to the edge of the loading dock, and he snuck me among a few boxcars; another völf had opened the door to a boxcar toward the end of the train. The völf quickly ran off, and I barely caught his scent. Inside was a large crate of various supplies.

Shirou turned to me. "These supplies belong to the train company. They will not be happy with you once the train stops, so be on your guard."

I nodded, trying to hold back my angst. I would be alone soon, leaving the only world I had known as an adult.

Shirou jumped up into the cab. "Sit. We have some time before the train is set to leave. I need to show you something else that might help you."

I jumped into the car and sat next to him, vertically kneeling, as he was.

He reached into his pouch, "You good on wrapping your arm?"

I nodded. "Yes."

"Ash gave me a pouch of blood vials for you. He told me it was blood specially made for you. Whatever that means."

I nodded, mentally questioning why he had not yet picked up on my bond.

"Use it sparingly. It looks like a sixteen-day supply."

"Sixteen?"

"Yes. The instructions state that each vial is for daily consumption. One ounce per day—that's it."

I nodded again and then changed the subject. "You mentioned seeing me as a tyke. Could you maybe tell me anything at all about those days?"

Shirou looked at me with a reluctant glare. "Can't recall a whole ton, honestly. One day we just noticed you. I understand that your father was given a message to return to Spears. I believe that was where he retrieved you."

I sighed. "Of course."

He slapped my shoulder. "Turn around, and hold out your arm."

I obeyed and paid careful attention as he unwrapped the bandage about my forearm. The burns from the white-hot flames had already begun to heal dramatically. My naked skin was slowly resuming its usual color. I watched Shirou lay the leaves against my skin, followed by a cool and refreshing dressing against the burns. Afterward, he layered the bandages over them, creating a subtle cast.

"You're healing unnaturally fast," Shirou noted, cutting me a quick glance.

Regardless of what had healed, I could not help but be grateful that I had managed a perfect escape.

"Thank you, Shirou. Thank you for everything." I crossed my chest with my bandaged arm and straightened my posture.

Shirou rose too.

"Light of Uridei," I said proudly.

For once, he let a smirk alter his intimidating glare. "Light of Uridei, Kovuco Blackstar." Shirou jumped down from the train car. "Wait! Kovuco?"

"Yes?"

"The judge is Josef Vyaminof. He is the wülkure assigned to hunt you down. Stay close to other Völfien and blend in as much as possible. He is very dangerous, Kovuco. Do not let him find you!"

I nodded as the train's departure horns roared to life. "What will happen if he finds me?"

Shirou sternly replied, "He will shoot you on site."

Shaar
Paskalis
Paskali Express, *storage boxcar number two*
Aoustí 17

I hid in the shadows and watched the departure from the open door of the boxcar. The train was now crossing a massive bridge made of iron and brass. The bitter scent of iron swept through my senses. Within moments, the train crossed over the woods, where I could see my old home in the distance. A calamity overcame me.

Will I ever see home again?

I thought of Tam. I hoped he was all right. I hoped he wasn't harmed.

By Uridei, I pray he is safe.

Where was my father? I'd promised to see him soon.

By now, I am sure he has heard of my disappearance.

I thought of Ash and wondered if they had found his body. What would I inherit from a battle-torn veteran of the Great War?

Am I worthy of this inheritance?

The train passed through an extensive collection of trees and a path next to the ocean. I turned once more and collected the sight. I knew it might be the last time I saw my coastal home. There was a final brief moment of light, and then, suddenly, I was cast into the darkness of a tunnel. Minutes later, I was surrounded by woods again.

Between the new, unfamiliar scents and harrowing anxieties, my mind began to wander.

Shirou never left András's side, so why now? Was my disappearance of dismay to him—a burden— because of his service to my father? Was it to clear his own conscience?

I know the law and the consequences that lie before me, but should I have stayed? Could I have presented my case, waited, and participated in the movement to rescue Ameilja?

Worse, had András been the one to initiate the judge to find me? His daughter was gone, and now the one protectorate that stayed behind had abandoned his post to actively pursue her alone.

There is no going back now. I am on this train, headed for Ameilja.

Hours passed, and I started to drift in and out. I was alone now. Yet somehow, I could make out a still silhouette of Ameilja's form. I reached out a paw, and she reached out a hand for it. I called out her name in an exhausted whisper, and then she was gone.

I sat there, tuning into her heartbeats as the minutes passed.

To ease the feeling, I took my first dose of her blood, hoping to quench the loneliness and worry of not knowing where she was. Her blood poured down my throat, reviving my mindset. It still didn't replace the need to physically taste her—taste the one I'm bonded to. I needed to preoccupy my mind; forget the feeling of her flesh against my tongue. I reached into my pack and pulled out the small lantern. I lit it with the flint and knife and then made a small campfire.

Behind me there was a cart stuffed with wool blankets. I took three: one for my bedding, a second to fold into a makeshift pillow, and the third for my shoulders. Next, I reached for the brown pouch and pulled out my bread, fruit, and gouda. I used my knife to slice the cheese into thin pieces, along with the apple. I thought of Dancer's expertise and made small sandwiches. I ate slowly, absorbing the taste and to help quench my hunger. I didn't have a glass but didn't back down from taking a swig of the red wine. It wasn't refined like the wine I'd had on Ameilja's birthday, but it was sufficient.

My mind lulled, then dipped into the memories of the Purge sparks. I still couldn't fathom the ability the bond gave me to connect into Ameilja's divine ways. I wondered how much she knew of me since our bond. The things I buried deep inside were possibly secrets no more. No more than hers were, although I dared not turn pages that didn't belong to me.

Quiet your mind, Kovuco.

I lay down and faced the woodlands. I closed my eyes and found comfort in the ghostly sense of Ameilja's touch. I imagined her small hand mystically covering mine. Her sweet humming voice was in my ears as I fell into a deep slumber.

CHAPTER TWENTY-THREE
MELANCHOLIA

Isarah
Demitori City, Obsidian District
Duskwell Hospital
Aousti 16

KIEFER OVERSAW ISABELLE'S REGISTRATION, EN-suring she was checked into Duskwell Hospital accordingly. Per Henrik's direct orders, no one could know she was there. That was one thing Kiefer could agree on with his centurion.

Kiefer needed to guarantee that Isabelle not only received the best treatment but also would be safe from members of the Commission. Duskwell was predominantly a hospital for the Völfien and the Orkésh, despite its location. It was also under Okra's jurisdiction, which only added to the approval of her being admitted there.

A human doctor dressed in a blue-and-white peacoat-style lab coat walked up to Kiefer. His brown hair was tightly bound in a knot on the back of his head.

"Dr. Grayzond?" Kiefer said, gazing down at his badge.

The doctor answered punctually, "Yes, Dr. Nils Grayzond. A plea-sure to make your acquaintance, Wülkure Yuska. I understand it was you who brought Isabelle Baadar in?"

"Yes, how is she?"

"She is stable, but I am sedating her as we begin her blood therapy. Due to restrictions set by the centurion, I have to administer blood slowly to all Völfien patients. I'm sure you understand." He eyed Kiefer for a brief moment. "She was tranquilized; I presume you administered this sedative drug?"

"That is correct."

The doctor paused, tapping his pen against his lips. "Interesting sedative. I'm not aware of this one. Where'd you learn it?"

Kiefer didn't answer. Just as a magician didn't give away his tricks, Kiefer did not share his talents. To elude the question, Kiefer continued. "Doctor, as you've been ordered, we must keep her safe, but can we protect her whereabouts? I don't want anyone to know she's here."

"I insist we continue this conversation in my office. It's through the garden."

Kiefer stuffed his hands in his pockets. "Very well."

Dr. Grayzond scanned through Isabelle's chart as he led Kiefer down several flights of stairs, and into a garden swollen with exotic plants and palms. It was an inner sanctum of the hospital, beautiful and peaceful. White sand pathways and benches sat under the shade, accompanied by the few birds and insects that visited the space.

"Wülkure Yuska, you know Ms. Baadar has a son, correct? There's a chance he could be a visitor."

"That is my understanding. I have questions about him."

"Well, it is a patient-doctor privilege. I cannot release any extended information regarding Ms. Baadar or her kin, but he—"

"Doctor, as I mentioned, absolutely no one can know where she is. It is highly unsafe for her right now. I need details on her son; he needs to know about her current situation."

"As soon as her son knows, rest assured, it will likely heighten her security measures. From what the paperwork shows, I have no doubts he's already involved."

"Because her son is a member of the Blue Coat syndicate?" Kiefer arched a brow.

Dr. Grayzond fell silent.

As soon as they arrived in the hospital's southern hall, the two left the garden. Dr. Grayzond took Kiefer into his office and asked him to take a seat in front of his desk. He started organizing papers in the folder he had been meticulously tending to.

Kiefer continued once he knew the doctor was paying attention. "I am already aware of his involvement in the Blue Coats. I need to find him, and I would greatly appreciate your cooperation." He asked less directly, hoping it would lead to an answer.

"I am afraid I can't do that, Wülkure."

"I am an æsir, Doctor."

"With all due respect, fuck your rank. That means little here in *my* hospital," Dr. Grayzond shifted his tone. "I am not in your jurisdiction and will die to protect the patients here. But under advisement, I understand that you, in particular, bear no prejudices with the völves. I will point you in the direction where you *might* be able to get close to the Blue Coats. That is the only way you will find Ms. Baadar's son. I, however, must warn you that the Blue Coat syndicate protect their own relentlessly. They won't like a wülkure sniffing about."

"Yeah. Trust me, I know. But to be clear, you're not even going to give me a name?"

The doctor smirked facetiously. "Wülkure, I am not and will never be at the privilege to discuss any of my patients."

"Patient." Kiefer corrected.

The doctor sighed. "Wülkure, I—"

"It's fine, Doc. Hippocratic oath—I get all that shit. What *can* you tell me?"

Grayzond chuckled. "I can see you're not one to give up lightly, are you, Mr. Yuska? The Blue Coats are a crime syndicate of humans and Völfien, as I am sure you already know. They're quite fascinating; they're capable of maintaining human identities in their best-shifted Rinkin forms and protecting themselves all while harnessing their brethren's gifts against their opponents. They take from the rich, give to the needy, and avenge injustice against their own and any member of the Fae. They have been known to help humans allied to them as well."

"Describe them as you like, but they still stand as opposers against the Commission. Ms. Baadar told me to find her son, and I believe finding him will save many lives. There's a far greater threat out there than my simply knowing a name, Doctor."

"How so?"

Kiefer didn't answer, dipping his head.

The doctor chuckled again. "Now we understand each other." He paused, thinking strategically of what to say next. "My colleague Jón Malsson runs a mobile clinic in Sapphire. Start there."

"A dryad, isn't he?"

"Correct. An aspiring actor as well."

Kiefer squinted at him.

Grayzond smiled and adjusted his coat. "I have no quarrel with you, Wülkure. Understand that I'm not blinded by greed and power in my years on this earth. I am guided by history and ethics."

Kiefer bowed his head. "You and me both, Doc."

"Splendid. Now, I have patients to attend to, Mr. Yuska. I will contact you when Ms. Baadar awakens, but I feel you'll be more informed after your correspondence with Jón Malsson." He gestured Kiefer toward the door with a forced smile. "I will walk you out."

☆

The Eastern Sea
The Renouncer
Aoustí 16

Ameilja sat in a conference room at the base of the airship. Her placement was at the room's rear, opposite the entrance. A large metal sign displaying the ship's name hung on the far wall to her right with the remaining walls primarily constructed of windows to oversee the clouds.

She had braided her hair and dressed in a casual green dress more suited for travel. She glanced out the large window closest to her as the airship reached a higher altitude. She then glanced at Tam, instantly relaxing her tensed shoulders.

Before she had attended to herself, she'd attended to Tam. He had quietly cleaned up and changed into his human clothes. Ameilja had hoped the guards would leave him alone so he could rest after his exhaustive transformation; she could feel the utter contempt they had for him. She didn't trust anyone aboard the ship. As much as Tam was making Ameilja his priority, she was making him hers.

Her gaze dropped to the collar around his neck. Against her wishes, Tam cooperated with the lethal piece of metal. There was a combination of spikes lining the inner layer, and if he changed back into a völf, the tips would pierce his throat and release a venomous concoction of vil-kanás and ózykas into his bloodstream, which would kill him instantly.

Ózykas, a fluid that built up in a bowl-like flower, was used to kill dryads, cease glamouring abilities in the fae, and was equally effective in clogging the airways of völves. Ózykas and vilkanás formed a deadly cocktail against the Völfien, especially should it enter the throat. There was no undoing a corrosive ózykas sting.

Ameilja softened her analytical gaze, studying Tam respectfully without making it obvious.

For a Rinkin, Tam was undeniably fully accomplished in his trans-formation. It took her by surprise. His short, dark brown hair appeared smooth, feathered back from a strong yet sharp facial structure. His golden eyes carried the intensities of his inner beast. He was a handsome human and behaved like a perfect gentleman. As much of a goof as Tam was known to be, it was clear he took his transformation seriously, just as he did his job as her protectorate.

He also refused to sit. He stood by Ameilja as if on duty without his fellow White Throats accompanying him. The silence of the space left him uneasy, keeping his Völfien senses alert.

Ameilja didn't expect Tam to explain himself; however, she began to piece together items she had never questioned before.

Ever since Tam had been brought into House Frost, he'd received his quarterly examinations off-site. She remembered Brother Tad as his sole examiner. Was his transformation a secret that Tad protected? Was her father, or maybe even Ash, involved? Ameilja's heart clenched at the thought of her father withholding another detail about her Court of Völfien—first Kovuco's Rinkin and now Tam's phenomenal shift.

What more is he hiding?

Tam cleared his throat. "Just know I only lied because I was told I must keep it secret."

Ameilja shifted in her seat. "It's not my right to your privacy or secrets, Tam. Are you safe? Nat was very interested in your transformation."

"Depending on what she is up to, Nathalii may know the truth."

"Which is?"

"I've always been able to achieve a perfect Rinkin transformation.

My entire life. Brother Tad would record my transformations and have them altered in my file." He crossed his arms, meeting Ameilja's stare.

"Tad lied?"

"Ash's idea. I was told I'd be taken away from you if I was discovered. For that reason, I obeyed."

Ameilja nodded. "I understand. You speak none of this unless I am present. Understood?"

Tam nodded, and Ameilja noticed he intermittently leaned toward her throughout their conversation. He inhaled, sniffing subtly, processing the scent, and then repeated.

"What are you doing, Tambor?" Ameilja whispered irritably.

"Just confirming."

"Confirming what?"

"Kovuco—his scent."

"And?" she asked nervously.

Tam didn't answer; his attention locked on the doorway ahead. "They are coming. Are you ready?"

Ameilja straightened her posture. Her breath caught in her throat. "As I'll ever be."

Moments later, four armed guards entered the room. They wore heavy armor, and each took a corner to stand, holstering a rifle. A few more people joined, followed by Nathalii's two female bodyguards.

The first one had her dark hair in a ponytail, finely braided. She wore a headdress that resembled a demon's horns. Her eyes beamed bright red, while she wore colors of violet and black with blood-red accents. The next one had fine white hair cropped eloquently at her shoulders. Her eyes too were red. Her dress was red and black with silver accents. A spiked headband lay atop her white hair, oddly making her look like a little girl.

It was laughable to Ameilja that her aunt thought such accents portrayed those corrupted women as innocent. Each of their dresses assumed a role of promiscuity and sexual desire of the darkest variety.

Nathalii confidently entered, topping off the wardrobe array with her similarly elaborate and enticing attire. Her features twisted into an excited grin as topless female servants entered the room after her and placed a feast on the table. Large nipple piercings hung from their exposed breasts. They wore skull masks, each designed with a horrific expression.

Many more dishes poured in: cabbage rolls served with rolls of sausages and sour cream with jalapeños. A bowl of bright polenta surrounded by a crown of flowers. Grilled and minced meat rolls marinated in garlic, spices, and mustard. Beef tripe soup served with red chili peppers. An entire pig platter served with pickle spears and an apple stuffed in its mouth. Crunchy and salty greaves. Two sweetbreads, one filled with sweet walnut paste and the other with poppy seed paste. A lamb haggis with a boiled egg inside and each slice topped with minced lamb offal and green onion. A fried doughnut-shaped cottage cheese and semolina mixture covered in sweet cream and blueberry jam. Finally, a beef salad that somehow had been baked to look like festive gelatin.

Once the topless servers left, everyone was finally seated. Nathalii sat at the end, opposite Ameilja, with her two bodyguards on either side.

Ameilja convinced Tam to sit at her right. The captain of the *Renouncer* sat next to one of Nathalii's bodyguards. Seated next to her other bodyguard was a man who looked like a priest; however, part of his attire suggested he no longer served the Order. The final guest sat across from Tam and was a redhead who was dressed similarly to Nathalii, only she didn't look like a dominatrix from hell. Her hair was tied into two braided buns on either side of her head.

"Such a splendid time to be gathered together, yes?" Nathalii purred, eyeing everyone around the table. "My apologies, we are short a few attendees; unfortunate circumstances led to their unexpected deaths." She cut a sharp glance at Ameilja.

Ameilja's features hardened.

"By all means, dig in." Nathalii added with a wink, specifically at Ameilja.

Everyone began digging into the feast. Wine and scotch were poured. Tam inconspicuously coaxed Ameilja to join, preventing her from appearing as an outlier or uncooperative, to keep her safe. She took a cabbage roll and a slice of the roasted pig with a few pickles and tossed a flower from the polenta onto her plate. Each movement was quick, portraying her distaste at being there.

"Ameilja, you have *exceptional* taste in völves!" Nathalii spoke up amid the clattering dishware. "So handsome, of course." She locked her inquisitive gaze on Tam as she slowly took a bite of meat. "I am unaware of the pretty white one you brought to your coronation. Oh, he gave me chills, but you most definitely can never go wrong with a creature that's practically immortal."

Ameilja furrowed her brows. "Immortality does have its perks, I suppose."

"Well, wouldn't it be grand if we could never grow old? Possibly never die? You know there are very few diseases that can affect völves. Orks are far more durable than humans, but völves are superior! Albean had good taste." Nathalii suddenly stood with her wineglass in hand. "Völf? Tam, I believe is your title?"

Tam tightened his stare.

Nathalii smirked playfully and then dropped her gaze to his plate. "Are you not eating? I thought for sure you would enjoy this fine pork. Or the meat rolls. Oh—wait, how rude of me. Maybe you're not hungry. Perhaps with that perfectly human cock of yours, I could facilitate a bit of—"

"Enough!" Ameilja snapped. "Never disrespect him—ever!" She pushed her plate away, zoning her viper stare on her aunt. "Cut the shit! Why are we here? Who are these people? What the hell is happening?"

Nathalii squeaked, enticed by Ameilja's rage, and covered her lips with a hand. "Oh my goodness, I completely forgot! My apologies, sweet Ami; allow me to introduce you. Of course, you've already met my two bodyguards, Vasilica and Sørina." She gestured a hand toward them. "And you should also know the well-known captain of this fine vessel and æsir of my fleet, Captain Skári O'Shalléd. Then we have former paladin, Kythis Graal—"

"Former?" Ameilja interjected, assessing the man that matched the age of her father.

Kythis lent a bow with his head. "Excommunicated, to be exact, Miss Frost." An elongated, tight grin stretched across his sleek face before continuing. "Found the Order a bit boring. I learned what was important from the Order and gained what I needed. Great art forms, especially when it comes to combat. The Purge is fascinating too, but I found the dark much sweeter. All those higher divinities are so bland. It was better to study curses than divine rights by Uridei. I guess my studies, combined with my *vast* intelligence, led me to formulate this entire operation."

Furiously, Ameilja emptied her glass of wine in Kythis's face. He didn't flinch, not even a shutter of his eyes. "Filth!" she cried out. "Egotistical filth!"

Kythis smirked. His perfectly groomed head of black hair still looked intact, even with red wine sloshed over him. He bore regal, enchanting eyes of fiery brown, despite the despicable, ugly truth he had just revealed to Ameilja. He was a traitor to the Order.

Ameilja turned back to Nathalii. "What the hell am I doing here? Answer me!" she yelled as loudly as possible. She wanted to show her disdain for all these people. They may have acted friendly, but she knew they were all snakes.

"Well, Ami, dear, funny you ask. There's much more I'd love to share. You see, I have a little adventure I want you to be part of. I've heard you like escapades, yes?"

Ameilja gritted her teeth. "I will not cooperate! Not for the likes of you or this former paladin."

"Oh, but you haven't even heard what it is! Maybe it will interest you."

"I mean this with the utmost disrespect: anything *you* and anyone in this room are involved with gives me no interest."

"She's a feisty thing, isn't she," Kythis tauntingly noted.

Ameilja glowered at him.

"Well then, perhaps this will change your mind." Nathalii cooed, picking up a small bell next to her plate and quickly ringing it.

In entered a familiar figure, one Ameilja didn't jump to, at least not as suddenly as Tam.

"Kärleiv?" Tam growled, shooting up from his seat and instinctively leaning in front of Ameilja. "No! I saw you die at the hands of the Purge!" He bared his teeth, dipping his darkened gaze in warning.

"Tam!" Ameilja snipped, urging him to settle.

Tam refused. "He's infected by the Näkk, Ameilja!"

"What?" A mortified whisper slipped through her lips.

Gooseflesh surfaced Ameilja's arms. She snapped her horrified gaze up at Tam and instantly noticed his golden eyes had dilated, and his muscles shifted with intent—he was an attacker staring down his prey. She quickly clutched his wrist, reminding him he could not turn back into a völf.

"Die? No, no, no!" Nathalii giggled. "This is *not* Kärleiv. Meet his twin, Kärfínn." She paused, soaking up Ameilja's bewildered expression. "You see, they both were granted extraordinary gifts. Quite unique, actually." She pivoted toward Kärfínn, eyeing him with fascination. "Kärfínn has been undead for quite some time. All because of intelligent, persistent men like Kythis here, Kärfínn and Kärleiv were reanimated and able to aid us on our quest."

"Not possible!" Tam snarled. "I saw him die! Die to the Purge."

"Yes, Kärleiv did—so sad! But not Kärfínn." Nathalii purred with excitement again. "Oh, just imagine what the near future holds when we can create a world of competent, civilized undead like these twins!"

Ameilja's stomach twisted. Her mind felt heavy. Whirling, weighted memories swept through her mental realm.

This can't be …

Twins …

She'd thought Kärleiv kidnapped her, but upon further inspection, she realized it had been Kärfínn who killed Jayña. She remembered that Kärleiv had wielded twin daggers, not a sword, as Kärfínn did. They'd been in on it together. They'd planned it the entire time. All along, they knew.

Ameilja closed her eyes.

Twins …

My vision … the night of my coronation. Twin fetuses in a womb. Blood-covered hands … Swirling fluids and white flames. Then a wild wolf emerged from a shadowed forest just as I was hurled back into reality. It must have been a warning!

Ameilja snapped open her eyes. *Uridei was warning me about the Näkk's resurgence!*

She looked over at Kärfínn and spoke up. "Another former member of the Order, and now you're—you're—"

"Undead," Kärfínn finished. "I was a paladin long ago, but the Näkk has me now. It's restored me. Made me new."

"It's defiled you!" Tam growled. "You're nothing but a husk! A manipulated project—a rotting—"

"Hold your tongue, völf!" Kärfínn hissed.

Tam leaned forward, sending a warning message with his body language. "Enough." Kythis raised a hand.

Ameilja squeezed Tam's wrist. He didn't break his stare from Kärfínn, who was settling in his seat at the end of the table.

"Allow me the honor of showing you *my* creation," Kythis said, turning his attention back to Kärfínn.

Kärfínn clutched his porcelain mask and unlatched the buckles that held it in place. He pulled back his hood before unveiling the face beneath the mask.

Ameilja's lips quivered uncontrollably as disbelief swept over her form; witnessing the most insidious thing she'd stood against now before her. *This isn't possible. This can't be …*

Kärfínn's flesh was a withered gray, but from his forehead to his lower jaw, ear to ear, was an exposed skeleton. He looked at her through empty eye sockets filled with glowing, diabolical greenish-black flames that intertwined in and out. The colors were hypnotizing—a dangerous sight. The power of the Näkk undoubtedly fueled his form.

Ameilja collected herself and squeezed Tam's wrist again. "Sit," she whispered to him. He was hesitant but obeyed, still keeping his eyes fixed on Kärfínn. She knew Tam could not protect her from the Näkk, especially a new, unique strain such as this.

This was far more powerful than she could even comprehend.

Uridei, save us.

Ameilja locked her gaze on Kärfínn, processing the words she desperately tried to gather as a multitude of questions fired off in her brain.

Inhale.

Exhale.

She closed her eyes once more, took another deep breath, then opened them. She placed both palms against the table and slowly stood, instantly gaining everyone's attention.

Ameilja eyed every single person sitting around the table, holding their stares direct and willing while she prepared to reason with her captor. Once ready, she spoke.

"So, I understand that you're the one who's spearheaded all of this, yes?" She looked at Kythis, searching his face. "You. You're the one."

A smug grin grew on his lips before she turned to Nathalii. "And you, what do you want with me, Nathalii?" Her tone remained calm. "You've wanted me for years. Now here I am."

The redheaded woman cleared her throat. "Might I interject?"

Ameilja shifted her gaze to the unknown woman.

Nathalii smiled and held her hand as if announcing the winner. "Please, Doctor. I am so sorry! I completely forgot to introduce you!"

Doctor? Ameilja thought.

"Not at all. My name is irrelevant compared to the plans that will concern Lady Ameilja." The redheaded doctor turned her gaze to her. "Miss Frost, naturally you have questions, so I'll keep this simple and to the point. You are here for a purpose. You are a mastered seer, a rare gem with impeccable power. The Näkk needs your power to progress, just like it once needed an Aureate's. Kythis here has built an entire movement with acolytes of the plague. For years they have been inspired by the possibilities of the Näkk." She briefly paused. "Those involved in this operation go beyond what you'll ever comprehend, so I highly suggest you follow suit. Your aunt here is one of the many elites who have funded the progress of this operation, and they will stop at nothing to see it through. They wish to find a cure to better our world—we all do. And you are our answer."

Ameilja shook her head. "Do you and these crazed followers truly believe the Näkk is our cure to betterment? Dress it up however you want, Doctor, but this is purely a chance to command the darkness. It's greedy desire—nothing more. Something history has shown to be a disaster for humanity. I'm aware of the Näkk's power; I'm aware of the undead. It's written in many historical volumes. This will not end well. To even consider Sabor's authority over the entire world, the Commission—"

"Miss Frost, if I may, why not?" Kythis strategically interjected. "The Näkk's power is our chance at eternal life and, quite possibly, control. It's better that we wield Sabor's power than anyone else. It presented itself again; it wanted to be found. Besides, haven't humans caused enough devastation and posed an equal threat to themselves? Your völf here even? The Fae? The Orkésh?" He sighed and took a sip of his wine. "Uridei, and his Aureate Albean, demanded we sit and watch this void we call humanity. What a joke. Shall we exist and do nothing, while a real master would seek to control a power more magnificent than creation itself?"

Kärfinn turned away and began putting his hood and mask back on. Ameilja wondered if his intrigue toward the Näkk had anything to do with his lack of faith in humanity. She full-heartedly agreed that the human race had caused despair; however, the Näkk was not the answer.

"Humans' living for eternity goes against our design; undead or not, it's just not possible." Ameilja locked her gaze with Nathalii and then with the doctor. "Surely you should know the risks."

Nathalii rose. "Through the research of some of the most brilliant alchemical doctors in Isarah and Fjorthúr, we were able to reanimate a corpse, like Kärfínn here. As you can see, he's far more advanced and controlled compared to the bloodthirsty undead of the war. The twins were our answer to immortality. Truly, the possibilities are endless, Ameilja, but we're currently capped. Our lovely doctor here believes we can fully unlock Sabor's power through the ancient practice of involving a being who can achieve transmutation naturally, like you, a seer. With natural abilities, that doesn't pose a risk, now does it?" She cocked her head.

"So what exactly do you require?" Ameilja's demeanor changed. She swallowed hard, curling her hands into fists. "Do you expect me to just surrender myself to you?"

"Yes," the doctor responded without hesitation. "More specifically, surrender yourself to the Näkk. As a seer, you're predestined to channel the Purge like no other, and we believe you can channel the Näkk the same. You have the desired vessel to which its power can attach and flow. A fantastical gift just like the Aureates … you should feel honored!"

"Honored?" Ameilja scoffed. She glared at the no-name doctor. "This will undoubtedly unleash the plague upon the lands again! Have you gone mad?"

The doctor sighed and folded her hands calmly on the table. "You've heard of the Sunspire facility, I'm sure. We have a plan, and we need you to maximize the power built and collected within its labs." She glanced down at her folded hands, then cut a glance back up at Ameilja. "Perhaps we can make an even better deal. If you help us, we can track down another seer, or someone with similar power, and then that person can replace you. You'll be free to live life as you please."

"No! I will never betray the Order or my people! And do you think I'm that ignorant; there are no other seers! How dare you assume I'd deliver a replacement—"

"No, no, Ameilja!" Nathalii interjected. "I do have the perfect replacement. Together we can draw someone else out. This is someone who can channel supernatural energy comparable to yours, maybe even more so than you!"

Ameilja eyed her sadistic aunt questioningly.

"We have been searching for an ork—not just *any* ork but an ancient one. It's known he's achieved the universal summoning of natural elements—you know, water, fire, and all the earthly things."

"You're talking about the Wöndin?" Ameilja huffed irritably. "You're setting me up! Those are just tales! Orks are not gifted with such powers. Some orks have even confirmed they are mere storytellings."

"We have good reason to believe he is here, and evidence of his existence has already revealed itself. I am determined that together we can find him and replace you."

"I don't believe you! Why me, Nathalii? Why do you need me, unless you mean to destroy me?"

"Leverage." Kythis cut in. His husky voice grated against her skull with every unwelcoming word he spoke. "To be honest, your dear aunt here does not wish for your involvement, believe it or not. But you *are* the confirmed source we can use. As our doctor here stated, if we find your replacement, you go free."

Ameilja watched as Kythis shared an unreadable look with Nathalii before taking another long sip of his wine, finishing off the glass.

She dipped her head, tuning into her chest rising and falling with each anxious breath. She slowly sat back down; each movement feeling hypersensitive. Her dress felt too tight; its fibers rubbed against her flushed skin. A loose strand of hair tickled the nape of her neck. Her thoughts raced—her heart pounded— then she snapped, opening the way for her outraged spiel.

"You're delusional! All of you! None of this makes sense. How can you even begin to imagine controlling the Näkk with *just* me? I am no Aureate! You act as if I am experienced with my powers. I've just recently learned to wield the Purge. How could I possibly wield the Näkk without becoming your undead pet? I don't believe you! I don't—"

"Silence!" Kythis bellowed.

Ameilja tensed.

"Yes, Sabor controlled the Näkk without dying because he was an

Aureate." Kythis irritably explained. "But your gift is well beyond the human condition, and the Näkk desires those powers to advance. A seer of your caliber could easily transmute its force and control it without succumbing to its deathly consequence."

"You don't know that! With what proof?"

"The Wöndin's son," he declared.

"What?" The word barely escaped.

"The Wöndin and his offspring exist. His son has been our testing template for years."

"H-how?"

"An entrusted team has harnessed the Näkk's strain, combined it with the ork boy's inherited powers, and emulsified it within the Sunspire's laboratories. There you have it: proof."

Ameilja shook her head, lost for words.

"The Näkk is ready for you, Ameilja. It's been waiting." A large, triumphant grin spread across Kythis's wicked features.

"Ameilja," Nathalii spoke up, "You *are* proof enough. Have you not considered your recent demonstration with your völf? The pretty white one; what's his name?"

Ameilja hesitantly answered, filled with terror as the truth was revealed, "K-Kovuco."

She remembered the wall of flames. Kovuco had survived the deluge of it. She had achieved the perfect transmutation of the Purge. She'd channeled it as if it were the air she breathed. She's fully aware of her power, but to actually speak it aloud would mean ...

"I know your master prefers private audiences, but I was able to see some of your performances." Nathalii continued. "I've even watched you take your adorable little adventures with your völf friends. Such a fierce, determined spirit you are, sweet Ami. Only a master seer could have created a force of Purge flames that profound. Oboro knew you were capable of sparing Kovuco. She knew you could—and so did I."

Ameilja's heart clenched. She felt tricked and even lied to. *Why the hell did Oboro allow Nat as an audience? And now I'm in danger of becoming her instrument.*

"Your gift is a burden at best, Ami dear. You were destined to achieve perfect transmutation." Nathalii's eyes glistened, and she beamed at

Ameilja, proud in that moment. "But you have already achieved it; you've officially ascended."

"Your perfect little *ascension*, huh?" Ameilja scoffed. "I already told you: I will never betray my people."

Ameilja glared at Nathalii and the doctor with more hatred than she ever had anticipated she could muster. Nathalii and her bodyguards remained unmoved, along with Kythis and Kärfínn. Captain O'Shalléd and the redheaded woman stepped away from the table, worried Ameilja might unleash her Purge on them at that moment.

All were lost in the pandemonium but unaffected by the forces Ameilja knew were at play. She wished her father; her mentor, Bernát; her handmaiden Jayna; her wülkure, Ash; and her White Throats were there. She found herself wishing, most of all, that Kovuco was by her side.

If not for Tam, she'd have destroyed everything in the room, engulfing the entire ship with her flame, bringing it to the ocean, and burying its conspirators, even if it meant her life.

That would have served an even greater purpose beyond what fate lay ahead.

I beseech thee, Uridei. Damn them to hell for desiring the blood of the innocent. Are none truly righteous? Do none truly seek the Light?

Nathalii turned back to Ameilja, noticeably upset. "Ameilja, I know this is hard to hear, but I never intended to bring you here to die."

Ameilja rolled her eyes. "Let's look at the logistics of this. The Purge stopped the Näkk once before. Why would you want a seer to control what they can destroy? It sounds counterproductive, does it not?"

"You're right," answered Kythis. "But after the power has fully risen within you, you'll feel no desire to destroy it, trust me. With your influence, I'm certain we will utilize all paladins' Purge solely to channel the Näkk. Just imagine: we'll reinvent the ways of the paladin—no, even better. We'll restore the Order of the Völfien beyond what it was in the old days. In this, we will reinvent the entire Commission. Maybe just get rid of it entirely if you wish."

"Restore what? You wish to restore everything the Commission stands against. Restore the evil, the war, the violence—"

"The world will inevitably find war again, despite what we're doing,"

Kythis stated. "But in this current structure, you know the Völfien will always be treated as the enemy. This fact alone should rejuvenate your calling to aid us. You'll bring your beloved Völfien race to a place of freedom and power once again. No control—"

"Stop manipulating me!" Ameilja cried out, slamming her hands onto the table. "Just stop!"

Kythis responded by slamming a fist onto the table so hard it cracked, causing Ameilja to jump. "Listen to me!" He rose out of his seat. "You can't surely be so foolish, can you? Your closest friends don't even support you or your advocacy to free the Fae races! Beyond even the Eastern Isles, the outside world beyond us will always question and live in fear." He laughed aloud in a derogatory manner. "Will the Commission ever stop mobilizing völves? Do you think the empress will ever tear down the protective decrees imprisoning the Fae to their fear-based rhetoric? Would she trade that all for someone of the likes of *you?*"

The quiet Captain O'Shalléd gruffly chuckled. "No. The empress will allow you to die. She'll let you die to keep the current ways of the Commission."

Tam took a step forward, and a protective, guttural growl rose up from the depths of his chest. He swallowed, trying to suppress his instinctive nature.

Ameilja's lips quivered and curled inward. Her face heated. "I know the empress disagrees with my wishes, but—"

"Then help me to ascertain her position, child!" Nathalii impatiently screeched, and her voice rose to a temper Ameilja was not used to.

Nathalii had always been known to be giggly and teasingly dismissive; now she revealed a side she had never had a reason to demonstrate—a passion beyond her mischievous ways.

"Do you want this boorish display to continue?" Nathalii pushed, sprawling out her dagger-like fingers as if grabbing at the air. Her movements mirrored the strain in her voice. "The war gave us purpose, and now we shackle progress. We must overpower anyone who stands in our way, and that includes the empress. We must unite all the races under a power far greater than any. This new world will all be under *our* control, Ameilja. Allow us the chance to become immortal, magnificently everlasting, with the power of the Näkk!"

Ameilja shook her head, wanting nothing more than to run.

The doctor reached out a hand for Ameilja. "Ameilja—"

Ameilja jerked her hand away and backed off; had Tam not caught her, she'd have fallen backward in her chair. He ensured she was seated safely again.

"Who are you?" Ameilja snipped. "You're the only one who doesn't fit. How does a doctor find any of this ethical or sane?"

The doctor stepped closer and looked down at Ameilja. She stood so tall and with such authority that it seemed she could smite her with a single word. "Miss Frost, my name is Dr. Sayáko Wendtfuss, and I will be telling you about the Sunspire."

CHAPTER TWENTY-FOUR
THE SCENT

Shaar
Zen'tund Plains
Paskali Express, *storage boxcar number two*
Aoustí 17

"AMEILJA?" I WHISPERED, BUT SHE DIDN'T ANSWER.

She was distressed. Her tears fell like arrows impaling me on the pallet boards I lay upon—each seared agony into my form. I curled and shivered subconsciously in my fading slumber. I scratched the flooring through the wool blanket I lay on.

Ameilja.

Suddenly, I was unexpectedly seized and forcefully brought to my feet. My eyes were closed, but I could smell them: humans. Ones who intended to harm me. I felt a fist against my snout and then my neck. A hand seized my shoulder; instinctively, my claws pierced his flesh, spraying gore as I pinched the tendons in my clenched fist. I threw the unidentified human overhead and shattered his structure against the pallet-board floor. We must have been in a tunnel, as the only illumination was that of my lantern.

The following human unveiled a pistol; at that point, I counted two as my senses realigned from my sleep. I held my paws out. Wide-eyed, I pleaded, "Wait! I mean no harm!"

"Say that to the man you just murdered!" he shouted, intent on pulling the trigger. Unfortunately for him, he used one hand and pointed it at my throat. It was pressed against me, point-blank, so in a flash, I grabbed the top section of the weapon and bent it against my left fore-arm; his wrist shattered, and the gun was freed from his grip. I tossed it out the open car door. I thrust an open palm to his sternum, and he was ejected from the car.

The final human looked at me with terror in his eyes.

I cleared my throat. "Speak. Who knows I am here?"

He backed away in fear, realizing I stood in front of the door to the next car. There was no escape from me, so his terror had overtaken him.

"Answer me, human. Who knows I am here?" I said it calmly, as if speaking to a child.

"The staff knows. We were sent to deal with you! The head conductor doesn't like stowaways!"

I nodded. "I imagine so. What was the plan? Shoot me and toss me out?"

The man nodded, still horrified. He was bold to answer, knowing I was capable of ending him as I had his colleagues.

I bowed to him. "I am sorry for their lives. It was self-defense. You would have done the same, no?"

He was hesitant, swallowing hard, nodding. "I would have! I would have, völf!"

I nodded at him. "Farewell, human."

I felt the train lift as we began our ascent. *We must be close.* I sensed the light, the fresh air, and the ocean again. I lifted my bag and tossed it over my shoulder. With a clawed foot, I smashed the lantern, extinguishing the faint glow and banishing us into blackness. When the natural light took over, I'd be gone. He'd only know me as a nightmare. One that had left him as the sole survivor.

I swung my massive form to the top of the boxcar, landing quietly so that the human would not hear my positioning. The train finally breached the light, and the burst of wind caused me to brace myself. I blinked several times to clear the spots floating in my vision. Beyond the jagged crags was the port known as Nomad's Landing—one step closer to Ameilja.

I have arrived. I have arrived in a new world. A world where men will want me dead. First, I'll save Ameilja. Then they can have me.

I mentally recalled the papers I had packed explaining that the in-between point was where I would board the airship. I had been given enough money to purchase a ticket for the flight. It would be an easy trek through this port; therefore, I'd be an easy target, and I feared the judge would be in search of me there.

As the train approached the landing, I jumped a few cars ahead and landed on a flatcar. I was still a stowaway, so I had to ensure I was not seen. After wrapping my face in the gauzy, dark scarf that wrapped my bottle of wine, I cast up my hood. The scarf aided the shadow effect my hood gave me. Not a single strand of platinum would show.

Once the train closed in, I leaped off the flatcar into the clearing below.

I hoped I wasn't noticed as a group of farmers approached the area. Fortunately, the conical caps they wore were dipped, and they didn't take notice of my presence. I dashed into the brush, safe from view. I listened intently to see if a search would be conducted after my onslaught with the train staff. Once it was clear, I needed to get to the other side of the island to purchase my ticket quickly. I briefly pondered if I should attempt stowing away again to avoid suspicious eyes, but I saw what trouble that had already granted me.

I needed to move onward.

The climate had warmed significantly, so I discarded the robe and furs I carried and straightened out my belongings so that I might appear a collected, casual traveler. Instantly, I reversed that strategy when I peered down at my feet and noticed how dirty they had become. The once cream-colored fur was now slathered with a warm brown shade.

A disguise?

I removed my jacket, leaving myself in my sleeveless undershirt and slacks, and began applying the mud to my exposed fur. I also managed to find a farmer's cap stuck in a nearby thornbush. I carefully lathered my face except for my muzzle, disguising my silvery coloring. I couldn't control the wetter mud excess dripping, but at least the conical hat provided an excellent shade over my blue eyes.

Cautiously, I meandered the beachfront and wended my way into the streets. As in most ports, prefab businesses and establishments were set up to lure in patrons boarding the airships.

This place was much different from what I'd personally experienced in the past. This port was gloomy and overcast. Discomforting smells lingered in the air, mixed with thick smoke from the nearby cigar stand run by an elderly, gruff-looking ork. One of his eyes was missing.

Strangely, a Völfien blood station stand was set up beside him. A woman managed the station; her wülkure jacket was armed and ready with banes of all types. I guessed it made sense to have a blood station at a port. It ensured my kind traveled with their required doses.

I glanced around and also noticed the disheveled buildings exhibiting extensive deterioration; all of it added to the area's dreary and run-down appearance.

I approached one of the parlors and ordered a cup of beef broth. It was filled with kimchi and whole chili beans. It was cheap and efficient, and I ate quickly, continuing through the streets while scanning for the Judge. Following the signs, I eventually got to the concourse.

It was not as crowded as I had hoped. The armed Sentry members naturally raised discomfort in me, but I quickly found a group I could blend in with. A group of völves in robes matching the Temple of Spears' colors were walking toward the ticket booth; I casually followed them, until a familiar scent trickled into my nostrils.

This scent. Tala?

A female völf with shiny wheat-blonde fur and captivating amber eyes was standing right before me—a female from my youth.

I clutched her shoulder. "Tala?"

Her familiar smile formed as she turned to me. "Kovuco? Is that you?"

I wanted to silence her, but I hesitated. I couldn't believe I had been able to sniff her out so quickly. "Yeah, it is!"

Tala was a small völf, even for a female of my kind, but she was known for her determination and had never backed down from an opportunity to prove to anyone of any race what she was capable of. Her personality was as big as her punch.

She didn't hesitate to hug me.

The two other völves turned to us, looking delighted to see me despite my not knowing them.

The first völf smiled. "So, Tala, this is Kovuco, huh?"

Tala blushed. "Yes. Kovuco, I'd like you to meet my comrades from Spears: Keyni and his mate, Makuee."

Keyni was a tall, lean black völf, but his fur was beginning to gray around his ears and eyes. Makuee was also a tall völf, but her fur was a maple blonde. After a closer look, I recognized their robes. They were missionaries for the Völfien community and were known as positive influences to our survival within the Order, focusing on understanding and healing the relationship between man and Völfien.

I bowed. "Pleasure to meet you. If I may, I need to get on the next airship to Blackwater. Are you—"

"Please join us!" Makuee cut in, snapping a glance at Tala. "We're passing through Blackwater as well. You should accompany us."

I was relieved. "Yes, of course." I handed her coins from my pouch. "I'll meet you by the entrance. Just—"

Tala reached for the bag. "That's fine. Stay among us; we'll cover you," she whispered, sharing a subtle wink.

I obeyed. *Thank Uridei I found allies. Even better, a friend.*

I waited by the entryway to the airship, covering as much of my face as possible. Moments later, I felt a claw graze my side. I turned, and Tala smiled warmly; her claws glistened from the dirty wetness of my muddy disguise.

"Why are you so dirty, Kovuco?" she chuckled. "I don't remember you being so unkempt."

I laughed nervously, unsure how to explain myself.

She clutched my arm and dragged me away from the loading dock. "Come on. We'll get you cleaned up. Nomad's Landing is rough around the edges, but the airship is nice."

"But won't we miss boarding?"

"No, we have plenty of time. Besides, you smell like low tide. They'll kick you into the ocean before you even make it to Blackwater."

"But, Tala, you don't understand. I must—"

"Kovuco!" she snapped in a whisper. "You're never going to get on that ship stinking as you do. We have time. Come on."

She led me to the entrance of the public beach access, where a stone wall with showerheads and a bench were set up. I stood still and watched her as she turned on the nozzle, removed the farmer's cap, and then pulled my shirt over my head. I quickly pivoted and slipped down my slacks.

Peering over my shoulder, I noticed Tala watching me, taking in my body. There was evident interest in her eyes.

"We have an extra robe," she said, setting it on the bench behind me, inhaling slowly. "It should fit you just fine," she added softly.

Not leaving, she sat on the bench behind me. I quickly washed off the mud and used the soap she'd set beneath the showerhead. Once finished, I shook off the water as best as I could with no towel present. Tala helped me by using her claws to brush through parts of the fur on my forearms, carefully avoiding my bandages. I continued to stand there naked, unsure of the moment. I didn't have much of a choice.

"Much better, huh?" she sighed.

Her coat reminded me of warm butterscotch, shimmering radiantly when the sun peeked through the overcast sky. I remember a conversation in the courtyard between Tala and another female völf during our past training. She had officially shifted into her Rinkin and explained some of its fine details; her human hair color matched her fur, while her amber eyes contrasted against her dark eyelashes, and the parts of the lingering transformation.

She was a stunning Völfien, both in her Rinkin and in her Medzio. Why she had an interest in me I'd never know.

Should I say something?

She unexpectedly slipped her fingers between mine, clutching my thumb within her clasp. She closed the distance between us and observed my eyes. I was unsure what to do. My heart rate increased as my pupils searched her eyes for an answer. If I'd wanted, I could have pretended I was the same völf she had known when I had no inhibitions to hold me back, but human morality, insecurities, and customs of Shaar had clouded that völf. Nudity was now regarded differently compared to back then, but Tala hadn't wavered from that world—or had she?

She looked at me with a longing I never had known. To experience a female looking at me with such intense sexual desire rose an innate feeling I had yet to tap into. It was as if fate had drawn us together, and there I was before her, vulnerable and exposed. Had I fallen into the trap of her Völfien design?

Her eyes yearned for me. She slowly wiped away a leftover blotch of muddy debris from my brow with her other claw. "Those blue eyes haven't changed a bit," she said. "They're …"

"They're what?" I asked.

She nodded longingly. "Just as I remember."

No, this can't happen.

She reached for my brow again, intent on embracing me, but suddenly stopped. When she stopped, she laid a paw against my chest. I tensed. She glanced into my eyes, subtly taking quick sniffs, and her ears twitched. Her desire found a crossroad, but what?

"There's someone else, isn't there?" she asked with quiet disappointment.

I couldn't answer. I didn't know how.

She suddenly wrapped her arms around me tightly. "I am relieved!"

"You are?"

She let go of me and nodded. "I knew the moment our paths separated that it had to be a sign, but I couldn't help but think of you often, hanging on to the idea that maybe we were meant to be together. But now I know for sure. It was never meant to be, Kovuco." She stepped back, seeming embarrassed that she had given away too much. "Get dressed! We need to get you to Blackwater." She then whipped around and walked off with confidence carried in her stride.

My muscles relaxed.

There had been a time when I'd wondered whether Tala had a thing for me. My father and most of our pack had wanted Tala for me, but I never had pursued her. There even had been a rumor that another female desired me. My challenging upbringing had held me back, my sole focus and distraction. My past had been the burden I carried in darkness. I still did. I'd wished I were better at that. I'd lacked confidence around females, not believing what they saw in me. But that had changed now, not because of Tala or so-called rumors but because of the strong-willed, intoxicating red-haired beauty I was bonded to.

Ameilja.

She was the mate I had always desired, despite my dark past. She was my driving force, my entire world beyond the oceans and meanings of our cosmos. Ameilja was my muse—my reason.

Knowing that Tala sensed someone else from my sullen heart gave me an additional determination—it lit the fire and recognition I needed within me to survive this mission.

I'm coming for you, Ameilja!

I closed my eyes once more and tuned into her senses. Unfortunately, her stress had not changed, but I knew she was well. She was well and awaiting me, and I was getting closer.

CHAPTER TWENTY-FIVE

INTO THE FRAY

Isarah
Demitori City, Sapphire District
Transparent Knives Theater
Aoustí 16

KIEFER KNEW AN AUDIENCE WITH HIS SUPERIORS was upon him, and he'd only briefly met with Okra to share his report on the Sunspire. His investigation continued.

He decided to go directly to the theater where Malsson spent most of his time. The theater was located in the Sapphire District, which was known for its illustrious yet contemporary architecture. The key to its structure was in housing the mansions of Demitori City.

The district was well known for the historic Djörfung Temple, the Demitori Museum of History, and the Transparent Knives Theater. That theater was where he would find the dryad Jón Malsson. His hobby was acting. Besides that, he was a skilled philanthropist, frequently traveling through the other districts for his medical practices. He was paid handsomely but also didn't make a lousy living as an actor. He often glamoured himself as a human to blend in and appeal to his human audience.

Kiefer knew what glamouring meant by definition. Glamouring was a magical ability possessed by the Fae to disguise their appearance by putting off pheromones to trick others into seeing only their disguise. He rarely witnessed the ability; there wasn't much need for it in Copper.

He passed through the establishment's luxurious lobby and onward into the theater, where he could see actors performing. The actors were preparing for a fight between a masked creature and demonic fiends. They were using wooden swords, but for the show, the actors used genuine blades, pierced bags of false gore, and shot blanks from antique pistols that would simultaneously spark fireworks off protective vests beneath their wardrobes.

Kiefer cocked his head, observing their act. Acting was a sport put on by trained professionals, or artists. It was an art to make something believable.

Kiefer knew how to kill a man, and these guys faked it and made it look like a genuine article for gasps and applause.

Fascinating.

"Jón Malsson!" Kiefer called out, allowing his voice to echo throughout the open space.

The actors stopped and turned to Kiefer. For a moment, he wasn't sure if they had made him a member of the act, as they appeared to be locked in their demonic postures.

Then one of the masked men unveiled his clean-shaven face and peered toward Kiefer. "Yes? I am Jón Malsson."

Easy enough.

Jón had sharp, elegant features and pointed ears. His skin was pale green, with the coarse texture of an oak leaf. His long black hair resembled silk, and he bore black eyes with a piercing stare.

"Might we have a word?" Kiefer asked, advancing toward the stage.

"May I ask who you are, sir?" he asked cordially.

"My name is Kiefer Yuska, wülkure of the Copper District. I have some questions about some affiliates of yours."

The Fae man turned to his comrades and spoke in a strange tongue, and they broke off from the scene. Malsson leaped down from the stage, walked toward Kiefer, and held out a hand. "Pleased to meet you, Wülkure Yuska. How can I be of service to our city's finest?"

"Finest, eh?"

"Of course. I have respect for our wülkure departments. I've medically aided many and been privy to intriguing conversations. You're known simply as a hunter but have a much more delicate role in our society. I've heard about you, you are somewhat the interpreter of the voiceless, those labeled falsely by human ignorance."

"Interesting observation. Enlighten me on your thoughts?"

"Sure." The actor offered Kiefer to sit on the chair before him.

"I'll stand."

"Okay—perhaps you would like to take a walk around the theater? It is beautiful, and you can appreciate its finer details more intimately when it isn't bursting with souls."

Kiefer shrugged. "Actually, we should speak in private."

"Oh. Well, of course. We should take it to the director's office. It's upstairs."

Along the way, Malsson spoke in a dither. He asked about Kiefer's interest in theater or other arts and even asked questions pertaining to the medicinal side, knowing the wülkure Pjauti training. Naturally, Kiefer answered with simple yes-or-no responses. Not that Kiefer wouldn't entertain conversation with a Fae, but in this particular situation, he studied the way Malsson became apprehensive in between his breaks in speech. Kiefer made him nervous.

Once they reached the office. Malsson pulled some chairs away from the director's cluttered desk. "My apologies, Wülkure Yuska. We're running into some setbacks with this new show, and it just has us a bit unorganized."

"It's fine. I only need a few minutes of your time. If you cooperate, I'll be on my way."

Malsson swallowed hard. "Okay. Well, what can I do for you?"

Kiefer brandished the pocket watch of the deceased Kristján Baadar.

Malsson took the pocket watch and popped open the locket, revealing the clock with the picture of Isabelle. "The Baadars?"

"You're familiar?"

"I am a friend of the family. Last I heard, Kristján was in Fjorthúr."

"Close," Kiefer said. "He was working at a facility known as the Sunspire."

Malsson paused. "Was?" His features saddened. He seemingly presumed something terrible potentially had come to pass. "Are they all right?"

"Isabelle is in the hospital, currently down and out. Unfortunately, Dr. Baadar was executed by her brother, Æsir Rotenfeld."

Malsson gasped, burying his face in his hands. He rubbed his temples and then collected his wits and returned to Kiefer. "Am I permitted to visit Isabelle?"

"I imagine you'll go despite my wishes. But I have questions before I give you any of that."

"Anything. You have my attention."

"Where's Isabelle's son? Isabelle told me we need to find him."

"Kouta. Her son's name is Kouta," he answered without hesitation. "I'm afraid he won't be easy to find."

"Reason?"

"Since his early adulthood, he's been a member of the Blue Coat syndicate. They are very dangerous when crossed and don't like the Commission. He is bound to have found out by now what is going on. The Blue Coats have connections all over the city."

"Tell me about that." Kiefer pressed; pleased to hear Malsson speaking transparently about information he had already gathered. "What are his distastes with the Commission? I have never heard his name brought up; it would be a major red flag to see a Baadar appear on our radar. Especially in league with the Blue Coats. I find this odd."

"Allow me to correct myself. It's the leadership within the Commission the Blue Coats dislike."

Kiefer acknowledged the dryad with a nod. "Can I ask who the pack leader is over Kouta?"

Malsson thought for a moment and then nodded. "It's a völf named Julius Richter."

"Richter?"

"Yes. You've heard of him?"

"Met him—well, his pistol to the back of my head. Recently, actually. I might be able to recognize his voice in a crowd. You had to think briefly about whether you could give me the leader's name. Why?"

"It's apparent you know of the Blue Coats more than I assumed. The Blue Coats have already approached me. Had they not, I would have never uttered a word."

"So Richter said it was okay for you to reveal his name to me? So he knows what I am up to then?"

"I can't answer that, but it's evident the Blue Coats are very interested in meeting with you, Wülkure Yuska."

"Richter, you mean?"

Malsson shook his head. "No. Zero."

"Zero? Who the hell is Zero?"

"Zero is the syndicate leader of *all* the Blue Coats."

Kiefer crossed his arms. "Why is he interested in me?"

"I cannot say, but I can tell you that word of whatever happened in the Sunspire has more than likely reached them. I wish I had more for you, but I am not privy to the details. I can make arrangements for you to meet with them. A masquerade is coming up in celebration of the play's first performance. Could we perhaps meet on that night?"

"Yes, but I have more questions. Regarding Isabelle, I know her to be somewhat of a legend within the ranks of the Sentry. She mastered both wülkure and wächter classes in her younger years, built to be a weapon. I also know she has an unknown disappearance lingering over her head, but I would never have imagined her to be a—"

"Völf?" Malsson finished; his black eyes locked with Kiefer's expectant stare.

"So you know?" Kiefer eyed him. "Figures. You Fae and your secrets."

Malsson huffed. "No, Wülkure, it's not because of our race's secrets. Kristján and I go way back; we studied in some of the same medical classes. I also attended their wedding. Despite Isabelle's outlook on our kind, she accepted my being a dear friend of Kristján's. It shocked me to hear of her disappearance. By the time she returned, I'm afraid I was at odds with Kristján's decisions—his affair. The rumors were true; he was having an affair with a colleague from Blackwater City. Isabelle remained reclusive and out of the public eye after she returned, avoiding the media attention against her step down from such a profound title within the Commission. After a few weeks, I mustered a visit with her to check in. I found it odd she preferred the solitude, opposite of the Isabelle I once knew."

"Did you notice it then?" Kiefer asked.

"Yes, during that visit, I realized she was a völf, but I was alarmed too." He paused briefly. "The Baadars never knew I was aware. I didn't dare question them. I didn't think it was even possible—a human having the ability to shift into a Völfien? It was like she had completely changed—her mannerisms."

"But how did you know she was a völf? How did she keep it secret this long?"

"I don't know how she's kept it secret, but I knew due to her lingering transformation. Her ears were pointed, and her eye color and shape had changed. It reminded me of the Völfien's Rinkin but much more humanly defined. Her foundational scent was still her, though—a human scent. While I visited, she eventually excused herself to the restroom, and I checked their cabinets. The evidence sat there on the top shelf: stored vials of blood. They were unmarked, most likely stolen. When she returned from the restroom, her hair was positioned around her ears to cover up what I had already noticed."

"What about Kouta?"

Malsson's jaw tensed as he drew his greenish lips into a thin line and then slowly parted them. "He's a völf too."

Shit.

"I didn't know he was one too, at least not until I met him. I saw him, and just like Isabelle, I instantly knew. Their eyes matched—mother and son."

"When did he join the Blue Coat syndicate?"

"As Kouta got older, his unique mindset and odd mannerisms were noticed by his peers. He was bullied harshly for much of his youth during school. Some of these youth were children of the Sentry and Academy of the Commission. I am sure you can see why his interest in the Blue Coats became a thing. But that's not all. He ended up biting one of the children. Humans biting humans doesn't happen; typically, you know, that sort of thing came off as odd. He dropped out of school before the age of sixteen. The Blue Coats are known for adopting young humans and völves so they can start training them early—especially the Völfien. Völfien members are more valuable if they can achieve Rinkin form to maintain their dual identities. I can guarantee they know about Kouta's and Isabelle's secrets."

Kiefer sighed.

"Isabelle and Kristján moved closer to Copper after Kouta's incident. Because of Isabelle's previously ranked position, the Commission only slapped a warning on him, demanding she keep her son in check. That didn't aid Kouta's feelings toward the human race. The last I heard, he still loathes the humans and turned toward favoring his Medzio form—if I can even call it that for someone like him. A hybrid? A human-völf?"

Kiefer rolled his eyes, cracking his neck, as he absorbed the information. "It doesn't matter what he and Isabelle are labeled as. They are Völfien in my book."

Malsson nodded. "With time, I came around more and eventually asked Kristján about Kouta—not sharing what I knew about their transformations, of course, but noting that Kouta always seemed distraught. Kristján never told me what happened, but he said he would do right by Isabelle for the rest of his life and be the best father he could for Kouta. Because of the affair, I think. Maybe guilt."

"So jovial." Kiefer arched a brow.

"Trust me, I internally questioned everything, but I didn't want to pry at such sensitive, unheard-of subjects. Their family had been through so much, and Kristján was excited to be a father. How could I ruin that small piece of happiness?"

"Well, I've seen Isabelle as a völf, and if you're confirming Kouta is indeed a völf, then that confirms Kristján is not the father. Do you know who the father is?"

Malsson shook his head. "No, I know nothing of Kouta's father. At one point, I felt suspicious that Isabelle had been raped." He paused. "Can I ask you a peculiar question? Pardon my ignorance, of course."

Kiefer nodded. "Go on."

"I have never heard of a case where a völf has been with anyone other than another völf. They are an intimate race dedicated to each other and run their lives purely on instinct. Is it possible that Isabelle was raped or could have consented to sex with a völf, and therein lies a link to her transformation? I knew Kristján very well; he was a smart man, and I know he must have hidden the truth about what happened to her during her captivity."

A völf and a human? Kiefer scanned the room, thinking he could have used a cigarette right about then. "I've read several volumes on the Völfien. They discussed the Rinkin form in detail. Anatomically, a völf who would be capable of transforming to safely and effectively impregnate Isabelle would likely be a völf with experience, mastery, and the ability to transform damn near fully human. Even with the same genitalia, the key issue here is that Völfien can't impregnate humans. It's impossible. The races differ."

"So we are told," Malsson added.

"It just seems unimaginable." Kiefer shook his head, brushing his fingers through his dark hair. "I have met a few mastered völves devout to their honor and culture. It's hard to imagine they would be interested in a human's ways or risk such a forbidden act."

"Truthfully, I thought the same thing." Malsson relaxed his shoulders. "I just hope she wasn't raped or violated."

"Seems unlikely. Völfien are romantically intentional, and they bloodlet."

"Yes, you're right."

"I'll just have to find out what I need from Kouta then," Kiefer said, turning his head away from him.

"Well, that may present some disappointment."

"How so?"

"Isabelle never revealed the father to Kouta."

"How convenient."

"At one point, Kouta tried bullying it out of me, thinking I knew. I swore to him I didn't. Eventually, I started seeing their family less, and he submerged himself entirely within the Blue Coats. Last I heard Kristján was working within the Sunspire."

Bully? "So is Kouta violent?"

"*Violent* is a bit harsh—he could be aggressive. He has his mother's temper. His rough upbringing doesn't help."

"A radical then?"

"Oh no! I wouldn't call him a radical. The Blue Coats' sole objective is to protect beastkind from humankind, but they have also liberated orks from gang initiations. They even have humans within their group. They merely want peaceful coexistence and fair treatment for all."

"Right. They are trying to change the hearts of a dominant race that probably never will." Kiefer rose. "Do you know how many lives that will cost? That would be a revolution."

"It is understandable."

"What about you, Jón Malsson? You were friendly with the Baadars and obviously are an ally to the Blue Coats. Would you participate in such a revolution?"

"If it guarantees the ceasing of violence."

"Unfortunately, there will always be violence, Malsson."

☆

The Eastern Sea
The Dreamcatcher
Aoustí 17

"What?" snapped Nav'i when he felt Dancer's claw drive into his shoulder. He turned and noticed the black ceramic mug of coffee. Nav'i gazed into the cup and examined the liquid with a shade of disapproval. "What's in it?"

Dancer, devoid of emotion, answered, "Mocha. Double espresso. No cream."

Nav'i eyed Dancer and then the mug. "This isn't Shaar Night Café; we're far from that now, buddy." He huffed. *Spoiled.*

Dancer didn't answer, which Nav'i assumed meant he understood. Dancer took a huge gulp of the coffee, reminding himself he would not be granted Ameilja's generosity. He then took a longing whiff, absorbing the coffee's most hidden notes.

"Why must these larger airships take so long to travel," Nav'i grumbled, settling in his chair. "I'm surprised Haruka didn't have us on *Black Arrow.*"

Dancer ignored his disgruntled comrade.

Nav'i tipped his gaze and observed that Dancer's coffee matched his. "You're the cook, so you should know: Anything special with the coffee on this ship?"

"The chef here grinds his own beans."

"Hm. Nice. Bet you're eager to go back."

Dancer released his control, and a smile answered Nav'i's question.

"Bet it was more a curse when you got shipped out of Rúnar, huh?"

"Never saw Rúnar. I stayed on the ship for three years before they rehabilitated me."

"So where did your passion for food come from? I always thought it was the Isle."

"A chef of the Isle, yes. I didn't talk when I boarded the ship, and they weren't comfortable letting me off. They wouldn't leave me alone, because I refused to sit, so they took me to the galley, where I worked alongside their chef. He taught me everything I know."

"Do you remember his name?"

"Chef Bon Kuromori."

"I wonder if he's still around. Old guy?"

Dancer shrugged. "Midforties."

"We should try to find him. It would be great for you to show him how much you've improved."

"How do you know I've improved?"

"I don't know. I refuse to cook or even accept certain meals or coffee unless you've touched it. Other than from our café back home. You've completely refined your craft in the years we've been packmates. You probably could teach him a thing or two from learning Tsunetomo cuisine."

Dancer fell silent, then turned and faced the back of the ship. Among the drifts of clouds, he could see the shimmer from the ocean emanating under the moon.

Nav'i locked on to his sudden and rare emotion. "Dancer? You okay?"

"I'm leaving the White Throats," he blurted.

Nav'i dropped his mug and nearly choked on the current sip. "What?"

"I'm leaving."

"What do you mean you're leaving?"

"Everything has changed. They will continue to change. I need to make my way."

"What do you mean? You can't just leave our pack!"

"Ameilja knows."

"Ameilja knows *what*?"

"She knows I'm leaving. I wrote her a letter of my concerns, and she ordered my resignation. Ash sent word to Friar Kuromori. He will collect me once we port."

Dancer had unveiled a scroll from his belt, and he handed it to Nav'i, who scanned through the completed order.

"You're serious?"

Dancer took back the scroll and carefully rolled the order. "You'd rather me stay?"

"No, I mean—how could you do this? Leave us when we're at this critical point?" Nav'i stood up and strut to the other side of the landing, shaking his head, frustrated. He turned back and faced Dancer, who resumed his usual calm posture. "Dancer, you've been a good friend, a brother. I don't understand."

"You have to follow your path, Nav'i. That path means we must part."

"What? Follow *my* path? Stop with your holistic bullshit! What are you talking about?"

"Why didn't you go with Tam?" Dancer asked, avoiding the question.

"With Tam? I don't even understand why he went back. Ameilja and Kovuco are fine. It's like he got spooked—ridiculous. Maybe its just a Blackstar trait?"

"Or they're just growing into the völves they are meant to be."

"Right," Nav'i sneered. "Yet I still can't believe this is happening. I can't believe Kovuco, honestly."

"What is your problem with Kovuco?"

"Kovuco? I told you! He's impulsive and reckless. He makes stupid mistakes and underestimates his value, only crippling his self-esteem. It pisses me off!"

Dancer twitched an ear. "So you admit you see he has value? As a Völfien, you should encourage his strength—"

"It's his weakness! He gets so much credit and validation. Ash always praises *little Kovey*, and as for Ameilja—" Nav'i paused before saying anything further that he'd regret.

With the current circumstances, he wondered if there was something beneath the surface that Ameilja favored in Kovuco over the others. Did it even matter? They were bonded now, and he was somehow happy for them both but also unsettled in knowing the conflicting road ahead.

"I disagree," said Dancer. "His weakness is his advantage."

"Disagree all you want," Nav'i huffed.

"When are you going to tune into yourself more, our race even, and see that our vulnerability, our rawness, *is* our power? Control is not the answer. Kovuco's weaknesses will lead to his purpose—you'll see."

"Sure ... I'll see," Nav'i mumbled under his breath.

"You have made quite a name for yourself since joining the White Throats. You also make mistakes because of personal, reckless actions. You have weaknesses too."

Nav'i knew Dancer had a point. He always had his points, and there was no pride, no matter how powerful, that could disqualify them. Shamefully, he felt it came across that he was jealous of the attention Kovuco received despite his strange, mysterious nature.

"It's obvious you've competed with him." Dancer added.

"I don't know why I competed with him so much. He—" Nav'i stopped again. "Something personal happened in our younger years. I've held it against him all this time. He gained the attention of a female völf I sought. He took my chance from me when we were growing up."

"He took your chance?"

"Kovuco earned it, and I missed the opportunity."

There was an awkward silence, and due to the tension, Dancer moved on. "Never mind Kovuco. His fate is sealed. Who is Nav'i going to be now?"

Nav'i wasn't sure how to answer. What did he want? He stayed merely out of obedience and dedication.

"It doesn't matter what I want to be," he stated gruffly. "That choice isn't mine to make. I have a duty to uphold. Tam shouldn't have abandoned his post, and you shouldn't either!" Nav'i snapped his gaze to the far window, tensing his posture. "You're not leaving, Dancer—not now."

Dancer sighed, "I was afraid you were going to say that."

A sudden, sharp sting radiated through Nav'i's neck. He whipped around and faced Dancer who was backing away defensively.

Nav'i clutched the site of the sting, feeling a small device protruding from his skin, "Dancer?" he snarled as a wave of shock swept through him.

"I'm sorry, brother."

Nav'i's vision began to blur and his body felt numb, "Dancer, w-what did you do?" he sputtered, coughing and holding his head.

Dancer stepped forward and pulled Nav'i toward him before he slipped into unconsciousness. "Goodbye, Nav'i," he said, as the large black völf slipped to the floor.

Dancer stood over him, silent. He sighed, relieved.

Suddenly, a figure approached from behind. Dancer inhaled, catching the scent. "It's been done, Lady Haruka."

"Are you sure about this?" she asked.

"Yes. It has to be this way."

☆

Isarah
Demitori City, Brass District
Grande Mariner Apartment Complex, room 504
Aoustí 16

Kiefer unlocked the door and pushed it open. Before he could glance up, the only living human in the world who could sneak up on him locked her arms around his neck.

"Where have you been, Kief? I have been so worried! I heard about the Sunspire; how could you make me worry like that?"

"Rae, I'm fine," he answered between her tender words and continued kisses along his cheeks.

"Are you sure you're okay?" She ran her fingers through his unwashed black hair, caressing him as if it had been months since they'd parted.

"Yeah. Yeah, I'll be okay. Don't worry."

"I—I made you some coffee." She scampered toward the kitchen, quickly pulled a mug from the cabinet, and filled it with his favorite dark roast. She knew his routine. "Would you like me to start you a shower?" she asked as she brought the mug to him.

He subtly smiled at her, took a sip, and sighed with relief.

"Good?" she asked, desperate for a positive review.

"Yeah." He nodded as he walked in and sat on the couch in his living space.

She ran into the kitchen again and started shuffling about, ensuring everything was tidy. "Can I get you anything else? Are you hungry? Or—"

"Rae!" he snapped.

She froze and glanced at Kiefer with uncertainty, hanging on his next word in suspense.

He mustered another exhausted grin. "Can you just come here?"

She walked over to him; he stood up, took off his jacket, tossed it over to the chair, and started loosening his tie.

She began helping him, and he released the silk material and let her remove it. Once it was removed, she laid it over his jacket, and he unbuttoned his vest. She took a knee and began unstrapping and untying his boots. Once he'd removed his vest, he sat down and allowed Rae to take both boots off. He then grabbed her wrist and pulled her close. "Come," he tiredly whispered.

Rae crawled onto the couch and nestled up against him. He held her head against his chest, close to his heart. He breathed deeply, exhaling a satisfied breath of relief at being home, where he belonged. He hoped she'd meet his tired energy.

He was calm. He wanted her to be relaxed too.

"I missed you, Kiefer," she whispered.

He didn't answer. He'd fallen asleep.

CHAPTER TWENTY-SIX
THE JUDGE

Shaar
Zen'tund Plains
Nomad's Landing
Aoustí 17

THE CAPTAIN OF THE AIRSHIP ANNOUNCED THAT we were set to depart on time, which still felt far too long while we idled.

I sat alone in a small passenger compartment, awaiting the völves I'd be traveling with. Now smelling fresh and clean in the robe Tala had given me, I still felt like a sitting target.

Eventually, Tala came back and sat across from me. I'd thought for sure she would sit next to me, but then again, I'd presumed the others would be following after her.

"Where are the others?" I asked.

She looked uncomfortable, answering, "They have another cabin. They, uh, needed to discuss some things alone."

Or they knew we had to discuss things alone. Judging by their noticeable reactions, they must have assumed we'd be officially hooking up.

Awkwardly, I spouted the only words that came to mind: "Uh, okay. I suppose that gives us more time to catch up, yeah?"

She nodded. "Yes, it does."

"So you're a missionary völf for the Temple of Spears?"

She nodded, relieved. "Yes. I applied under pressure, honestly."

"Under pressure?"

"It was because of our lead, Makuee. She knew I was disappointed after you left. I couldn't stay, feeling like I had failed to live up to the expectations we were presented with. My emotions got the best of me. Are you honestly surprised, Kovuco?"

"What do you mean?" *Does playing dumb work at this point?*

"I know it never happened, but surely you caught on that I had feelings for you. Or at least that I was pursuing you."

I scratched the back of my skull. "Yeah, it was fairly obvious. But doesn't every male hope he's sought after?"

"Even if he doesn't want it?"

"I never said I didn't want it." I waved my claws defensively. "I just never knew how to. My mind was focused on other things."

Tala smiled. "You're a more traditional male than you think, Kovuco. The female likes you, but you don't necessarily have to like the female, huh?"

It sounded shallow, but it could've been true. Growing up, I had become warier after my trial, knowing I could be dead before considering a female companion. Tala was beautiful, far more than most. She was kind, highly charismatic, and ambitious—all traits I remembered my father stating to me, and my brothers also had agreed.

"She'll be a suitable mate, Kovuco. And your tykes would be beautiful! Potentially a new shade of platinum beyond what mankind has ever seen," my father had said numerous times, with my elder brothers smirking at my expense. Funny that my platinum fur was what made me so outlandish, yet he encouraged a whole new shade.

During those days, Tala had felt out of my league. She always had strived to be the best at everything she did and lead in every way possible. I did find that attractive about her, even her extroverted nature. At the time, maybe I'd felt it was a bit too extroverted, but I could have hidden behind it when I preferred to dip into the shadows. Again, it hadn't been my priority.

"I just never thought it possible, Tala. Not you and me. Not anyone."

"Why not? I know your father admired the idea of you and me. Don't think I didn't hear his bit on the new platinum tykes either."

I laughed nervously. "He said that aloud to you too, huh?"

"You know your father. He always spoke his mind. I loved the idea of being a Blackstar. I used to write it on the binding of my journals: *Tala*

Blackstar. I even thought of names for our kin. But you drifted into your studies, further from my goal to impress you, so I waited."

"Waited?"

"Yeah. You know, I waited for your interest to spark. Surely you'd take notice and pursue it, but you never did. You applied for House Frost, which made sense, considering your father's past with the Frost family and the call for young males. Even if I had applied, I wouldn't have had the right shade rumored to be Lady Ameilja's favorite choice."

I chuckled. "Yeah, we did become the White Throats, didn't we? But it's a name we have owned proudly."

There was another awkward pause, and I reached for Tala's paw. She took my index finger and gave me a ready glance. I knew that glance. She wanted honesty and was prepared for the truth. After everything, she deserved that.

"Tala, I hope I didn't hurt you. If I did, I'm sorry."

She smiled and shook her head. "You don't have to apologize, Kovuco. Selfishly, we often choose mates because of what our packs designate for us. It's hard to find an imperfect völf since our society demands perfection in all we do. You and I made sense outwardly, but when I got closer to you, I realized there was a path I wasn't meant to tread."

"Tala, I am truly sorry. I wish I had been more open. I pushed too many away when I needed support from those around me. I have always admired you. Everyone loved you and clung to your every word. I'm sure they still do."

She smiled widely. "I needed the challenge of Spears. I needed humility. Did you ever hear of my family's past?"

I shook my head. "No, I don't think so."

"Well, my mother and father mated young, nonbonded, and like your birth, it was not approved by a lead. Realizing their foolish nature, they parted but decided to raise me as their daughter within our pack."

"Wait! Amarok isn't your biological father?"

"No. Do I look anything like him?" She laughed. "He's my stepfather. My real father is Kekoa."

I caught my breath. "You're telling me that Kekoa is your father?"

Tala chuckled. "Yes!"

"I feel so foolish! But it makes sense. You and Kekoa are so much alike!"

"Well, now you know. We völves disregard gossip too much, unlike humans." She rolled her eyes. "We value gifting, and my father, Kekoa, and Amarok gifted me with values I could seek in a mate, and the two never saw each other as competition or opponents."

"How are things with your mother?"

"You know, I never asked. I assumed they were young and dumb and took advantage of a situation, and I was the result. They were so young, Kovuco—my mother was barely nineteen when she had me. They were good friends and remained good friends. Therefore, barely anyone knows the truth, and they're okay with it. I'm okay with it."

"I'm happy you told me this, Tala. I hope you find someone to make you happy. You deserve that."

The truth at that moment was sobering. Little Tala always had proven to everyone that her small size wouldn't stop her. I never had known of her circumstances and never had considered what challenges she'd faced. Also, what emotional strength had been necessary for her to adjust to claiming both fathers and for both her fathers to live amicably, raise their daughter, and continue to be productive members of our pack in Kyottó.

"Well, I still think you're a catch, Kovuco. Who stole my chance to swoop in?"

The question I wish she wasn't so bold as to ask. "Yeah, well, it's not quite a thing yet, Tala. I, uh, am not sure where it's going just yet."

Tala crossed the threshold between us and sat beside me, leaning back against the window. "C'mon. Tell me about her. You can still do that, right?"

Do I have to? I thought dimly. "Well, she serves the Order too. A dedicated student."

"Boring, Kovuco! Tell me about *her*! How'd this scent saturate you so profoundly?"

She said it as if I were doused in the scent. As if it had been brought to life during a passionate night of sex. Little did she know it had been created in my death throes.

"Um, she's beautiful, of course. No, she *is* the most beautiful creature I'll ever lay my eyes on. I think I believe in love at first sight because of her."

"Details, Kovuco. Details!"

I paused for a brief moment and envisioned Ameilja's every detail, hyper-fixating on the feelings spiraling through my being. I then shared the details Tala pushed for. "Her eyes are bright green. It's as if a soft moss grew over bright blue ice. She's intelligent and loves reading and new adventures. She's not afraid to overstep. Her mind is captivating, and I love how her thoughts never stop." A smile formed across my face. "She pursues everything she does with perfection and grace, all while accepting someone like me."

"How'd you know?"

"Huh?" I snapped out of my trance.

"How'd you know she's the one?"

I thought for a moment, feeling as if I were burrowing her down a hole that wasn't exactly what she was thinking. Ameilja wasn't mine. The scent we carried was explored not by lovers but by desperate fools trying to stay alive.

"I guess it's how she looks at me. Part of why I'm not a hundred percent sure yet."

"What do you mean?"

"She has these little gestures, these little touches. They feel intentional, and it leaves me questioning."

"Questioning what?"

"What's next for us. Like she wants me to know she'll always be there, and so will I."

Tala rested her chin on her knuckles, staring at me dreamily. "So romantic—something only the Völfien know. A bond to be shared for eternity," she whispered.

A sudden fear bellowed in my stomach. Did Ameilja understand a völf's concept of eternity? We were the only race besides the Aureates who lived for what felt like an eternity. With eternity, we had even stranger customs regarding sex, friendships, feeding, housing, and familial traditions. I couldn't think of any other race that started a sexual relationship with bloodletting.

Hypothetically, if a völf could be with anyone besides another völf, there would be an end to that eternity. Humans died quickly; they were so fragile compared to us. Völves also didn't care about concepts like legality or virginity. Those were more intimate human concerns, human to human, but were those going to be thoughts and concerns for a human being with a völf? Would I be able to cope with those concerns? Sure, every völf had a first time, but there was no pain, only the pain and importance of surviving your mate's bloodletting, because that meant you earned an eternity together.

My father grieved for his first mate, whom he'd spent centuries with. When she'd died, their bond had died with her. Then there was my unknown mother, a relationship other than mine that hadn't borne fruit. I didn't even know if they'd bloodlet.

I cleared my throat. "So I suppose we'll see where Uridei takes us."

She nodded. "I have a good idea of where he's leading me. You too, Kovuco."

I looked away, maintaining my smile, hoping it was convincing enough to move on before I said too much. I doubted Tala would have been as happy if she had known the truth of the scent. The truth was that I had a forbidden bond to a human, a human I could never have.

The Eastern Sea
Nomad's Landing airship
Aoustí 17

Tala had fallen asleep. She'd moved back to her side of the compartment and curled up.

I decided to read from Tala's Book of Light, taking that quiet time to pray and meditate. In the midst of doing so, I heard a knock on our door.

"Yes?" I whispered loudly enough to breach the door, hoping I was quiet enough to allow Tala her continued rest.

"I have a letter addressed to this car."

"To?" I asked.

Tala stirred, and I decided to rise and open the door, potentially waking her.

I opened the door, and a gentleman approximately five feet tall, with a well-trimmed goatee, grinned. He wore a leather mantle with gold buttons and a top hat. His shirt was a deep lavender, and he wore large, circular glasses. His overall impression was baleful; lurid; and redolent of the powdery scents of quince, patchouli, and tobacco.

As finely dressed as he was, it wasn't the first thing I noticed. I glanced down to see a gold-barreled revolver pointed at my heart.

"The letter is addressed to you, Kovuco Blackstar."

"Josef Vyaminof?" I asked.

The judge unveiled a second revolver and pointed it against the wall in plain view of Tala, at the angle at which he suspected she would be lying.

"Please don't!" The idea of watching Tala die struck me with horror. I shuddered, almost breaking down in desperation.

I quietly exited the car and lightly shut the door. Josef's revolvers were unmoved, confidently held in position to fire, despite his small size. I could smell a deep odor of fresh vilkanás. It was so strong that I nearly urinated on myself, fearing how close it was. The pungent spores sweltered under my eyelids, causing them to swell.

He pivoted, with the revolver trained for Tala pressed to my back so he could nudge me to step forward. "Walk!" he snapped in a gruff whisper.

His voice was soft, silky, and flawless in his every delivered word. His speech was short and deliberate. I remained silent. We were already toward the back of the airship; its hallways were empty and devoid of souls. The judge's sinister presence seemed to repel anyone from intervening in what would happen next. Fear loomed in my imagination like a feeding frenzy of sharks awaiting me at the end of the ship. That might have been all I was suitable for in the next final moments I had left.

With every step I took, I counted, thinking that number might be my last. I wanted to be brave, and for some strange reason, I wanted the judge to believe I was courageous until the end. However, I wanted the sweet moments to resonate in my head—my closure with my father, Tala, my packmates, and Ameilja.

Ameilja ... my love.

I continued my count. *Six. Seven. Eight. The eighth month of the year is Aoustí. Nine. Ten. The tenth of Aoustí is Ameilja's birthday.*

I felt a gap of terror hit me. *Twenty-one. Twenty-two. Twenty-three. Twenty-four. Ameilja's year. My Ameilja is twenty-four—humans in this day and age average seventy-five to ninety years. I wish I could see Ameilja's face for another sixty years, or maybe more, if I was not meeting my fate.*

I suddenly felt a strange sensation flood my mental realm. Memories of Fenris crashed through my mind. Her words reverberated against my skull. She visited me with a purpose—for my purpose.

Wait! I'm not ready. I'm not ready to die!

We got to a lonely staircase. The stairs spiraled to the bay of the airship. Lifeboats lined the walls over an open hatch, and supplies and luggage were scattered about the rear of the space—my death chamber.

The judge stopped walking. "Up to the hatch, völf."

Reluctantly, I obeyed. Once I stood before the door, I turned around to face him.

He gave me a curious look. "You want to watch?"

"Watch you shoot me? Yes."

He shrugged. "Up to you." He pointed his right arm and pulled back the hammer on his revolver. His finger clutched the trigger, prepared to squeeze.

"Wülkure Judge Vyaminof, may I ask you a question?"

The judge's eyebrows rose with curiosity. "Question?"

"Who ordered my execution?"

"Does that even matter? Is it not the law of Shaar—"

"I understand the law, but it does matter which House ordered my execution."

"The royal family proposed the order, as it always has. Fair?"

"No!"

"No?"

"*Which* House ordered my execution?"

The judge looked upon me through his spectacles. I was sure he wondered why it mattered. That law was in place because of Shaar's using Völfien as protectorates. Why should I have acted surprised? But it did matter to me. It mattered if András, my father's dear friend, the father of the woman I loved and even obsessed over, had called for my execution. If he'd ordered my death, some strange part of me wanted to know so I could accept or object.

Did he not believe I protected his daughter enough to bring her back in the face of her darkest hour?

"Was it Frost? Did High Abbot András Frost order my execution, Judge?"

The judge sighed. "If it gets you to shut up, no. Abbot András Frost did not order your execution."

I nodded and took a deep breath, holding back the tears of relief in my eyes. "I demand sanctuary, Judge! I come willing, and I must speak with Father Frost. It's about his daughter!"

"Sanctuary?"

"Yes. It is my right. As a protectorate for the lady of the Order, I have the right to stand before my leaders and plead my case. I may have information valuable to the abbot. Please!"

The judge shook his head. "Indeed. But the truth is, you are now a ghost." He rested his index finger on the trigger with no remorse visible in the slightest through the dark spectacles on his face. "And you, Kovuco Blackstar, have been a ghost to me since you laid eyes on this revolver."

I surveyed the room. I had been deciphering all around me since I made my decision—the decision to live.

"It's time." he whispered sharply.

Even though I wanted to watch my killer take my life, I closed my eyes, folding my paws in prayer. "Light of Uridei, merit me to your will. Grant me the hand to Purge. Give me the courage to stand in the way—"

The judge joined the prayer. "Forgive us our transgressions. Cast out the darkness; make way your fire. Speak Uridei; your servant is listening."

My eyes opened, and the judge didn't stand before me. Tala had bridged the gap. She held a bo staff in her paws.

"No!" I roared.

Tala smacked the staff's tip against the judge's hand, and the revolver was cast away. The firearms were chained beneath his shirt sleeves; that way, in case the guns were disarmed from him, it would not be difficult for him to retrieve them quickly.

He drew up his second revolver as Tala prepped for her next swing. The judge was skilled and fast. I grabbed Tala, forcing her face into my chest, as I charged for the judge. I grabbed his wrist with my spare paw, and with all my might, I drove my claws through his thick leather gloves, praying that the bones snapping would call the battle. The grimace on his face suggested he was determined to win.

He slung his revolver upward with his other hand, reaching out for it. Before he could clutch the handle, I had to act first. This act was one I knew the judge did not expect me to make, and it involved my jaws.

My teeth locked around his shoulder and tore through muscle, blistering tendons beneath the boundless pressure I could muster. I bit down and prayed the muscles would relax. They didn't. I felt his tensed muscles fold as he reached for the revolver again. I felt the barrel press against my temple, and in an instant, I forced another bite into his throat. His larynx crushed against my teeth, and his final breath was unable to find its way beyond the tourniquet of my jaws.

The judge fell limp, and his revolver fell to his side by the chain latched to it. The sound of his body hitting the floor echoed through the chamber. I immediately spit out the leftover bits of blood, careful not to swallow any of it, in the event his blood was tainted.

Tala stared down at the judge's corpse. Even in death, his face remained blank and cold-blooded. He was a wülkure of the Commission, and killing him made me a murderer.

A judge could carry out his will freely, and to stop him meant standing against the Commission. This would only complicate my mission. In their eyes, I was a dead völf, one of the vicious beasts they labeled us as daily.

"Kovuco! You killed him!" Tala gasped, horrified.

"I had to!"

"Kovuco, you'll be—"

"What was your plan exactly?" I snapped.

"Disarm him and maybe rough him up a bit?"

"He would have killed you! You know who he is, right?"

"No, I have no idea. Should I?"

"He is one of the most vicious wülkure in the Commission!" I fell backward, landing on my rump with a thud.

She knelt beside me. "I'm sorry! I didn't realize a wülkure was out to get you."

"What were you planning on doing? You attacked him. What made you think he wouldn't just shoot you for disarming him?"

Her stressors seemed disenfranchised by the realities she'd ignored in the first place. As I was covered in the judge's blood, my demands seemed of lesser priority.

"Well, I was trying to create a way for your escape, you idiot!" She got up and stomped off, massaging her temples, with a headache brewing in her skull.

"And then what? Do you think he'd have ditched you? He would have killed you, Tala!" I said, frustrated.

"Yes, but you would've lived on! You have someone to chase after! I don't anymore." She smiled slightly amid the moment's madness.

Her words filled me with sadness. "It would have haunted me if he'd killed you for my sake. Besides, I haven't gotten her yet. It might not ever happen, Tala! Ever!"

"Why do you keep saying that? The scent coming off you is so strong, Kovuco. Why do you think I told you about my parents? I wanted you to feel less guilty about—well, you know."

"About what?" I urged.

"Well, you're not a virgin anymore—that's for sure! Even though you're supposed to be when working as a protectorate for the Order."

I shook my head. "You're wrong. I am still a virgin, Tala. I didn't have sex with her."

"How? The scent off your lips is almost overpowering; your energy is driven toward someone intensely."

"Intense as in blood, right?"

"Yes, but I doubt you had a bloodletting session without at least having a throe of passion." She chuckled. "C'mon. That would be crazy! I mean, unless you needed it because you were dying." She paused and snapped her gaze toward me; my gaze couldn't lie. "Kovuco, did you bloodlet to survive?" her eyes widened in horror.

"Uh, yes. I would likely have died. She shot me."

"Shot you? What völf in Shaar uses firearms?"

"She's not—" I paused and buried my face in my bloody palms. *Damn it.*

"She's not what, Kovuco?"

"She's not a völf!"

"Not a völf?" Confusion coated her tone.

"No! Damn it, she's not a völf, Tala!"

"She's human?" Her voice quivered.

I nodded.

"What the hell, Kovuco? What was so powerful that you couldn't keep your paws off a damned handmaiden?"

My eyes widened. "Not exactly a handmaiden either."

"Who?"

My silence was revealing.

She followed the trail and went straight for the top. "Wait! Don't tell me. No, Kovuco. No. Are you talking about … Ameilja?"

My stare intensified.

"Ameilja Frost? *The* Ameilja Frost? Daughter of High Abbot András Frost? The crowned seer? Your lady of the Order?" She paused and swallowed. "Kovuco, are you—are you bonded to Ameilja?"

It did me no good to lie or to even try. I thought it best not to nod, but I did. I acknowledged the truth.

"Kovuco! I—I don't know what to say." She dropped to her knees, staring at me.

"You could say it's foolish," I said.

"I don't want to say that. It's—I don't know—unfounded?"

"Impossible," I added.

"I mean, Kovuco, she's one of the highest sought-after women in the Isles. The man who sent the judge after you is likely a suitor."

"If they know she's missing." I sighed. "But I know, I know! It was an accident. I can't explain it. But everything I said is the truth: it was love at first sight. I didn't do this on purpose; it just happened."

"Does anyone know?"

"My packmates. My father."

"Nav'i?"

"Nav'i? Uh, yes, Nav'i knows."

"What did Nav'i say?"

"Nav'i wasn't pleased, but he pushed me to pursue the truth. Even though Ameilja may never work out for me, I have to pursue her in the circumstances I have fallen into."

"You know, from our youth, Nav'i used to study chimeras, transmutation, portals, and such. What if there was a way you could achieve full Rinkin form? Maybe you could, to some extent, have a chance."

"It's impossible to reverse the more noticeable anatomical differences from the humans. It'd be strange."

There was silence for a moment. Tala turned toward the body of the judge. I hated that she looked guilty.

"I'm sorry, Kovuco," she solemnly whispered.

I smiled at her, hoping it would comfort her. I couldn't blame her. I'd have felt sorry for me too.

"It's like you said: we'll just have to see where Uridei takes you," she added gently.

I nodded. "Yeah. We will see."

"I don't judge you. I still meant what I said. You're a very special völf. I am honored to know you."

I chuckled. "Might have dodged a crazy one, eh?"

"No, Kovuco! You're my friend. You'll always be my friend. You've always been an acquired taste, handsome, and so has your father. Maybe it's just who you are. You will do disservice to your true calling if you don't explore its meaning."

"Thanks, Tala."

It was quiet until she finally stood up, walked to one of the windows, and stared into the distance. She sighed and began taking off her blood-splattered clothes.

"We're almost to Isarah. Get undressed. I have some civilian clothing for you. Get to the nearest temple, get off the street as soon as possible, and be as deliberate as possible with your commute."

"What about the judge?"

"Well, since you killed him, it will only haunt you later. Just try to avoid claiming sanctuary."

"Why?"

"Well, until you know which House called your execution, you can't trust anyone now."

"Don't worry about me, Tala. I must continue my journey."

"Well, whatever you do, just be careful."

I turned my gaze to her and smiled. "I will. Thank you, Tala. And I hope you find what you're looking for."

She nodded wearily. "You too, Kovuco."

CHAPTER TWENTY-SEVEN

DESOLATION

Isarah
Demitori City, Brass District
Grande Mariner Apartment Complex, room 504
Aoustí 17

KIEFER WOKE, AND RAE WAS CURLED INTO HIS
bedsheets with him. Her naked form straddled him longingly. A gentle
smile formed on her soft lips as he brushed his fingers through her hair.

"Hi," he whispered.

"Hi," she softly responded.

He remained there and wished he could for the rest of the day. Just
when he'd convinced himself he'd earned a day to sleep in, a steady
tapping at his door echoed throughout the apartment. He counted the
pauses, realizing whoever was there wasn't going away until there was
an answer.

He rose and quickly dressed in slacks and a shirt—enough to be
presentable, other than his exposed feet. Pulling his fingers through his
hair, he ensured his pistol was loaded, taking with him a .357 revolver
in the event there was trouble.

Kiefer cracked open the door just enough for the dead-bolt chain
to catch. He sighed. It wasn't anyone he wanted to see, and he was
happy to be accompanied by a weapon: Dr. Tobias Frahm stood in
his doorway.

Frahm flashed an awkwardly pleasant expression. "I heard you were
a coffee drinker." He held a bag of coffee beans from the Escape Goat

Coffee Company, a prominent coffee and tea house in the Brass District. It just so happened it was Kiefer's preferred roast.

What the hell is he doing here? Kiefer eyed the coffee bag and then Frahm. He stepped back into his apartment to undo the dead bolt. He opened the door and allowed Frahm to come inside.

"Ah, much obliged," Frahm said as Kiefer shut the door. Then he turned to face the end of Kiefer's revolver a split hair from his nose. Frahm didn't flinch.

Still, that fucking smile remains plastered on his face. Even with a revolver powerful enough to behead him.

"Allow me the honor of making your coffee. Should you choose to kill me, that is your wish."

"If I wanted you dead, I'd've let that völf crucify you in the Sunspire. I *chose* to keep you alive."

"All for this moment then, yes? Killing me removes me from the electorate to become the head doctor—"

"Kitchen!" Kiefer barked. He directed Frahm into the kitchen. "Set the coffee down, and sit," Kiefer ordered.

Frahm listened, doing so with casual confidence. He saw the coffee dripper was full and pointed to it like a hidden prize. "Already brewed coffee, eh? Sorry. I knew I was slacking by sleeping in."

"Speak your business, Frahm."

"I take it you mean the elixir and bringing that ork back to life. It was beautiful, wasn't it? Just a taste of your blood, and the undead are bound to your will."

"Beautiful? No. Explain." Kiefer tightened his grip on the weapon.

"I named it Narkänum. Narkänum is what we have been concocting. After all these years, and many prototypes, we had successfully entered a productive stage. The neurological components synthesized through alchemical immurement hypnotize the undead to our will. We used it on the Wöndin's son, the ork boy you witnessed. The Wöndin's offspring's inherited power has aided in our study for years now." He paused. "My employer is also currently traveling abroad with a member of the un-dead. This undead member is very special and quite unique. I'm still trying to wrap my brain around what we've been able to accomplish with that prototype. My employer can control his every move and—"

"With your employer? You're telling me the undead walk among us? That fucking plague is beyond the Sunspire?" Kiefer gritted his teeth, gripping the revolver tighter.

"Calm yourself. He doesn't wander as a bloodthirsty threat. And it's currently just one; well, there was another, but he has perished—but that's not the greater concern. Now that Dr. Baadar and Dr. Tiem are dead, I only have one other colleague, Dr. Wendtfuss, to turn to, and she wishes to take the Sunspire's research in a very deadly direction."

"Deadly how?"

"Deadly as in forcing a member of the Order to die rather than using the individual already dead to the Näkk. We can turn the tide of this maddening experimentation, Kiefer, and solely use Narkänum to bring back Sabor's power. We've lost the Wöndin's son, but I don't believe sacrificing another powerful being is necessary."

"So why are you here? What do you need with me?"

"I pray for your willingness to volunteer your time. You've already been within the Sunspire and seen what we've accomplished. Wouldn't you like us to turn the tide?"

"Pray? Thought you hated the Order," Kiefer sneered.

"Please. Did I not just say I was opposed to the sacrifice arrangement? The Order would have me refrain from revenge, Kiefer. That's why I left the Order. The Book of Light remains a vessel of information to which any man of intellectual sophistication should consider; however, loosing my wife is a trauma I must navigate through. I believe my wife was mad. She was led astray, and I was blind to her weakness. That's something I must carry to my grave. Something I will have to forgive myself for before asking Uridei's forgiveness."

"I am not buying it, Frahm. You have a god complex, and you'll have to have me forcefully imprisoned to get my aid in your sick game."

"We'll see what my employer has to say about that; it's only a matter of time before you find out that—"

Rae stealthily ventured into the space, aiming her PSR at Frahm.

"Rae!" Kiefer gasped. "Go back to the bedroom! Now!"

"Why is this scum even here?" she exclaimed, refusing to take her eyes off Frahm.

"Rae! I've got this. Drop the rifle."

378

She refused to move a muscle.

Frahm rose. "It's fine. I should leave. But I will be waiting, Kiefer. At this point, I have concluded my work at the Sunspire. We have all but to harness the weapon, and we can start winning this operation and using it for great things. There is no need to kill a seer, as Wendtfuss intends. Just think about that, will you? If I personally wanted to force you, you never would have left the Spire."

"I'll remember that threat clearly."

"Not a threat, although I guess it could come off that way. Despite what you think of me, I want what is best for humanity. I still believe in Uridei, and Uridei grants us free will."

Frahm dipped his head to Rae. "Madam. A good day to you." Frahm pressed past Kiefer.

Kiefer remained unmoved even after the door shut behind the crazed doctor.

Rae lowered her rifle. "What is going on, Kiefer? Who the hell was that guy? Why did you have a gun on him?"

"No one. He's nothing. Just a nutcase doctor from the Sunspire."

"I heard about the cult massacre, but what's all this about needing more of your aid and about someone from the Order needing to die?"

"Nothing, Rae. Just nonsense. You heard him: free will, and I am more than unwilling." He walked back to the bedroom.

Rae followed. "Nonsense? A doctor of the Sunspire doesn't just ask for your help to harness a weapon—a weapon of a historical figure who is a madman! I heard what he said, Kiefer; don't play dumb with me! And now members of the Order are being sacrificed? Really?"

"Because he is a madman, Rae!"

"Tell me what's going on!" Her voice rose, and Kiefer snapped.

He forced a hand over her mouth and harshly backed her against the wall. A tremble of anger writhed through his fingers as he covered her lips "Enough! You and I are done; I am leaving, and when I return, I expect you gone. Understood?"

With tear-filled eyes, she shook her head, muttering a "No" under the force of his palm.

"I forbid you to return. This is the end of you and me. Do you understand? Tell me you under-fucking-stand, Rae!"

She shook her head more forcefully, unwilling to succumb to this angry fit she knew all too well. All to try to push her away.

Kiefer grabbed her shoulder, hurled her onto the bed, pulled out his pistol, and pointed it at her head. "You are leaving, and you're never to come back here! Never seek me out!"

She leaned into the pistol. "What are you afraid of, Kiefer?" She arched her brow.

"Why do you even want me? You realize you're not the only one, right?"

"What?"

"You're not the only one I am fucking! I fuck around on you constantly!"

"Fuck around?" she asked with a tick of sarcasm.

"Yes! I am fucking other women. I have had six other women consistently since I have been with you. That doesn't count those not afraid to see me again."

"I know, Kiefer," Rae huffed. "I fucking know! Your colleague Szonja is one of them. One who isn't afraid of you."

Kiefer remained unchanged, but Rae saw right through him. She knew he was shocked that she knew of Szonja.

"I know about them. All of them."

"Why then? Why do you hang around so much? How can you risk the humiliation and still stay? Stay and risk being killed for me? Why?" Kiefer pressed.

"Because."

"Because why?"

"Because I love you!" The words slipped effortlessly through her lips. "I know you have other lovers, but you're my only, Kiefer. I can't see myself with anyone else. Just you. Maybe that makes me crazy, but better I be crazy than be without you."

"So stupid! Stupid and insecure!" Kiefer spat, belittling her.

"Damn you, Kiefer! You never let me in! And even though I know this, I hold on to the hope that one day you will. If you think I'm *so* stupid, pull the trigger—fucking do it! Or just beat me—ravage me as you do with other women in bed. I know it's what you like—pain to numb the real insecurities within *you*. I see you for who you really are, Kief! Please do what you will, but I will never leave you. Not when you need me right now more than ever." Rae paused, inhaled an elongated, shaky breath, and eyed the weary man standing before her.

Rae settled her tone to a light whisper. "I mean, look at you; you're fucking exhausted."

Kiefer relaxed his shoulders and lowered the gun. Pieces of his dark hair fell in front of his face. He looked into Rae's attentive eyes as they glistened under her thick tears. Under their grief, she was filled with courage and determination. No matter what Kiefer did, he knew she would not leave him alone; she wouldn't allow him to turn his force into a fear tactic. But Kiefer couldn't allow her to become a weapon. Not against him. He couldn't let her die because of him.

"Enough!" he snapped, violently breaking the silence. He grabbed her by the arm and pulled her into his hallway. He tossed her toward the front door. "Get out!" he screamed. "Get the fuck out of here, Rae! Don't come back!"

Rae stumbled to her feet. "No! I'm not leaving you, Kiefer!"

"I won't ask again, Rae! Get—"

"No!"

"Out!"

"I love you, Kie—"

He cut her off by sharply slapping her cheek. He hit her hard enough to send her to her knees. She began to yelp out sobs.

Rae regained her footing and left without turning to face him. Tears streamed down her reddened face. "Fuck you!" she wailed as she fled.

The counterblow of silence immediately whipped through his apartment. Defeat flooded the space. Kiefer curled the hand he'd laid on her into a tight fist. His nails embedded into his palm so deep it began to bleed. His arms trembled.

Did I really just hit her? What have you done, Kiefer?

He felt more alone than he ever had in his entire twenty-nine years of life. He wanted her but knew her leaving was the best way to protect her from what was likely coming for him. He couldn't bear the thought of her being hurt. It was better that she believe he was the monster.

Kiefer felt hollow and somewhat afraid. With no known family, abandonment and desolation were his shadows. He turned, dropped the .357 onto the floor, and shuffled toward his couch. He sighed and buried his face in his trembling hands. He never had laid a hand on a woman—aside from a fugitive or one who desired it during sex. This was wrong. Painfully wrong.

What did I just do?

Rae was innocent; she didn't deserve his wrath. She was the only one who fullheartedly did not show fear of him, physically or mentally. Then again, although he didn't admit it, she was the only woman he desired not to be afraid of him. Now that probably had changed.

Rae had been the one who leaned in first to kiss him—a kiss he'd experienced passionately and felt a sensational spark in. With her, for the first time, he'd risked sex to completion without pulling out. It had been only a couple of times, but Kiefer never made the same mistake twice. Kiefer made love to Rae; despite his denial in using the word. She'd been the first he went to bed with when the sun went down and stayed with after the sun rose and the first he took to dinner and then took for breakfast the following morning.

Although he didn't outwardly admit it, Rae was his future. Rae was the first female he'd wanted to be there when he made it home safe. She was his comfort—his solitude.

Rae was Kiefer's definition of love.

Now he didn't know if he'd ever be able to experience her genuine affection again. His future was unknown. She was gone, and rightfully so.

Kiefer pulled his fingers through his hair, tugging it tightly as he dug his fingernails into his scalp. His entire world was falling apart; so much was out of his control.

I'm sorry. I'm so sorry …

For the first time, Kiefer wept.

☆

Fjorthúr
The Sunspire
Lab 1
Aoustí 20

Dr. Sayáko Wendtfuss stared down at the floor, recalling the report that Isabelle Baadar had shot and killed her own brother, Anton Rotenfeld.

She was well aware of the expertise of the Baadars, but she'd had no idea it would end in bloodshed. Of course, she hadn't expected Isabelle to turn into a Völfien either.

Wendtfuss had argued with her colleague Frahm about having Isabelle returned to the Sunspire for experimentation. Sure, the Völfien were not beneficial to their experiments with the Näkk, but she found it curious that a well-known ex–Commission member had acquired that new ability. Frahm had attested that it didn't add up but urged Wendtfuss that she had to accept that it was in Wülkure Yuska's hands for now, and eventually, she could pursue her interests after the renegade Völfien woke from her coma.

"Dr. Wendtfuss?" said an assistant from Lab 2.

Wendtfuss turned. "Yes?"

"Everything is ready. I have just heard word from control that Kythis Graal has arrived on the island."

Wendtfuss looked around the lab, pleased with the work completed in such a short time. Kythis would never know that these labs had been vastly flooded and covered in offal less than a week ago.

"Excellent. Continue preparation. Now that Kythis has arrived, he will ensure we have samples of the Näkk."

"Very well, Doctor." The assistant paused. "Any word on how we are going to replace the ork boy? Excuse me. I mean Dakka."

Wendtfuss gave the young assistant a stern glare, clearly not in a jovial mood. "I said continue preparation."

The assistant bowed, feeling shame for upsetting his head doctor. He quickly resumed his orders, thankful to be one of the nine surviving people of the original team.

Wendtfuss turned to one of her new security leads, Benny Albrecht. "Wächter?"

Benny nodded and led the doctor to the elevator platform. Once he and Wendtfuss stepped in, he got on his comm unit. "Wächter Albrecht to control. Do you read, control? Over."

Toffel's voice sounded through the unit. "This is control. Over."

Since Toffel had been able to hack the Spire from the bunker, he was far too valuable to silence, so under strict security and triple the pay, he had been promoted to æsir as a permanent lead on the control level.

With the approved order of Kythis, Wendtfuss had also threatened the other wächters involved in taking back the Spire, swearing them to silence.

Necessary steps had been taken to execute any survivors she deemed untrustworthy.

Wendtfuss, Frahm, and the new team would stop at nothing to keep the secrets of the Näkk hidden. If any word got out or if any contracts were broken, a swift execution would be the result. Or the traitors would become the next test subjects in their lethal game.

"Take us to the foyer. Over."

Albrecht sighed as the elevator platform began to ascend. The clockwork mechanism within the shaft's walls began to turn and lift the platform away from the underground labs.

"Something wrong, Wächter?" Wendtfuss asked with a tinge of annoyance.

"Not sure I trust Toffel. Seems like a mistake to keep him alive."

Wendtfuss laughed. "I suppose you would have liked us to eliminate my nine other staff members as well?"

"Well, no, but Toffel is a complete outsider. He was just a last-minute add on; he had no idea about the Spire's dealings until his involvement per Captain Bayde's orders. He really should have been executed."

"You said the same thing about Ólaf, Wächter. And he signed the same confidentiality contract you did. Anyone who can hack the Spire from the bunker is a worthy tech to have on staff. Your team is well aware of the risks, and he's been appropriately accommodated."

"Yes, Doctor."

The elevator stopped at the bridge level, and they stepped into the foyer, which was now fully equipped with new security. A team of four stood by, now led by security lead Rikard.

Rikard stepped forward. He cleared his throat. "Dr. Wendtfuss."

Wendtfuss greeted him with a nod and then stared forward. He spoke into his comm unit. "Rikard to control. Do you read, control? Over."

Toffel's voice sounded through the unit. "This is control. Over."

"Open the front doors. We are in place. Over."

The front doors' internal clockwork mechanism unlocked and

slowly dragged the doors open. The sun's glow bled into the foyer, along with the warm, salty air. A pair of airships hovered over the shallows.

The new defensive measures were underway as a secondary bunker was being built. Since the ork raid, Kythis had ordered that advanced security measures be increased, and new prefab shelters were to be constructed. With Nathalii's deep pockets and knack for architectural design, she would ensure the entire beachfront of the Sunspire was actively guarded and luxuriously housed.

Kythis Graal stepped down from his airship's platform. His dark hair was slicked back, glistening in the sun. He walked confidently, holding his chin high, as he inspected the beachfront efforts with pride on his walk toward the Sunspire's entrance. His long leather jacket whipped against the wind, instantly ceasing as soon as his foot breached the foyer. All eyes turned toward him. He grinned the type of grin that made even Wendtfuss nervous. An eerie presence wafted around his tall form, permeating the space he stood within.

Kythis casually studied the foyer, eyeing the room as if looking for evidence that an attack had ever transpired there. Wendtfuss tensed, waiting for his response. The fact that he had nothing to say at that moment was a good sign—the exact reaction she wanted from her superior.

"Lord Kythis, I hope your trip was comfortable." Wendtfuss spoke up.

He turned to the doctor and lent another keen smile. "I am even more comforted to see that the Spire appears to be in good repair. You and Frahm did well with cleanup."

Wendtfuss cringed at the idea of Frahm taking even half credit for the work she had put into getting the Spire back into operating order. She took the opportunity to gloat. "My lord, I have taken measures to ensure the bridge is completely staffed with a new crew. We now have increased efforts to have a morning crew, a graveyard crew, and a split crew to prevent such an infraction ever again."

"Very good." He approved.

Wendtfuss nodded. "Speaking of the cult, Chef Ádrez Cháput was killed. Appears an infected ork mutilated him."

Kythis's brows shifted. "That's a shame. He was only following orders."

"My lord?" she whispered, scanning her surroundings to ensure there weren't any unauthorized staff members within earshot.

"Ah yes, I am the one who arranged the break-in."

"I had no idea. Why?"

"Kristján was becoming a problem. Tiem had advised me that he was getting cold feet about our dealings with the Näkk. I know Henrik and others were quite fond of him, so it was better to have an assassination take place than to convince Henrik to have him killed. Don't want to look like the bad guy, do I?" He winked.

Wendtfuss swallowed nervously. Rikard and Albrecht shifted where they stood, feeling a bit on edge that Kythis dared to say that aloud in front of them. They were all sworn to confidentiality; however, they knew any news acquired increased the risk of their being executed or never having a chance to leave the island ever again.

Kythis sensed this and laughed. "Lighten up, everyone. It didn't work—which brings me to my next concern: the völf."

Wendtfuss nodded. "Yes. We have installed a secondary sprinkler system that is infused with a féja-based compound. If any members of the Fae breach, they will be subdued quickly."

"That's it? Féja sprinklers?"

"We actually had another safety precaution installed as well. Our very own wächter, Benny Albrecht, suggested another mechanism be added to our exhaust system. Should we have a breach involving Völfien, there is another powder-based compound that contains vilkanás."

Kythis's smile grew wide across his freshly shaven face. It stretched the wrinkles starting to settle in, giving away his age. He turned to Benny. "Interesting. Where have I heard your name?"

"Perhaps from the war. My grandfather was killed while pursuing the Danheim House."

"Ah, back when we were silly enough to cooperate with the Order. I believe I do remember that name. Your grandfather was—"

"Killed by a völf. Supposedly accidental."

Kythis nodded. "Dr. Wendtfuss, I think this is most impressive. I think it's a travesty that such a mind is only serving us as a wächter. I will be taking Mr. Albrecht back to Demitori with me after my work here is done." He turned toward Benny. "We will ensure you have a place in our operations going forward, especially with how things are advancing with our studies."

Benny smiled widely. "Yes—wow. Thank you!"

"No, thank you, Benny," Kythis said as he winked at the eager wächter, then turned back to Wendtfuss. "But not to worry, Doctor; I will have more crew at your disposal. In the meantime, let's get your samples. I am sure you are eager to get started."

Kythis and Wendtfuss followed Benny to the elevator. Once again, Benny contacted control, and the platform began its descent to Lab 2.

Once the foyer was out of sight, along with the listening ears of Sunspire's regular staff, Wendtfuss cleared her throat. "My lord, may I ask, what are we to do about our predicament? Am I to receive the seer?"

"I have granted lovely Baroness Nathalii some time to pursue her interest in the Wöndin."

"Excuse me for pressing, but Nathalii is only chasing a ghost. There is no such thing as an ork who is capable of transmuting elements like a seer. Really—"

"We are following leads, Doctor." He hastily cut in. "You have my full support, *but* I have personal interests I must continue pursuing. Have you forgotten that it was Fallz'den's son who brought the Näkk back to us in the first place? He is no mere ghost. Surely something fantastical thrives in his DNA, and surely the official news of his son's death will draw him out. I'm quite shocked we haven't seen movement yet." He turned to face Wendtfuss, tightening his glare. "Continue your research, and ensure the samples are prepared. Understood?"

"Yes." Wendtfuss obediently responded, recalling the large ships outside of the facility. "I presume you have more test subjects for me?"

"I do. Henrik signed off on another prison in Isarah. They had thirteen more prisoners scheduled for death row."

"Hm, perfect." She said as a tinge of impatience coated her sigh.

Kythis snickered. "Don't be so ungrateful, Doctor. I know you are eager, but all great things take time. The answers are within reach; it's just a matter of time—maybe even just hours."

"And you're still certain about Ms. Baadar?"

Kythis eyed the doctor out of his peripheral. "Yes, she's being handled."

"Expertly?" She boldly questioned.

Kythis turned toward the doctor. Her lips quickly tightened—eyes locking within his firm glare—realizing she had overstepped.

"Are you questioning *my* decision?" he spoke slowly, as if he were tasting the words right off of his tongue.

Wendtfuss swallowed, subtly shaking her head followed by rapid blinks, stumbling on what she would say next.

Kythis leaned in, closing the distance between him and the doctor's face. The smell of his sharp cologne swept through her nostrils. "You have nothing to worry about, Doctor." He calmly spoke, holding his composure as if he were a snake preparing to bite. "As I've stated to Henrik on more than one occasion, Kiefer Yuska is *far* more capable of handling that bitc—" he paused, correcting his derogatory tone "—that *woman* compared to any other wülkure out there."

Wendtfuss swallowed again, nodding.

"Good. Glad we're on the same page." Kythis jeered, leaning back up, and straightening his jacket. "Kiefer Yuska will gather all the pertinent information I will ever need. He's quite intelligent you know … after all, he is my son."

Wendtfuss snapped her shocked gaze to Kythis, giving away she had just learned of this news. Before she could say another word, the elevator platform jolted, settling at Lab 2.

The doors opened, revealing a short hallway with a guarded steel door at the far end. Behind the door revealed a large space that held a built-in prison with a centered lab space. New, iron spiral staircases led up to each platform to access each of the three floors, where both human and ork prisoners were stored.

Along the outer cages were twenty-six-gauge wires emitting 7,700-watt electrical pulses every three seconds. The amperes were so strong they could be seen as they pulsated, even if nothing touched them.

The area was heavily guarded by wächters with even heavier weapons.

Kythis looked to Wendtfuss. "Just think: all these useless lives will have purpose." He stepped further into the space, listening to the rustling noises within the prison cells. The test subjects protested in fear by screaming, cursing, and threatening. Kythis laughed, scanning the cells with ominous joy. "All thanks to the Näkk."

CHAPTER TWENTY-EIGHT
THE INHERITANCE

Isarah
Blackwater City
Aoustí 19

I STEPPED OFF THE AIRSHIP, INSTANTLY TAKING
in my new surroundings. It was strange compared to Shaar. Blackwater
City was a gravitational phenomenon filled with networks of bridges
and ports that hung over the ocean. Buildings floated on surfaces just a
few feet from the sea.

The architecture was industrial and uniquely mechanical.
Cobblestone roads with large gaslit lanterns lined the clanking-sounding
streets that thrummed through my olfactory receptors. Steam bellowed
from the rooftops, even through some of the establishments' upper windows, engulfing the sky above.

These people. This world.

The people there wore clothing made of thick leather-like canvas,
and embroidered metalworks of gold and steel. The men wore fancy,
elaborate hats, and the women did too. I could at least differentiate that
the men wearing dark goggles with badges stating their craft were the
tradesmen, and there were many in Blackwater.

Whereas we valued ornate, naturalistic trinkets, the people of this
world strived for mechanical solutions purposeful and strategic to their
daily lives. Their plumage was a statement made in the most obnoxious
of ways, but who was I to judge? To them, I stood out vastly.

Blackwater contained a plethora of personalities in one place—many cultures, primarily the human race, but even the Fae meandered confidently through the streets. The Fae there were adorned in colors, charms, and magnetic elements, and some appeared glamoured wearing attire telling a story unlike anything I'd have imagined seeing back home in Shaar.

I awkwardly smiled as some caught me staring; however, I noticed many who found me equally peculiar. I didn't mean to be rude, but I was currently witnessing pages I'd read come to life in real time. I'd read in detail about the Orkésh, the eloquent dryads, and the minotaurs. Now I was up close and personal with many different species, free to speak to them without the duty as a protectorate. I was a sight; however, strutting in my platinum fur and Shaar'an-style jacket added to the uniqueness of my presence there. Despite my current circumstances, it was a relief to see the other side of the world. I liked it. There was much more to experience.

Thankfully, I was overall disregarded as the people moved swiftly through the busy streets, focused on his or her destination. Cars I'd only read about sped through the streets, leaving behind putrid-smelling vapors. If one wasn't careful, he or she could easily get run over.

Sweat began to bead along my temples. The weather was also much warmer, and the sun was blisteringly bright against my blue eyes.

I finally caught sight of some völves with even longer, thinner fur than mine. It layered finely down their backs in beaded braids, some entwined with colorful feathers. They were busy speaking with a few Fae, laughing and sipping from steam-filled mugs, as they eyed art pieces displayed in a shop window. I then caught sight of two wülkure watching them, standing just a couple of yards away. The cultures might have changed, but the Commission did not.

I took that as a sign to dip low and get lunch. My priority right now was to get instructions to the closest temple. I was currently on a large port and assumed I would have to cross a network of bridges to get to the actual soil of Isarah, but I had to know for sure. I also needed to get farther from the airship station since both rides had left bodies behind me. Indeed, my presence would eventually be known to someone.

I found a quaint hole-in-the-wall restaurant on a street corner, called Tag's. Familiar scents lingered in the air: foods and spices of Shaar.

Thank Uridei!

There was a dragon painting on the outside, over a bowl of ramen. I could smell glorious eggs, noodles, and pork. Rather than confuse my system, it was best to stick to my typical cuisine, especially with all the new meats I was beginning to consume. I ducked under a sail-like shade and entered the small establishment. There were two available tables. Like the Shaar'an seating, the tables were low to the ground, with an array of pillows to comfort those who sat at them. There was a small bar near the kitchen.

I scanned the room, absorbing its elements. The walls were made of shudders and what appeared to be other doors, all painted with a whitewash encapsulating them together. Framed images of watercolor dragons and phoenixes cleverly balanced the ornate pottery of leafed plants. A voice rang out from behind the counter at the head of the restaurant in a tongue I recognized as Shaar'an: "Have a seat! I'll be with you in a moment!"

I bowed and sat at the closest table.

I waited patiently until a heavily tattooed dwarf with a forked beard approached me with an exhausted notepad. "What can I get you?"

I was caught off guard. He was casual and spoke loudly; even for a nearly seven-foot völf, my ears folded timidly.

I cleared my throat. "I've never been here before. I mean—" I began speaking in Shaar'an, until the dwarf stopped me.

"Sorry, friend. Saw your jacket and just assumed you spoke the more eastern tongue. You are Shaar'an, yes?"

I nodded. "Yes. Do you have gyoza with pork?"

The waiter shot me a confused look, furrowing his brow. He stood shorter than my sitting height. "Generally, that's what makes gyoza, gyoza, fella."

"Uh, right." I laughed. *Kovuco, you idiot.* "I'll have some gyoza then. How much? I only have—one second." I reached into the pouch strapped to my belt and unveiled the Shaar'an coins. I wondered now if I could even pay for the meal. "I'm not sure if my money's good here. I just got into town."

The waiter shifted his eyes. "You have a credit, völf?"

"A credit?"

The dwarf huffed. "I mean, it's obvious you just got into town. Who brought you here?"

I would drop a name that might be familiar but that could place me in danger. I best skip lunch.

"I should go. Sorry to waste—"

A human woman quickly tapped the dwarf's shoulder. "I've got this, Kóji. Fetch the gyoza, and start two dragon specials."

The dwarf laughed. "Eh! What the hell are you doing back in Blackwater?"

"Here for business, Kóji. Now, get those dragon specials going! I have places to be, and so does our traveling friend here."

I felt embarrassed, but the woman gave me a wink. "It's the best they've got!" she said. "Get it every time I'm in town!" She leaned in and whispered, "I don't want it to go to his head, but that dwarf can cook a mean special too."

"You didn't have to," I said.

"No worries! Enjoy. I hope you like a spicy broth."

"Order's up!" the dwarf yelled out from behind the counter.

She grabbed her packaged tray and darted for the door. "See you, Kóji!"

"You staying at the Varka-Tanu again?"

"Yes! You gonna be serving breakfast?"

"As per my usual."

"Wonderful! I'm hoping to head back to Demitori City soon. Maybe I can get a few other Commission members to drive back with me. You know how I hate traveling alone."

"Just pick up a hitchhiker; there are plenty!" He huffed.

She cast a quick salute before pressing through the door.

"Thank you!" I called. Not sure if she heard me, I slinked back into my seat.

The dwarf, Kóji, brought out a steaming bowl of ramen crafted with chicken bone broth and topped with ground chili pork and braised pork belly. Additionally, he set down a small plate of pan-fried pork and vegetable gyoza with sauce.

"Type-three dragon special, Mr. Völf," announced Kóji.

"Type three?"

"Special blend. It's a favorite of the local Völfien here in Blackwater. Just don't tell the Commission." He smirked.

My mouth uncontrollably watered as the smells penetrated my sinuses, reminding me that I needed to eat. "It smells outstanding."

The dwarf bowed. "I added a few extra dumplings for ya. You look kinda starved." His small, stocky form eyed my massive, famished form.

"It was kind of that woman to pay for me. She didn't have to go out of her way to feed a strange völf."

"Don't worry about it! That overly chipper human eats like a völf, so she knows what's best for ya! Besides, I'd do anything for my favorite out-of-towner. There's no finer wächter, or sweetheart, than Rae Arow."

☆

Isarah
Blackwater City
Aoustí 19

I elusively crossed the bridge within Blackwater City, stopped a female völf, and asked for directions to the nearest temple, hoping it was the Vaterlünd Temple.

She pointed me to a new-age-looking building made of olive wood and dark metals. An iron fence wrapped in vines sprouting little red and orange flowers surrounded the structure.

I cautiously walked in through the archway and into the outdoor atrium and immediately was startled at the sight of an elder sister. She was wearing her modest attire and kneeling by a little sister, attending to a cut on her finger.

I fell to my knees, clutched my thighs, and bowed low. "Apologies, Sister. I did not mean to intrude." I got up and walked toward the archway.

The sister called, "Sir?"

I turned, still dipping my head.

"My name is Sister Cácilie. You are safe here in the atrium; however, this location is the female monastery. We have a male monastery about three blocks from here called the Vaterlünd. Wait outside, and I will take you."

She turned back to the little sister and whispered to her. The little sister got up, folded her hands, and bowed low to me. She placed her index and middle finger together and pointed them upward while curling her other fingers together. She then put the two upward fingers against her lips. "Light of Uridei, sir," she said with a gentle, frail voice. Her intent moved me, and I returned the gesture.

"Light of Uridei, Sister," I said.

She hurried off, and Sister Cácilie led me through the archway and back onto the cobblestone path. Her gait was slow due to her age. "Are you new here, sir?"

"Yes," I answered. "My name is Jón O'Kuma. I come from Shaar. I am seeking Brother Rui. Do you know him?"

The sister nodded. "Yes, Brother Rui is a monk of the Order. I noticed your prostration. Are you a follower of Uridei?"

I nodded. "Yes. I am from a seaside temple in Shaar."

"I've always wanted to visit Shaar. May I ask your business here in Blackwater?"

"My business, I'm afraid, is very sensitive."

"Understood, Mr. O'Kuma. My apologies for intruding."

"Not at all, Sister. Allow me to apologize. It has been a difficult few days for me. I did not mean to come off as secretive."

She smiled at me. Her warm, delicate eyes gave away that she no longer wished to ask questions, since I had already established the sensitive nature of my business. I wanted to break the silence but decided her honor should affirm my own.

She guided me through the network of streets until we reached the Vaterlünd. It was a more significant temple, with accents of white and an ashen green. She directed me to the door and stopped. "Well, Brother Jón, here is where I depart. Brother Rui will be here, as he doesn't venture out much anymore. I hope you find what you are looking for. Know that the Sisterhood of the Light is always an ally."

I bowed to her and returned the finger gesture. "Light of Uridei, Sister Cácilie."

She bowed and departed slowly down the street. The finger gesture was much subtler than the chest beat I was accustomed to. It showed restraint and control among the brotherhood and sisterhood of the Order.

I opened the large black door by pulling the steel ring in its center. Cautiously, with all senses alert, I entered the atrium. Its marble floor depicted Albean. Elegant writing scripted within the marble stated, "Albean, the savior of humanity, stood as an example of dauntless strength and regal bravery, notably his gracious humility and the power of divine forgiveness."

I questioned what Albean would have thought of humanity now. Would he still have thought it was worth risking opposition to raising a beast-like race to fight alongside the humans? A greedy, dominant race who now shackled the race meant to be equal among them?

Albean, oh, how times have changed.

I pressed through the atrium and into the main level of the temple. The walls were adorned with significant works of art, all dedicated to the glory of Uridei. The entire room was a wonder to witness. I walked to the candlelit altar, knelt there, and prayed aloud in my Völfien tongue. My voice echoed through the empty room, circling the intricately decorated walls and wooden pews.

A man's voice suddenly spoke as I quickly finished praying: "So hurried, dear brother. Something troubling you?"

I whipped around to see a monk; the top half of his head was bandaged entirely, with his eyes covered.

"Sorry. No, Brother. Just very nervous."

"I see that. You're a foreigner, yes?"

"Correct, Brother. I am from Shaar. Across the ocean."

"Hm, Brother? Are you of the Order?"

"I am. And the Commission. I am a protectorate."

"Protectorate." The title rolled over his tongue. "Do you protect an abbot or a paladin?"

"Seer, actually, Brother." *Did I just give myself away?*

"Protectorates of a paladin, an abbot, and even a seer are often paladins. Which class are you?"

"None, Brother. I am Völfien. Respectfully, you must have me confused with an armiger."

"I know you're Völfien. I might be blind, but those clattering claws secure the truth. Do members of Shaar also not recognize the Völfien as worthy of being paladins?"

"No, Brother. We are serving the Order as protectors only. It's un-heard of for Völfien to be granted such a title. Ever since the Commission denounced us."

"Ah, yes. That's correct. Forgive me; my mind is going, and I've been within this temple for many years." He paused. "Sit with me." He tapped on the bench beside him.

I walked over to take a seat, when he flashed a hand before him and said, "My name is Brother Rui. It is a pleasure to meet you."

I knelt and took his hand with both my paws. I kissed his ring. "Brother Rui, my name is Kovuco. Kovuco Blackstar."

"I know." He sounded annoyed. "Please sit, will you?" He tapped the bench again.

I sat where he patted, and we sat there in silence. Even as I slumped over, I still towered over his aged, frail body.

"You should ask." He interrupted the silence.

"Huh?"

"Ask me. Ask me how it happened."

"Uh ..."

"My wounds. I felt your bandages—could feel the leaves beneath them. It's the same dressing I use on the bandages about my brow. Surely you must wonder why I am blind."

"I do. May I ask?"

"Hatred, dear brother. Hate caused this. If one says he loves Uridei but hates another, he's a liar. I almost destroyed everything I have come to love by simply hating another. It cost me my eyes."

My jaw clenched.

"As I shared, I know who you are, Kovuco. Ash told me about you." He paused, looking around, even though he could not see a thing. "I must tell you a tale of Brother Ash back when we were young. Are you listening?"

"Yes."

"Brother Ash and I are brothers by law; he married my sister, Carleigh. Ash was a gifted marksman, as was I, a paladin. During our time in the war, we were faced with many trials. Ash's love for Carleigh was an unfavored romance and, as you know, had to be approved by the abbot. I was against my sister's marriage to Ash. I believed Ash was un-worthy of her. He came into the Order as a man, not a boy, as I did. I had much more devout experience. Ash took his skills to the wülkure role. I saw darkness in him, while Carleigh, and even the abbot of Spears, saw goodness in their union."

He took a moment to slow his breathing. "My anger and ego drove me to make Ash my rival. There was an attack on our temple. Carleigh and an entire House were mercilessly murdered. They took captive the younger sisters where they faced being trafficked. For three long years, we pursued them until we finally found them."

Jayna.

He relaxed his lungs again. "Ash and I imprisoned the man who killed my sister. Rather than return him to Spears to face trial, I opted we torture and kill him. Ash pleaded that we not take revenge on the man but return him to Spears, as we were ordered. I moved with the revengeful decision to use Uridei's flame on the man. Ash intervened. He utilized his Pjauti skills to reverse the effect, causing my flames to erupt, blinding me permanently. He vanquished the darkness inside me and freed me from my dissidence. Afterward, I stepped down as a paladin and vowed only to serve men of the Order, even lost men seeking sanctuary, for the remainder of my days. It's my duty to be a servant to them, criminal or not, and learn to forgive. Ash's sister has cared for me selflessly ever since. I am lucky that Uridei's love stretches over us. Otherwise, I would not live the fulfilled life I do, even without my eyes."

"Ash reversed your flames? As a Pjautist? How?" I asked.

Rui smiled. "It's the wülkure's ways. They know a paladin could still turn against the will of Uridei, just as any sinful human can do. Evil nature lives in all of us, Kovuco, but we must learn to use that energy for good. In that case, Ash reversed my flame. He was a man of the Order, after all and knew my intentions were wrong. It does not often happen, Kovuco, but my anger was unjust and not common within the paladin ways. Call it what you want, but I call it a miracle of redemption. I've turned this mess into a message, one that influenced change."

His story was hard to hear. Brother Rui had been blind since he was young, yet he lived a fulfilled life, reconciling through his punishment. I was sure his message had impacted the lives of many.

"Brother Rui, you mentioned that Ash has a sister. Ash was my dear friend, and I would like to pay my respects."

"Who brought you here?"

"Sister Cácilie of the sisterhood. She wore teal colors."

"Sister Cácilie is Brother Ash's sister."

An image of her face flashed before me. She had his eyes, fierce and bewildering; her smile was confident and boisterous. She passed as far more elegant than old Ash. I wondered if she had his crazy dirty-blonde hair under her veil.

I grew solemn. I remembered Ash's fate in Shaar, wondering if his body ever had been found. "I should hope to revisit her if that's okay. I gave her a false name due to the circumstances of my mission. I owe her great respect for Ash."

Brother Rui rose. "Walk with me. There will be plenty of time to make amends to Sister Cácilie. She understands desperation more than most of us within the Order. She deals with the most persecuted and neglected of our populace—orphaned children, lost and abused women, homeless elderly."

He held out a feeble arm, which I quickly cradled as I followed his direction. He used his cane to tap around the stone floor, leading me back into the atrium and through an arched door to the right. Past several rooms with bunks similar to my dorm back in Shaar, we eventually reached the end of the hall, where a stone spiral staircase descended. It looked eerie and mismanaged, especially for a blind man to utilize, but there was enough room on the stair width for me to continue guiding him. He turned a dial on the wall, and the gaslights flared brightly, lighting our descent.

We reached a basement far beneath the temple. Before us was a large wooden door with a seal. The seal bore a familiar sigil.

The sigil of the ancient Völfien Order.

"Now, Kovuco, you must break this seal."

"How, Brother Rui?"

"Well, only a paladin can. He must use the Purge, and the fire must be strong enough to break it."

"I don't understand. Ash told me I needed a passcode and gave me a key." I reached into my pocket and placed it in Brother Rui's palm.

His bony fingers curled around the piece of metal. He nodded and smiled widely. "Indeed. Behind the seal is a lock. When Ash and his comrades crossed the ocean, we made this seal together, and it was sealed with a high-level Purge flame. Remember, I returned deeply wounded and gave up my paladin gifting. I have not since used the Purge. You alone must break it to retrieve Ash's inheritance. Not I."

Is Brother Rui even listening to me?

"Brother Rui, I am not a paladin. I am just a Völfien protectorate. I can't break the seal."

"Unwilling to even give it a try, Kovuco Blackstar?"

I shot him a flustered glance with the security of knowing he could not see it. My chest heaved as I gazed at the lock. Suddenly, the blind monk seized my paw, the one wrapped in rowan leaves.

"Are you not a Purge user, young völf? These wraps suggest you are."

I pulled my grip away, cradling my bandaged arms. "It's difficult to understand."

"I received a message from Ash that you'd be capable of breaking this lock. I am sorry, but the trustee must obtain this man's inheritance. Unless the news I received was false. It was my understanding you could use the Purge."

How does he know I used the Purge?

He then reached into his jacket and pulled out a scroll. He carefully felt the broken wax seal, confirming he had the proper documentation. He swept his fingers across the textured text. He nodded, acknowledging the details. "Yes. He told me a young völf by the name of Kovuco would come and could open the seal, and he alone could cross into the room to obtain the inheritance."

I grew confused and frustrated. Ash had fallen into the ocean to his death before I had managed to use the Purge, and even then, I merely had obeyed Ameilja's words in my head. It had been quick and all through our unique bond. I sighed deeply without letting myself lose patience with the old monk. Before speaking, I took a deep breath. "I will try, Brother."

He held out an arm, and I took off my jacket and laid it in his grip. I caressed my bandaged arms, remembering my fur and flesh lighting up in Uridei's white flames, Purging Kärleiv.

Had I regarded rage? Vengeance?

I remembered my strategy, but the desperation that had pumped through my veins had illuminated my success. I'd purged not in vengeance but in fear—fear of death and fear of losing the one I loved. Now I stood there hopeful in my forbearance that I could feel her again.

Ameilja?

I placed a paw on my chest and took a deep breath. Somehow, I felt her hand on mine while we synchronized our beats. We found each other's breath and each other's pace.

Ameilja, lend me your fire.

My paws clenched with the dagger-like claws drawn, and the white flames spurted from my fingertips. It almost felt effortless this time, less painful. I placed a paw on the seal and braced myself for the surge. I could feel my veins pulsate under my flesh, and my muscles began to buckle, holding their ground like stone. My teeth gritted, and my eyes went white until they too steamed from the heat of Uridei's light. With all my might and muscular power, I attempted to lift the seal as the white flames began to spark blue and gold. My entire form heated.

I hoped Brother Rui backed away as I felt the seal lift. I clutched the seal with my other paw and could feel the heat spread through the other half of my strength. I let out a massive roar, but a voice unlike mine reverberated from my throat. Unrecognizable. Immortal.

Suddenly, the seal lifted and smashed against the ceiling, splintering into flaming hot coals. I fell to my knees and felt the flames continue to burn on my arms and shoulders. I concentrated, carefully channeling the energy, until the fire calmed and quieted, simmering slowly into popping blue and green flashes.

I inhaled.

Ameilja?

I exhaled.

I felt the flame repair me this time, restoring my flesh. Hair follicles were instantly restored, and new hairs sprouted. I drew a knife quickly from my belt and harnessed the energy through metal properties. Barely any burns were left over.

The resplendent inferno rested into my fur as if transmuting itself into living matter. It didn't die; it merely responded to my form, becoming one with me again—soft and platinum, to its original state.

I examined my arms, my face, and my teeth. All were there, restored. Clean.

I looked at Brother Rui. His broad smile was unbroken as he clapped wildly and said, "Good show, Brother Kovuco! Good show!"

I took the key Ash had left me and remembered his words: "White Powder has fallen."

"Brother Rui?" I said.

"Are you serious, Kovuco? I have waited twenty years to witness this door open, you melt away the seal on the first try, and *you* have questions? Ask, Kovuco, quick, before I expire!"

"I never gave you the code."

"What code?"

"White Powder has fallen?"

Rui shook his head, leaning on his cane. "I am sorry, young Völfien. That code is only used when Ash Ulrendt has perished."

A voice unexpectedly called out, "Fat chance of that, Kovey!"

DARK IS THE WAY

Isarah
Demitori City, Sapphire District
The Masquerade
Aoustí 21

"I LOOK FUCKING RIDICULOUS," KIEFER MUTTE-
red as he adjusted his white tie made of smooth silk. His collared shirt
was deep red, matched with the silver snake embroidering of his black
vest. Large and ornate buttons accompanied it.

He wore a jacket embellished with complex swirls symbolizing the
wavering currents of the ocean. He stared at his reflection as he sleeked his
hair back. He did so to put on his masquerade mask, shaped like a ram,
which he hoped would attract the Blue Coat völves, who would likely be
looking for him. He finished by applying a few spritzes of his cologne. Its
scent wafted a warm spice with a lingering aroma of teakwood.

Rae's favorite.

He eyed the mask. Kiefer admired the ram for its unique, determined bravado, including its ornate horns, but more so, he'd chosen it
because it symbolized the animal a hungry wolf would hunt in the wild.
It was the one piece of his wardrobe he approved for that night's agenda.

He harnessed a pistol to his side and a decorative dagger at his hip.
He tucked a blowpipe into his black boots and a pair of throwing knives
under his jacket, against his chest. A small pouch carrying bane-filled
vials hid easily under his thick coat.

He didn't wish to attract too much attention, so he blotched on a black powder base around his eyes to conceal his identity beyond the slate mask coloration. The rustic coloration of the mask's horns would distract any wandering eyes should someone from the Commission expect to see him that night.

"Time to party." He smirked.

When Kiefer arrived at the masquerade, the celebration had already overtaken Sapphire Square. The gaslights' glow lit up the streets in bright colors: blue, green, gold, and white. Streamers of the same colors were strewn throughout the streets. Performers danced through the masked people, twirling and performing magic tricks or just blowing raw alcohol onto torch flames to create puffs of fireballs for shock value. Whimsical, melodic music swayed the atmosphere. In the center of the excitement, circles were forming in which hallucinogenic drugs were being administered to add to the acts they could consent to in the public light of the streets. Kiefer moved fluidly through the routs of exotically dressed people; he could smell the rich foods and fine alcoholic drinks distributed among groups. It didn't take long till he noticed the Blue Coats stalking him.

Bingo.

They lingered close, wearing dark jackets with tinges of blue and leaflike designs on their lapels and cuffs. Their jackets were roughed up, as if they'd seen casual battles. Antique pistols fashioned into modern-day weaponry hung on their sides—a distinguishing sign of a Blue Coat. The manufacturer was unknown, but the weapons were considered a criminal carry.

He stopped in the courtyard, the center of the street. Festivities continued around him, but a pair of masked Blue Coats stood in every corner. Some he could make out as völves in their Rinkin form by their protruding incisors, their clawed hands with lingering fur, or their ears that were still elongated and pointed. Others were the human members.

"Mr. Yuska!" Malsson greeted him.

Shit, was he that easy to find?

Malsson wore an outfit much like his costume for the play. A woman wearing a feathered dress of black and blue accompanied him. Her mask resembled a dragonfly.

"Pleased to see you again." Malsson bowed. "I have some business to discuss, but would you mind giving this lovely creature a dance?"

The woman gave Kiefer a modest bow, which he returned.

"Did you get my message, Malsson?"

"Yes, I did. My people kept an eye out for Miss Rae. It appears she left early in the day for Blackwater City by train. They tracked her down to an address." Malsson gave Kiefer a small piece of paper.

Kiefer opened the delicate paper and read the address. He nodded—her mother's address. He lit a match and caught the paper on fire, allowing it to smolder away in his palm. "No one knows of this, correct?"

"You have my word. I will tell you, she looked very dismayed."

"She was," he answered, returning to the woman and his mission.

The woman held a hand out, intent for him to take her to the center of the street, where patrons danced. She smiled before returning to the festivities, saying, "My name is Sóley."

Kiefer took her hand, and he was swept onto the dance area within the open town square next to a grand fountain surrounded by tiny faeries emitting light from the dust that fell from their wings, all for additional effect. Kiefer rarely sees these types of fearies, but he's noted they prefer water and friendly company. The woman named Sóley began her dance with him. She looked Kiefer in the eye, moving out of memorization, as she hummed the tune softly.

"Sóley?"

"Yes?"

"Aren't you a whore?"

She laughed softly at his blatancy with a tinge of playfulness in her tone. "Courtesan, actually. I'm far too exotic to be a whore, Mr. Yuska."

"Is there a difference?"

"I am more courtly and of good wealth, and my clientele are of a higher class. I don't stand at street corners or in line for choice pickings."

"I see."

"The fact that you recognize my *whoredom* above my actual role brings me satisfaction in what a wülkure knows."

"So there's more to Sóley, grand courtesan of Sapphire, eh?"

"Of course. Much more, Mr. Yuska. Do you not recognize me?"

"Are you intending to be dismissive? Of course, I can't see who you are beyond your mask."

"Interesting, I would think a man who does not drink alcohol, only coffee, would have a better memory."

Kiefer cocked his head slightly. "Am I missing something?"

"The more dense, the higher the alcohol content, if you note the faster flow of the tears, the dyer the taste." Sóley licked her lips slowly.

Kiefer's lips parted, shocked. "Emilíana?"

"I am also Fae, Mr. Yuska," she answered swiftly.

"Fae?" Kiefer scanned her features: she had no pointed ears, her skin was that of a human's, and he could see her warm hazel eyes when he glanced through the mask's eye slots. "You're glamoured?"

"Indeed. My identity as a Fae is protected as a human of my choice."

"Your eyes are different from last time."

"Yes."

"You're not from around here, are you?"

She shook her head. "I'm a rare breed, Mr. Yuska. I come from another realm."

Kiefer eyed her questioningly. Once again, another tale he'd heard but had never believed. "Ethrylian?" he asked.

She didn't answer but smiled teasingly. He dropped the matter by lowering her into a gentle dip; her fairy-tale homeland was not important. As he brought her back up, the Blue Coats caught his attention again. They moved in slyly through the roaring laughter, jovial hollers, and melodic folk music, exchanging energy that they were there for him. Kiefer, of course, was used to being approached with fear and hostility, and he felt nothing but confidence as the hunters closed in. He knew he wouldn't resist when they decided to capture him.

"To be honest, Kiefer, I had been watching you," Sóley causally admitted. "I knew you'd be at the Blind Tiger that night. After poor Teo, you didn't think we'd let you off that easy, did you?"

Kiefer furrowed his brows, and quickly assessed the Fae female he currently danced with. It dawned on him she wore the same shade of blue.

Shit! How did I miss this?

Without a moment for him to ask, she took a spiked clip from her hair and clicked it onto his tie, clearly marking who he was. "Remove this, Wülkure, and you'll be eaten," she whispered in his ear, and then she led him into a spin. She slipped from his fingers and left him alone in the center of the square.

The lights dimmed to soft blue, and the music began picking up. The Blue Coats on the corners of the town square vanished, but he could make out the luminescent eyes that glared toward him from the shadows. Rather than decipher his next move, he stopped and stood still.

He closed his eyes and waited.

This is how it happens. No weapons. No resistance. Take me. Take me to Zero.

☆

Isarah
Demitori City, Pearl District
Darmouthe Manor, the Ami-Rose Suite
Aousti 19

I don't want to wake up, but I'm also not asleep. I'm stuck in a trance, standing in the city streets. There's commotion stirring around me. Am I back in Shaar? It feels like Shaar ... but a location I have yet to pinpoint. Is that—it is! I see Kovuco!

Ameilja saw him, a younger coming-of-age version of Kovuco wearing an amber-dyed jacket with red trim; his bag was strapped over his broadening shoulders.

She saw he was younger by just a few years, but by then, being in Tsunetomo, Kovuco would have taken lives as a rite of passage into adulthood. He was at the age where he would have recently been accepted as her protectorate.

Ameilja noticed he was his usual self. He still averted and passed others in a crowd with sad, sullen eyes.

Why are you like this, Kovuco?

She followed, walking parallel to him from across the street, until he intersected with the other White Throat protectorates and Ash. He perked up enough to engage his comrades, smiling at them when they addressed him, but she could see past his smile; he remained dark, conscious of his presence and finding opportunities to escape the spotlight.

She noticed that at times, he would stare at the floor, adrift, always detached, and somewhere beyond in his thoughts.

Ameilja eyed her other protectorates: Nav'i read a book; Dancer sipped coffee from a thermos; and Tam looked ahead, confident and full of his lively, overbearing energy.

"Does anyone know if Ameilja *actually* likes coffee?" Tam asked, glancing over his shoulder.

Dancer nodded. "The lady loves coffee."

"Seriously, Tam?" Nav'i said, slamming his book shut. "Are you even paying attention when we're on the job? All she drinks is coffee. You've been at her side longer than we have."

"Yeah, but she's always adding so much cream and syrups. She seems to have more of a sweet tooth like I do. Dancer, come on; you agree, right? Help me out here," Tam urged.

Ameilja's attention was immediately diverted toward Kovuco. As soon as her name was uttered, she noticed a shift in his demeanor. *What's going on, Kovuco?*

Weaving through the crowds of people, she continued to watch him. Her surroundings lulled in and out like slow pulsations.

Kovuco's ears shot up, and his eyes widened at her name's mention. It looked as if he tried to suppress it. Suddenly, he stopped walking to process something. Everything else went silent, forbidding her a chance to spy on idle gossip about her.

Ameilja didn't understand what kept Kovuco feeling so alone. Maybe it was his upbringing or the backlash from society in judging those mysterious blue eyes.

Tam repeated her name.

There it is again; he hears my name, and he's suddenly hypnotized.

Ameilja assessed Kovuco thoroughly. Did his position over her bring him purpose? Perhaps it brought him genuine happiness. All that time, she'd noticed consistent withdrawn energy from him, but maybe she had foolishly neglected to truly understand him. It all had started when they'd met, the day she'd asked him to be her final völf.

He's always been patient and charming. But was that all just a show? A setup to keep me at bay from whatever was going on—just a protective barrier?

She thought back to the coronation and their dance together. Her memories recalled the moment when they had paused; he'd had wonder in his eyes that she'd never before witnessed from him. At every other moment, he'd appeared distant and withdrawn.

That day of my training …

She thought of the day she'd mastered the Purge and of the smile Kovuco had shown just before she swept the flames of Uridei over him. He ultimately had surrendered to her.

Was that his edge? All this time did I just give him some brief satisfaction over his sadness? Does he feel his entire life's purpose is just protecting me—risking himself for me?

Oh, Kovuco, you're meant for so much more! Protecting me should not be your life's purpose.

How cursed he must have felt now that he had drunk from her. He was now bound to her but not in a way he might have desired.

Why does this haunt me? Why do these feelings torment me? I saved Kovuco, but maybe all I have done is curse him. He's at risk of facing devastation if I die. Will he feel lost? Would he heal from the break in our bond?

Ameilja recalled a recent, brief moment when she'd felt a female völf's presence around Kovuco.

His heart had raced. Her presence sped his heart rate and then ceased. Maybe Kovuco has had someone all along. Why didn't he tell me? He can resign as my protectorate at any time; he doesn't have to stay.

"What have I done? I've damned him," Ameilja whispered as she stared at him from across the street. "I'm so sorry, Kovuco."

He knows I want to save the Order from complacency. He knows I want him by my side, unshackled by the Commission's unfair regulations. I am so tired of it all, yet here I am, waiting to become the perfect sacrifice for the acolytes of the plague. But if I die before they utilize me, the world will remain what it is, and Sabor will remain in the void. Shall I just sacrifice myself to save the world? Should I just end it all to save humanity and free Kovuco of this forbidden bond?

Ameilja stepped off the sidewalk like a ghostly apparition; she floated across the cobblestone streets, closing the distance between herself and Kovuco.

He could not see her, but she stood there closely assessing his features.

"I'm proud of you, Kovuco. Your heart has undergone so much.

You've been betrayed, beaten, overlooked, and almost killed, yet you've stayed loyal. You stay yourself—you."

Warm tears spilled over her soft cheeks.

Why me, Kovuco? What am I missing here? Why would a human like me bring you purpose? I've only brought sadness, rebellion, and turmoil to you. I don't understand.

Ameilja continued to watch him as time slowed.

I hope Kovuco will live past this. I hope he finds someone to love. I hope he realizes it's not his fault. Uridei's will is beyond our understanding.

Within her reverie, Ameilja closed her eyes and opened them again to see she was back in reality. Her cheeks were wet. Her heart felt heavy.

She lay on her bed near Tam, who lay on a nearby couch. She turned toward him.

Ameilja could tell he'd tried his best to stay awake, but she was relieved he finally had given in to rest. They had arrived in Demitori City early yesterday morning and been forcefully delivered to her room, ironically named the Ami-Rose Suite, in Nathalii's manor.

Ameilja rose from her bed and inspected the door; they were still locked away. She wondered if anyone would be coming soon. She'd refused all her meals so far, demanding her White Throats' whereabouts.

She glanced over at Tam again. She studied him. His head was sunken into a large throw pillow; pieces of his dark hair had settled around his brows. His intense features were now settled and gentler while he slept. As much as she hated how Nathalii had spoken of him, she couldn't deny that he was attractive. Any man would have dreamed of obtaining a physique and features like Tam's, whereas Tam's were natural.

She couldn't put her finger on it, but something radiated from him, an energy that was intimidating and forcible.

Adémaro also had a way of forcing you into submission with one look, the same way the sight of Mother Vhera or our savior Albean would.

Tam is a Blackstar …

She remembered feeling a numbness in her arm after waking from the blow to her head. She had been knocked unconscious the entire time while Kovuco used the Purge, yet she felt his presence the moment Kovuco called to her. Mentally, they were still connected.

Is this truly how profound our connection is? Does Uridei have an even greater plan for us? Kovuco has used the Purge twice now. I remember feeling his stress; he needed me. I lent him my power, but how could this be? He is my protectorate, not a paladin; how is this even possible?

"Adémaro?" The name slipped from her lips.

I remember seeing Kovuco's father once years ago. Even a younger Adémaro sent chills down my spine. He was undoubtedly the most magnificent völf I've ever seen, nearly perfect. Kovuco is beautiful, attractive even, for a völf, which was indeed passed on from his father.

A startling, abrasive knock sounded at the door, disrupting her investigative thoughts. Tam instinctively woke and immediately stepped in front of Ameilja. He waited and listened with all senses alert, till he abruptly fell to his knees, crying out from an unknown phantom pain.

"Tam! Tam, what's wrong?" Ameilja panicked, running to aid him.

The door opened, and Nathalii entered, holding a hand out as if pinching the air. With the deadly collar still secured around his neck, Ameilja feared he might change into his Medzio form to elude the pain.

"What are you doing?" Ameilja yelled. "Stop!"

"Subduing the völf, Ameilja. I can't have him biting."

"Stop it! He's clearly human!" she pleaded. She leaped to her feet to stop Nathalii.

Kärfínn swiftly entered and caught Ameilja by the neck. He drew a knife from his side, and she gasped, thinking he intended to use it on her, as he had on Jayna. He forced himself into the room, pushing her backward, until he could hold the blade against Tam's neck.

"No! Please! Please don't hurt him!" Ameilja cried out. Tears began to fall.

She hated that she cried. How her tears must have fueled their malicious control over her. Her inability to read the cruelty of Kärfínn beneath his devilish mask brought fear to her. He moved against her form with prejudicial aggression and maintained eloquence in every insidious movement he made.

"Good!" He tossed her to the ground. "I knew you could be reasoned with."

Ameilja coughed and crawled toward Tam. She hovered over him. Tam lay on the ground, struggling for air.

"Ameilja, I am sorry we had to get so rough, but you gave us no choice," Nathalii said.

"He didn't do anything!" Ameilja snapped.

"How am I choking?" Tam asked between rasping coughs.

"Don't worry; the ózykas is only injected once you take your Medzio form. This is just simple alchemy," Nathalii answered coolly as she pulled apart the rings on her pointer finger and her thumb. The clawed rings were separated, and Tam's chokehold was released.

Crazy bitch!

"Unfortunately, we can't find your völves. All three are lost at sea. Nav'i and Dancer, the two black völves, boarded their ship but vanished between Shaar and Rúnar. Oddly enough, the paladin Haruka is also missing. As for your platinum völf, the Blackstar one, his body hasn't been recovered. There—you've got your answers. Happy now?"

Tam squeezed Ameilja's hand. She was unsure if he was upset by the news or wanted her to stay quiet.

"I don't believe you. I want my völves! Kovuco is alive! Don't speak of him like he's some corpse!"

"What about your father?" Kärfínn hissed.

Ameilja glared at him. "What about my father?"

"It's only a matter of time before he crosses the ocean and comes for you."

"Does my father know of the fate I will face?"

"Of course not." Nathalii laughed. "We wouldn't want him to worry, now, would we?"

"He *will* interfere!" Ameilja sneered, boldly standing to her feet.

"There is an order to these things. Your father will have the opportunity to fall in line, or he'll become an enemy. Same with Malkovich if he dares to get involved. Or they'll be killed."

"My father is a light in this world! He will never be labeled as an enemy, nor will agree to your sick game!"

Nathalii smiled her usual mischievous smile while she eyed Tam. He maintained his distance from her, recuperating from the pain she'd blanketed him with a mere few moments ago.

"Hm, interesting you say that. Maybe you're right; András will never be labeled as our enemy, but that's because of the choices he'll have to make."

Ameilja shook her head. "You're wrong!"

Nathalii chuckled like a demented child. "The Völfien started as mere wolves; now they are the most deadly creatures I have ever seen. Why do you think your father admires them so much? If you only knew, dear child. Your precious father has his secrets. He is the man he is today because he found betterment in a very dark place. And as for all the Völfien, even Tambor here, will they always follow the light?"

"Yes!" Ameilja pressed. "Light will always conquer!"

Nathalii dipped her gaze. "Light is just a wavelength, sweet Ami; easily suffocated. When the lights go out, darkness remains. It reigns superior, stronger, like the authority of the Näkk. Your father, and all those around you, *will* fall in line with its power."

She caressed Ameilja's cheek and tucked her blood-red hair behind her ear, using only her sharp deep-green-painted nails. She then pinched Ameilja's earlobe and wrapped her arms around her tightly. Ameilja wanted to push her away but was too afraid of the repercussions.

With an icy whisper, Nathalii said, "Ameilja, my love, dark is the way."

☆

Isarah
Demitori City, Sapphire District
Ember Lounge on Feen Street
Aousti 21

"My name is Orvar Meyvandt, syndicate leader of the Blue Coats," said a human man of average height, narrowing his eyes at Kiefer.

Orvar looked pale and weathered, with long dark dreadlocks hanging from his head. Considerable amounts of charms hung from the few dreads that lay over his broad chest.

The Ember Lounge was dimly lit, barely lighting the features of those around him, including Orvar. The smells of rich alcohol, suede, cigar, and hookah smoke filled the air Kiefer breathed. Kiefer noted whitened, visceral dual scar marks over Orvar's right eye. A third scar peeked out among a few dreadlocks on his forehead. He presumed it must have been a völf scratch by how it looked and healed.

The Blue Coats trained within, and their tactics included hand-to-hand combat, so at times, you knew you were facing Blue Coats by the scars they carried, all to prove their loyalty and worth. They were an elegant yet rugged syndicate, experiencing the Isles from a less glorified perspective.

"As you may have heard, I go by Zero," the man verified.

So this is the famous Zero, eh?

He was dressed in fine clothing: a dual-buttoned vest with a silk ascot tucked in neatly and a long blue jacket embroidered in dark flowering patterns. The top section of his dreadlocked hair was tied into a spiked headdress, giving him antlers for his masquerade ensemble. Nearly every finger bore a massive metal or gold ring with diamonds. His fingers were scarred with evidence of stitching, as if his fingers had been sliced off at one point. His nails were tinged black and overgrown, filed sharp yet maintaining a cloudy white color.

Kiefer assessed the room, casually dipping his eyes in each direction. Although the lounge was dark, he noticed the ornate furniture and decorations, including a deep blue chaise, where he sat alongside Sóley. Across were two dark green wingback chairs. Four völves were behind Zero, and another four were behind Kiefer; the shadows hid their identities. A small dark fox sat in the green wingback closest to Kiefer. Its beady black eyes never locked with Kiefer's gaze, but it seemed to sit and listen intently. A crow was sitting on the back of the couch by Sólely, and another dainty fox was on her lap as she drank wine from a crystal glass.

Zero sipped on whiskey as he spoke sternly to Kiefer, spurred by the few glasses of hard liquor he had undoubtedly overindulged in that evening. Beyond the lounge were other lounge stations where similarly dressed and scarred humans and völves conversed, occasionally shooting glares at the wülkure hawkishly. Not a single völf appeared distracted, which made them the fiercest, most intimidating pack of völves he'd ever seen. Those who weren't watching the wülkure kept to their lounges' festivities, drinking from chalices of deep red liquid or smoking cigars and hookah pipes. All alert, the völves had partners to watch one another's back when they turned for a drink.

"Malsson tells me you're on the prowl for one of my Völfien," Zero stated matter-of-factly.

Kiefer lifted his chin slightly, gesturing for him to go on.

Zero may have possessed the craft to appear patient, but he moved like an assassin; he was watchful and aware, getting to the point. "If you are worried about Lady Baadar, there is no need. My people have eyes on her. She will not be touched or visited by someone we disapprove of."

"And Dr. Grayzond?" Kiefer said.

"Dr. Grayzond is a Blue Coat doctor. My mandate only spearheads his animosity for the Sentry. I'll assume you experienced his protective, obnoxious nature."

"I'm beyond that. Back to Isabelle."

"Certainly, rest assured your colleagues will not want to tread near Duskwell under any circumstances. Besides, she won't be the one they are after anyway. Killing her provides no behoof to their cause. She has served her purpose in simply becoming a mother and stepping away from the Commission."

"Ah yes, a mother. Her son is the völf I seek."

Zero took a long sip of his whiskey and swished the contents in the glass. "He is here. But what do you think you need with him?"

"Isabelle asked me to find him. Said only he can stop this madness within the Sunspire."

"Madness? You mean the Näkk?"

They know? Kiefer hesitated. "A team, including Baadar, have been experimenting with the Näkk, yes. They are raising the dead, and doing other insidious shit. Isabelle breached to stop him. She mentioned her son. My focus is to learn more to use this against those still trying to control it."

"That's very interesting. What do you, as a wülkure, know?"

"I know there appear to be two practices involving the Näkk. One involving emulsions and one leading to sacrifice. I also believe someone of great power, a social elite, is funding this whole operation."

"Hm. Have you considered looking at your own centurion, Wülkure?"

Kiefer eyed him, questioning how the Blue Coats always got their info. He answered, "I know the centurion is involved. It's confirmed."

"Now we have some trust." Orvar chuckled, taking a quick swig of his drink.

"Have I not been honest with you this entire time?" Kiefer said.

"May I call you Mr. Yuska?" Orvar eluded his question. "My calling you a wülkure assumes you're here on business, and I'd like to think of this meeting as, well, not dealing with the Sentry."

"Sure, if I can call you something as daft as Zero," Kiefer added. "The Näkk can infect the ork race, not just the humans. There's an elimination process being carried out between the two surviving doctors. Their operation lost fifty percent of their leads, so there is a direct opposition of ideas; therefore, one will be removed, while the other's tasks will take precedence. It's bound to get messy and lead to more death beyond the Näkk's strain."

Zero nodded. "Makes sense. Humans always manage to fuck things up; they're always seeking something greater to fulfill some internal life complex and are never satisfied. Back to your inquiry, Yuska. You're seeking Isabelle's tyke. Tell me—what do you, a human, think of the Völfien? Perhaps not just my Völfien but the race generally?"

"They are rather intimidating at times," Kiefer admitted, building trust verbally. "But they are not vain and do not attack unless provoked; they protect their own better than any species I have come to face in my years as a wülkure."

"Fair. I, a human, personally began surrounding myself with Völfien company intentionally. Völfien are disciplined, intelligent, and passionate; they have a knack for reading. Hell, my legibility increased because of them. Their race are eternally ingenuous and pacifistic; they prefer to die by their traditional values. Humans, unfortunately, learn these traits, but once they divide themselves from a moral compass, they thirst for the things our Völfien brethren recognize as blessings. Still, our race treat them as monsters—a shame."

Kiefer sighed. "I recognize this. Against my better judgment, I believe that to protect humanity's interests means I am at the same crossroad."

Zero smiled as a Völfien stepped out from the shadows. It was Richter.

"Firstly," Zero said, "justice for Baadar is paramount. Rotenfeld is dead, but we desire the destruction of the Sunspire and anyone associated with that place. Two reasons. One, the number of people who have died in that place. A worthy slaughter is deserved to show the conspirators and their acolytes that their hand in an innocent faculty is futile. As much as we fear prospects of the Näkk, the priority of the Blue Coats is to hold the Commission accountable for these atrocities."

"It sounds like we are on the same page. Two?"

"Two is quite simple: Baadar's son won't rest until he's gotten revenge on those responsible for the death of the only man he called a father. Anyone who has stepped foot in the Sunspire or who stood by while Baadar was executed in cold blood is now being collected."

"I imagine I meet that list." Kiefer shifted in his seat. Suddenly, Kiefer felt the cold hollow of a barrel pressed against the back of his skull.

A lucid voice said, "Now is the time to make your case, Wülkure."

The voice was less gruff and mellow, yet the speaker spoke from the back of his throat to emphasize his hatred.

Zero rose from his seat, walked to a side table in the far corridor of the room, and filled his whiskey glass from a decanter of honey-colored liquor. He lightly tossed the glistening whiskey in the tumbler, sniffing the fumes and smiling pleasantly. "A fine fucking year. Fine fucking year indeed. We have more of this stuff, Sóley, no?"

"Plenty, dear," she said as she took another sip of her wine. She then whispered in the fox's ear. It leaped down onto the floor and scurried into the shadows.

Zero paused again before returning to his seat next to Sóley. "Mr. Yuska, I'd like you to meet the young progeny of Isabelle: Kouta Baadar."

Kiefer didn't turn but knew the pistol wielder, Isabelle's son, stood behind him. Revenge radiated off his form; he was ready to kill Kiefer with one blow.

"Pleasure to meet you finally, Kouta," Kiefer said. He was interrupted when he heard the hammer of the pistol click and then the sound of a bullet being loaded into the chamber. Kiefer blinked and twitched slightly.

Zero took another sip. "Now, on to Isabelle's request. Now that you have our Kouta, what do you think comes next?"

"Not sure," Kiefer answered with a lull of irony. "Sort of seems like I have met the end of the line."

"Oh, not tonight, Mr. Yuska! Remember, as you've been told, to-night is not a night for killing—only hunting, scoping, and learning. Kouta suggested I kill you tonight. To a brazen observation, I agree. You do meet this vengeful list we mentioned; however, I have suspicions that on closer examination, you may be removed from that death list. If you survived Isabelle, I think she wanted you alive. I have asked that Kouta maintain this until he has more information. She told you that Kouta is part of the Sunspire's undoing, so why not keep you alive until we know more?"

The pistol was removed from Kiefer's head, and Kouta turned the corner to sit across from him. A fox who sat there leaped onto the floor as he did. Kouta crossed his left leg, a perfectly human leg tucked into a cuffed boot made of hardened, studded leather. Kouta was a tall, slim man with brown eyes lined with dark makeup to hide his appearance under his mask. Kiefer presumed this appearance was all to complement his wolf mask hanging from his jacket's lapel. He had a full head of long, messy blond hair that he kept tied back in a low bun. He wore a pale blue fur-lined coat, black boots, and a blue floral-patterned scarf around his waist. He looked like the prime example of a Blue Coat: angst and elegance all in one.

Kiefer didn't make eye contact with Kouta. He examined him quickly in his peripheral vision. *That's Isabelle's boy, and he sure as hell looks nothing like old Kristján.*

Like Isabelle, he bore the slightest references to the hunter form of the völf.

"With what you know now, Mr. Yuska, bear in mind that my Völfien are always watching; my men are always watching. All walk among the Demitori public; tread lightly if you consider turning your back on the Blue Coats."

"I'm here to stop this madness that we damn well know will impact us all, no matter our role or positioning," Kiefer stated. "I'm here because of your mother's words. She thinks you can stop this, yet you seem to have no clue as to why."

Kouta reached into the front pocket of his jacket and unveiled two cigarettes, eluding a response.

Their space fell quiet, all eyes were on Kouta. "I'm curious, Yuska."

He finally spoke up. "Ever fuck one of the Fae before?" A smirk played on his lips as he leaned across the coffee table. Sóley leaned in and lit the two tips. He sat back down and handed one of the lit cigarettes to Kiefer. "We smoke the same cigarette, you and I," he added casually.

"No, I've never bed a Fae," Kiefer answered, annoyed.

"But you've had your tongue down one's throat," Kouta tauntingly chuckled, cutting a glance at Sóley.

Kiefer took the cigarette, ignoring Kouta's bullying, and examined the filter with the writing "Tithe 77 Menthe." *Unfortunately, we do smoke the same cigarettes.*

Kouta took a deep drag from the cigarette and allowed the thick smoke to spew through his teeth. "I guess we will just have to help one another until my mother wakes up, huh?"

Kiefer locked his eyes on him.

Kouta smirked; the unrest in his glare spoke louder than the silence. Before Kiefer could say another word Zero finished his drink and set the glass on the table before him. "Welcome to the syndicate, Mr. Yuska. Moving forward, you're one of us now."

CHAPTER THIRTY

PANTOKRAÐOR

Isarah
Blackwater City
Vaterlünd Temple
Aoustí 19

MY GAZE FELL UPON A GHOST, OR SO I THOUGHT.
"Ash?" I gasped.

"You thought they could get rid of me, eh, Kovey?" Ash said sarcastically as he limped over to me.

I didn't have words. "Damn it, Ash! You're alive? Thank Uridei you're alive!"

"Don't get mushy on me. Now, turn and open that damned door! It's been a long time waiting!"

I stepped back and slowly turned around—anything to keep that old man in good spirits.

I took a deep breath as the key fob echoed; the lock creaked and snapped as I turned the skeleton key within its mechanism. I pushed open the door and stepped into the abyss that had not been occupied in twenty years.

It was vastly dark. A chill filled the air. I noticed a couple of unlit candle sconces hanging off the wall closest to me. I swiftly concentrated the Purge and snapped my fingers, and the tips of all the wicks in that room were lit as if they were connected through the same underground gas pipes that lit the streets.

"Amazing, Kovey!" Ash's raspy voice heightened.

The room now glowed, and the inherited majesty unveiled itself before me. Ancient weaponry, paladin swords, and several other weapons forged by the religious Order had been placed with intention. Weapons layered the room, along with armor and additional leather attires suited for holy warriors. In the center of the room was an altar, where a large bullwhip lay on a red pillow; its essence drew me to it.

I turned to Ash, who stood in the doorway; Brother Rui waited in the hall.

"Pick it up," Ash urged.

I turned back to the whip, approaching it slowly, then wrapped my paws around it, feeling the fine plaiting of consecrated black leather against the padding of my palms. It had been threaded eloquently and masterfully into a lethal wrap. The handle was ten inches long but compact enough for one to carry it easily. It was delicate yet heavy, like the body of a medium-sized snake.

"Kovuco, that whip is eight feet long, representing the eight sacred trees of the Fae. Much of this weapon's construction comes from magic within the Rowan's roots. It is of the highest quality, triple-plaited, with a fair bolster in its handle. It's completely waxed, giving it a fine matte finish, and able to withstand the elements of any alchemist or dark force."

He paused, taking a moment to watch me eye the ancient piece. He stepped toward me. "The core is completely shot-loaded, adding weight to the front end with two finely twisted tapers at the end. Between the threads, you'll notice tiny stones that will sharpen under the Purge, making it a deadly weapon against the users of the dark, notably the Näkk."

Every detail, from the knot-like handle designs to the Völfien-head pommel on its end, was a marvel to behold. I continued to examine the weapon.

"Triple-plaited, shot-loaded, and wax-coated," I said to Ash, the keeper of this tome.

"Yes," he answered. "Its name is Pantokraðor. It means 'almighty, and all-powerful,' and I assure you, with Uridei's blessing, it needs no other title. So sure of its crafting, the dwarf who enhanced it was sure it was a worthy piece for someone like you. You alone."

I snapped it overhead; a fine crack echoed throughout the room. I instantly felt exhilarated and satisfied with the sharp snap. As at a crack of thunder, my ears twitched; a joy emitted, tinging the fibrous tissue around my heart. I hoped Ameilja felt the same joy I felt at that moment. I hoped she could feel my deepened determination to protect her with this ancient weapon.

Before I'd left for Tsunetomo, my brother Sangállo had taught me how to use a bullwhip. I'd always preferred this weapon because it gave me control if I needed to subdue someone without killing him.

"This whip is mine—has been mine?" I disbelievingly asked, tapping the pommel with my claw. The pommel of heavy metal displayed a roaring völf head with embedded diamonds for the eyes. Bits of blue were splashed in the cuts.

"Yes. It's always been intended that *you* would wield it. It's like it was meant to be all along, divine timing. Your brother Sangállo assured me you would be trained and ready when you made it to this moment. Even better that you can now somehow wield the Purge. I wish I'd seen you, Kovey. Taking out Malkovich's bodyguard with the purge. Heard all about it from Shirou."

I turned to face him with amazement still plastered across my features.

"Check out that ring too," he added, nodding for me to look.

I looked to the ring that split the handle from the eight feet of the whip. A ring of solid gold was crafted into the metal with absolute precision and artistry. On the other side, the Völfien alphabet was inscribed around it.

"Order of the Völfien," I whispered, realizing its origin.

Ash continued, pacing the room. "If lit with the Purge, a layer of plait flashes gold. The whip becomes a razor of golden fire. It'll match your rare coat of platinum, Kovey; it'll surely make you a real devil to face." He chuckled. "Like all dwarven masterpieces, this whip, Pantokraðor, is Galfnik's masterpiece!"

I turned to Ash. I couldn't help but question my being the intended owner. "Why? Why is this meant for me? Why would I, the bastard tyke strapped to my father's shield, need a weapon like this?"

"Galfnik was directed by the abbot of the Temple of Spears to construct this whip by order of someone else—who I'm not sure. I was not permitted to use it or have knowledge of who ordered its creation, nor were Brother Tad and Brother Rui. No one has ever interacted with that weapon, not even Galfnik." Ash chuckled, "The old dwarf whispered, 'The whip is now finished,' and ordered it to be locked away immediately. I then asked him, 'Does it need to be tested?' The crazy son of a bitch said, 'No, the first crack belongs to its master!' You, Kovuco Blackstar, are that master; you have cracked it first. If you need answers, I recommend you visit the abbot of the Temple of Spears. You will have to go there for answers."

I nodded and sharply inhaled, expanding my chest slowly. I looked down at the majestic whip.

I am coming for you, Ameilja. Pantokraðor and I are coming for you. I will take down, and Purge till death if I must, anyone who dares to harm you!

I toughed the plaited leather and sniffed in its fine materials, still excited by its brilliance. I thanked Uridei for the intent of the weapon and that it had been crafted for me. It felt like part of me, and now it was united with me.

I grinned and locked my gaze with Ash, happy that the old man was alive and that I was now part of something larger than myself. Larger than I ever had thought imaginable.

Isarah
Blackwater City
Vaterlünd Temple
Aoustí 21

Word had spread quickly. The authorities were now looking for a white-furred völf they deemed a "rabid murderer." Another rumor littered the streets that I'd murdered my master in Shaar. That story had also fabricated rumors that my master, András Frost, was some awful, abusive handler. I was not sure which lie disgusted me more. The rumors were starting to create an uproar within my race, creating more distrust against the humans due to the unknown truths.

The one detail that stood out to me was that nothing had surfaced about Ameilja's disappearance; the gossip was all focused on me.

Fine. Let the humans think what they want of me; it's not as if previous judgments were any better. If they think I'm the villain—to hell with it. I will proudly be labeled a murderous, rabid völf for Ameilja. I am her beast! I dare anyone else to try to stop me again.

I presumed that Ameilja's captors were expecting me. I couldn't openly run around as Kovuco, the platinum-furred völf, so I had to blend in.

Brothers of the Vaterlünd assisted me in tinting my platinum fur. Ash added hot black coffee mixed with cinnamon and a dark plant-based dye in a glass bowl. He informed me it was henna, which typically brought about red and brown colorations, but adding a dark roast of coffee would darken my fur, coating me completely black like my comrades Nav'i and Dancer. The mixture would also grant me a temporary unique scent, at least superficially. The added cinnamon would help the intense smell.

The application was hot and uncomfortable around the more sensitive regions, but it had to be done. Once it dried, it hurt to move, as it pulled my fur and skin, encapsulating me like a statue. Layer after layer, I became a muddied mess, spiked in the thick, paste-like compound. It dried under the sun for three hours and then was brushed and applied again. The process was repeated into the afternoon, until I could no longer recognize the old Kovuco. I still had my cream-colored bits of white fur from my neck to my navel. *Thank Uridei my groin didn't need to be dyed.*

My platinum was gone and lost in a now coal-black coat. To see myself look nothing like my father filled me with newfound hope that I could escape my status as a criminal escapee. No one would know who I was. I dressed in clothing from the armory. I wore a green Vaterlünd shirt, black slacks, and some green prayer beads hanging from pieces of my exposed neck fur. No longer did I look like a Shaar'an völf. I was now a völf of Spears, a völf of Isarah.

The entire time I was under color transformation, I could feel Ameilja struggling. More so than I've ever felt or witnessed from her. It heightened my inner stressors, so I decided to take that allotted time before traveling to Demitori to pray and meditate on Pantokraðor. I too struggled; my focus kept falling back on her.

I'll protect you. Stay strong. Please stay strong.

"Kovey!" said Ash, breaking my peace like a crack of thunder.

I nearly jumped out of my skin, unsure if it was the dreaded nickname or the fact that the only voice that ever uttered such a nonsensical name would speak beyond my trance.

The old hunter sat beside me on the bench, facing the small, circular window that overlooked the horizon—the horizon that led to Ameilja.

I looked to Ash: his dirty-blond hair was held up in a bun, and he was dressed like the people of Isarah, no longer a Shaar'an wülkure, enforcer of Völfien. He was officially with his people now. He didn't smell like bourbon or cigar smoke. He smelled clean and of incense.

"So what's next for you? Think you're gonna settle here in the Vaterlünd?"

"I can't be in the city, Kovey. I need to be out there: In the mountains, amongst the trees. But don't be so quick to rid yourself of old Ash yet. I will be in Demitori soon after I have secured my passage into the city. Remember, I died the other day. Not many beyond Shirou know I am still alive."

I paused, allowing the thought to pass over so I could dig deeper. I had questions about the old wülkure's survival. "How'd you do it?"

"Do what?"

"Survive. I thought for sure you were fish food. Did Shirou find you?"

"Shirou the mighty völf. Saved old Ash before it was too late," he muttered.

I turned back to the horizon. I was satisfied that Shirou was a light when everything went dark. I was thankful he could undo the worst of this journey so far. Now Ash seemed at peace.

"Kovey, we have to find a way to get you to Demitori City."

"I can manage a ride."

"A ride?"

"Yes. I met someone on my way here. Her name is Rae. She's someone I think I could blend in with and manage a perfect escape."

"Rae, eh? Tell me about her."

Ash seemed curious but critical of my choice, so I treaded lightly. I needed to convince him.

"She bought me lunch. I overheard her mention that she should be attending breakfast at a place called the Varka-Tanu. She also mentioned that she hoped to pick up a few Commission members to return to her hometown soon. That hometown being Demitori City."

"Why is she looking for Commission members to drive back to Demitori?"

"She's a wächter."

Ash grinned. "Wächter. Soldier. Excellent pick, Kovey. Stay away from hunters—all wülkure. You might have a new look, but you know we're trained to look beneath the surface. They will find you out."

I nodded and continued. "Also, I know she accepts völves. The dwarf told me she's friendly and that she eats like a völf."

"Damn. A human eating like you?"

"Yeah, she's quite small too." I arched my brow.

"Those wächter women are fierce. I'm telling ya." He shook his head and straightened his goatee. "What's your angle going to be?"

"A völf interested in alchemical studies."

"No. Too much."

"Better I make up an elaborate lie to see who will support me there. You know I am bad with lies, Ash. I'll be found out. If I am going to make friends in this city, it has to be humans willing to dream beyond the pattern of this world. I can't conform. I must find those willing to discern what is unjust and unpleasant, or they will become enemies when it comes time to rescue Ameilja."

Ash thought for a moment and said, "All right, Kovey. You've made a valid point. We'll see if the völf-stomach lady has the same appetite you have for breakfast then. If you think it's a bad idea for any reason, know that public transport will suffice. But you'll miss it if you try to attend breakfast. You sure this Rae's gonna be an ally?"

I thought back to the gentle-faced girl from the restaurant. Her kind eyes had looked at me with genuine care, and I recalled the playful wink she'd flashed toward me. I remembered the words from the gruff dwarf chef: "That overly chipper human eats like a völf, so she knows what's best for ya! Besides, I'd do anything for my favorite out-of-towner. There's no finer wächter, or sweetheart, than Rae Arow."

This Rae must be a kindhearted individual for a Fae dwarf as rough around the edges as he to compliment her so boldly. It was a relief to witness another Commission member other than Ash extending genuine care toward our kind.

"Yes, I'm confident she's an ally," I finally answered.

I internally questioned if she'd see through my charade. Would she know I was the platinum murderer from out of town?

Only time will tell.

CHAPTER THIRTY - ONE

THE RECKONING

Shaar
Tsunetomo
Frost Manor, András Frost's quarters
Aoustí 21

ANDRÁS SLAMMED A FIST AGAINST HIS MAHOG-
any desk, glowering at his captain. "Ridiculous!" His voice rattled the
atmosphere.

His brothers of the Order had recently explained that the attack on
Frost Manor had been cleverly designed to keep him stationary. His
Völfien protectorates, Shirou and Lain, stood on either side of his mas-
sive desk with the propriety of royal guards to a king.

Lain clutched his tonfa sword. It was smaller than his usual and resembled one reserved for Ameilja's White Throats. He glanced at Shirou.
Shirou sighed, heightening his senses. He felt just as annoyed as András
but devoid of the emotional attachment his master had for the situation.

"I am Abbot András Frost! I demand you grant me an audience
with O'Shalléd!"

András's airship captain stood with knees shaking as he answered
his lord. "I am sorry, Father Abbot, but there is no passage opportunity
at this time. All passage across the Eastern Sea has been ceased until
further notice. It might take a few days, depending on—"

"Unacceptable! You expect me to sit back and wait? A madwoman
has kidnapped my daughter! Do they expect us to comply with such
insolence? I'm ready to show up with my own ship!"

The captain bowed. "Please, Abbot. We have at least located his whereabouts; give me more time to patch in and negotiate with æsir Captain O'Shalléd."

"Æsir?" András huffed. "A traitor like him no longer wears such a title. I need a *leader* who will stand before me and discuss realistic terms. A leader with a suitable reason for me not to bring his entire fleet to the sea!"

Bernát lingered in the corners of the abbot's office, waiting for the onslaught of the airship captain to commence. Once the captain departed, he stepped forward.

"Lord Frost, I am sure arrangements can be made, but you must be patient. We cannot risk your death against that fleet. There's much we still don't know; blindly flying you in would not be wise."

"How can I be patient, Bernát? My estate has been bombed, Jayna has been murdered, Kovuco is missing! Ameilja, my daughter—the crowned Seer of the Eastern Isles, has been taken against her will. She could be dead, I have no answers for our people, and you want me to be patient?" András slammed his fist into his desk again.

"My lord, I mean no disrespect, but remember, I have trained your daughter since she was small. She's the closest thing I have to a child, but we cannot continue threatening Nathalii's captain and her security. We still must find out who all are involved and why. The empress didn't hesitate to send the judge after Kovuco; why not do the same for Nathalii and her fleet?"

András scoffed. "I will never rest if something happens to Kovuco. We don't have answers as to his motives yet, but Nathalii is an easy find. We know her positioning while she sits on her ship with my Ameilja. I do not want to send a judge, because if he is successful, which they usually are, I don't want him to kill Nathalii."

"You want to keep Nathalii alive? After everything—"

"Yes, I know. I haven't—" András paused and turned to the wall between his protectorates.

"Abbot? Haven't what?"

"I haven't told Ameilja the truth about Nathalii."

"I know. But I think she will live on," Bernát urged. "Especially with the current circumstances."

"But what if she finds out the truth? And then she learns I have pulled the trigger on Nathalii so hastily?"

"Ameilja should have known the truth, András. Why you have let her become an adult without knowing the truth is beyond me. Does Tanja know?"

"Dear Uridei, no!"

"My lord! How could you not tell your daughters that—"

"Bernát, enough!" he shouted, facing him with an icy stare. "At this rate, she will find out soon enough!"

"And Tanja?"

"Pray that Tanja does not find out. If she finds out, it will only fuel more reason for her to act out."

Bernát shook his head. "I am sorry to have questioned you, but the tides have turned, and I'm afraid it will come back to bite you. Know it is only because I care for your family, and I have been privileged with this knowledge."

"Bernát," András said, lowering his voice in surrender, "what do you think Nathalii wants with her?"

Bernát fell silent, unsure how to answer.

The door suddenly pushed open, and András's captain rushed back in. "My lord, I have news!"

Behind the captain, several armigers entered, surrounding Jakob Malkovich. The armigers were armored and fearsome, but so was Malkovich in his leather cuirass and battle coat.

"Malkovich?" András gaped. "What are you doing here?"

"Word is spreading. I heard that you were being barred from leaving Shaar. And Ameilja is missing?"

András approached his colleague with a scowl. "They have my Ameilja, Jakob!"

"Your concern must be great. Trust me; we will not allow this to go unpunished. We will get her back."

"How? I have been pleading for hours all while ensuring my people are safe. Nathalii took her without cause. Your bodyguard Kärleiv murdered some of my men, including Ameilja's trusted handmaiden, Jayna. I don't understand any of this nonsense. I need to save my daughter! I don't know whom to trust. I will not wait any longer!" András whipped around, his form swelling with rage.

"I'm here," Malkovich urged, sharing a confident smile. He stepped forward. "We will retrieve Ameilja. She is a member of the Order, the high seer of our empire, and therefore, we are justified in making a stand."

András turned back to Jakob and shook his head. "This stand will surely lead to punishment. I cannot place your forces in jeopardy."

"With news of Kärleiv's betrayal, understand I bear responsibility here. I have yet to gain understanding of his motives, but you must permit me to join you." He stepped closer to András, lowering his voice to a whisper, "You know my feelings for Lady Ameilja."

"Jakob, I know your intentions. I trust you with my life." András ensured. "Surely you realize what you're saying. If we leave these shores and challenge the *Renouncer*, our actions will lead to more bloodshed. We could be labeled as traitors by the empress for not following her order to stay off the sea. I cannot risk your reputation or—"

"András, please. With so many royals, including her son, creating problems at this time, the empress has much on her plate. She is heavily guarded at this time while answers are being pursued. This is not the first time travels have been paused due to an unidentified issue. Empress Sinnika will keep the news to a minimum and move forward with absolute precision, as usual."

"No disrespect to the empress, but we both know Sinnika moves at her own pace."

"Yes, and she knows that kidnapping a crowned seer is high treason. No matter her intentions, we *will* pursue Ameilja as an act of the Order. Nathalii and O'Shalléd have committed a betrayal against the Commission. We have every right to execute this plan; better we ask for forgiveness than permission."

András's weary gaze locked with Jakob's. He looked around the room, clenching his fists. "But how? I only have two ships assigned to my name; would my paladin force even be able to withstand the *Renouncer*?"

Jakob placed a hand on András's shoulder. "Let us see them try to stop *my* armada."

"Your armada?" András eyed him.

Jakob stepped aside and allowed András and his two protectorates to walk down the hall to the outside landing.

"Jakob?" András gaped, taking in the scene.

Fifteen airships idled in the distance. The sun blared its approval over the majestic vessels. If such a force began its descent for a city, authorities would be forced to evacuate civilians.

András smiled with fervor. All his threats to try to bend Captain O'Shalléd were now a reality. His two Shaar'an warships, combined with Malkovich's armada, meant he now had an abrasive force to bring to the battle.

He looked to his two Völfien protectorates, who had eager grins spreading across their muzzles. "Are you ready, boys?"

The two völves pounded their chests. Lain licked his incisors and said, "Just when I thought this was starting to get boring, eh, Shirou?"

Shirou answered with a howl of excitement. The howl was so intense it reached all the protectorates throughout the walls of the Frost estate.

They were going to Isarah.

Shaar
The coast near Frost estate
The Black Arrow, *Haruka's airship*
Aoustí 21

Nav'i's eyes snapped open, and his nostrils flared, inhaling familiar scents. A darkened space surrounded him.

Am I home?

He sat up in the bed, wearing only his slacks and shirt, and quickly scanned his body.

"I'm alive?" he questioned, relieved.

He gazed through the shadows and saw Haruka sitting cross-legged on a chair. She was sharpening arrows and fitting them into a quiver after carefully inspecting the sharpness of each arrowhead.

"Lady Haruka?"

"Nav'i. How are you feeling?"

Nav'i scanned the room, "Where's Dancer?"

"Dancer is safe. He's a free völf now. You've been sedated—Dancer's idea. He insisted we do it this way; he knew you'd try to stop him from leaving."

Nav'i sighed aloud. Part of him was happy for his friend, part was pissed at being drugged to unconsciousness, and part was sad that he might never see the acerbic black völf again.

Fortunately, that happy part was all he needed to focus on his present circumstance.

Nav'i couldn't help but feel nervous around Haruka as she sharpened her arrowheads confidently in the shadows. She carried her confidence as if she were a Lady of the Order. Technically, she would have been if not for the loss of her parents. Her dark eyes demanded authority, even over a large völf just a few feet away.

"How long was I asleep?" He questioned.

"Just a couple of days. It had to be that way until we confirmed plans."

As much as he wanted to argue this decision, he didn't dare question her. His auditory sensors picked up, "We're back home? Idling near Tsunetomo?" he said, snapping his gaze to the airship window.

"Yes. We never made it to Rúnar. We're here, in my ship now, to pick up Abbot Frost. We are preparing our armada for a full assault near the shores of Isarah."

"What? Why?"

"Ameilja has been captured."

"Captured?" Nav'i shot up as a snarl roiled within his chest. He was unnerved that even in his distress, Haruka remained composed, still sharpening her arrowheads.

"Yes. By Baroness Nathalii Darmouthe."

"Her aunt? How the hell did that happen? Tam didn't get on the airship with us, and Kovuco was with her!"

"It was an inside job, Nav'i. Unfortunately, Malkovich's bodyguard has been allegiant to that wicked wretch. Who the hell knows why." She sighed. "It's assumed Tam has also been captured."

"Is Tam safe? Kovuco? Are they"—Nav'i gulped—"dead?"

"I cannot say, but this kidnapping has escalated into quite a turn of events. Tam is likely being used as a bargaining chip for Ameilja's cooperation; Kovuco has murdered the judge sent by the empress; æsir

Captain O'Shalléd is leading the fleet that kidnapped Ameilja; and Tanja and her not-so-innocent husband are still missing. It stands to question whom we can trust right now. If Tam and Kovuco are alive, their time is limited unless they're quick on their feet."

We can only hope, Nav'i thought.

Kovuco's confessed love for Ameilja hopefully meant he would be tactful and elusive. He was positive their bond would aid in the hunt.

Nav'i collected his words, "Nathalii? What would an egotistical elite of Isarah want with her niece?"

"Interesting you label her that way. I'm now curious: What's your view on the social elites?" Haruka asked him, holding back from answering his question.

"By definition, they are the so-called masterminds who have been pulling the strings on our society and the likes of the Commission. Their money speaks for them. Their money gives them power. The baroness and her riches never sat right with me but never to the point where it would lead to this."

"Who else doesn't sit right with you?"

"Who else?" Nav'i asked, perplexed.

"What about Abbot András Frost?"

Nav'i tensed. "Is this an appropriate conversation we should be having right now?"

"Answer me, Nav'i."

He hesitated. "I believe he has his secrets."

"Elite secrets?"

"No. More like regrets. Regrets he hides. Shirou and Lain know. They hide it in their scent and rarely leave his side. And besides, everyone knows he resigned from his elite seat after migrating to Shaar."

"So he says." She arched a brow. "How about Malkovich?"

"He is *curious*."

"Curious?"

"Yes. They all are. Even our empress has hidden secrets and would die to keep them. It is her son who's missing with Tanja, yes? I have doubts about all of them. Humans have their ways. Anyone who fought in the later years of the war I consider curious, Lady Haruka. We're, unfortunately, the generation having to piece it all together."

"I can't disagree." She paused. "Jakob wasn't in the war; but, he might as well of been. Let's focus on him."

"I don't like the way he looks at Kovuco."

"How so?"

"I've only noticed it a few times. If Kovuco is present, there is always a scheming sort of stare. The stare a predator lends when he has narrowed in on his prey. The stare was far colder than I had ever witnessed at the coronation. I never want to assume bad intentions, but are you suggesting Malkovich is part of this plot?"

"There is more to Malkovich than meets the eye, Nav'i. Whether he participates in their affairs I cannot tell, but you do know there is a history between the Blackstar family and the Malkovich family, yes? The Blackstar's trials were held in Jakob's House. Ever wonder if there is more to that? Maybe Jakob hasn't approved of Kovuco all along; maybe it's because he's a prospective suitor for Ameilja and notices her favor toward Kovuco, or maybe there's something deeper between the two families." She raised her eyebrows, emphasizing her points.

Nav'i fell silent. He scanned the dark room, eventually settling back on Haruka's eager expression. She stared at him so intently it urged him to respond.

"Familial affairs are not my business." He firmly stated.

"Even though Kovuco is one of your packmates?"

"His business is his own." He pushed. "I will honor that despite what affairs lie between the two families. I am honored to be in league with a Blackstar. Both Tam and Kovuco."

"Very well. I personally do not favor Malkovich, to be honest. Yes, he took the lead after my parents passed, and I can't say he's done a bad job, but I have my reservations. I look forward to breaking from the Commission's grasp, and his, and my only way out is through the elimination of Malkovich."

Nav'i straightened. "Kill him?" he said, treading lightly into even considering a discussion regarding the assassination of such a high-ranked member.

"Yes." Haruka's eyes darkened.

"This sounds personal." Nav'i pressed. "I ask that you do not share such things aloud, especially to me."

"Apologies. Those are ties I will have to rectify in my own time. But I do wonder, don't you have an obligation to protect your friend?" She cocked her head in question as she placed another sharpened arrow into the quiver.

"And what if Malkovich isn't involved in any of this?" Nav'i challenged. "What if he is just a good guy who finds Kovuco peculiar? Most do, after all."

"Hm. Do you find your packmate peculiar, Nav'i?"

"I find Kovuco very peculiar. But Kovuco's and my problems stem from our youth quarrels. As I said, I am honored to be in league with him."

Haruka sighed, knowing she made the black völf unsettled. "Let's just put this conversation aside; the current issue is saving your lady. And right now, I need a völf's help."

"I assume that's me." Nav'i sighed, wondering where she was going with this.

"There's currently an even greater threat looming out there, and Jakob will stop at nothing to keep his finger on the pulse of this threat. You said one thing right regarding the social elites: their money gives them power. They are as dangerous as they are suspected to be, involving themselves with dark, twisted games and financiers of necromancy play, and there are only two ways to stop them. I possess one ability, but you possess the other, increasing my odds. I first approached Dancer since I knew him as a tyke, and he preferred freedom—freedom I was happy to fulfill—but he advised that you would be best for my task."

"What exactly is your task?"

"In order to successfully save Ameilja, we need to destroy the threats. I know how to handle the Purge—not to the extent of Ameilja, but as a paladin. I have a good hold over it. With that, we have an advantage."

"I don't understand." Nav'i shook his head. "Your Purge flames?"

"And your teeth," she added with certainty. "Both are suitable banes against the undead."

Nav'i flinched. His eyes dilated, processing her words. He then crossed the space and paused a couple of feet before Haruka, glaring down at her. The room fell silent to the point he could hear a faint ringing in his ears.

"Yes, you heard me right: the Näkk is here."

"How is that even possible?" He took another step toward her.

"Because of greedy, unethical bastards—that's how." She huffed, placing her final sharpened arrow into the quiver. "You are pledged to Ameilja, but I am afraid she is in danger of a much larger plot to bring back Sabor's power. And as the Commission orders, we must answer that call to save her. Knowing our enemy, I could use a völf of your prestige."

"Prestige—you mean you're not asking me to be your protectorate?"

"Hell no. I don't need a protector; I need a fellow hunter. Do you think I'm going to sit back and look pretty? I'm a lady of strength, Nav'i, one you don't fuck with!" Haruka locked her gaze with his and stood up.

Nav'i cocked his head, delving into information that he knew was against the law for a völf of his stature to acquire. "These necromancers you speak of—are you suggesting the theory that only the teeth of a Völfien and the flame of Uridei can stop them?"

"That is what is written."

"What makes you think that utilizing my prestige will even work? We don't know the slightest as to what the enemy may be hiding."

"I know more than you think. I have my ways of overhearing Jakob's privileged news. He has his inside connections."

Nav'i perked up his ears. "Has Jakob told András?"

Haruka shook her head. "No. His focus is aiding in saving Ameilja first. Telling András the news of the Näkk would be a major distraction. He will tell him at the opportune moment, as any centurion should."

Nav'i relaxed his muscles and loosened his clenched fists. It dawned on him that he was happy she was an informational gatherer, constantly involving herself with House Malkovich's gossip and private news. "Before I agree to help you, Haruka, tell me what you can."

Haruka nodded. "That's fair." She adjusted her blouse. "On the thirty-first of Lyul'ai, a facility known as the Sunspire sent a distress signal, but it only reached the centurion of Isarah, Henrik Böestrum. He has a singular communication channel, preventing other Commission branches from being alerted. This drew up the suspicion that an elite member was responsible—Nathalii, to be exact. You do know that Henrik is Nathalii's nephew, right?"

Nav'i shook his head. "How would I know these things?"

"Well, piece it together. Someone with a lot of power, money, and familial connection could easily pay off a centurion to override actions between other centurions, and to keep them from hearing Sunspire updates."

"You have my attention."

"Scientific and alchemical research has been developed there for years, but the plague has been held within its labs. Everything back-fired. Gruesomely. As you know, it's been recorded as a war between the Purge, Völfien, and the undead. We need to take out this operation with everything we have and save Ameilja from their morbid plans. You were created for this purpose, Nav'i! All of us were. Völfien, paladin—"

"And Ameilja."

Haruka grinned, narrowing her eyes. "So are you in, Nav'i?"

Nav'i nodded, processing the harrowing news. "I'm your völf until we free Ameilja."

"Good." She stepped up to him.

He raised his chin, towering above her.

Haruka took Nav'i's paw in her hand and shook it stoically. "Nav'i, we have a deal."

CHAPTER THIRTY-TWO

THE WÄCHTER

Isarah
Blackwater City
The Varka-Tanu
Aousti 24

"YOU WEREN'T KIDDING," ASH SAID, PATTING HIS mustache with the napkin from his lap. "She's a sweet little thing, ain't she?"

"Sh!" I quieted him harshly. "Someone might hear you!"

"She might have a taste for völves too, Kovey. You're not the only xenophile in the world, you know. Maybe she eats like a völf 'cause she's trying to attract one."

"Don't be ridiculous, Ash." I huffed, looking around to ensure no one else heard him.

"Okay, okay! Sorry, Kovey. That was insensitive."

There was a brief silence until I finally moved past his comment and made eye contact. I nodded. "You're forgiven. As long as you don't leap to your death again."

Ash shared his ornery smile. He began tapping his fingers on the tabletop, building anxiety through my bloodstream. "So what's the plan?" he asked, folding his hands across his stomach.

"Well, I am going to go up, get a pan of breakfast, sit at her table—"

"Nope!"

"Nope? What do you mean *nope*?"

"Oh, hi. I'm Kovuco—"

"I'm not going to give her my real name!" I snipped.

"What's your new name?"

"Jón."

"Jón? Rather common. Common human name, not even a Völfien name, for that matter."

"I couldn't think of a good name that wasn't of Shaar'an descent or Orkésh."

"Orkésh?"

"Yes, the name Kovuco is Orkésh! Are you really going to push me right now?"

"What? No, it's not."

"It is."

Ash shook his head, making a face I did not care for. "Nope. Won't allow it. You don't jump from one weird ork name to another. The name has to be Völfien."

"Drop it," I said forcefully, trying to counter his continued effort to *nope* anything I said.

"Well, I think you have a pretty odd idea there, Jónsi. I'll get this!"

"No nicknames, Ash. It's Jón. Wait—where are you going?"

Ash suddenly rose from his seat and flashed a hand before my nose, silencing me as if I were a young child. "I'll be back!" he said.

"Ash!" I grunted.

It was too late. Ash headed toward the crowd where the dwarf Kóji stood, talking to Rae and a few others.

Ash, confident and casual, approached the group and began making remarks to the dwarf. The dwarf nodded and gestured with his stubby hands: "Two."

Ash nodded, acknowledging the dwarf, who turned to the crew of chefs. That allowed Ash to intervene in the group of wächters, including Rae. There were three men. Two had thick, groomed beards, while the other had long black hair and appeared of Shaar'an descent, but his skin was darker.

I tried to shift my glance to something else and make it look like I was focused on something other than what they were doing. I retrieved my journal from my belt and quickly resumed notes I had invested in while at the Vaterlünd. My ears twitched, picking up the sounds, trying to find familiarity through Ash's twangy accent, prepping for whatever narrative he was working up.

Something about weapons? Whatever the hell any of this means. Wait—he's asking about transport?

"I've got a buddy who needs transport to Demitori. Unfortunately, he's not too fond of airship transport—you know, sensitive ears."

A bearded man chimed in. "Understandable. Now that you say that, I wonder if that's why you never see many völves on airships."

Rae said, "It's not their way, Copeland. The Völfien believe in the path made by Uridei. The airship is a manufactured structure that removes the natural experience of the road."

Ash interrupted. "Right. Well, he is needed soon. Do you guys know anyone who—"

Rae said, "I'm needed in Demitori myself. Honestly, I'd be happy to help out. Is he—"

"Yeah, he's fucking famished, actually. Do you want to take him this? Any proverbs on a Völfien appetite? 'Cause he's got one hell of an appetite!"

I heard the harsh scrape of the cast-iron skillet from the countertop, which distorted any response other than Rae's acknowledgment, and then I heard a light-footed strut toward me.

Deep breath, Kovuco. She doesn't know who you are. Keep it casual. You're Jón, the coal-colored völf. You're used to talking to females. Humans—human women—

"Jónsi?"

I turned my head and met her expression. Her kind eyes met mine with a subtle smile. Each hand grasped the handle of a cast-iron pan filled with home fries topped with bacon, bratwurst, egg, onion, peppers, tomato, and cheese, and off to the side was a warm baguette. There was a drizzle of spicy cream mustard; its savory, ethereal odor forced my muscles to swallow drool ready to spill from my nervous lips.

"Uh, yes. I'm Jónsi. You can call me Jón too if you like."

I held out a paw for a shake when she set down the steaming pans. Her hand, a hand that appeared only suitable for delicate tasks, clutched my paw with a grip I would never have expected.

"Nice to meet you, Jónsi."

I should have corrected her. Now I am stuck with this ridiculous nickname.

"I'm Rae. I don't mean to interrupt, but your friend over there was chatting with us, and he mentioned that you missed the public transport to Demitori."

"Yeah. We missed our flight."

I realized she dodged the accusation that I was afraid of airships.

"I met a Jónsi down south once. I always thought it strange, and then he told me his name was Jón, which was too common. His lover called him Jónsi, which seemed to resonate throughout the ranks as his permanent name."

I laughed nervously, trying my best not to scratch my neck anxiously. "Jón is a pretty common name. My, uh—well, Ash there has always called me by a shortened name too, so it stuck."

"I think it's a handsome name. It's unique, softer, and deserving of a story. What's your surname, Jónsi?"

What is with this human? Asking a völf for his surname? Is she even a wächter?

"O'Kuma."

"O'Kuma? Jónsi O'Kuma. I like it!"

"Thank you. It's my name, after all."

She chuckled. "You're funny."

I'm funny? Uh—find something to talk about, Kovuco. You have to keep this together.

I quickly scanned her body for something to discuss besides her firearm or the kukri strapped to her side. I knew nothing of guns but could always inquire; she might have forgotten Völfien were not privy to man-made firearms. It was intentional that our fingers would never be compatible.

I noticed a small book peeking out from her bag. I recognized it by its binding; it was a historical romance I'd read when I was in training. It appeared to be written in a different language.

"Is this your first time reading this story?" I asked, pointing to the novel.

She beamed, seeming delighted that I'd dared to ask. "Yes!" She pulled the book from her bag. "You Völfien and your reading—gosh, I love it! Please, no spoilers! I just got through chapter one."

"You speak different languages?"

She nodded, still smiling.

"I enjoyed it. Read it when I was young."

She held the book and examined the cover. "My father sent it to me as an early birthday present. I had many brothers, so I hadn't much time for the girly romance stories. At least that's what they called them." She laughed. "I guess that's why I ended up in the Commission." She gave me another smile and placed the book back in her bag. "Sorry, but do you live around here? You don't mind if I sit with you, do you?"

"No, please sit." I started eating from the pan, hoping it would disguise any awkwardness I could not deflect.

"Well, I wasn't considering returning to Demitori for some time, Jónsi. But this might signify that I must be brave and make the trip."

"Be brave?"

"Yeah. My boyfriend and I—or whatever he is. I need to settle things with him, but he might not want me around."

"Why not, if that's not too personal?"

"It's fine." She poked at the food in her pan. "As you can see, I am in a dangerous line of work. He pushes me away because he wants to protect me, forgetting that I always face similar dangers."

"I mean, that makes sense. The best way to protect those close to you is to push them away. Then no one can use them against you."

"To be honest, Jónsi, I told him I loved him, and it might've scared the hell out of him." She laughed again, this time lowering her gaze.

"I can relate." The words slipped from my lips like a dark whisper in an octave that might've made a mere human uncomfortable, but Rae was no mere human.

She gave me her attention, silently demanding that I explain myself.

I cleared my throat. "I had someone say she loved me once. It scared the hell out of me too. It was innocent, an illusion of endearment, and I knew that. I wanted to respond to her, but I could not. Fear kept me from speaking the truth." Rae's eyes searched mine, tuning into the words I shared. "Love means so much more than what we often realize. We use it sparingly, yet Uridei calls it the greatest of virtues. While many define love as romance or a warm feeling you get, Uridei's definition is fundamentally deeper. Love is alive, based not on what we feel but on what we do. Love is self-sacrificial, selfless, putting another's needs before your own. It's an action."

"Wow," Rae said, shifting in her seat. "If he looked at it that way, that would surely scare him off. But he's no Uridei follower. I can tell you that."

"You're right, Rae. Love is scary, but it takes humbling oneself to bear the burden. Once you do, you have to understand that you'll never be able to love perfectly but acknowledge that if you utter those words to another, it's like a contract that you will always try. Even if it takes a lifetime or eternity."

Rae smiled. "That might be all the motivation I need."

She seemed lost in thought for a moment when I noticed the crowd of men and Ash approach to sit at our table.

"Jónsi!" shouted Ash. "These gentlemen have agreed to take you to Demitori!"

The black-haired man placed a hand firmly on my shoulder. "Indeed, Mr. Völf. We'll be delayed, but what's a scolding now and then?"

Rae shook her head. "No need, Hattori. I'll take Jónsi. I have a few things I need to work out personally. You guys take the next airship after the assignment is complete."

"You sure, Rae? It's not a bother?" asked the man with a perfectly groomed beard.

"Please. I'm sure."

The black-haired man shrugged. "Sounds like a plan to me. No one ever rips Rae anyway."

Rae tossed a piece of her baguette at the man. "Ah, fuck off, Hattori!" she scoffed with an ornery grin.

"It's true!"

She shook her head as the man, with a badge displaying the name Copeland, gave her a playful shake about the shoulders. Some inside joke had transpired before me, and I just grinned through it.

"Before you leave, drink this. You will insult that blistering dwarf if we don't toast to his fresh-squeezed orange juice," said Copeland, setting two tall glasses of orange juice before Rae and me.

We all turned toward the counter, where the dwarf continued barking orders at his brigade of chefs.

"Kóji!" shouted Copeland.

As soon as the dwarf turned his attention, following Copeland's lead, we raised our glasses.

Copeland shouted, "To the greatest dwarven chef on Isarah!"

The dwarf bowed, and we gulped down the juice.

It was the best damned orange juice I had ever tasted.

☆

Isarah
Blackwater City
Aoustí 24

Rae and I turned the corner, and she pivoted toward a strange, boxlike vehicle. It was a general-looking motor vehicle, small and compact. I noted that it looked sturdy and capable, impressed by the design.

"It's a wächter-issued all-purpose vehicle. Four-wheel drive."

"Four-wheel drive? Aren't all vehicles four-wheel drive?"

"No. Most are two-wheel. This is an off-road piece of machinery."

"I don't think I have seen any vehicles with two wheels. Unless you're referring to the bicycle-looking ones."

Rae rolled her eyes and chuckled. "Have you lived under a rock? You've got a lot to learn about the world, Jónsi. Get in!"

I walked up to the door and pulled the handle only because I had seen other humans do so. I desperately tried to act as if I knew some practical notions about the vehicle, but I didn't.

I got inside and squeezed into the tight spot, but my legs were so long that I had to prop them up on the edge of the seat, and my head hung between my knees. I closed the door, neglecting my tail, which was still dangling out the side of the vehicle. I slammed it in the door, yelping loudly.

Rae laughed and reached for a handle under my seat, and the seat launched backward. Suddenly, I was gifted with enough legroom to sit comfortably.

Annoyed, I dragged in my tail, removed my jacket, and tossed it into the back along with my suitcase.

"You good?" she asked, trying not to giggle at my dismay.

I nodded. "I think so. Of all the things Albean could have done for us, he didn't think to create us without tails. They can be a nuisance sometimes; it's like if you had to wear a cape all day, unsure if you'd get it stuck on something, or torn."

She laughed again. "I needed these laughs," she said with a toothy smile. She then started up the vehicle, and it roared to life. I watched her step on the gas pedal, and we hit the road for Demitori City.

We took a network of bridges that ventured onto a more extensive road that stretched a great distance. Rae explained that this highway would take us to our destination.

"Do you have a place to stay in Demitori?" she asked.

I nodded. "Yes, the Temple of Spears will house me." My thoughts were directed to my brothers; I wondered what they would think of my circumstances.

"My boyfriend has a spacious apartment near the Copper District." Rae continued, grabbing my attention. "You'd love Copper! It's the largest district known for its Fae inhabitants and Völfien. Assuming I work things out with him, you're welcome to stay there rather than in the temple. That way, you'll be closer to the city. Only if it suits you, ya know." She paused. "I can't wait for you to meet him. He also works in the Copper District; I swear he trusts Fae more than most humans."

"Trusts Fae more than humans?"

"Well, he works with the Fae, specializing with your kind, actually—Völfien."

I shifted in my seat. "What does your boyfriend do?"

"Oh yeah, I forgot to tell you. He's an æsir over the District."

So he's a—oh no! He's—

"He's a wülkure."

CHAPTER THIRTY-THREE
THE HUMAN

Isarah
Demitori City, Obsidian District
Duskwell Hospital
Aousti 25

"THIS SHOULD DO IT," KIEFER CONFIDENTLY spoke to his reflection as he dressed in his civilian clothes: dark pants, black leather boots, a white shirt, and a purple tie with white stripes layered in subtle forty-five-degree angles.

He then put on a gray pin-striped vest and slipped his pocket watch into the lower pocket. He brushed his hair back, and put on a top hat he kept for formal occasions, along with a pair of dark spectacles to shield his eyes. He was never one to wear hats or spectacles, but it made for a great cover when he wasn't in his usual wülkure attire.

This was to fool not only his new partners within the Demitori underworld but, hopefully, his colleagues within the Sentry. His goal for the day was to remain under the radar.

He headed toward Duskwell to remove Szonja from her post. Otherwise, he risked her being killed by Zero's völves. He realized it was a premature decision to get her involved; especially when she didn't know all the details. The Blue Coats were currently docile, but without fully understanding their militant capabilities, he needed to tread lightly until he'd earned more face time with the disgruntled völf, Kouta.

He arrived in the courtyard of the hospital. Szonja stood at the fountain before the dual sliding glass doors. She held her sword firmly as she casually sipped her coffee.

He made his way to her, and she looked up. "Kiefer? You decide to show yourself?"

"Who was in charge while I was away?"

"Okra met with me a couple of days ago, but as soon as he saw Yegor's and my books, he signed off. Why?"

"You have to leave this place. It's not safe."

"What? What are you talking about? And why are you dressed like that?"

"Never mind my attire, Szonja. The Blue Coats. They are watching Baadar. If we step near that room, we're asking for it. She's safe now but—"

She grabbed his tie. "Kief, I hear you. Let's get outta here. Then will you tell me what the hell is going on?"

He ignored her question. "I'll deal with Okra soon. Let's go."

She gave him a sly smile, and her tongue glided against the back of her teeth. It was a smile only a lover would see. "Sure. My place?"

"No."

Her seductive look quickly faded, and she peered at him through bedeviled eyes. "What's wrong?"

"There's someone else."

"Okay. And?"

"I love her, Szonja. I fucked up majorly, and I need to earn someone like her back again."

She studied him, digging deep into his soul for truth. "Do you *really* love her?"

He closed his eyes and sighed.

She snapped her fingers, and his eyes widened again as he braced for retaliation. A smirk formed on her pink lips. She leaned forward and gave him a light peck on the corner of his lips. "You were a lousy lay anyway."

She was letting him off easy, and he knew it.

"I'll miss those bad workdays, though," he teased.

"Too bad," she said. "Now, let's get outta here. It would be best if you got me up to speed before you get us killed. Can't love anyone if you're dead."

Kiefer led Szonja away from the courtyard. In the corner of his eye, he caught a glimpse of a familiar, disturbed, charismatic smile.

Kouta.

Kiefer tried to lock on his position, reaching for Szonja's pistol, but as soon as he turned back his gaze, Kouta Baadar was already lost in the shadows.

☆

The Eastern Sea
The Black Arrow, *Haruka's airship*
Aousti 25

Thick, murky clouds rolled through the skies, their fog grazed the dark waters below. Light showers of rain pommeled the floating ships while anthems of thunder cracked the atmosphere. The massive *Renouncer* was surrounded by a square shield formation: four defender airships, all a quarter of the *Renouncer*'s size, unaware of Jakob Malkovich's imminent attack.

"We have our orders." Haruka said to the black völf at her side.

Nav'i walked alongside her in his new gear. Instead of House Frost's red ascot, he wore a green one representing House Malkovich. He wore a jacket with leather pauldrons and a Commission-issued belt. He felt, for once, recognized for who he should have been: a member of the team and a respected member of the Order, a völf of Albean.

"O'Shalléd's fleet is currently idling near the coast of Isarah, at least fifteen miles out from the port. He has four defender ships. Nathalii has taken Ameilja to her manor in Isarah, so we're clear to commandeer the fleet."

"Got it." Nav'i nodded.

"If we do this right, we'll take them down quickly. Besides, their fleet is now much more minuscule compared to ours." She chuckled at the thought.

Haruka's ship, *Black Arrow,* and another airship of House Malkovich, *Rising Night,* led by paladin Mordehn Crögah, were designed for stealth and speed. They were a hybrid, distinctive design specifically for Malkovich's House, with *Black Arrow* being gifted to Haruka.

Black Arrow was a small, angular ship resembling a boat, fueled by the hydrogen gas filling its balloons, which kept it high above the rolling ocean waters.

Both vessels pierced through the thick clouds and set for their target. Rather being greeted by a smaller, less lethal ship, O'Shalléd would be greeted by some of the fastest battleships the skies had ever seen.

Each vessel was equipped with Jakob's most high-ranked marksmen; a combination of approximately twenty-five armigers and paladins. The armigers were lined up and armed with crossbows along the front of the deck while the stationed paladins at the edge of the deck were wielding reverse crossbows as their primary firearms. Below the deck, gunports were manned by a small wächter crew who operated the cannons. Every member held a proper position and duty.

Haruka and Nav'i stood centered among the readied crew, as the swollen clouds misted there forms.

"I promise you, Lady Haruka, you'll be the first paladin to step foot on the Renouncer's deck," Nav'i affirmed.

"Very good." Haruka responded, holding onto her confident grin.

The airships began to pick up speed, cutting through the dreary skies. The drizzling rain pelted their skin, dampening their attire. The engines' whistling nipped at Nav'i's ears, but he withstood it. Seconds passed, and the blanket of fog was ripped apart by the daggerlike ships.

"Steady!" Haruka called out.

For a brief moment, the sun's bright glare seeped through the clouds. It glistened against their eyes, granting them favor in that moment. Then the rear of one of O'Shalléd's defender airships came into view.

"Uridei be with us," Haruka whispered loud enough that only Nav'i could hear.

The wächter crew didn't hesitate. *Black Arrow* and *Rising Night* fired massive volleys from their gunports. The cannonballs shredded the defender ship instantly, taking lives and creating massive explosions due to its dormant equipment. When they bypassed the vessel, its hydrogen-filled balloons erupted into a ball of fire. The heat could be felt where Haruka and Nav'i stood. They watched as the defender ship descended through the fog to meet its watery grave.

"Well, that was easy," Nav'i scoffed, eyeing the obliterated vessel.

"Don't get too comfy." Haruka voiced.

Crögah's ship was ordered to circle the *Renouncer*, providing fire support, while Haruka's ship was ordered to make impact. Large blades were released just below the center gunport, designed for penetrating the sides of a ship's hull.

Haruka turned and grinned at Nav'i, and his ears twitched. She knew he was listening and whispered, "You're my völf, right?"

He nodded and drew his twin tonfa swords. "For now."

"First to board?"

"The first!" he proudly growled.

"Good! Now, brace yourself!"

Nav'i took a knee, grounding his footing. He lent his forearm to Haruka for support. By the time she clutched on to him, *Black Arrow*'s blades had ripped into the hull of the *Renouncer*, locking it in place. The impact swayed the crews' readied stance.

Upon impact, a three-second trigger mechanism unleashed a concentrated burst of flaming shrapnel that killed some of the *Renouncer's* crew and set their surroundings on fire. Immediately, the front layer of armigers, including Haruka, fired explosive bolts at the captain's cabin and toward the quarterdeck of the massive vessel. The bolts smashed through windows, and some found their mark along its quarterdeck.

"Hell yeah!" Haruka cheered as adrenaline pumped through her veins.

Three cannons fired, weakening the *Renouncer*'s hull.

Haruka tossed her crossbow to a nearby paladin, who quickly reloaded a bolt, just as she looked up and noticed the *Rising Night* soaring overhead. It made contact with the *Renouncer*'s quarterdeck by demolishing much of it with explosives. The burst caused a whiplash of air, pulsating the atmosphere. Haruka felt the lingering vibrations through her grounded stance.

The crew of the *Renouncer* immediately responded, attempting to stop the attacking vessels. Dozens of its crew members began to board Haruka's ship with axes and blades; some wielding rifles with bayonets fastened to them. With a vicious rage, they began attacking Haruka's crew. Some of her armigers fell to their deaths in mere seconds.

"No!" Haruka screamed. "Nav'i! We must charge the deck!"

Nav'i took in the melee as it played out before his eyes. He snapped from his hyper-fixated gaze and fiercely impaled two charging *Renouncer* members with his tonfa blades. He slashed a third across his throat, beheading him. Blood sloshed Nav'i's form, coating him in a victorious crimson.

"Nav'i!" shouted Haruka, shouldering her crossbow. "Now!"

Nav'i sheathed his blades and took to her side. Quickly, he lifted Haruka into his arms and leaped onto the enemy deck in a single graceful bound. He met Haruka's promise to ensure she boarded the enemy's deck first.

The remaining crew from the *Black Arrow* immediately followed suit and managed their way onto the deck. Simultaneously, the *Rising Night* hovered nearby, releasing the few paladins and armigers on board.

"Nav'i, watch out!" Haruka yelled.

A member of the *Renouncer* clutched his rifle and aimed it for the völf. The gun fired midair just as Nav'i's tonfa sword was thrust into the man's stomach. Nav'i tossed him to the side and slashed another approaching member across the face. The blade split the top half of the man's skull, and he fell dead at the völf's feet. Another began his vengeful charge with an ax. Haruka fired a bolt through his shin. He fell, but before he could hit the ground, Nav'i tackled him and began tearing at the man's throat with his jaws. He ravished the meat and blood and rose to his feet once he had mutilated the corpse. His muscles contracted, absorbing the fresh blood.

Haruka swiftly turned on her heel and shot another bolt through a crew member, which gave her enough time to examine her surroundings. Two of the *Renouncer*'s defender airships were repositioning to aid O'Shalléd's crew. Just as she was about to warn Nav'i, explosions unexpectedly lit up the skies, taking the two defender airships with it.

"Jakob!" Haruka gasped.

The two defender ships were each met by a pair of Malkovich's battleships. One of them she knew carried both Jakob and András. Haruka whipped around, looking toward the east. Flashes of light and fire continued to light up the sky. She noticed the fourth defender ship dipping out of harm's way, retreating in a cowardly manner, as it turned its keel for home.

"That's right," she pridefully huffed. "Go tell dear Nathalii what's transpired over these seas!"

Another crew member suddenly charged for Nav'i, who was focused on another slaughter. Haruka drew her sword, screaming in rage, and deflected the crew member's blade swing. She brought her knee to his gut and then reversed the blade, letting him fall against its sharp edge, slicing through his throat.

"Die!" She roared.

The crew member gargled and choked, spewing blood from his mouth. Haruka pulled the blade from his wound, wiped blood from her brow, and then looked back to Nav'i, who was slowly rising from his meal. His armor was doused in gore. His dilated gaze locked with hers. Haruka paused as she processed the thought that the scene looked terrifying. Nav'i breathed heavily, and his nostrils flared over the scent of blood, scanning for more souls to meet his fury.

"Nav'i?" Haruka cautiously grabbed his attention. "A rather successful raid, I must say. And we were first to board, thanks to you."

Nav'i nodded, inhaling slowly. "Are you going to give me a hydrostein?"

Haruka narrowed her eyes, grinning widely. "No. You're currently my völf. You get rewarded for that sort of thing. Digest his taste. He's yours."

Nav'i smirked, wiping his mouth with the back of his paw. He scanned their surroundings, instantly noting that the *Renouncer's* crew was diminishing. By then, Jakob's battleship had breached the other side of the ship.

A sudden scream, followed by hoarse cursing, erupted from the quarterdeck. Both Nav'i and Haruka diverted their attention as a pair of Malkovich's armigers appeared, escorting O'Shalléd away from his quarters. Haruka could see Jakob and András closing the distance between them, followed by András's protectorates, Shirou and Lain.

"Jakob Malkovich! I should've known!" O'Shalléd hissed through gritted teeth. "The centurion will have your heads for this infraction!"

"Ah! Henrik, you mean?" Jakob scoffed, his booming voice echoing through the skies. "*That* centurion has much to speak for himself, and Shaar's forces will be sure he meets judgment, Captain. You should be concerned about your present circumstance. Kidnapping a seer is high treason. Oh, and stopping an abbot from pursuing his daughter seems rather risky, don't you think?"

"'Twas the order of the baroness—is she not family?" O'Shalléd eyed András, cocking his head.

András drew his blade and held it to the captain's throat.

"Easy, Father András," O'Shalléd cooed.

András grounded his tensed form and spoke through clenched teeth. "You come to *my* land, dine in *my* House, and murder members of *my* Order, and you dare use the baroness's lineage to alleviate your crimes?"

"I was just following orders. I'll—"

"Silence!" András bellowed, gripping his sword so tightly his knuckles turned white.

András's body shifted in preparation to murder O'Shalléd; his respiration accelerated and trembled. O'Shalléd's hyper-tensed eyes locked with his, searching for a hint of grace. A small bead of anxious perspiration slid down O'Shalléd's temple, past his eye, and over his cheek. It extended beyond the edge of his mandible and splattered onto the blade that was pressed painfully against his throat.

The brief moment of silence was eerily deafening between the two men.

András's upper lip curled. He shifted his arm, prepared to slash, then abruptly halted and sheathed his sword with a single stroke.

An audible sigh of relief slipped out of O'Shalléd's mouth.

András snapped a glance at Haruka and then stormed off; his protectorates followed. "May Uridei have mercy on your soul!" András grumbled aloud.

Jakob met Haruka's stare. "Find something O'Shalléd can do to contribute to our efforts, will you?"

Haruka smirked at him, brushing a piece of gore off her shoulder. "Can't think of anything, honestly."

Jakob ominously shifted his features, hinting his approval to Haruka before he followed after András. Haruka caught the cue.

"Nav'i, you know that this is the ship that carried Ameilja to Isarah, yes?"

"Lies!" exclaimed O'Shalléd.

"So full of shit!" Haruka snipped. "Seems you've never faltered from the egotistical asshole I've always known you to be. We *know* what's going on, O'Shalléd; you can stop with your pathetic pity party."

Screams could still be heard about the ship, along with intermittent explosions and gunfire, confirming that any of the *Renouncer's* survivors were being handled.

O'Shalléd glared at Haruka, fuming at her audacity. "Killing me will be a grave mistake!"

"Ugh, I've heard enough of this pathetic man's voice," Haruka whined obnoxiously, intent on probing his pride.

"I'll see you in hell, you orphaned bitch!" O'Shalléd spat, spewing saliva from his lips. The two armigers holding him tightened their grips.

Haruka turned to Nav'i. "You're not too full for another helping, are you?"

Nav'i made eye contact with the captain. He forcefully sheathed his tonfa swords and growled, baring his sharp teeth dripping with saliva and blood. "Nah, I'm just getting started!"

Isarah
Temple of Spears
Aoustí 25

Ameilja wore her Commission uniform and, for once, agreed to wear it how it was preferred.

She pulled up the cowl over her head and put on her headscarf. It was required to keep her red hair and face hidden, per Nathalii's orders. The only item Ameilja insisted she wear outside the customary sisterhood attire was her mother's necklace. When her security detail, a caravan of four vehicles with armed acolyte followers of Nathalii, arrived at the Temple of Spears, they let her go in alone. They at least granted her the time to meditate and pray.

Still, the acolytes were to inconspicuously secure every door and window to ensure no one could break in or, in Ameilja's case, escape.

Ameilja gazed upon the statue of Fenris, the matron of Völfien, before entering the great Temple of Spears. The rich detail of the temple was beyond human understanding, but it had not changed since her last visit there when she was young. It remained with its original design. The Völfien of the land, not humans, had built it—a remembrance of the old ways, the Order of the Völfien alongside the Religious Order.

The choir sang as she began her steady walk down the aisle toward the altar. She rested her hands on her chest, grasping the cross-shaped necklace.

When she arrived at the altar, she knelt before it. She took a deep breath and delved into her thoughts. She hoped that in this place, she could manage reassurance and maybe even a vision—anything to give her hope.

She wondered how many souls had been lost because of her. She thought about her handmaiden Jayna, who'd died protecting her. What had become of her protectorates? Of Ash? Were they accompanying her father? What about Haruka? Had they safely made it to Rúnar?

Uridei, please cast a shield of protection around them.

She tried to pray, but mostly, she worried. She worried about Tam. Was it wise that she'd distanced from him at this moment? Was every waking moment leading closer to something terrible happening to him for his staying by her side? She knew it would break his heart, but she considered seeking the known Blue Coats in the shadows to take him away from her to protect him, but with Nathalii having her hands on everything, it was unlikely.

Uridei, please hear me.

Even more heavily on her mind was Kovuco. She recalled the sensation of his seizing her power to use the Purge. Never could she have imagined such a feat.

I sense his emotional state. I sense a change in him; he is stronger. More confident. More focused in mind and form.

Ameilja felt an intense concentration in Kovuco. A determination was rising within him. He was becoming much more fierce than the gentle Kovuco she was used to.

Where are you, Kovuco?

She revitalized their first synchronization, remembering the first heartbeats beating in unison as the bond set in. It surged an unexplainable warmth through her arteries and veins, caressing her mind, as it lulled her entire form into its intimate embrace. The feeling reminded her of when Kovuco had lowered her onto her soft bed and gently tucked her in safely.

The bond was calm, intensely impassioned yet sensationally unparalleled.

Ameilja slowed her breathing and focused on the thump in her chest. *Kovuco* … She could feel the rushing wind, the ocean spray, and that continued strength. Then the feeling of stretching veins and pulsating arteries … a sensation of pain, until suddenly—

Ameilja, said Kovuco.

She quietly gasped, tightening her eyelids. She didn't want to break the connection, as she sensed him so fiercely that she felt as if he were right behind her, the heat radiating off of his form, meditating in the same posture.

"Kovuco, I am here! Are you safe?" she whispered.

Yes. I am close. I'm going to get to you soon! But I need time.

"Why?"

I have to be strategic. I'm also mastering my ability to Purge. But our union makes everything so different—better. You make me better, Ameilja!

A tear formed in her eye. "I am so proud of you, Kovuco. Is it everything you dreamed it would be?"

Dreamed?

"Our bond showed me that your deepest dream was to be a paladin—the old ways of the Order of Völfien. I—I didn't know."

There was silence.

She choked on her own words, trying to keep her composure and continue without crying.

Ameilja, are you safe?

His words broke her. The tears came. They poured down her cheeks despite her eyes being closed. "No. They are going to kill me, Kovuco." Ameilja's voice cracked through her hushed whispers. "Nathalii has not agreed to it, but I cannot imagine any other outcome. The pursuit of my dream has earned me a death sentence. If I don't cooperate, they will kill our friends and our family; they've already killed Jayna!"

You must stay strong, Ameilja!

"I know." She opened her eyes and gazed up at the ceiling, tempted to tell Kovuco her exact location and her news of the Näkk, but hesitated. She swiped away her tears. "But I admit I am scared. I am so scared, Kovuco. Scared for our people, for you, and of the imminent future."

Stay strong, Ameilja. Persevere, and know that I will save you!

"I'm fighting!" she assured. "But, Kovuco, *you* must stay strong! How often do you need to physically bloodlet? Are you facing any weakness?"

I'm managing, but I will have you within reach soon. I will refuel our connection, Ameilja. Soon I will taste you again.

Ameilja closed her eyes, replaying his words. "Kovuco, word is spreading about you. Nathalii knows about you and the judge. She's going to be looking for you! Rumors are spreading, Kovuco. You will be discovered! You—"

Ameilja's breath caught in her throat again. It was the truth. She knew he would be discovered. With his platinum fur and the oceanic blues in his eyes, he'd be spotted, even with his new divinities. Deep down, she also feared someone would find out about their forbidden act. She was not sure how anyone would, but it heightened her nerves.

"I can't lose you, Kovuco."

There was no reply.

"Kovuco?"

Silence.

"Kovuco? Kovuco!" she urged.

His presence was gone, and she was alone again. His reminder to stay strong lingered.

"I will, Kovuco. I will stay strong."

Isarah
Demitori City, Brass District
Grande Mariner Apartment Complex, room 504
Aousti 25

Kiefer completed day three of lying low since his underground connection to the Blue Coats. He was eager for Isabelle to awaken but, thankfully, hadn't spotted her cunning offspring lingering around his property.

Kiefer wasn't afraid, though; he hadn't earned his title as the top beastkind wülkure for nothing.

As for Kiefer's team, Szonja's and Leif's cases kept them busy, and after harsh ridicule for double-booking himself, Yegor returned to his assignment with Tree'veld, getting his foot in the door through Zara Doz'hura. Rumors were spreading among the orks. All those loyal to the Orkésh ways were whispering about the return of the Wöndin. Whether it was true, only time would tell, and maybe would birth a connecting piece to Marius's ideals on the gang having involvement with the Sunspire.

These predicaments created new challenges for Kiefer. He had to keep his team at arm's length of the truth while simultaneously process-ing the events of the Sunspire, which were still escalating behind the scenes, and investigating Kouta's purpose.

"Who the hell is spearheading all of this?" Kiefer moaned, annoyed, leaning his forehead into his palms.

Kiefer wouldn't admit it, but the burden of these events felt beyond his expertise. He rubbed his eyes till they turned red, allowing the pres-sure to distract him from a lingering headache. Kiefer clenched his jaw and pushed the thoughts from his mind. He had much more to attend to through a mountain of reports. New information had been sent re-garding a lady seer's missing protectorate. Another völf issue.

This specific völf was reported as a high priority for all districts to be alert to, assuming he was an actual threat. Kiefer questioned why a völf had more attention than the traitorous leadership within the Commission. How had none of this surfaced?

He had read through the alert. The seer, Ameilja Rose Frost, was a Shaar'an-born woman and daughter to High Abbot András Frost. He read that a troublesome protectorate of völves surrounded the seer; two of them were Blackstars. The main concern was Kovuco Blackstar, who had been fathered by the less popular Blackstar and almost had been cast out as a demon völf. He had faced a gruesome trial within the temple of House Malkovich.

Kovuco was also notated as highly aggressive, but every völf had been labeled as aggressive, and fluctuating between moderately and highly aggressive was never a huge indicator, in Kiefer's opinion. *Highly* usually indicated deaths in the past thirty days. He had reportedly killed the judge since he left his post.

Kiefer leaned back in his seat and scanned the notes, skipping to the section describing the Court of Völves.

Any pictures? Descriptions?

He flipped through the pages. "Here we go."

Tambor Blackstar: golden wolf with gold eyes—related to Kovuco. Danflor: black wolf with brown eyes—was once enslaved. Nav'i: coal-black wolf with green eyes—standard. Kovuco: platinum-white coat and crystal-blue eyes ...

He's a murderer with the eyes of a demon. Interesting. What defines platinum fur?

"This völf must also be spattered in a bloody rage," he sarcastically whispered to himself, shaking his head. "I wish I had a picture, but it appears the Frost family refused one or misplaced it."

A knock suddenly sounded at the door and disrupted his concentration.

"Who the hell could this be?"

He rose from his seat, grabbed his pistol, and meandered over to the door after straightening his collar. He loosened his tie slightly.

He cracked open the door, and froze. The visitor stood before him wearing a short gray skirt in an academy cut. She wore tall combat boots over black-and-white plaid stockings and a neatly pressed military coat over a white blouse. A Commission ascot was attached to the collar. Her brown hair was tied back, allowing her delicate cheekbones to show in the light, and her rich brown eyes were sad yet calculated.

"Rae?" he subtly spoke.

She nodded. "Hi, Kief. I, um, know you told me not to come back, but I wanted to say something. Something I need to get off my chest." She bit her bottom lip. "Then I'll be gone. Promise."

Kiefer unlocked the deadbolt and opened the door. "Okay."

Rae inhaled, readying her words. "Well, I know things ended on a bad note between us, and despite your reckless actions, I realize I overstepped. I told you I loved you and honestly, I think I said it because I wanted you to let me stay. But I thought about it, and I realized I used it selfishly at that moment. Love isn't selfish, its selfless. The truth is, I love you so much, Kiefer, so much that it aches, and I do genuinely enjoy caring for you." Rae's eyes tightened. She clenched her jaw, holding her ground. "I truly feel that way, and I don't know if you feel the same about me, but I do know what I deserve, and it's the Kiefer I have fallen in love with, not the Kiefer who feels the need to protect me and push me away. When have I *ever* said I needed your protection?"

There was silence. Kiefer was dumbfounded and wondered if he was even awake. Was he dreaming? Was she back, standing there as beautiful as she always was, sharing her heart, her emotional transparency?

Rae took his silence as a hint. "Well, I suppose I'll see you around. Take care of yourself, Kief."

She started to walk away, when Kiefer cleared his throat, "W—wait!"

Rae stopped and turned, locking her eyes with his.

"I'm sorry I slapped you. I'm sorry I said all those things to you. There's no excuse for my actions; I'm the fucked-up type, apparently, dark in my ways, and it's hard for me to be the man you need. I am not sure I'll ever be the man you need. Or the man you deserve." He shifted where he stood, lost on what to say next.

Rae smirked. "As I said, Kiefer, I love you. I know what I want. What you decide in this life is up to you." She waited momentarily, wondering if he would say anything more, when he reached out a hand. She looked at his hand and back into his now tear-filled eyes.

"Stay." His throat bobbed as he drew his lips into a tight line.

She slowly approached him and reached for his hand, taking it in hers. "You sure?"

He nodded, closing his eyes. "Please."

She smiled. "Okay, Kiefer." Without asking, she locked her arms around his neck.

He was hesitant to touch her back, harboring the guilt of what he'd done to her.

"It's okay," she whispered.

When he'd finally convinced himself it was okay to embrace her properly, he nuzzled his face into the comfort of her warm neck. "I love you," he said, sharing the three words he had relentlessly feared, now letting them slip effortlessly from his lips for the first time.

460

Rae kissed his cheek and whispered in his ear, "You hungry?"

☆

Isarah
Temple of Spears
Aoustí 25

"Ameilja!" A voice called out from the entrance of the temple.

Ameilja stood up from the foot of the altar and turned toward the front corridor, adjusting her eyes from the sanctuary's darkness.

"Coming," Ameilja quietly called, and she walked toward the light to meet her acolyte escorts.

She reached for her necklace and realized it was gone. A quiet gasp slipped from her lips. "Wait!" She quickly turned back.

A cloaked monk stood at the altar. He knelt over, picked up her necklace, and turned his attention to her.

"Thank you!" She sighed with relief.

"I believe you dropped this."

"Thank you so much, Brother. This is very dear to me."

"I know," he answered as he placed the necklace in her palm.

He knows? She regained her composure and adjusted her eyes to face the tall man as he slightly pulled back his habit's hood. She had never seen the man before, but she stared up at him as if he were a ghost who'd taken conscious form. She wondered if she was the only one there who could see him. She locked her gaze with him, and a pair of crystal-blue eyes stared back at her.

Who ...

She assessed him quickly. His hair was light, a couple of pieces caressed his forehead. Sharp masculine features stared back through reclusive, diamond-gleaming eyes. Those eyes chased the slight luminance of the oceanside back home. His inviting smile was that of a good friend who reminded her to be strong and courageous.

"It's no trouble, Lady Ameilja." He smirked.

She looked down at his feet; the soles lay flat against the floor, as human as hers. She couldn't see his ears, but his fingers and nails were clearly human. Her heart raced but lulled when she realized the heart-beat wasn't just her own.

He spoke again. "I'm sorry. My mistake—I know better than to call you *Lady*."

Her breath ceased, and time blemished into blurs.

"Ameilja," he corrected in a deep voice, one she was more accustomed to.

She gasped but kept collected, still looking upon the human man as if he were an apparition.

He smiled gently, lent her a bow, and said, "I'll see you soon."

He turned and walked down the aisle toward the corridors. He walked right past her security and beyond them. Ameilja's lips parted, and a whisper slipped away.

"Kovuco?"

GLOSSARY

Abbot/Abbess; Father/Mother — Spiritual leader and overseer of a temple or House of the Religious Order of the Commission. Follower of Uridei. This is the highest position within the Religious Order.

The Academy — The branch of the Commission that houses and educates aspiring alchemists and their research.

Æsir — Title held by a Commission team leader specifically within the Sentry branch.

Alchemy; Alchemist — A broad term often used to define medieval chemical science and philosophy. Examples include the ability to bend natural elements to man's will; indefinitely prolong or advance life; or traveling between realms.

Armiger — Role within the Religious Order of the Commission. Armigers are the armed forces for a temple or House. Follower of Uridei. An armiger is eligible once they turn fourteen years of age. Once trained, armiger are crafted a sword forged to encompass a lifetime of servitude to the Light, pledging their life to conquer the forces of darkness and defend the weak. NOTE: A paladin would knight an armiger to uphold the principles of the blade.

Aureate — Godlike being like but not equal to their sole creator, Uridei. They were ancient beings endowed with supernatural powers, and abilities. The Aureates had ruled over the lands inhabited by humans, Orkésh, Fae, and other creatures during the beginning times. Their power had been intended only for the blessing and welfare of all, ensuring Uridei's creation transpired fruitfully.

Bloodletting — The act of bloodletting is a bonding ritual between lovers that is only practiced between Völfien mates, bonding them for life. When Völfien become lovers, they drink the other's blood, linking their lives together symbiotically. The effect of this act is complex, binding memories, feelings, even biological functions such as heartbeats. The act is irreversible until death.

The Blue Coats Syndicate — A crime syndicate that seek to defend members of the Fae against unjust treatment. They operate outside of the Commission. Ran entirely by humans and Völfien. They exist within Obsidian District and Brass District, known for wearing eloquent yet rugged blue coats and utilizing antique revolvers. They are led and organized by the infamous outlaw called Zero.

Centurion — The Commission's assigned commanding general over a region's Sentry branch. An Abbot/Abbess would also fall under their centurions lead. The Centurion is in direct allegiance to the Emperor/Empress.

The Commission — An institution built under the influence of the Aureate, Albean: Humanity's savior. The Commission was created to ensure the human race comes to order and peace amongst all races and cease forces that seek to destroy them. It is comprised of three branches:
— The Sentry, involving the wülkure and the wächter roles.
— The Religious Order, involving armigers, paladins and abbots.
— The Academy, involving alchemy roles and departmental studies.

Demonology —The study of demons and the arts of the blue flame, and the Void. Those who use the Purge are to demonstrate knowledge in challenging the existence of demons in the world.

Dien — A non-combative servant or attendant specially trained to work for the Commission, and the royal family: Emperor/Empress.

Divinities — The study of Uridei's Light and the Purge. Divinities support a bonded relationship with Uridei's Purge flames to enhance a Paladin's ability to use it.

Emperor/Empress — The Eastern Isles is considered a growing empire and is led by a sovereign monarch who is addressed as "Emperor" or "Empress."

The Fae —The race of Fae are known as non-human members of society. This race consists of any member inspired by the nature of the world. Examples of the Fae race are the Dryad, or the Beastkind, such as Minotaur and the Völfien. An Aureate was said to be the curator of nature, forming the mountains, forests, and deserts and placing creatures and their Fae protectors in them. It's believed the Fae were endowed with fantastical abilities and rise to be the strength of those landscapes. NOTE: Orkésh are controversial to this definition per the Pjauti, the Art of Fae Banes and Venoms.

The Fae Calendar — The Eastern Isles' Fae Calendar comprises Völfien words. Much like a traditional Calendar, it is made up of twelve months. Their months are aligned with trees of the land:
— Sturnyule
— Solmauð
— Harujasa
— Avíthen
— Mítraven
— Lyun'i
— Lyul'ai
— Aoustí
— Lúnasa
— Hallotyr
— Elftyr
— Zwolftyr

Féja — A powder-like substance that consists of various plants and metals, creating a stunning tranquilizer for members of the Fae. Féja is crafted by Wülkure or practitioners of the Pjauti.

Glamour — Per the Pjauti, glamouring is a magical ability some of the Fae possess to disguise their appearance by putting off pheromones to trick others into seeing only their disguise.
NOTE: This ability is still under study.

Hydrostein — An intense sedative used to force a beast to regurgitate (sometimes used on an Ork). The side effects include vomiting, retching, blindness, fatigue, and muscle tension. Hydrostein can be dangerous as it can send Völves into an uncontrolled rage due to the abrupt change in their system. On rare occasions Orks have been known to die to a Hydrostein.

Medzio — Völfien word for "Hunter", is referred to as the primary form of a Völfien.

Monk — A man who has been sworn, as a non-combatant, to a life of poverty, chastity, and purity. As a monk, you learn from the book of Light, memorizing its scripture.
NOTE: Monks are a male role, women are known as "sisters" within the Sisterhood of the Light.

The Näkk — The Näkk is a wicked, deadly plague from unknown origins. It is known to be an infection that can raise the dead into flesh-eating revenants. It was first discovered by the Aureate, Sabor.

The Religious Order — The religious branch of the Commission. Implements a moral onset of values from the Book of the Light, following Uridei. The Religious Order's structural influence came from the originators from the war, the ones who fought the tides of darkness with Albean's Purge Flames. This is what led to the creation of the holy warriors known as the Paladin.

Ózykas — A fluid that is built up in a bowl-like flower, is used to kill dryads, cease glamouring abilities, and is effective in clogging the airways of völves.

Paladin — Role within the Religious Order of the Commission. The holy knights of the Order, paladins are the sword and Purge-wielding warriors who promise to live on through the ages as the protectors against the forces of darkness, and all that threatens the Light. An armiger must earn the ability to wield Purge flames in order to be promoted to a Paladin.

Pantokraðor — A whip whose name means almighty, omnipotent, and all-powerful. The whip was explicitly constructed for Kovuco Blackstar by an unknown source.

Pjauti — The Wülkure's study, or art, of the Fae, banes, and venoms.

Protectorate — Protectorates are of the Religious Order but originate from the Order of Völfien. A protectorate is most often a bodyguard to an Abbot, Paladin, or a Seer. The position is given to an accepted Völfien who must learn to wield weapons tailored to the Völfien, and independently study the Book of Light.

Purge Flames — Uridei's white flames, an elemental gifting endowed to the Aureate Albean, the savior of humanity. Specifically used against dark, demonic forces.
NOTE: An ability attained by a paladin.

Red Fang — Sword of Ameilja Rose Frost, an heirloom from her mother. A dagger, with no name, accompanies it.

Rinkin — Völfien word that means "brother to man." It is the near-human form of the Völfien that requires a complex transformation.
NOTE: Völfien can see their "human" self in their reflection.

The Sentry — The branch of the Commission acting as the secular, combatant sector. The Sentry includes the Wächter and the Wülkure roles.
NOTE: The Sentry is under command of their region's Centurion.

Narkänum — A neurological emulsion synthesized through alchemical immurement designed to raise and manipulate the dead. It bears controversial usage and is technically still under a trial basis; little is revealed beyond the walls of the Sunspire, but it is formulated to mock the wielding of the Näkk.

Svarfætúr — A predominate Orkésh gang that resides within the central cities of Isarah. This Orkésh syndicate is called the Svarfætúr, run by Declan Chappequa, who relentlessly pushes to reign superior by the ways of their ancestors in hatred and malice. Seeks divisive tactics and unfair agendas.

Vilkanás — Völf's Bane, a blue-violet root utilized in slaying Völfien. Its qualities are known to attack blood and oxygen, constricting blood flow, acting as a deadly poison.

Wächter — A role within the Commission's Sentry branch. Wächters are the enhanced combatant force, and wield heavy weaponry and become master operators of aircraft or sea vessels. They study the seas and skies. They could be programmers, technicians, mechanics, engineers, pilots, and possibly other creatives.

Wöndin — The Wöndin is an ancient Ork believed to exist within the society of the Orkésh. The Wöndin is not only known for influencing unity but is also considered magical. Beyond the fantastical traits, many Orks cling to this legend, hoping it is real. Belief in the Wöndin provides a path of purpose amongst not only Orks but the Fae as well.

Wülkure — A role within the Commission's Sentry branch. Wülkure are known as the hunters of the Fae if they step out of line. Wülkure are known for their combat prowess. They are also masters at understanding and utilizing Fae magic, venom, or concocted emulsions to protect humanity in their everyday lives.
NOTE: They study the Pjauti.

ACKNOWLEDGMENTS

In 2005, I was young and indifferent. Like most young men, I was searching for meaning and, by the grace of God, grew up and learned along the way. If you expect life to be easy, you're in for a very unfulfilled and disappointing human experience. You only learn from hardships; rise stronger and faster from enduring pain and suffering, and I have enjoyed the race and hope I can run as long as I possibly can. It's this drive that conjured up this tale of Kovuco Blackstar. He's young, torn, and searching for meaning, doubting and second-guessing himself, all the while pursuing happiness. I hope you enjoy his race no matter how dark, bloody, and frustrating it might be and no matter the outcome. It is a tale I hope speaks to a suffering world that will never be a utopia but will always be worth rising each and every day fighting the good fight and never ceasing to learn or experience.

For that, I have a few members of my wonderful family for not only enduring and loving me but also supporting my creative journey and personal hardships.

First, I would like to thank my mother. Mom. Hardworking, through thick and thin, no matter what I put you through, you were always there, loving me unconditionally. Thank you for always being my mama bear. There is no mama bear more fierce than you. You will always rise above, never forget that.

To my grandparents, for always pushing me to be the best of the best. To always listen to me and pour your wisdom into my life. I have much of my strength, sanity, and unstoppable dedication because of both of you! Your hard work is always noticed.

To my siblings. Laughter has been the best medicine, and my joy is substantiated by the fun we have together. In a family of introverts,

_y_ breathe life into our family, and I can't imagine a greater
_ı_ us.

_ı_ny beloved wife and muse, we have been through so much to-
_ı_, you and I. Storytelling has been a romance we have shared since
one. I am happy you have supported me over the years and literally
_ı_shed me to achieve this lifelong conquest. Fantasy is our lifeblood,
and it continues to fuel this crazy love story that is yours and mine. You
are the reason I believe in love at first sight, the call to protect and to
chase after one another till death do us part. Thank you for being a part
of this writing journey. I couldn't have done it without you! I love you!

To my daughter. Like Kovuco, I dreamed of you with your mother.
We named you and imagined you at such a young age, and with pro-
phetic predestination, here you are! Our little light in a dark place; long
blonde hair with forest leaves stuck in those strands of gold. You are the
reason I'll never quit, and I hope you continue to keep me young and
active. I hope you never cease to be a light, even when other lights go
out. Your creativity will go far in this world!

To all my friends and family as well. There are so, so many to thank!
Many of you have supported me even as early as High School and my
home school days, where my only source of social interaction was other
home-schooled kids and/or from church. Family isn't always blood,
but the friends you keep and never part from. I thank God for every
one of you.

First and foremost to my best friend, Brandon, the creative behind
Blackstar's cover, illustrations, graphics, and never ending ideas, banter,
and talks. I couldn't have asked for a better guy to push me through. I
have you to thank for bringing Blackstar to life through your artistic
talent and creativity. Even when you drive me to my boiling point, it's
always for my betterment to humble me and push me to be the best
version of myself. Thank you, and as always, being a friend I can turn
to. Also, to your wife and son. Behind every great man is an even greater
woman, and without our wifely support, there would be no fruition in
this dream! A special thank you to both our wives for putting up with us.

To my editor, fellow writer, and best friend, Patricia. Patricia, ever
since our youth, I knew you'd never go away, and I am so happy you
didn't. You are an amazing person, inspiring and dedicated. Thank you

for being my first reader and first fan of Blackstar. You have played an amazing part in developing this story, ensuring I could tell it (legibly). I also want to thank Patricia's husband, Matt, for putting up with nonstop banter, late-night editing sessions and our double-date nights (including *zoomies* with our dogs.) Thank you for your support! Happy to call you a dear friend.

My revered yet gentle father-in-law. Thank you for always being a calming presence in our lives while also being the Tasmanian devil of a defender too. We love you.

Throughout this journey, I have been honored by those who have helped me develop this craft and helped make Blackstar what it is today.

Grandma K, you are the best adopted grandma we could ever ask for and your support has always been appreciated.

Kat "Kitty", my adopted sister-in-law! Thank you for being there for not just my wife but my family. Always a beloved sister and friend!

Also, thank you to Patricia's dad, Dave, a Fantasy enthusiast, for being one of the first readers to pour into this project. I so appreciate your support for Blackstar and hope you can continue to be a source of knowledge and insight.

Every writer has had a beginning, as a student, and therefore I want to thank the first teacher to help me hone into this craft. Thank you to my High School English teacher and fellow writer, Jodi. Jodi, I will always remember my time in your class, both Freshman English and of course, Creative Writing class. Thank you for believing in me and being a teacher who cared enough to push me to be the best I could be.

A special thank you to Adam with WhipWorks for all your expertise and assistance with crafting the Pantokraðor. Looking forward to having a replica brought to life in the future.

A shout out to Brennan and my sister Katie for medical and trauma advice (for the story), and Megan as another first-time reader and major influence! Your feedback was beyond helpful!

Shoutouts to ALL of my childhood friends and family, and the best set of couples to be a part of my marriage and early steps into parenthood. You know who you are and drinks to you and for as long as we can!

In closure, it is worth mentioning, it took reading and the love of reading to start writing. There are so many stories that have inspired me to work tirelessly on this dream. My love of writing came from the brilliant works of J.R.R. Tolkien, especially the Lord of the Rings trilogy and the incredible masterpiece, the Hobbit. So many lessons, and I hope I can repeat the process in masterful storytelling.

A shout-out to my wolves at the Colorado Wolf and Wildlife Center, specifically Nav'i and Tala. Many of my Völfien characters were named after these majestic creatures. Animals have always been an amazing gift in this life, and the wolf has been a nominal piece in my vision for Blackstar.

I also want to thank my Barber for putting more care into my hair than I do. Thanks for making sure I look good on my author photo.

Another shoutout to my team at Archway Publishing for helping me achieve this dream!

Above all, I thank God. The Creator of the universe, the Alpha and Omega, Beginning and the End. There would have been no days beyond 2005 without a forgiving and loving God. I owe my life to our creator, and the lessons passed on. Speak, your servant is listening...

Lukas Ryan.